REVIEWS OF *THE SAVANNAH PROJECT*

From bestselling authors

"*The Savannah Project* signals the arrival of a new member to the thriller genre. Chuck Barrett. The tale contains all of the danger, treachery, and action a reader could wish for. The intrigue comes from all directions, slicing and stitching with precision. A worthy debut from an exciting talent."
—Steve Berry, *New York Times* bestselling author

"From the tree-lined streets of Savannah to the mossy stones of an ancient Irish castle, *The Savannah Project* weaves a fast moving tale of murder, mystery and suspense. Chuck Barrett has written a winner here. A must-read novel for thriller lovers."
—William Rawlings, bestselling author of *The Mile High Club*

From book reviewers

"*The Savannah Project* is a bona fide suspense thriller. Rife with abundant mystery and intrigue, author Chuck Barrett's standout tale takes the reader on a tortuous path of all-engrossing action and adventure. A highly recommended instant classic."
—Apex Reviews

"*The Savannah Project* is an exciting thriller that will prove hard to put down."
—The Midwest Book Review

A taut, pulse-pounding thriller."
—*ForeWord* Clarion Reviews

"Chuck Barrett's *The Savannah Project* grabs your undivided attention from the very first sentence and does not let you truly exhale until the very last, chilling-to-the core line…"
—Olivera Baumgartner-Jackson/Reader Views

THE
TOYMAKER

Also by Chuck Barrett

The Savannah Project

THE
TOYMAKER

A NOVEL OF SUSPENSE

Chuck Barrett

Switchback
PUBLISHING
An Imprint of Wyatt-MacKenzie

Cover design by Mary Fisher Design, LLC, www.maryfisherdesign.com

FIRST EDITION

ISBN: 978-1-936214-68-6
Library of Congress Control Number: 2011943072

Barrett, Chuck.
        The Toymaker: a novel of suspense / Chuck Barrett
        FICTION: Thriller/Suspense/Mystery

Published by Switchback Publishing
An Imprint of Wyatt-MacKenzie

www.switchbackpublishing.com

This book is dedicated to my parents,
Charles and Doris Barrett,
who have always been in my cheerleader section.

Some people say, "The devil is in the details." The truth is, the small difference between successful and failed missions is equal to the sum of the unattended, minuscule, seemingly trivial details. *The Toymaker* keeps you on this thin line as the story unfolds.

The REAL *Toymaker*

Wasted with no vision of a future
Dying futile in a land of dreams
Vision of what once might have been
Fade into another day

Anonymous

CHAPTER 1

Lake Burton, Georgia
March 29—11:30 P.M.
Present Day

FRANCESCA CATANZARO DRUMMED her fingers on the command console. Tonight's mission should be straightforward—get in, make the kill, and get out. Yet she still couldn't shake the first-time jitters. She looked at the two operatives sitting across from her and feigned a smile. "Picture of your wife?" she asked the eldest, a large black man who had introduced himself as an ex-Marine called Johnson.

He held up the photo for her to see. "No, my daughter. She'll be a teenager tomorrow." He slipped the photo inside his black jacket.

She glanced at the much younger man sitting next to him, legs bouncing with the energy of a teenager while he was putting on black face camo paint.

"Nervous?" she asked.

"Hell no, ma'am. I have no family." He motioned with his head. "Came along to cover grandpa's ass."

"Shut up, Aaron," Johnson said. "Just keep painting that crap on your face, pretty soon you'll look like me."

"Don't call me ma'am." She smiled at Aaron then turned to Johnson. "Any idea who's pulling the strings on this one?"

"The father of one of Director Bentley's new recruits." Johnson said. "I guess they go way back. Bentley called your boss for his...technical expertise."

She laughed, opened the rear door to the black van. "Good luck, gentlemen."

The two men jumped out and slipped into the darkness.

She closed the door and looked at the tall, carrot-topped man sitting next to her. He was leaning back in his seat with his hands clasped behind his head, a Cheshire cat grin on his face. His cocky demeanor was not something she cared for.

"I thought you said they were cousins." Matt said.

"To be so smart you can be so naive. Cousins is another word for CIA." She pointed at the metal case. "Launch Jasper." Francesca nicknamed the electronic drone *Jasper* after the British slang for wasp.

Matt toggled two switches and a three-inch replica of a wasp came to life.

The miniature drone was the invention of her employer, a man she affectionately called *The Toymaker*—given his business was providing specialized equipment for the world of espionage—or 'technical expertise' as Johnson put it.

Jasper was an advanced, miniaturized spy plane that was a replica of a wasp. Equipped with an infrared video camera, microphone, and weighing less than a small AAA battery, the electronic wasp was powered by three small watch batteries with a useful life of 45 minutes. Just like a real wasp, the drone was propelled by flapping its silicone wings allowing it to hover, climb and descend vertically, move sideways, and travel at speeds up to eleven miles per hour.

Operating a unit resembling a radio control for a model airplane, he brought the wasp to life, hovering it between them. "Ready, boss."

Francesca opened the door. "Okay, you're on."

The drone flew out while she watched the monitor. The drone started its half-mile flight toward the lakefront mansion, flying overhead of the two operatives as they jogged up the steep hill. Five minutes later the home came into view on the monitor. As the drone approached the mansion, Francesca was able to distinguish the architectural details of the stone masonry. The building looked dark and empty, but she knew it wasn't. Somewhere inside was the assassin Ian Collins.

"Take Jasper around back." She instructed Matt.

He maneuvered the drone around the side of the house capturing video of the densely wooded lot surrounding the manor, then behind it, the lake and a two-level boathouse a hundred feet below. The drone panned the rear of the property. A long sloping backyard ended at a stone wall which plunged thirty feet to the lake. Stone steps, the same stone from the house and the wall, led to the boathouse.

"Take a look in the windows." She said.

Matt guided Jasper toward the back of the home. "Only a couple of lights on. Maybe he already went to bed."

"Maybe." She said. "Johnson, how far out are you?"

"We just got to the driveway." Johnson's voice in her headset.

She motioned to Matt. "Put their helmet cams on three and four." The two screens lit up with night vision views from the two operatives' video cameras. "Johnson, can you get a visual through the front windows?"

"Negative. Blinds are all closed. Front door locked."

"Jasper's in the back yard. Couple of lights on back there. Check it out."

"Roger that." Johnson said.

"Matt, pull back. Let's make sure no one's watching."

The view from the drone zoomed out from the rear of the house. "Back yard looks clear. Be careful." She said to the operatives.

"Roger that, mom." Aaron said. "Glad you're watching our backs."

She watched while Matt held the drone's position steady. The drone's camera picked up the operatives coming around the corner of the house. She scanned the video feeds from the drone and the helmet cams on her monitors, studying every detail from each viewpoint.

She'd been in their shoes when she worked for Italy's External Intelligence and Security Agency. Her reputation for successful operations in Italy earned her respect in a male dominated field. She'd loved her job, but, as with any government job, there was too much bureaucratic red tape. It was a year ago when she met the eccentric old man she called the toymaker. He recruited her into The Greenbrier Fellowship a week later. Six months specialized tradecraft training, followed by six months fieldwork, and now she had her first assignment as mission leader.

"Johnson, what do you see?"

"Initial assessment. Two lights on downstairs. Looks like the glow of a TV upstairs. No movement detected. Get this, though, the alarm light is green. It's not armed."

"Check the door." She said. "See if it's locked but don't open it."

"Unlocked." Johnson's voice. "I repeat, not locked."

"You and Aaron check the other doors. Maybe we can find an unlocked door that doesn't open into a lighted room." She watched the monitors as the two men separated, each checked doors and reported them locked.

"All locked but the one." Johnson said.

"Let's take Jasper inside for a look." She motioned to Matt. The view in the drone's monitor zoomed in as it flew toward the house. She watched as the drone approached the door. "Johnson, let Jasper in then take cover until Matt can sweep the house."

"Roger that." Johnson said.

Francesca watched while Matt guided the drone from room to room. Five minutes later she concluded the lakefront mansion was empty. She told Johnson to let the drone out and return to cover while Matt scanned the rest of the property with the drone.

"Where do you want to start?" Matt asked.

"He has to be around here somewhere, move out toward the lake. Let's see what's out there." She studied the monitor. From the drone's angle looking toward the lake, she saw a finger pier to the left and a two-story boathouse to the right. Something on the pier caught her attention. "There." She pointed to the spot on the monitor. "Looks like someone standing on the dock, check it out."

Matt maneuvered the drone toward the finger pier. "What is that?"

"I don't know." She said. "Get closer...but not too close."

"No cigar. Just a wooden owl decoy on a post." Matt said. "Used to scare birds off the dock. Where to now, boss?"

"Pull up and scan the boathouse."

The drone climbed vertically and rotated toward the structure. The lower level of the boathouse was covered with tongue and groove siding, no windows, and two boat slip openings facing the lake. The upper level had a large railed sun deck and a sheltered post and beam veranda equipped with a full outdoor kitchen and a stone fireplace.

"Here." She tapped her finger on the monitor. "The glow under the veranda. Check it out, but make sure he doesn't spot Jasper."

"No problem." Matt smiled. "I'll make a low pass."

As the drone moved in closer, she recognized her target. "Bingo. We got him boys. He's on the upper level of the boathouse. Start working your way down there."

Francesca's team had tracked assassin Ian Collins, also known as Shamrock, to the cliffside mansion 90 miles northeast of Atlanta on Lake Burton where he'd been hiding since fleeing Savannah, Georgia. The two operatives were tasked with the hit under her direction, them CIA, she and Matt, The Greenbrier Fellowship.

By Francesca's orders, Matt hovered the drone fifteen feet above and twenty feet back from Collins. She noticed Collins glance at his watch then stand. "Target's moving, take cover." He walked down the stairs and disappeared into the lower level of the boathouse.

"We've lost sight. He's gone inside. Collins is all yours, Johnson. Be careful." She motioned to Matt. "Find them. I want a visual of the takedown."

She maintained a constant vigil, scanning each of the monitors while Matt maneuvered the drone into position and followed the operatives' progress. Johnson and Aaron split up and were approaching the boathouse from adjacent corners. At the bottom of the stairs was the only door into the lower level and it was closed.

She turned to Matt. "Find a way to get in there."

Francesca watched the drone fly over the boathouse, rotate, and descend vertically. As the opening came into view, she saw what looked like closed garage doors extending down to water level.

Before she could determine her next move, she heard a groan as Aaron's helmet cam went dead.

"Aaron? Do you copy?"

Nothing.

"Matt, find him." She turned back to the monitor. "Johnson, man down. Locate Aaron." She saw a shadow move across Johnson's monitor then his helmet cam went dead too. "Johnson?"

Nothing.

"Johnson?" She turned to Matt. "Shit. Get that drone over there now."

He guided the drone to the front of the boathouse, panning down as it homed in on the boathouse door. "Oh God." She saw someone's feet being dragged inside and then the door closed.

"Matt, You have to get Jasper inside. I don't care how you do it. Just do it."

"I'll try. But if it gets wet…" Matt said. "We're dead in the water. No pun intended."

Francesca pulled out her silenced pistol and chambered a round. "Get the drone's video feed on my phone."

"Where the hell are you going?" Matt asked. "Our orders are technical assistance only."

"CIA orders, not mine. This is my op and I don't want their blood on my hands." She opened the van door. "Call it in."

Francesca closed the door leaving Matt to handle the command center. Something had gone wrong. Collins got the jump on the two CIA operatives and the mission was on the brink of disaster. She ran up the steep hill toward the mansion. She glanced at her phone. "Matt, how are you coming on the video feed?"

"Almost there. Another few seconds and you should have it." Matt said. "Jasper's inside the boathouse—oh shit, this is bad."

Francesca watched as the video feed came through on her phone. The inside of the boathouse was rustic. Both slips were empty, a small planked walkway wrapped around the outer perimeter and down the middle separating the two slips. Cables used to hoist boats from the water hung from long metal pipes attached to the rafters. Johnson and Aaron were suspended over the water, hands tied above them and secured to the cables. Boat anchors were attached to their feet. The Irish assassin was larger than she'd expected, with a white blaze in his dark hair and a bandage on the left side of his head. He hit Aaron with an oar, held up something, and was speaking.

"Matt, I need audio."

"Here it comes." Matt said. "Sorry."

"Are you going to let your partner die?" Collins held a picture in front of Aaron's face. "Do you want to see her without a father? Now, tell me who sent you."

She saw Aaron turn his head away. Collins tossed the oar onto the planking, pulled out a knife, and held it against Johnson's face. "Tell me who sent you or your friend will never see his daughter again."

"Go to hell." Aaron spit at Collins.

On her phone screen, Francesca saw Collins gouge the knife into Johnson's right eye. Johnson screamed behind the duct tape gag. She closed her eyes at the horrific image.

"When I said he'd never see his daughter again, I meant it literally." Collins said. "His fate is in your hands. Now I'll ask you again, who do you work for?"

Collins flipped the switch on the wall. The metal pipe overhead started turning, slowly unwinding the cable and lowering Johnson into the water. "He still has one eye. Talk and I'll raise him."

Aaron said nothing until Johnson's head went under. Johnson was thrashing about in the water. Francesca couldn't believe what was happening.

"Stop. Pull him up." Aaron begged. "I'll tell you what you want to know. Just pull him up."

Collins stopped the boatlift while Johnson's head was under water.

Francesca ran down the driveway until she reached the mansion, alternating glances from her phone to the path ahead, while keeping her 9mm Glock raised in front of her. "Matt, can you get the drone any closer?"

"Not a chance." Matt said. "Any closer and he'll spot it."

Collins voice again. "Who do you work for?"

"CIA." Aaron said. "Now pull him up before he drowns."

"Bentley. I should have known." Collins leaned against the wall. "Is Jake Pendleton behind this?"

"Pendleton. Yeah, that's him. Bentley called him 'JP.' The two old men go way back." Aaron said. "Now pull him up."

"Old men?" Collins said. "This just gets better."

Francesca ran down the sloping backyard toward the boathouse. She slowed when she reached the wall, descending the stone steps as quietly as she could. She watched in horror as the assassin picked up the oar and bashed it against Aaron's head. Blood ran down the side of his face. Collins flipped a second switch on the wall and Aaron's body began lowering into the lake. He tossed the picture into the water and opened the door.

On her phone, she saw him open the boathouse door at the same time the light beamed outward from the doorway. She was twenty feet away, looking straight into the door and right at the Irish assassin. She dropped her phone and fired three shots at Collins. The man staggered back into the boathouse. She ran toward him and fired two more rounds. The assassin staggered backward and fell into the water next to Johnson.

She raced through the doorway, both men were submerged. She'd seen what Collins had done to Aaron. He was probably dead. No one could have survived that blow. She needed to save Johnson. She flipped both switches, reversing the boatlift. The cables tightened. Bubbles rose to the surface where Johnson went under, none where Aaron went down.

She grabbed a boat hook from the wall and frantically reached for Johnson's cable. Probing to hook any part of him. Next to her, Aaron's lifeless body rose out of the water. Johnson was thrashing like a fish below the surface. She grabbed his collar, pulled his head above water, and ripped the tape from his mouth.

Johnson coughed and spat water from his mouth, gasping for air.

"It'll be okay, Johnson." She reassured him. "Help is on the way." Blood was oozing from his gouged-out eye socket.

He shook his head and coughed.

"Don't talk." She leaned closer. "Just take a—"

Collins popped out of the water with a knife in his hand. The blade slashed across her left cheek from her eye to her chin. She recoiled to avoid the killer's grasp, headset falling into the water. Francesca grabbed her pistol, aimed, and fired into the water where Collins went under until her magazine was empty.

She fell back against the boathouse wall, cradling her cheek, sliding down the wall to a seated position. The pain was unlike anything she'd ever felt. So intense.

A soft buzzing sound caught her attention. She looked up and saw the wasp a foot in front of her.

"Matt. Help. Get help." She said to the drone.

After two minutes she pulled herself to her feet, the drone matched her moves, and then it suddenly backed away and spun around. She turned and saw him.

A white blaze down the middle of his brown hair.

One blue eye and one brown eye.

CHAPTER 2

**Six Months Later
Gibson Desert
Australian Outback**

JAKE PENDLETON STUDIED the camp through his AN/PVS-9 night vision goggles for the fourth October night in a row. He and his friend turned colleague, Gregg Kaplan, were manning an observation post overlooking an al Qaeda training camp run by Mustafa Bin Yasir.

The rock-strewn ridge had proven to be an ideal vantage point for intelligence gathering since the entire terrorist camp was visible from the perch with virtually no blind spots. Hidden between the mulgas, an evergreen eucalyptus shrub, Jake and Kaplan, a former U. S. Army Special Forces soldier, built short half-moon shaped walls out of rocks. Roughly eighteen inches high, the walls served as blinds where they monitored all movements within the camp. Patterns of the al Qaeda cell's sentries, location of the communications tent, and all other vital information had been recorded and sent to an analyst at Langley.

Moonless nights offered additional cover, this phase of the moon chosen deliberately. Darkness had become Jake's ally. A lesson he learned quickly as he adjusted to his newfound role with the CIA's Clandestine Service. It reminded him of a phrase he'd heard Kaplan say several times—the motto of the 160th SOAR, Special Operations Aviation Regiment—*Death waits in the dark.* Jake preferred the comfort of darkness.

At the direction of CIA Director Scott Bentley, Jake and Kaplan were sent to the Outback to apprehend Yasir.

According to Bentley, recent chatter had linked Yasir's radical cell with plans for other terrorist attacks, potentially on U.S. soil. In cooperation with the Australian Secret Intelligence Service, or ASIS, and the Australian Special Air Service Regiment, SAS, Jake and Kaplan recorded the nocturnal activities and patterns of Yasir and each member of the cell. Since the attack was planned for the middle of the night, every behavioral detail was noted.

Yasir had been implicated in the planning of the 9/11 attacks although no conclusive evidence linked him to the conspiracy. His association with terrorists known to have hijacked United States airliners and the recent intelligence community chatter had elevated Yasir near the top of the FBI's most wanted terrorists list.

"Do you think about her much, Gregg?" Jake whispered—undetectable at three meters.

Kaplan said nothing.

"Annie. Do you ever think about her?"

"Not as much as you might think." Kaplan turned to Jake.

"Everything about that day in Savannah is etched in my mind. The blood. The carnage." Jake was silent for a minute, then continued. "Not a day goes by I don't think of Beth. I just can't seem to let her go. How did you get over Annie?"

Kaplan removed his night vision goggles. "It's easy to let go of something you never had."

"I should never have left her. I should have been by her side. I'm the reason she got shot in the first place, then I just left her alone."

"Bullshit, Jake, she wasn't alone, she was in a hospital. With her parents. Recovering. How would you have known? How would anyone know? Quit feeling sorry for yourself. It's time to let her go and move on."

Jake lowered his head, feeling the pain like it happened yesterday, not six months ago. The day she died, Beth had been one month from her thirtieth birthday, three months before their wedding day. If he could go back, he would tell her not to come to Savannah to see him. Would have done anything to keep her away from there.

Jake turned and sat down against the rock wall, his back to the ledge. He fished around in his pocket and pulled out an energy bar. "Gregg, we're wasting time. Let's just set up this attack with the Aussies and get on with it." He broke it into two pieces, handed half to Kaplan.

"Patience, Jake. We don't want to rush things."

"Rush things? We've been sitting on our asses up here for the past four nights. You call that rushing? It's time for action."

"You're right." Kaplan said. "We've gathered all the intel we need."

Beyond the ridge where Jake and Kaplan were observing the al Qaeda camp laid the Buckshot Plains. Dawn's first light revealed the vast, dry region, its red sand hills and desert grass stretching as far as the eye could see.

Nestled close to the cliff with its recently mounted camouflage netting, the terrorist camp had all but disappeared from satellite imagery. Aerial photos captured the camp prior to the netting and a CIA analyst mapped the camp and sent scaled diagrams to Jake and Kaplan.

In addition, an ASIS analyst built a 3D terrain model of the camp. It looked like an architectural student's final project. Every detail of the terrorist camp was depicted with amazing accuracy.

From the ridge overlooking the camp he could distinguish details through the camouflage netting, verifying the accuracy of the CIA's analyst's original diagram, recording any changes, and relaying the intel back to the analyst for modification.

"Let's go then." Jake slipped his NVGs inside his desert camo shirt, stuck the remainder of the energy bar between his teeth, and crawled away from the ledge making his way toward the trail leading toward the SAS camp. Jake waited while Kaplan left instructions with the two SAS soldiers who came to relieve them.

Kaplan was a good friend. They had endured a lot together in a short amount of time. They met earlier that year under strange circumstances. He was an NTSB accident investigator from Atlanta and Kaplan an air traffic controller in Savannah, Georgia. He interviewed Kaplan during the investigation of an aircraft accident in Savannah. Kaplan was the last controller to communicate with the small jet prior to the crash that occurred a few days before St. Patrick's Day. Proceeding with suspicion, Jake's investigation turned deadly. It cost him the life of his fiancée Beth McAllister and   left him with a burning emptiness.

Empty. And angry.

Jake left the NTSB at the urging of his former Navy boss, now director of the CIA, Scott Bentley. The director had lured Jake and Kaplan from their former government careers and recruited them into the CIA's Clandestine Service where Jake channeled his anger into every covert black op. With each mission, the pain subsided a little. With each hit, he felt better. He became his own therapist.

He'd seen the CIA shrink—Bentley had insisted he and Kaplan both go to the psychiatrist at Langley. Kaplan's long-time girlfriend, Annie Bulloch, was killed in Savannah on the same day Beth was shot.

St. Patrick's Day.

The bloodiest day in Savannah's modern day history. It was something Jake and Kaplan held in common. It should be a bond between them, but Jake knew it wasn't.

The loss of Beth changed him, forced his anger to surface—anger he didn't know he had until his first covert assignment two months after her death. He wasn't supposed to kill his target, his assignment was to capture him and return to Langley. Something went wrong and he panicked.

His heart raced. Beads of sweat rolled down his face. His anger churned inside him like a volcano ready to erupt. Thoughts of Beth, the Irishman, and death ignited his volatile state of mind. His grip on his semi-automatic tightened as he aimed at his target. Seconds later he felt relief as his victim lay covered in blood. Once again, he'd avenged Beth's death, a secret he'd kept from Bentley and the CIA shrink.

Along with relief was affirmation. A declaration in his own mind that Laurence O'Rourke, the man who shot Beth, was dead. He was killing O'Rourke over and over. Every time he aimed his pistol, he saw O'Rourke's face. Every time he squeezed the trigger, O'Rourke died. He recalled the blood spurting from the man's neck. The man lying on the stone floor in the Friars' chamber, a red puddle under his neck and head. He watched the man's face grow ashen, heard gurgling as the man tried to speak, watched the man grow still and die. Once again, he had avenged Beth's death—then came exhilaration, followed by calmness and tranquility.

A sound on the trail caused Jake to look up. "It's about time, I was about to leave your ass here." Jake could barely make out Kaplan's dark features behind the balaclava. With his dark skin, black hair, and brown eyes, Kaplan's size, six-one, two hundred-ten pounds, was his only discerning feature from the terrorists in the camp.

Kaplan smiled. "When we get back, I'll call Bentley. Get the green light for tonight."

"We should have already taken them out and captured Yasir. We could have squeezed out the location of the other attacks and not risked missing our next target."

"Provided Yasir knows anything about them." Kaplan motioned for Jake to take the lead down the trail. "These cells don't usually share information about each other's activities. Only the handler knows all the locations…and handlers are more difficult to catch."

The three-mile hike from the ledge overlooking the terrorist camp to the SAS base was characteristic of the mountainous Australian Outback—rugged. It took them over an hour traversing the rocky terrain to reach the camouflage canopy covering the basketball court sized SAS camp. Australian sentries were concealed in the hills surrounding the camp blocking every access. Their job was to ensure the unit's presence in the desert remained undetected by the terrorist cell. Even if the cell had access to satellite imagery, which was unlikely, the camp would be virtually undetectable.

Centered under the large canopy was the TEMPEST secure tent. The copper mesh tent contained another copper mesh room inside, which provided extra radio frequency shielding for all the equipment housed within its curtain walls. A tent inside a tent. The radio frequency shielded enclosure was part of the 'Executive Travel Kit' as Kaplan had called it. The shielded tent technology eliminated the possibility of electronic eavesdropping by providing a high degree of radio frequency attenuation. Other equipment housed in the tent were receivers from SIGIT Group which were used to monitor everything transmitted or said inside the terrorist camp.

The terrorist cell would be scanning for signals, so the TEMPEST provided extra precaution to prevent being detected. The success of the mission depended on the element of surprise.

Jake followed Kaplan into the small enclosure that housed the Integrated T2C3 Secure Communications Workstation. Its main feature was the secure satellite phone and link terminal allowing for secure voice and data transmission and reception.

Inside the dimly lit room, Jake saw an Australian SIS analyst monitoring the secure data link terminal. The same analyst was always at the terminal. Monitoring the TEMPEST's level of integrity and analyzing signals received from the terrorist camp was his only job—and he always seemed to be there. *The man must never sleep.*

Without looking up the analyst said, "Bentley wants you to report in. He is waiting for your call. Said there has been some new development and your mission might be scrubbed."

CHAPTER 3

Ios Island, Cyclades
Greek Islands

REVENGE.

Ian Collins had obsessed about it every day for the last six months. First, his reputation as one of the best assassins in the business had been ruined when he failed to deliver on a contract in what was made into a public spectacle by the meddling of one man. Then several days later he was wounded in a shootout at a mansion in Georgia. Now, he could no longer support his lavish lifestyle and was forced to live like a rat in hiding.

His last paying contracts had been lucrative but it had left him a pariah. Without work for six months, his cash reserves had dwindled. He needed work.

Collins sat on a rock atop a hill looking down at the town of Ormos on Ios Island. His sanctuary. His retreat. And the rock—his favorite place for reflection, contemplation, and planning.

The perch offered a beautiful vista of Ormos harbor; a tranquil sheltered waterfront nestled amidst the Greek Islands. He'd seen a postcard photo taken from the very spot he now sat. A cruise ship in the harbor had just dropped anchor. Soon tourists would flood the streets of his small retreat, buying over-priced trinkets from the merchants near the waterfront.

Collins owned a small villa on Ios Island, one he'd paid cash for several years earlier while his cash flow was abundant. Whenever he felt threatened, whenever he got that uneasy feeling Interpol was getting too close, or whenever he just needed a break, this was where he came. Here, he was off the grid.

And *off the grid* was where he had to stay. His travel would be limited. All expenses paid with cash. No paper trail could be left to follow. Not yet.

Collins, a former Irish Republican Army hit man turned assassin, once had a lucrative business. He was good, maybe the best. During a time when society seemed to adopt an attitude of solving its problems by eliminating them, he was in the business of eliminating people's problems—and business was good.

Society labeled him a psychopath. He preferred "product of his environment." He'd grown up with violence. In his younger days in Northern Ireland, it was a way of life.

He hadn't always been ruthless. He remembered the turning point, now a haunting memory. He was a teenager when an escaped convict came to his hometown of Londonderry. The man beat him, tied him up, and forced him to watch while the man raped a woman, the aunt of Collins' best friend. He felt helpless and scared but another emotion emerged that day as he watched how powerless the woman was to defend herself. Domination over the weak. The convict was the mighty lion who had stalked his prey, taken what he wanted, and then, satisfied, walked away.

Collins mastered the skills of an assassin. His hits were clean. Executed with precision and accuracy.

Keeping a low profile was not easy anymore. After the botched assassination attempt in Savannah, Georgia on St. Patrick's Day, his likeness and description had been telecast worldwide, and since that day, he was at the top of Interpol's most wanted list.

The logical thing was to disguise his appearance. Although distasteful to him personally, he kept his hair bleached and dyed to match the natural white streak in his hair leaving him with a full head of white hair. Dark brown contacts in both eyes masked his mismatched irises, one vivid blue, the other light brown. All traits associated with his Waardenburg's Syndrome, a hereditary medical condition passed to him by his father.

During childhood he'd dealt with the ridicule and joking about his different eye color and white streaked hair. He ignored the teasing and pretended it didn't bother him. But things changed after he witnessed the rape. He began to get in fights, each one more brutal than the last, until he beat a boy to death. He hid the body and was never implicated—another runaway teenager the authorities ruled.

Fear was soon replaced by the thrill of domination. There were other children who later disappeared and were never found. But they got what they deserved. And so will the meddling American.

In the distance Collins could see the Greek island of Silkinos. A beautiful backdrop as the sun sank lower into the western sky glistening off the crystalline waters of the Mediterranean Sea.

Revenge. How sweet it will be.

He sat on the rock and plotted.

Plotted his revenge. He wanted to make the man pay for destroying his livelihood. He wouldn't kill the man—not at first anyway. Killing the man was too easy. Collins wanted him to suffer. Just like the girl who teased him in school, he tormented her first by putting her cat's head in her lunchbox. Later she disappeared.

The meddling man who had ruined his reputation would feel Collins' wrath. Soon, the man would know it was he who killed his fiancée. Collins would take great pleasure delivering that message. The man needed to feel guilt, needed to suffer.

Then, Collins would kill him.

Collins left his perch at the top of the hill and started down the path toward his villa. His plan became clear. A smile crept across his face.

Collins knew how he'd kill Jake Pendleton.

CHAPTER 4

"WHAT DO YOU mean the mission might be scrubbed?" Jake looked at the ASIS analyst. The last thing he wanted was a delay. He could feel anxiety welling up inside him. He needed this mission. The missions were his therapy sessions. It was only during the missions where he had the opportunity to avenge his fiancée's death. He wouldn't let this terrorist escape.

The Integrator 2100TS secure phone beeped. "Ask him yourself, that's the director now." The analyst got up from his chair and pointed to the phone, "All yours mate."

Kaplan stepped forward and pushed the speakerphone button. "Kaplan."

The voice was CIA Director Bentley, "Gregg, is Jake with you?"

"Right here, sir." Jake said.

The ASIS analyst walked to the door flap, stepped out, and secured the copper mesh door. A potential weak spot for leakage, the door was sealed with a copper infused version of Velcro then verified safe using the T-Set to check for signal leaks.

"Good. I'll let George take it from here."

Jake first met George Fontaine six months prior when he'd arrived at CIA Headquarters in Langley and received his initial briefing on the two Irishmen who had escaped the day his fiancée was mortally wounded. At just under six feet, Fontaine was overweight with brown hair and a crooked nose, which matched his crooked smile—the smile never seemed to leave his face. But most of all, Fontaine was competent.

Competent and thorough.

The same way Jake had been when he was an intelligence officer for the U. S. Navy. The way he had been when he served under Bentley. A trait Bentley demanded from his subordinates. 'Leave no stone unturned. No possibility unexplored. No detail ignored.' was Bentley's dictum. Jake held fast to it in the Navy, as did Fontaine with the CIA.

"Jake. Gregg. We've picked up intel and chatter that an American might be in the camp. Goes by the name of Khan, Hashim Khan. He declared himself a traitor and now ranks high in al Qaeda, handling and planning cell movements and attacks. His photo should come across the wire any second now. He's number three on the FBI's Most Wanted Terrorists List—even higher than Yasir. Khan has been blamed for planning several terrorist attacks around the globe including the failed Detroit airliner bombing, the DC subway attempt, and the Times-Square car bomb attempt. We believe he's planning another attack or *attacks* and is in Australia with Yasir."

"Sounds incompetent to me." Jake said.

"Might seem that way, but those failed attempts were in the U.S. In other parts of the world he's responsible for dozens of attacks and over a hundred deaths. We need more time to figure out his intentions. If we move prematurely, Khan's associates might move without him and we'll never know his intended targets.

Jake looked at Kaplan while he spoke to Fontaine, "That's a load of crap, George. We're ready for this op. We can get in and out, capture Yasir *and* Khan. Then we'll let Gregg do that interrogation shit you guys taught him." He glanced at Kaplan.

"Jake's right, sir." Kaplan said to Bentley. "We have all the data we need. It's time to make our move. Whatever Khan is planning, I'll get it out of him."

There was a faint click on the speakerphone.

Thirty seconds later another click, Bentley's voice. "Gentlemen, perhaps you're right. Now might be the time to move. Jake, my concern is you. There is no room for compromise here. It is imperative they *both* be captured and interrogated. If Kaplan can't break them, then I'll send someone down who can."

"I can break him, sir." Kaplan said. "Just give us the green light."

Jake smiled. He knew Bentley had decided to let them go ahead with the mission. He would control himself with Khan and Yasir. He had no choice. After the last mission, Bentley had talked to him about his trigger-happy tendencies and put him on notice.

Two weeks ago, Bentley looked him in the eyes, "Jake, the definition of clandestine is 'executed with secrecy.' That's why we're called the Clandestine Service—secrecy is our mission. You can't leave a trail of dead bodies everywhere you go. It raises too many eyebrows. I have a member of the Senate breathing down my back about your last operation. Says I need to learn to control my people."

"I'm sorry sir." Jake said. "But in my defense, the mission you're talking about, I stopped the bombing of the market. Those two men I shot were about to kill a lot of innocent people. You know how dangerous Afghanistan can be."

"Again, Jake. Clandestine. I don't give a damn that you killed those two goons. They deserved to die. I *do* care that you got caught on camera. It was hard to justify our presence over there. Just promise me you'll be more discreet."

"Yes sir."

The radio cracked then Bentley's voice, "The mission with the Australians is on for tonight." He said. "I'll let Fontaine give you a briefing but before you sign off, I want to talk you about another matter."

Jake noticed something out of the ordinary in Bentley's usual calm voice.

Humming sounds filled the room as the data encrypted computers came to life. The monitor displayed a diagram of the al Qaeda camp. Jake recognized it immediately. The encrypted fax machine hummed the arrival of a new fax.

"Jake, you and Gregg take a look at this." Fontaine said.

The next forty minutes were spent planning and discussing the exact timing of the raid on the training camp. The execution had to be flawless or else Australian SAS soldiers could die. Jake and Kaplan could die.

Kaplan would brief the SAS soldiers on the raid. Each soldier would know his assignment. Each soldier would know his target. Each man in the unit was a trained professional and Jake was certain the mission would succeed. He lived for these moments.

Fontaine finished the briefing and Bentley's voice crackled in the speaker. "Jake? Gregg? You still there?"

"Yes sir. We're right here." Jake looked at Kaplan who returned the stare. "What do you have for us?"

"Isabella Hunt has gone missing."

CHAPTER 5

"WHAT?" JAKE SAID.

"Gone missing?" Kaplan asked. "How so, sir?"

"Just that." Bentley's voice in the speaker. "She was working an op in Aden, Yemen when we lost contact with her. We believe her cover was compromised and she's been taken captive. We've tracked her as far as Sana'a, Yemen where we had our last confirmed ID. After that visual, they went underground, perhaps literally. We don't know if she's still in Sana'a, whether they've moved her to another location, or if she's even in Yemen. The trail has gone cold. We have assets combing the streets and countryside, asking questions from every source in the field. So far we've turned up nothing."

"What makes you think she blew her cover?" Kaplan asked. "She's good. She doesn't panic. It's unlikely she tipped anyone off to her identity."

"We're confident they're on to her." Bentley hesitated. "No other scenario makes sense."

"We have to go after her," Kaplan said.

"First things first, gentlemen. Neither of you is going anywhere until this mission is complete. I need you both focused on the job at hand, not distracted. I hesitated even telling you about Isabella until the mission was over and under normal circumstances I would never have revealed anything that would jeopardize team focus, but since both of you have worked with her, I thought you deserved to know. When you get back, both of you will come here first and we'll discuss our options for rescuing Isabella." Bentley paused. "Gregg, I know you and Isabella have worked together over the past few months—but I need you at a hundred percent on this raid. Don't let this distract you from your primary mission."

"No, sir." Kaplan said. "But after we finish here, I want to help find Isabella. You have nothing to be worried about."

Matter of fact, Jake was worried. Kaplan seemed to be getting close to Isabella Hunt. Too close. After she was shot in the leg when they were in Ireland, Kaplan had taken more than a platonic interest in her recovery—and she in his.

Jake and Kaplan became good friends during their ordeal in Savannah and Ireland, but the abruptness of Beth's death caused Jake to distance himself from everybody. Kaplan and Hunt tried to comfort him. It was obvious they wanted to be understanding, compassionate friends, but the trauma of his loss made him bitter and he resented their intrusion into his pain. A suffering he'd rather not share. He couldn't explain why, but he wanted to *feel* the suffering. He needed it. He deserved it.

His friend had tried to draw a common denominator since they both lost a loved one. But like Kaplan said, his girlfriend, Annie, had a secret side. He said he never really knew her and felt betrayed. Betrayed by her double identity. Betrayed by her involvement in the Savannah conspiracy. Jake didn't buy any of it. Kaplan was making excuses, probably to himself, to mask how he really felt.

Kaplan and Hunt's budding relationship wasn't lost on him either. He'd noticed them spending more time together. He was still grieving the loss of Beth, so how could Kaplan flaunt his newfound friendship with Hunt in his face like that? How could he even have a relationship with Hunt? It wasn't right. It was too soon.

"Don't worry about Gregg, sir." Jake grabbed Kaplan's shoulder. "As always, he'll give you his best."

"No problem, sir. I'll remain focused." Kaplan glared at Jake. "But like I said, when we get back, I'm going after her."

"Don't forget who gives the orders, Gregg." Bentley said. "Right now, back to work. Get some rest. Keep your wits about you tonight men and bring those two terrorists back *alive*."

† † †

18 Hours Later
3:45 a.m.

Jake and Kaplan, together with a team of nine specialized SAS soldiers were secured in their prearranged positions surrounding the terrorist training camp. Counting Jake and Kaplan, four ground teams of two each and three strategically located snipers.

Two snipers positioned themselves along the surveillance ledge, both with optimal viewpoints of the camp below. A third sniper, the only man not paired, was situated along an adjacent ridge covering the only potential escape route for the terrorists.

Every man was dressed in full black. Black clothes. Kevlar vests. Boots. Nomex gloves. Guns. Faces painted black. Black helmets outfitted with earpieces and voice activated microphones and night vision goggles.

Eleven men, set for a surgical strike against the camp under the command of Gregg Kaplan. Only at his direction would the precision assault begin.

During their briefing with Fontaine, they had developed the strategy based on the timing of the guards and the direction of their watch rounds. The total number of terrorists in the camp had been determined, confirmed, and reconfirmed through several nights of constant surveillance. Visual and satellite imagery, using thermal detection, had projected a camp occupancy at sixteen. Eleven highly skilled soldiers and operatives with the element of surprise on their side against a rag-tag group of sixteen terrorists in the desert, in the middle of the night—in Jake's opinion the deck seemed stacked.

In and out, he thought. There would be bloodshed. He'd capture Khan and Yasir, then he'd call for ASIS and SAS to clean up the mess.

Kaplan keyed his microphone. "Everyone in position? Check in."

In prearranged order, all nine SAS soldiers checked-in, their positions secured and ready for the first strike. The snipers lined the ridges with the task of eliminating the patrolling sentries and to provide overhead cover, if needed. Four two-man teams advanced on the camp, each team given a quadrant to secure with instructions to neutralize any threats.

Jake looked at Kaplan. "Here we go, buddy."

Kaplan nodded. "Yep. Keep your head down."

Kaplan switched on his voice-activated microphone. "Snipers, take down the sentries on my mark."

Four terrorist sentries patrolled the camp at any given time, two working the perimeter of the camp clockwise. The other two counter-clockwise. It had been nearly an hour since the shift change, which Jake concluded had been ample time for the previous four guards to fall asleep and long enough for boredom to dull the guards' awareness.

When the guards on the cliff side of the camp passed each other Kaplan said, "Engage." The ledge snipers fired the silenced rifles, 7.62 NATO match ammo. The only sound was the al Qaeda sentries falling to the sand. Body shots. Each bullet perfectly placed, right through the heart.

"Sentries one and two down. I say again, one and two down." The voice whispered through the earpiece.

A second later, another muffled pop. "Sentry three down. Repeat, three down."

As if he recognized the sounds, the fourth sentry began to run. Before he could take two strides, another silenced round dropped him. He fell face down into the sand sending his rifle crashing against the side of a wooden crate.

The sound of the thud caused the strike team to instinctively duck.

"Sentry four down. Repeat, four down."

"Hold your positions." Kaplan said.

"Movement at tent one," one of the snipers said.

"Hold fire."

A man stumbled out of his tent, rubbing his eyes. He walked over to the 'P-spot' as Jake had labeled it on the strike diagram. "That's the spot they all go to pee."

"Sniper three, how's your angle?" Kaplan asked.

"Clear shot."

"Take the shot when he starts to shake it."

"Say again."

"When the man starts to shake it, take him out. Understood?"

"Roger that."

Jake nudged him with his elbow. "You know, you're a sicko."

"At least then we'll know where both hands are." Kaplan smiled.

Another silenced shot. It was high, striking the man slightly below the base of the skull. The impact from the high-power sniper load nearly decapitated the man. He fell forward into the mulgas rustling the limbs as his body rolled through the tiny branches. The sound carried through the camp.

"We better move fast, Gregg. That had to wake someone up." Jake readied his Glock.

From all the observations, they had determined the training camp had two dormitory tents sleeping seven each. Two from each tent had sentry duty at night. The largest tent, Yasir's tent, housed only two occupants, Yasir and one other assumed to be Hashim Khan. Near one corner of the camouflage netting was a communications tent and a supply tent—both should be empty this time of the morning.

Kaplan made the call. "All teams, go, go, go."

CHAPTER 6

Hajjah Palace
Hajjah, Yemen

ISABELLA HUNT'S HEAD didn't just hurt, it debilitated her. Contusions on her forehead and the back of her head felt like a vise had been placed on her ears and her skull slowly crushed. With the pulsing of each heartbeat, the pain intensified.

She scanned the room, even with blurry vision she could tell she was in a holding cell of some kind. Metal bars mounted in the single window were caked with dust and dirt that matched the brown glass. A rough-hewn wooden door directly opposite the window had a four-inch square peephole—a peephole someone opened and closed every few minutes, checking to see if she had regained consciousness. Not yet, she needed time to think of a way to escape.

Dry, stale dust caked her tongue and throat. She could feel the dehydration, her body longing for a drink of water. She'd been in this country too long. The dry, arid desert had taken its toll. She coughed.

The peephole opened and a man brought some food and a tin cup with a few swallows of liquid. Both were horrid, but she didn't care. Isabella was disoriented, her head throbbed and vision blurred so she reaasoned food would help. She ate and drank, but it made her drowsy and sluggish.

She still didn't know what had gone wrong. One minute she was doing her job—assistant to a shipping magnate in the port city of Aden—sitting in her office updating an export contract, when a man she'd never seen before rushed through the door, grabbed, and hit her. She fell onto the desk face first and smashed her forehead against the computer monitor. When she tried to stand, something smacked the back of her head and the office went black.

Had she blown her cover? More importantly, when would Bentley send someone after her?

She knew he would. Sooner or later. She hoped it would be Kaplan. They'd worked together on her last two missions. Both times posing as a couple. The first time as vacationers in Italy, they consulted a man named Vincent Corsaletti, a man who was known for his powerful connections. Vinny, as he preferred to be called, helped them locate an escaped prisoner from Gitmo, Guantanamo Bay Naval Base detention camp. Corsaletti was a Sicilian information broker.

With Corsaletti's help, Hunt and Kaplan assisted Italian authorities in raiding the Islamic Cultural Institute in Milan and apprehending an al Qaeda facilitator who worked for Yemen's Political Security Organization and responsible for shuttling terrorists around the globe.

Their second mission together sent them to Tripoli, Libya, posing as a newlywed couple and potential customers for a Libyan shipping company. Corsaletti informed them the owner had ties to Ian Collins. They attempted to extract information from the owner to help them locate and apprehend the assassin known as Shamrock. The owner disavowed any connection to Collins, refusing to discuss the matter any further. Hunt and Kaplan were escorted out and they were left at a dead end.

She thought of the mission often, it had been different than the others. For her, it was special. A turning point in their friendship. Her thoughts were interrupted when the outside bolt on the huge door swung open. The black void that appeared outside the open door disappeared when two large men stormed into the room. The larger man picked her up, placed her in a wooden chair, and held her down while the second man grabbed her arms and pulled them behind the chair.

She recognized the feel of flex cuffs being slipped around her wrists and kicked the larger man in the groin. His grip relaxed causing the chair to tip onto its back legs. The man in back lost his grip on her hands. Free of the flex cuffs, she leapt forward, head butting the first man in the gut, knocking him to the floor.

She spun around to take a punch at the other man when she felt the sting in the back. Every muscle in her body contracted and she collapsed on the rough-hewn floor.

"American Tasers. Work well, yes." A third voice said.

She'd been tased once before. She didn't like it then and nothing had changed. Affectionately called "riding the bull," it was something all operatives had to endure during training, but there was nothing *affectionate* about it.

By the time she regained use of her limbs, she had been repositioned back in the chair, flex cuffed, and strapped to the chair with duct tape.

"Who do you work for?" The third voice asked.

"You know who I work for." Hunt said. "Your goons kidnapped me."

Knuckles crunched the side of her face. Blood spurted from her lips, splattering against the stone wall behind her.

"We can do this either way. The hard way or the easy way. I don't care, I have all night. Again, who do you work for?"

"Hilal Shipping." She braced herself, expecting another blow to the head but instead some sort of stick was rammed into her gut.

She gasped for air but the void in her chest wouldn't fill. She lurched forward against the restraints, begging for air. Finally it came. A small sip at a time. Her lungs burned. Her gut hurt. What seemed like minutes were mere seconds.

She raised her head, tried to focus—he was smiling. The left side of his face burned, no eyebrows or eyelashes. His left hand missing two fingers. His disfigured face not as appalling as the stench from his rotten teeth. His gums were brown, teeth black.

"What is your job at Hilal Shipping?"

She struggled to speak. In broken breaths she said, "I'm administrative assistant to Ahmed al-Hilal. Owner of Hilal Shipping."

"How long have you worked at Hilal?"

"Six weeks."

"And before, you worked for the CIA, yes?"

"No, I never—"

The next blow broke her nose. Blood flowed over her chin, dripping onto her lap.

"Leave us." The man commanded.

She heard two sets of footsteps walk away from her. The man lifted her chin with his stick. She felt his hot breath against her face. Smelled the stench of rotten gums.

"You will tell me the truth or you will die. I'll leave you to think about how our next meeting will go. But I promise you this, I won't be as polite."

Footsteps walked across the room.

The door slammed and bolted shut.

Isabella's chin fell to her chest. Pain radiated through her weakened body. Blood dripped from her nose and mouth as her lips formed the words, barely audible to her own ears, "Gregg."

CHAPTER 7

THE SAS STRIKE team had been regimented to perfection. The operation meticulously planned and each soldier knew his task. Jake watched Kaplan drill the soldiers time after time, covering every angle and every possible scenario. If something were to go wrong, each man should instinctively know what to do. Stay the course, don't over react, and maintain focus.

Underneath the canopy the terrorists used low light kerosene lanterns and flashlights to avoid detection from the air by overflying aircraft or satellites. In the nighttime desert, even the smallest output of light could be seen from miles away.

Team one entered the camp's perimeter first. Their task was to secure the communications tent, disabling any opportunity for outside transmissions.

Mounted on support poles underneath the netting were floodlights that went undetected during surveillance. A detail neither Jake nor Kaplan had contemplated was about to turn the mission into a tragedy. The floodlights were activated by trip wires randomly strung around the perimeter—tripwires that also went undetected...until the first SAS soldier stepped on the wire.

The area lit up like a football stadium at night, blinding the soldiers wearing the NVGs. The men ripped off their night vision goggles but the initial blast of light had temporarily impaired their vision. Now six men stood sightless in the middle of an enemy camp.

Sitting ducks.

Jake and Kaplan were outside the perimeter when the lights came on. Far enough outside to escape being blinded by the NVGs. The eleven-man team was now a five-man team and Jake and Kaplan were the only ones at camp level who could still see.

Within seconds after the camp lit up, Jake heard the terrorists yelling inside the tents. The six-blinded soldiers dove to the sand and rolled.

"Gregg. We have a problem."

Kaplan charged forward motioning Jake to watch Yasir's quarters. "Snipers, fire through the netting. Take out the dorm tents."

Teams two and three, the teams designated to hit the dorm tents, were deepest inside the camp and the most exposed when the first of the terrorists scrambled into the open.

Sniper rounds peppered the tents.

Screams of agony filled the desert night air.

Jake crouched to a firing stance on one knee. He took aim at the tent closest to his position. Three men ran out, two covered in blood, all firing wildly in the air as they ran into the night.

Jake noticed Kaplan in the same one-knee stance firing into the other tent.

More shots rang out. Silenced rounds continued to spray the tents. The snipers had done their job. The movement stopped and the camp went silent.

"Jake, Yasir." Kaplan was up and running for the terrorist's quarters.

Jake moved faster and was waiting when Kaplan arrived.

They stood outside, Jake heard whispering. "Drop your weapons."

Kaplan looked at him. "What are you doing?"

"Giving Yasir a chance to surrender." Jake said. "Just like Bentley wanted."

A voice came through the headset. "Team one operational, communications and supply tents secure."

"Good. Go help the others. Make sure both dorm tents are neutralized."

Jake and Kaplan parted the tent doors with the barrels of their pistols.

Kaplan looked in, "Mustaff Bin Yasir?"

Crouched in back were two people, one Yasir. Jake recognized him from the preponderance of photos he'd studied. The other an Asian woman, not Hashim Khan, the American traitor they were looking for.

Yasir and the woman were huddled in the rear, Yasir holding a knife to her throat using her tiny body as a shield.

"No shoot. No shoot." The woman pleaded.

"Drop the knife." Kaplan stepped toward the pair, his barrel switching from Yasir to the woman to Yasir.

Jake moved next to Kaplan. "Let her go—now."

"No shoot. No shoot." She screamed.

Jake felt his anger swell. He couldn't be responsible for letting another woman die because he failed to react fast enough.

† † †

A sudden clap of thunder blasted in his ears and caught Kaplan by surprise as he watched the pink mist fly from the back of Yasir's head. The terrorist fell backward into the canvas tent and tumbled to the desert floor.

He saw Jake still pointing his gun at Yasir's lifeless body, now crumpled on the floor in a bloody pile.

The woman started screaming in a language he didn't know. After what Jake just did, Kaplan didn't have time to deal with the Asian woman so he hit her in the head with the butt of his gun rendering her unconscious.

Securing her hands and legs with flex cuffs, he turned to Jake. "What the hell did you just do? Alive, Jake. Alive. Bentley wanted him alive."

Jake lowered his gun. "He was going to kill her. We need her more than him."

"How the hell do you figure?" Kaplan pointed toward the unconscious woman. "We don't even know who she is."

"Look at her. She's Asian. Why would an Asian woman be in this camp? Don't you think that's a little odd? Whatever her reason for being here is something we need to find out. That makes her our priority."

"What the hell's wrong with you, Jake? I don't know you any more. You've gone off the deep end. Ever since Beth died, you shoot everything and everyone in sight. The whole concept of 'capture alive' eludes you. You're careless and irresponsible. And your behavior endangers the safety of those around you."

"Shut up, Gregg. I did what had to be done. It was Yasir or the woman."

Kaplan shoved Jake in the chest, knocking him two steps backwards. "You're no better than an assassin. You're like, like...Ian Collins. Or worse, Laurence O'Rourke."

Kaplan saw it in Jake's eyes, he'd struck a nerve.

Jake raised his pistol, aiming it at Kaplan's head. "Don't ever talk to me that way again."

"Jake, two things you better get through that thick skull of yours. One, you need help. Serious help. When we get back, I'll talk to Bentley."

"And two?" Jake asked.

Kaplan heard Jake's sarcasm. "Two. If you ever point a gun at me again, you better use it...or I'll kill you where you stand." Kaplan paused to let the words sink in.

He turned and walked out of the tent.

CHAPTER 8

Two Days Later

JAKE TIGHTENED HIS seatbelt as the Challenger jet descended into the West Texas desert. It was the same Challenger he flew on to Ireland back in March when he discovered the secret cache of weapons buried beneath the ancient Irish ruins of the Creevelea Abbey. Since March, he'd flown on it numerous times. Bentley sat in the seat across from him and hadn't spoken a word since they left Langley. For that matter, Bentley hadn't spoken a dozen words to him since he returned from Australia.

He knew Bentley was upset he'd shot and killed Mustaff bin Yasir, but Bentley's refusal to even acknowledge his presence upset Jake. Yasir got what he deserved. After all, he was about to kill the woman who Jake now knew was an operative with an intelligence organization of some sort. He learned the woman's pleas to stop him from shooting were legitimate—she was close to learning the location of other cells. She needed Yasir alive, he was her only connection to Hashim Khan, the handler of the cells.

As Jake discovered after he returned to Langley, Yasir planned to reunite with Khan after the cell's attack on Sydney. Yasir and the woman had been booked on a freighter owned by the Hilal Shipping Company in Yemen, the same company Isabella Hunt infiltrated, and from which she had disappeared. Too much of a coincidence not to be connected.

When he and Kaplan arrived back at Langley from Australia, Jake was sent home, told to get some rest, and pack.

No destination given.

Jake knew Kaplan had been in contact with Bentley prior to and during their flight back to Washington. Kaplan was summoned directly to Bentley's office and Jake was sent home. He could only surmise that Kaplan would be going to Yemen in search of Isabella Hunt—only he wanted to go too.

"Sir." Jake had to break the silence. "Where are we going?"

"Jake, there's someone I want you to meet." Bentley closed his portfolio and gave his seatbelt a tug.

"Why the silent treatment?"

"Because I had to decide what I was going to do with you."

"And that is what...fly me across the country so I can meet someone?"

Bentley stared at him. "Yes, but first we're going to eat lunch."

"Where are we? We've been in the air for hours."

"West Texas. Not too far from El Paso."

"That's a long way to go for lunch. It must be good." Jake thought he saw a slight curl in Bentley's lips. Then it disappeared.

The jet descended toward the desert floor. Jake looked out the windows on both sides and saw nothing but tumbleweeds, sand, rocks, and cliffs. As if out of nowhere, an asphalt runway appeared beneath the aircraft as it gently touched down and taxied to a large hangar. Parked in front of the hangar was the longest golf cart he'd ever seen with a driver dressed in full cowboy regalia.

Jake followed Bentley down the air stair to the tarmac.

Bentley turned and pointed back at the aircraft. "Go get your bag, you'll need it. You're not returning with me."

The sound of those words sent a chill through Jake. He grabbed his bag and followed Bentley.

The cowboy stepped from the cart and motioned to take Jake's bag. "Director Bentley, Mr. Pendleton, Welcome to Wrangler's Steakhouse. If you'll hop in, I'll take you to your table."

Cowboy tucked Jake's bag away in a covered trunk on the rear of the cart. The cart's seats were made of plush leather with studs securing it around the thick padding. Tassels hung from the outside of each seat and whipped in the wind as the cart pulled away from the hangar.

Jake ran his hand across the leather. "Is everything here this nice?"

Bentley kept looking forward, "E. W. doesn't do anything half-ass."

The cart pulled under a thatch portico attached to the large adobe style building. Jake counted five parking lots, two of which were full. He glanced at his watch, "A lot of people for lunch, I hope we have a reservation."

"This is nothing," Cowboy said. "Wait til suppertime. It's Friday night, all seven lots will be full and there'll be a good two-hour wait for a table. Happens every weekend. Holidays are worse."

"Seven parking lots? I only counted five."

Cowboy pointed to a hill behind the restaurant. "Two larger ones beyond that ridge."

Jake turned to Bentley, "Will I be staying here tonight?"

"No."

"Mr. Pendleton, I'll deliver your bag to you this afternoon." Cowboy pointed toward the glass entryway. "Right this way gentlemen."

Cowboy took them to a table in an empty part of the restaurant, "Your waiter will be right with you."

Jake's curiosity grew until he couldn't stand it any longer. "Sir, what's going on?"

Bentley placed his portfolio on the edge of the table. "You promised me you'd control yourself in Australia...yet you didn't."

Jake inhaled to speak but Bentley's finger was in the air signaling him to remain quiet.

"I realize you thought you were saving the woman. She was undercover, sent to infiltrate Yasir's camp. She's a South Korean posing as a North Korean arms dealer. It took her nearly six months to gain Yasir's trust. She was supposed to arrange a weapons transfer for Khan. Her intel indicated that Yasir's camp was one of three cells planning attacks around the world. She claims she tried to stop you, our link to Khan is dead and we don't know what other cities are targeted. Now we might not be able to stop the attack or attacks."

"Sir, it all happened so fast. By the time I realized what she was saying, Yasir was already dead. I thought she would be more useful to us than Yasir. I had no idea a plant was in the camp."

"That's why you follow orders. You don't have the bigger picture." Bentley paused. "Are you familiar with Senator Richard Boden, Committee Chairman for Homeland Security and Governmental Affairs?"

"The old man with Donald Trump hair who's always chewing gum?" Jake nodded. "Yes sir, I know who he is."

"He wants me to hand you over to him. He has so much as ordered me to do so. He wants to make an example of you. Drag you through the coals publicly and then lock you away. I won't let that happen. Not to any of my operatives. I take orders from the President, not Boden. So I'm putting you someplace where you can lay low. Let this whole thing blow over, and sooner or later it will blow over."

Bentley unrolled his cloth napkin, placed it in his lap, and rearranged his silverware on the table. "Things have changed, Jake. Times have changed. The Clandestine

Service is not what it once was. Society has trouble accepting what we do. Congress is slowly neutering the CIA. Everyday we lose power and prestige. *The People* want things done, want to feel safe and secure, but they don't want to know the truth. Do you understand what I'm saying, Jake?"

"I think so, sir. The good ol' days are gone and the wheels of bureaucracy are grinding the company train to a halt."

"Crude…but accurate. In many ways, we've already ground to a halt. More and more covert operations are being farmed out to contractors and paid through over-budgeted slush funds and dummy corporations. The government has reached a point where it can no longer have assassins as employees. The public has an unrealistic expectation that all problems can be solved diplomatically. Society has grown soft and refuses to accept the true, evil nature of our enemies. So we have been forced to find other ways to accomplish our goals—goals that must be accomplished for the welfare of this nation as well as many other nations."

"How long before all this blows over and I can get back to work?"

"I don't know. That's why I'm putting you out of sight for a while. And in the mean time, maybe you will learn a little about yourself…and why your problems can't always be solved by simply pulling a trigger."

"But Admiral, I'd like to help Kaplan find Isabella. We're a team."

"Jake, first of all, you and Kaplan need a little time apart." Bentley's tone startled him. "Kaplan is a team player. Isabella is a team player. You, on the other hand, are not a team player and you had better learn to be one very soon or there is no place for you in my organization. Do I make myself clear?"

Jake now understood the impact of his actions in Australia. Bentley had never spoken to him like that and obviously had given him all the leeway he could. He would do what ever Bentley asked of him. He would control his anger—he had to. He would become a team player.

Their waiter interrupted them. He brought two menus, two glasses and a pitcher of water. While he poured water in the glasses he asked if they wanted cocktails. They both declined.

Out the window Jake saw an old covered chuck wagon with a steer skull attached to the front of the canopy. A peacock perched on the hitching rail. In the distance an old barn surrounded by cactus served as a reminder of the ranch's history as a stopping point for the old Pony Express.

"When do I meet this man?" Jake asked.

"He'll let us know when he's ready for us. In the meantime, enjoy a good meal."

"What do you mean, 'when he's ready for us?' Is he here?"

"He owns the place, Wrangler's Steakhouse. He's been watching us since we got off the jet."

CHAPTER 9

Sana'a, Yemen

KAPLAN, AND THE young man known only as Chase, pulled up in front of the safe house in the Company's Toyota Land Cruiser. The ride from Aden to Sana'a was long and lack of food and sleep were taking its toll. Kaplan hadn't slept in over twenty-four hours or eaten in over nine. The back of the U. S. Army C-130 that flew him from Washington to Yemen was loud and uncomfortable. First order of business was to eat and sleep. Daylight was only nine hours away and he wanted to be on the move by sun up.

Chase was younger than Kaplan expected, mid-twenties, and shorter too. Maybe five nine. He looked strong, and cut. He had a close-cropped beard—a chin curtain with no mustache. With his jeans, t-shirt, tennis shoes, and backpack, Chase looked like a college student.

From the information Kaplan gleaned during his pre-mission brief, Chase was part of a Delta Force Squadron temporarily based in Oman, now on special assignment in Yemen. As the United States' primary counter-terrorism unit, Delta was a versatile group of soldiers capable of assuming many covert missions, hostage rescue among them. Since Delta was a highly secretive unit, they were granted autonomy and tremendous latitude. They were allowed relaxed grooming and clothing standards and told to blend in and not be recognizable as military personnel.

Kaplan had studied the maps along the way with a Maglite held between his teeth. There were so many small villages in the outlying areas surrounding Sana'a that Isabella Hunt could be anywhere. The mountainous area was steep, rugged terrain, so a rescue attempt would be challenging. On the other hand, if they had taken her into a valley or the flat desert, infiltration and exfiltration would be simpler.

"Mr. Kaplan, are your familiar with Delta and its mission?" Chase asked.

Kaplan laughed.

"What's so funny? That wasn't a joke."

Kaplan reached down, rolled up his sleeve, and let his Maglite flash across his upper arm. "What do you think?"

On Kaplan's arm was a tattoo—Airborne—the insignia of the Delta Force. An arrowhead shield with a superimposed sword. "Good."

Kaplan went back to studying the map.

"Rank?" Chase asked.

"Sergeant Major." Kaplan turned off the Maglite. "You?"

"Captain."

"Captain?" Kaplan folded his map. "How old are you?"

"Twenty-six."

"Great." *They promote them younger and younger these days.*

According to Chase, one of the local sources had seen Hunt but was afraid to talk. Someone was needed to lean on the source and leaning was one of Kaplan's areas of specialty. If the source knew anything, as Chase had indicated, Kaplan would squeeze the information out of him.

Chase turned off the ignition to the Land Cruiser. "Before we go in, let me brief you on our brick." Kaplan remembered the term 'brick' referred to the small Delta team.

"Counting me, there are five of us, four men and one woman—"

"A woman? In Delta?" Kaplan was astonished. "I thought women were forbidden in Delta."

"Most of the time that's true but we're called a *funny platoon*. Have you ever heard of that?"

Kaplan shook his head.

"A *funny platoon* is an intelligence gathering outfit, that's our sole purpose." Chase explained. "Almost always under cover. Here, we are college students under a foreign flag, Canada, studying architecture of the region. We're all on a first name basis and never refer to each other by rank…ever."

"Understood." Kaplan said.

"We've only been here a day. We received the mission brief yesterday morning and we were on the go within three hours. We flew out of Oman and traveled to Aden and have been awaiting the arrival of our college professor—namely you."

"College professor, eh." Kaplan smiled.

"I have to be honest, the brick's been a little nervous about you. Rumors. We've had a couple of unpleasant experiences with Clandestine Services before." Chase grinned. "You being Delta will help put their minds at ease. Let's go."

Kaplan followed Chase into the safe house where three young men were playing cards while a short young woman stood watch. Barely five feet tall with dirty blonde hair, she wore sweat pants, flip-flops, and a t-shirt that read, *I'm Not Short, I'm Fun Size*—not what Kaplan was expecting. Certainly not fitting the mold Kaplan had envisioned of the Delta Force team.

"Look who I found." Chase said. "Professor Kaplan just informed me   he's a fellow alumni."

Kaplan pulled up his sleeve revealing his Delta tattoo.

The four soldiers smiled.

Chase introduced Kaplan to the members of the brick. He pointed to the woman. "She thinks she runs the place."

"Don't listen to him, Mr. Kaplan—"

"Gregg." Kaplan corrected.

"Professor." The woman paused until Kaplan grasped the protocol. "I only try to keep the boys focused."

"Believe me, she's got her work cut out for her." Chase said. "Don't let size fool you though—there's a lot of fire in that small package."

Someone had prepared a meal and brewed a fresh pot of coffee. "Do you mind?" Kaplan inhaled his food, washing it down with three cups of coffee. When he finished eating he looked up and all eyes were focused on him. The short woman was smiling.

Chase pointed to a door. "You'll bunk in there. The room's empty so you won't be disturbed when the team rotates watches. Take the one on the right." He pointed to the woman. "She'll grab the bunk on the left in a few hours. We lock up at ten and lights out at eleven. We're just outside the al-Rawdah district—it's dangerous for Americans here so we keep guard all night."

"But we're Canadians." Kaplan said in jest.

"Doesn't matter, all Westerners are the enemy here. And we're always faced with some element of danger."

"Then, I'll take a watch too." Kaplan said.

"Not tonight. You've been awake a long time. Get some sleep. You can pull a watch tomorrow night if you'd like."

Chase pointed to another door with a crescent moon sign hanging from the door. "The outhouse is over there."

"Outhouse?" Kaplan asked.

"Okay, it's not a real outhouse, but the facilities are somewhat...primitive. You know, third world country and all."

Kaplan laughed. "I'm sure it'll be just fine."

"One more thing." Chase patted his sidearm. "Keep your weapon within arm's reach at all times. If someone yells, get ready for action."

CHAPTER 10

JAKE SWALLOWED THE last bite of his t-bone steak, folded his napkin, and tucked it under the edge of his plate. He leaned back in his chair. "Now that was a good steak."

"I didn't think you'd be disappointed." Bentley smiled.

"So what's next? How long do we wait?"

"Relax, Jake. It won't be much longer." Bentley said. He pushed his plate to the side and drank the last of his iced tea.

"Sir? Why all the secrecy and cryptic answers? Who is this guy?"

"Jake, let me ask you something. How many surveillance cameras have you noticed?"

Jake studied the room. Glancing at the rough-hewn beams, the antler lights hanging from the ceilings, the pictures and paintings mounted on the walls. After a few seconds he said, "I don't see any."

"This compound has over five-hundred cameras mounted throughout. He has twenty monitors tucked away in a secure location. His computer analyzes every guest's motions and body language—he programmed it himself—and alerts security of any behavior not fitting his parameters. A security guard, disguised as a chef, will then approach the table and ask a few questions, you know things like, 'How is your dinner?' 'Is everything satisfactory?' 'May I get anything else for you?' The kind of stuff you'd expect but in such a manner and in such an order as to invoke certain subconscious psychological responses. Then his computer, based on its interpretation of the responses and body language will issue a threat assessment. Further action, or inaction, is based on the computer's assessment."

"You're yanking my chain." Jake said in disbelief.

"No, Jake, I'm not. The man you're about to meet is probably one of the smartest, if not *the* smartest person I know. He's in his early seventies and has been in the intelligence business a very long time. He can't afford to be careless or let his guard down."

"He's a spy?" Jake asked.

"No, he's not a spook and he's never been a spook. But the entire intelligence community, CIA, NSA, Special Forces—and not just our country but also several ally countries, have relied heavily on his technology for decades. He provides us with specialty items to help us accomplish our missions. He's been doing it for over fifty years. Hell, I've known him for thirty. You know that copper tent and the TEMPEST setup you used in Australia?"

Jake nodded.

"You're about to meet the man who invented the technology that made it possible. It is his design."

Cowboy interrupted them. "Director, Mr. Pendleton, this way please."

Jake gulped down the last of his sweet tea. He and Bentley followed Cowboy through a maze of rooms then down a long rustic hallway of knotted pine paneling littered with posters from movies, mostly Westerns, which were filmed on the property. Cowboy called it the *Movie Showcase Wall*. Wagon wheel lights hung from the fifteen-foot ceilings. They entered an unmarked room at the end of the hall.

Cowboy opened the door allowing Jake and Bentley to enter first. "Please make yourself comfortable. It should only be a few more minutes."

Cowboy walked out and left them alone. Bentley sat down in one of the two over-stuffed leather chairs facing the oversized mahogany desk. A small gas fireplace on an interior wall was flanked by bookshelves crammed with an assortment of hard cover books.

Jake studied the books. The books were all old and he didn't recognize any of the titles. "The fireplace. It doesn't belong with the rest of the room. I would have expected a wood-burning fireplace with a large mantel and brick hearth. Not a gas fireplace"

"Very observant." Bentley leaned forward, propped his elbows on his knees, and interlocked his fingers. "You're right, though. It's not a real fireplace. I mean, it is but it isn't. By the way, if it's any consolation, I didn't know either."

Jake looked at Bentley. "You're doing it again, talking cryptic. Didn't know what?"

"I didn't know there was an operative planted in Yasir's camp." Bentley said.

Jake heard a thump behind the fireplace and stepped back. Out of the corner of his eye he saw Bentley rise and start walking toward the fireplace. Just as he reached it, the fireplace shifted back several inches and slid to the side behind the bookshelf.

Jake stared into an empty elevator. "That explains the fireplace. What the hell kind of place is this?"

"Follow me and I'll show you." Bentley stepped inside. "Come on."

The elevator doors opened thirty seconds after they closed. Jake guessed they must be at least a hundred feet below the restaurant, but Bentley told him it was only fifty.

Jake scanned the expanse in front of him. Two different worlds separated by fifty feet of rock and dirt. Above, the serene relaxed atmosphere of the restaurant with its vistas of the West Texas desert. Below, the hustle and bustle of a factory floor. A sterile factory floor. Workers wore blue aprons with matching caps and latex gloves. A light buzz of action could be heard as people scurried from station to station. On either side of the expanse were two rooms with exterior staircases leading to work areas atop the rooms.

"As you could tell from the Steakhouse above and the workshop down here, he's somewhat of an eccentric man. And he has a few quirks. But don't we all?" Bentley pointed to the far corner. "Recognize that?"

Jake noticed the mock-up of the TEMPEST tent. "I do."

"That's his showcase area." Bentley smiled.

Jake started to move away from the elevator when Bentley grabbed his arm. "Not yet, Jake, stay here. If you wander off, we'll have an upset host. Even I don't have carte blanche to walk around freely. You'll see *what* he wants you to see *when* he wants you to see it."

"Isn't that a bit much?" Jake furrowed his brows. "I mean, we are on the same team."

"Sit tight, Jake. You'll understand after you meet him. He's a man of—"

"Scott Bentley, you old pirate. How the hell are you?" The old man rounded the corner from behind the elevator, grabbed Bentley's arm, and shook his hand so hard Bentley's shoulder was bouncing up and down.

Jake noticed immediately the man looked familiar, but he couldn't place where he'd seen him.

Bentley motioned toward Jake. "I'd like you to meet Jake Pendleton." Bentley motioned back toward the old man. "Jake, this is Mr. Wiley."

Jake shook Wiley's hand and noticed the old man didn't greet him with the same enthusiasm he gave Bentley. "You look familiar, have we met?"

Wiley glanced at Bentley. "No, I don't believe so."

"I know I've seen you somewhere before." Jake couldn't shake the feeling of familiarity with the old man. Where had he seen the man before?

"You two follow me." Wiley turned and walked away.

The old man stopped at the closest station, spoke in Spanish to a young woman who was hand-winding metal coils then motioned for them to follow again. Jake looked at the old man, early seventies, same height as Jake, 5'10", and appeared to be in good physical shape as he darted from station to station while the three men made their way across the open floor.

Jake noticed Wiley's gray hair, parted slightly off center, showed visible signs of receding. After almost every movement, the old man pushed his metal-framed glasses up on his nose and swiped each hand through his hair, one slightly behind the other, as if combing his hair with his fingers without actually running his fingers through his hair, more like patting it down. *Must be one of the quirks Bentley was referring to.* Jake thought it made him more interesting. Left swipe, right swipe. Always in that order, right hand never more than two or three inches behind the left.

The three men stopped in front of an office with an unmarked door and a plate glass window overlooking the factory floor. Bentley instructed Jake to wait outside while he and Wiley entered the office alone. Fifteen minutes passed, Jake wondered why he was being excluded and what the two men were discussing. He was getting anxious but he knew sooner or later he'd find out why he was here.

Wiley's showcase was next to his office. It reminded Jake of Radio Shack, only more impressive. He saw Wiley pick up the phone then hand it to Bentley, realizing for the first time it was a soundproof room. Jake never heard a phone ring or an intercom or even voices for that matter. Bentley put the phone down, glanced through the window at Jake then continued talking to Wiley. Jake's puzzlement over why Bentley brought him here gave way to concern.

After twenty-five minutes, the door to the office opened and Wiley walked out and moved across the complex floor.

Bentley came to the door. "Jake come in here please." He pointed to the plush leather chair. The same type as in the office upstairs. "Have a seat." He closed the door.

"What's going on?" Jake asked.

"There's been a development with Isabella. I have to leave earlier than I'd anticipated. I'm leaving you here with Mr. Wiley."

"But sir, with all due respect." Jake pleaded. "If there's been a development with Isabella, I should join Kaplan and help him get her out."

"Jake, listen to me." Bentley's voice now stern. "Until I tell you otherwise, you take orders from Mr. Wiley. Get to know him. You'll learn more from him than you ever could from me."

"But—"

"No buts, Jake…that's an order."

CHAPTER 11

JAKE WATCHED BENTLEY'S jet slice into the West Texas sky without him. A feeling of emptiness came over him as the jet's rumble vibrated through his body. He felt like a child abandoned on a stranger's doorstep—in a way he was. The emptiness started when Beth died. And now, the black hole was growing inside him.

Cowboy drove the golf cart toward Jake, stopping only inches from him. Jake noticed a bulge in his cheek from a wad of chewing tobacco.

"Come on. Mr. Wiley is waiting. I believe he has a full afternoon in store for you."

Jake crawled in the front seat next to Cowboy. "Did he say what I'm supposed to do?"

"Nah." Cowboy spit on the tarmac. Wiped his mouth with the back of his hand. "He never gets too specific but if I know Mr. Wiley, he's going to give you the grand tour himself. And that will take a while."

"Sounds just great."

"Try to keep an open mind."

"Easier said than done." Jake said. "I just got dumped here by my boss and left with a man I do not know."

"It'll be fine, wait and see." Cowboy led Jake to the upstairs office, opened the elevator, and said, "Jake, press the 'B' and Mr. Wiley will meet you at the showcase."

"You seem to know a lot about Wiley's business."

"If you'll pardon the pun...I wear many hats around here. I know most of Mr. Wiley's business." Cowboy reached in, pressed a button and the elevator door closed.

Wiley was waiting for Jake when he arrived at the showcase. "Sit down, Jake. Let's talk."

"Mr. Wiley, if you don't mind me asking. Why am I here?" Jake said.

"The simple version is Scott needed you out of his hair. You're a problem he doesn't have time to deal with."

"Problem?" Jake snapped.

Wiley looked at Jake. His eyes seemed to penetrate. He didn't speak at first, leaving a long void of awkward silence, then smiled and did the hair swipe thing again. "Jake, you have an anger issue."

Jake started to speak when Wiley raised his hand. "Hear me out."

Wiley paused. "I know about your fiancée. She was critically injured in the shootout in Savannah. You thought, as did everyone, she was recovering and it gave you a false hope. Unfortunately, she had a relapse and died. You're angry because she was taken from you. You never got to see her again. Never got to hold her. Bentley told me how reluctant you were to help him, but you did help him. And while you were tracking down her killer, she died. Somehow you feel guilty, like it's your fault. Well, you're wrong."

Wiley shifted in his seat, pushed his glasses up with his thumb and index finger and massaged the bridge of his nose. "It didn't matter where you were, Beth was going to die. Accept it or not. The anger you embrace clouds your judgment. I imagine every time you pull the trigger, you picture Laurence O'Rourke's face."

Wiley stopped talking as if allowing the words to sink in. Jake knew the old man was right, but how could he possibly know? How could this old man possibly know what Jake was thinking? What Jake was feeling? But he was right.

They sat in silence for a couple of minutes. Wiley stood. "Jake, have you figured this out yet?" He waved his arm out toward his workshop.

"I think so. You're a toymaker. You make toys for spies."

Wiley laughed. "I guess you could put it that way, yes. Another one of my emissaries calls me 'The Toymaker.' But there's a lot more to it than that, as you will soon learn."

"Emissaries?"

"Yes, Jake, emissaries. People who work for me that I send on missions of a secret nature. You, too, will be my emissary. In a manner of speaking, that's what you are with Bentley. Operative, agent, emissary. Call it whatever you wish, they are more or less the same. I prefer emissary—it's not so widely understood."

"People *you* send on missions?" Jake stood and walked over to the TEMPEST tent. "I thought you just made electronic spy toys."

"More than that. I also work in conjunction with an organization that is...let's say, free from bureaucratic red tape. I provide the manpower and resources to accomplish certain tasks other agencies can't because their hands are tied. Remember the Korean woman your friend knocked out in Australia?"

Jake nodded.

"Su Lee works for me. She's an emissary. She'd been gathering intel for months. That's what Scott and I were discussing while you waited out here."

Wiley looked at his watch. "That talk can wait for later. We have things to do now."

Jake started feeling like he was the only one left out of the loop. A secret Bentley and Wiley shared. He pointed to the copper tent. "We used one of these in Australia."

"I know. I sold the Australian Secret Intelligence Service four of them. Let me give you a little background about myself. I promise not to bore you for long."

"Somehow I doubt I'll be bored."

"I have degrees in chemistry and biological science. My original partner died a few years ago, he had degrees in electronics, chemistry, and physics. I first learned about electronics in the Army—Korea. I've been told on numerous occasions that some of the things I build are impossible. But I have one advantage over them, I'm not encumbered by academics. Impossible only means you haven't found a way to make it work yet. The word itself creates a mental roadblock. Don't tell me something won't work, can't work. Just sit down and make it work. I start from the desired end product and work backwards to make it work.

"I've been in the electronics industry for over fifty years. I've worked in production, engineering, administration, management, and sales. I worked for a group with Bell Systems, part of the old Western Electric, doing things similar to Jack Northrop or Lockheed Martin's Skunk Works. I'm sure you've heard of them."

Jake nodded. "They built the SR-71 Blackbird."

"They were into a lot more than that. And they're credited as being the first in the business, but they weren't. Lockheed Martin and Northrop were just the biggest and the most commercial. Most of us, and there are many companies like mine, have been in the business for a really long time. Like I mentioned, I got my start in the Army on a team that restored communications in war damaged Korea back in the fifties. Later I worked for a defense contractor in the DC area that specialized in QRC. Stands for 'Quick Reaction Contracts.' Which is exactly what it sounds like. We provided this for several agencies where we were scripted to break the rules, not abuse them, but to get the job done."

Wiley walked over to a shelf and removed an item. "My companies were founded to do nothing but these kinds of projects. The first thing I ask a customer is—can you buy what you believe you want from someone else? If so, please do. And, if not, tell me what you think you need and I'll take a look at it."

Jake followed Wiley. "Yeah? Who are your customers?"

"My customers are who you think they are. CIA, FBI, NSA, all the Special Forces, DOD, Homeland Security. The list goes on. And don't limit your thinking to domestic. Two of my biggest customers are the British SIS and Mossad."

"How? This place is too small to do as much as you say." Jake walked over to the couch and sat down.

"Jake," Wiley followed him to the couch and sat down. "I read your dossier. You served on the USS Mount Whitney as an intelligence officer."

"Yes sir, that's correct. Is that relevant in some manner?"

"Only in that you should know my companies outfitted the Navy's electronics. All the surveillance equipment you used...my design. Most of the items we produce are not needed in large quantity, so we don't need an assembly line. My products are highly specialized and are mission specific. When things are designed for the commercial market, they rarely get down to the kind of detail required by my customers. They say the devil is in the details and that is the basic truth of designing and building this stuff. The reason I spend so much time on what appears to be such a simple part is if it were made in mass production, it wouldn't meet my customers' standards. Those coils you saw my employees hand winding will have to be tuned to reach their intended values. The parts you've seen are mostly inductive elements required in precision filters. Most of them are used for Improvised Explosive Device disabling technology."

"I had no idea." Jake said. "IEDs have killed and maimed many soldiers. I wasn't even that familiar with them until I went to work for Bentley."

"Knowing people's lives are at stake and taking that responsibility seriously is what it's about." Wiley said.

"You said something earlier." Jake shifted on the couch just in time to watch Wiley make another hair swipe. "You said you had a degree in biological science?"

Wiley nodded.

"Are there any biological weapons here?"

"First of all, I don't make biological weapons, precisely. Nothing is produced at this facility that has any biological use at all. This factory is strictly radio frequency and microwave emission oriented. My Belgium lab has the only biological laboratory I own. You'll get to see it tomorrow."

"Precisely?"

"Biological weapons carry with them the stigma of WMD, weapons of mass destruction. My biological lab is more genetics oriented." Wiley made another hair swipe.

"What does that mean?"

"You'll find out tomorrow." Wiley said.

Something Wiley said earlier stuck with Jake. And it bothered him. *You, too, will be my emissary.* That line carried with it a lot of implications. Implications Jake wasn't sure he liked. None of which he liked. And why would he be going to Belgium?

"My guess is your Belgium factory is located near Imec. That would tie into everything you do, RF and microwave emission technology *and* biological research."

Wiley smiled. "Bentley was right." Hair swipe. "Your analytical skills are impressive. But if you don't learn some self-control, you will have a short career and quite possibly a short life-span."

CHAPTER 12

"Is THERE A reason I have to go to Belgium with
you?" Jake's perplexity at the situation Bentley had thrust
him into, was eating away at him.

"Of course there is." Wiley was calm, showing no
irritation at Jake's attitude. "I'm getting you out of the
country so Scott won't have to lie to Senator Boden. The
senator sees no need for the CIA, he's an advocate of the
NSA and is pushing Scott to turn you over so he can arrest
and prosecute you."

Wiley got up and walked over to a rack, pulled an item
off a shelf, tossed it up in the air and then caught it with his
other hand. "But Scott won't do that because of loyalty to
you...or rather your father."

The last comment stung. Once again he'd received
preferential treatment because of his father's influence.
Living in his father's shadow had become the bane of his
existence. He was certain he'd lost that stigma when he took
down Laurence O'Rourke and discovered the secret hidden
in Ireland.

"Jake?" Wiley asked.

"Yes."

Wiley held up the small item he'd removed from the
shelf then tossed it toward Jake. Jake caught it one-handed.

"You know what that is?" Wiley asked.

"It looks like something you plug into the back of a
computer. It has a serial connection."

"That's correct." Hair swipe. "It's one of the first
things my partner and I created for the CIA. It started as a
filter for a radio. It distorted and altered the signature
emission. Later we adapted another version for a computer,

which made it virtually undetectable. With the filter attached, no transfer of data could be captured. It allowed our computer total secrecy when hacking into another computer. Made it untraceable. A huge advantage gained in virtual espionage."

Wiley held his hand up and Jake tossed the filter back. Wiley meticulously placed it on the shelf where it came from and motioned for Jake to follow him.

Jake spent the next two hours following Wiley around his facility, listening to him explain the function and the reason many items came into existence. The man was remarkable and Bentley was right, he did have a number of eccentricities.

Jake was following Wiley back to his office when the old man stopped mid-stride and glanced at his watch. He could see the old man making a mental calculation.

"Jake, we need to leave now. It's just under a nine-hour flight with a quick refuel in Goose Bay, Canada. We should be in Brussels by ten at the latest. We'll eat and sleep on the plane."

Wiley took off toward the elevator and motioned Jake to follow.

Cowboy met them as the elevator opened into Wiley's office. "Sir, I have your overnight already loaded and Mr. Pendleton's bag is still in the cart."

"Great." Wiley said. He turned to Jake. "We'll take my Citation. That way we can get there fast."

They followed Cowboy to the stretch golf cart.

Jake laughed. "Citation and fast should never be used in the same sentence unless you have a 750."

Wiley looked him in the eye. "I have two Citation 750's and a Lear 23. The Lear is in Brussels. My other Citation is on assignment at the present time."

Wiley was smart, like Bentley said…and obviously very rich.

The golf cart pulled into the hangar. The Citation's air stair door was open and Jake saw one pilot standing by the door while the other pilot was sitting in the cockpit. The Citation 750 was boasted as the fastest business jet in history with a top speed of over six hundred miles per hour.

"This is my personal Citation." Wiley climbed out of the cart and walked toward the aircraft door. "Wherever it goes, I go. This aircraft stays with me at all times. I never know when I might have to jump and run. Airline schedules are too unpredictable."

The whirl of the right engine spooling up filled the air. Cowboy handed Jake his bag. "Say hello to Kyli for me, would you?"

"Sure. Whoever that is."

The Rolls-Royce turbofan engine fired flooding the tarmac with the smell of burning kerosene. Jake stepped up the air stairs as he heard the whirl of the left engine spooling. The co-pilot followed him into the aircraft, closing the door behind them.

Wiley had already buckled his seatbelt. "Sit down, Jake. These two jet-jockeys won't waste any time getting us in the air."

He slipped his bag into the compartment by the door and took the first seat next to Wiley. He twisted his neck around and observed the cabin. Four leather seats up front in club-style configuration. Behind the seats were two bunks in sleeper-car configuration. Located in the rear of the aircraft was a galley and restroom.

In his years as an NTSB investigator, Jake had never encountered a cabin configuration like this one, certainly none with bunks.

Jake looked at Wiley. "Looks like the toy making business is very lucrative, how old is your Citation?"

"I bought this one new three years ago. Then it went to the shop for the retrofit. That took two months. But it's ideal for my style of travel. If I have work that needs to be done then I have everything at my fingertips. Internet, phone, fax, the works. All encrypted, mind you. And at my age I need to get my rest or I'm not worth a crap the next day, especially with all the time changes I make." Wiley looked at his watch. "Speaking of which, we lose eight hours between here and Belgium so when we leave Goose Bay, I suggest you follow my lead and try to get some sack time. The bunks are comfortable. You're in the top bunk."

Jake gazed out the aircraft window while the Citation taxied into position. The surge of takeoff thrust from the Rolls-Royce AE 3007C1 engines forced him back into his leather seat. In a quick few seconds the Citation lifted off and banked to the left.

He returned his gaze out the window. "How large is your ranch?"

"Right now, as far as your eyes can see." Wiley said. "I own somewhere around thirty thousand acres, give or take a couple of hundred."

"Holy cow. That's big."

"This is Texas." Wiley paused. "That's considered a hobby ranch."

Four hours later, about one hour after finishing the onboard meal prepared for them from the Wranglers' Steakhouse, the Citation landed at CFB Goose Bay. A former United States Air Force base, now a Canadian Forces Base. A Canadian Forces fuel truck pulled up next to the Citation and started fueling the aircraft.

"How'd you pull that off? Jake asked. "The Canadian military fuel?"

Wiley smiled. "Connections."

Within fifteen minutes, the Citation was in the air bound for Brussels. Jake was amazed at the efficiency in which Wiley's travel had been conducted. Not a minute wasted by anyone, not the crew, not even Wiley himself.

The phone next to Wiley beeped. Wiley picked it up, listened for a moment and said, "Thanks."

Wiley unbuckled. "Jake we should arrive in Brussels around 9:30 a.m. which is…" He looked at his watch. "A little over four and half hours from now."

Wiley stood up and put his hand on Jake's shoulder. "You should get as much sleep as possible. In all likelihood if you survive the next few days, they'll prove to be life altering."

With that statement hanging in the air, Wiley disappeared into his bunk.

CHAPTER 13

KAPLAN ROSE WITH the sun feeling refreshed. He'd slept for over six hours—now it was time to get down to business. The business of locating and rescuing Isabella Hunt.

He found Chase and his team members at the table with a map weighted down on the corners by coffee mugs. In the light of dawn, they looked younger than they had the night before and they were all dressed alike. Jeans, t-shirts. Two in tennis shoes, three in hiking boots. And everyone had a backpack on the floor next to them. North Face, JanSport, Dakine—just what you'd expect from college students out exploring the world. Kaplan studied each one and noticed something odd, or maybe not so odd after all. They all had forgettable faces and features. No one stood out. No one had striking features. Perfect for covert ops.

The team had been talking about someone when Kaplan walked in. He assumed the name he heard was the source.

"Barakah? Is that our man?" Kaplan asked.

Chase smiled. "The source is Baraka Binte Talibah. But yeah, she's our source."

"A woman?" Kaplan showed his surprise. "How'd you manage that?"

"Actually, she came to us—in a roundabout way," Chase explained. "She approached one of us right after we arrived, something a local asset had arranged."

"When do I get to meet her?"

"That could be a bit of a problem." Chase said. "She doesn't know about you, yet. We are to meet later this morning. But first we need to discuss ground rules."

"Ground rules?" Kaplan asked.

"Yes. Her security is of upmost importance to us. She cannot be compromised. She will contact us when she can talk. She'll tell us when and where." Chase explained.

"Do you trust her? Could she be setting us up?"

"There is always that chance, but we are good at what we do. Besides, the circumstances that brought her to us pretty much assure us she's on our side." Chase explained how she came to them after her husband was blinded, had his tongue cut out, and her teenage daughters had been tortured and executed. Payback for her husband leaking information to a Yemeni police chief that led to the siege against al Qaeda militants in the small village of Hawta. Thousands of people fled as government forces moved into the village with tanks and armored vehicles. She was spared only because she wasn't home at the time.

"These people are brutal. Even more so with their own countrymen and women." Chase said. "I offered her protection but she refused. She witnessed the abduction and thinks she knows where they took Ms Hunt. She'll confirm it and get back to us."

"So we just wait?" Before Chase could answer, Kaplan's own words reminded him of Jake's impatience in Australia.

"That's right." Chase said. "We wait."

An hour later Kaplan, Chase, and Baraka Binte Talibah met in an abandoned white-washed home on the south end of Sana'a. The bomb-blast-wrecked home had been left in shambles nearly a decade earlier when insurgents attempted a government takeover. She was reluctant to meet with Kaplan present but Chase convinced the woman that meeting with him was the only way to ensure the safety of the captured woman.

"The woman is being held in…how you say…compound in Hajjah. Walls on all sides." Baraka explained.

"Where is this Hajjah?" Kaplan asked. "What's the terrain like?"

"All Hajjah is hill. Woman is in Old Hajjah Palace. One road in. One road out. Will not be easy." Baraka looked at Kaplan. "I help you get in. Must go at night."

Chase interrupted. "No Baraka. You've done enough. We can't ask you to put your life on the line. We can handle it from here."

"No. No." Baraka gave Chase a glance then returned her stare to the older, wiser Kaplan. "I go first, make sure no one get in way. I get you to Palace then you rescue woman."

Kaplan looked at Chase. "She's right. We need her. She can help. Without her, we might not stand a chance."

CHAPTER 14

KAPLAN SENT BARAKA away with plans to meet back at the same place later that afternoon. He and Chase returned to the safe house and briefed the brick. Then Kaplan called Bentley and CIA analyst George Fontaine via the Delta squad's encrypted phone.

"Before her cover was blown," Bentley said. "Isabella had relayed information about the Yemen cell's plans for a coordinated attack. Three attacks were to take place within weeks of each other across the globe. One in Australia. As you know, that cell has been eliminated. One in Europe and the other in the United States. Based on messages she'd intercepted to Hilal, Isabella believed the Yemen cell was planning an attack in France, probably Paris."

"Paris is a long way from Yemen. Was she sure?" Kaplan asked.

Actually," Fontaine said. "Yemen is closer to Paris than Sydney was to the cell you and Jake took out."

"What we need you to find out," Bentley said, "are the sites for the two attacks. Verify Paris is one, and find out what you can about the U.S. attack. We have no intel. It could happen anywhere and we're helpless to stop it unless you can glean some information from the Yemen cell."

Kaplan sensed a delay in Hunt's rescue and that bothered him. He needed to get her out of there. "Sir," Kaplan said. "We should get Isabella out of there then we'll find out what she knows and act accordingly."

There was a hushed sound on the other end of the line. Kaplan knew Bentley and Fontaine were talking. He looked at Chase and shrugged his shoulders.

"Sir?"

"Gregg." Bentley again. "We need to get to the cell leader before he gets a suspicion we're coming for Isabella. You need to find him and extract what you can. Then, and only then, go after Isabella. It's imperative we stop those two attacks and the only way to do that is make them think they are still safe. By now they know the Australian cell was taken down so they'll be extra cautious. Do what you have to Gregg, but find out when and where those attacks are going to take place or hundreds, maybe thousands of innocent people will die. The mission comes first."

"So Isabella is expendable?" Kaplan asked.

"Gregg, don't make me answer that."

"Yes sir." Kaplan felt a pang of regret. "So where do we go from here?"

"We'll gather what intel we have and send it to you. In the meantime, get out there and find out what you can from the locals. Any sources the Delta team has, use them. Squeeze them if you have to. We'll get back in touch in four hours. Understood?"

"Yes sir." Kaplan said. "I'll be standing by."

Kaplan disconnected the call to Langley and turned to Chase. "What sources do you have here other than Baraka? I don't want to jeopardize her, I need her help to get Hunt out of there."

"You heard Bentley." Chase said. "Find the handler first. Hunt can wait."

"I heard what he said." Kaplan pointed his finger at Chase. "But I will not let Isabella die at the hands of these lunatics."

"Mr. Kaplan." Chase interrupted. "You should prepare yourself for the possibility that she's already dead."

"I won't believe that...not for a moment."

"And if you're wrong?" Chase asked.

"I'll kill everyone that had any part in it. Then I'll kill their families. I'll send a message loud and clear to all these towel-headed radicals."

The room was silent. No one spoke. Finally Kaplan said, "Now, do you have a list?"

"We've only been here a day so our list is short." Chase pulled a steno pad out of his backpack. "Baraka gave us two names that might be useful, one better than the other, and both are only a short ride from here."

"Pick the best one from the list." Kaplan looked at Chase. "We're burning daylight, let's go."

CHAPTER 15

Leuven, Belgium

JAKE AND WILEY stepped off the train at the Wijgmaal station. The brumal fall sky left with it the threat of drizzle and cooler temperatures. A young woman in a white lab coat with a purple streak in her shoulder-length hair stood next to a Mercedes convertible waving in their direction.

The flight to Brussels took less time than Jake had estimated. Wiley and Jake were waved through immigration; a routine Wiley was accustomed to in Brussels. After a few cordial exchanges between Wiley and the officer, Wiley rushed toward the SNCB train depot. Jake didn't think a seventy year old man could move that fast, he was almost running to keep up with Wiley.

The train ride from Brussels to Leuven took fifteen minutes. Wiley hopped off one train and onto another leaving Jake struggling to keep up. Within five minutes the train for Mechelen left the station stopping at the first station just under five kilometers north of the Leuven station—Wijgmaal.

Jake and Wiley walked over to the Mercedes.

"Here, Jake." Wiley handed Jake his bag. "Put the bags in the trunk."

Jake took his bag as the young woman gave Wiley a tight hug and a kiss on the cheek.

"You made good time." She said.

Jake closed the trunk and walked around the car to Wiley.

"Jake, this is Kyli Wullenweber." Wiley looked at Kyli. "This is the man I told you about, Jake Pendleton."

"Jake." Kyli stepped close and put out her hand. "It's a pleasure."

Jake grasped her hand. It was soft. And warm. "Nice to meet you." He felt stupid, is that all he could say?

She was taller than Jake first thought. He was 5' 10", she couldn't have been more than a couple of inches shorter. She had thin lips, ivory complexion, chestnut hair, and soft brown eyes that sparkled when she smiled. They held eye contact, without speaking, hands still locked.

"Okay you two." Wiley opened the front passenger door and got in. "Let's go. I don't have all day."

Jake flushed, released his grip on her hand, and broke eye contact. He could feel the heat on his face and he tried to turn away.

Kyli smiled as she walked around to the driver's seat while Jake got into the back seat. "Buckle up, it's a hell of a drive."

Wiley smiled and winked at Kyli. Jake tensed in his seat as he buckled his seatbelt.

She inserted the key and the engine roared to life. She slammed the convertible into gear and floored the accelerator thrusting Jake into the back of his seat and spraying gravel across the parking lot.

Forty-five seconds later the Mercedes screeched to a stop in front of a building only two hundred feet on the opposite side of the railroad tracks. Jake took a deep breath and looked back, he could still see the train.

"God, I thought we'd never get here." Kyli said.

"Get your bag." Wiley ordered. "Leave mine in the trunk."

Kyli got out and handed Wiley the keys. "Here you go."

"Jake, I'm leaving you with Kyli." Wiley said. "She'll give you the nickel tour. I'll let her explain it to you."

Wiley gave Kyli another hug. "See you later, babe."

Babe. Jake felt disappointment. *Babe. Surely the old man and Kyli aren't—*

Wiley slipped into the driver's seat and sped off. Jake stared at the Mercedes as it disappeared out of sight.

"Where's he going?" Jake asked.

"He has a previous engagement." Catching Jake off guard, Kyli looped her arm through his as she guided him toward the front entrance. "You belong to me for the rest of the day."

Jake felt himself flush for the second time. "Is he coming back today? He said we have work to do."

"He might or might not show up this afternoon, but don't worry, he gave me a long list of things he wants you to do." She scanned her access key card through the device next to the front door. Waited for the buzz. "Let's go."

Inside the front door was a small lobby and reception area. Behind a desk sat a receptionist. Light brown-hair, blue-eyed, and early twenties, the receptionist was speaking on the telephone in what he guessed was Dutch. Beside her was the control system and monitor for the video/audio intercom for allowing visitor access.

Kyli said, "This is our office manager, slash accountant, slash security manager...she pretty much holds this office together."

The woman waved without interrupting her phone call.

"This way, Jake." Kyli slid her key card, punched in a password on a keyboard next to the door, and waited for the click. She pulled open the door. "Pay attention to the different levels of security. It's increasingly complex as we move deeper into the lab's more sensitive areas." She pointed to a bench next to the wall. "Just leave your bag there."

Jake followed Kyli into the first work area, which was remarkably similar to the work area in Texas. "Mr. Wiley said you have a biological section here." Jake wanted more information.

"We do." Kyli smiled. "There are two more security levels. The biological lab, we'll go there next, and then the vault."

"The vault?"

"Yes. Only Mr. Wiley can get in there. He's installed a failsafe system…in case something were to happen to him…but I don't know what it is." She reached into a closet and pulled out a lab coat for Jake and two lab caps. She handed him a coat and a cap. "Here. One size fits all."

He slipped on the lab coat and cap and followed her to a door.

She scanned her key card, typed in her password, and then spoke into a microphone. "Kyli Wullenweber."

A computer voice spoke. "Voice authentication confirmed. You may enter Dr. Kyli."

† † †

Athens International Airport
Athens, Greece

Ian Collins passed through security with ease. His new disguise worked as designed, blending him in with the crowds. By now he assumed Interpol had scanned his profile and nothing triggered any alerts. No facial recognition. Not even his 6' 7" stature had warranted the slightest second glance. High tech still had its flaws.

His confidence restored, he was making his first venture from Ios Island since he fled the United States back in March.

His recovery from the gunshot wounds took two months to completely heal. Fortunately the woman's aim was bad and the bullets didn't penetrate any vital organs. She'd fired five rounds at him and only connected twice, one of them a flesh wound on the leg. The other lodged in his side. He found a local doctor in Clayton, Georgia to remove the two 9mm slugs and stop the bleeding. After the doctor bandaged the wounds, Collins killed him and stuffed his body in a closet in the back of the doctor's office.

Leave no witnesses.

He sat down in a seat facing the large plate glass window overlooking the tarmac and the jet way at the Athens International Airport. He had a one-hour wait before his British Airways flight to London was scheduled to depart, plenty of time to check some last minute details. Then he had a three-hour layover at London's Heathrow airport before his flight to the United States was scheduled for departure.

London would be the true test of his disguise. Security might not be as easy to fool that close to Ireland. His face and reputation were notorious in England. Interpol and Scotland Yard would still be looking for him to cross through Customs. A gamble he had to take. He had to become mobile again if he stood any chance of restoring his line of business. He didn't have any other skills. Killing was all he knew. And killing was all he wanted to do.

Traditional means of transportation were still the easiest, most convenient, and many times, the cheapest way to travel. But it wasn't the safest. His former ally in the shipping business, the Libyan, was no longer a viable option—not since the man and woman came snooping around, asking about Collins' whereabouts. Information the Libyan didn't know and therefore couldn't reveal. As far as the world was concerned, Ian Collins had disappeared off the face of the earth. He intended to keep it that way.

For now.

Collins was flying west, which made for a long day with all the time zone changes. He planned to sleep on the overseas flight to the United States. He would need it. Tonight he had to stake out his next target.

He opened his laptop computer to check and confirm his hotel reservations in the United States. He double checked the status of his rental car and noticed the British Airways Airbus 320 pulling into his gate. Another thirty minutes before the first boarding call.

He'd planned his revenge with intricate care, no detail overlooked. His greatest challenge was not being recognized when he traveled. The gray hair and beard, brown eyes behind wire-rim glasses, and the meticulously placed theatrical make-up gave Collins the appearance of a man twenty years older. He even added age spots to his hands. The business suit and high-end luggage offered further deception of his true identity. He enjoyed the thrill of the ruse. Its high risk was exhilarating. As was plotting his revenge. Even without compensation, he knew he would enjoy this job.

Jake Pendleton would feel his wrath.

One piece at a time.

One *painful* piece at a time.

CHAPTER 16

MEtech Labs
Leuven, Belgium

"DR. KYLI?" JAKE was surprised. He was learning something new every minute it seemed. "Doctor of what? And why not Dr. Wullenweber?"

"Mr. Wiley's idea of a joke." She held the door open for Jake.

"Well Dr. Kyli, what kind of doctor are you?"

"I'm not a doctor of anything yet. I'm working on my dissertation for a PhD in Biological Science. Kind of boring, huh?" She laughed.

Jake stepped inside and Kyli closed the door. "On the contrary, it sounds impressive."

"Don't be impressed. I was raised around scientists and engineers, it's in my blood." She motioned to Jake. "Come on, Let me show you around."

Kyli spent the next hour showing Jake the different areas of the bio lab and introducing him to several of Wiley's employees.

"MEtech is basically a fully equipped biological and electronics laboratory." Kyli explained. "We have 2D and 3D simulation equipment, software, and a full complement of biological and electronics testing equipment. If there is anything we don't have, we get it from IMEC. The electronics lab designs RF and microwave custom antennas and subsystems as well as some QRCs."

"Remind me again. What are QRCs?"

"Quick reaction contracts."

"Oh yeah." Jake smiled. "I remember now. Wiley told me about them."

"As I was saying, the bio lab handles genetic research and testing. This is where I work most of the time."

"What exactly do you do?"

"It's complicated."

"Try me."

She smiled. "Don't want to bore you, but since you asked, most of my work deals with DNA testing. I take a DNA sample, process it, and look for genetic weaknesses."

"Weaknesses? Jake held up a vial from Kyli's lab station. "What type of weaknesses?"

"A genetic Achilles' heel. But I concentrate on flaws that would prove fatal, such as cardiac issues, susceptibilities to cancers, brain and circulation issues. Things of that nature." She pointed to a sample DNA string diagram mounted on the wall. "I look for those problem areas in a DNA string that indicate a potential cause of death."

"You can do that?"

"Yes, I can. Science has made historic advances in genetic research over the last decade. You'd be amazed at what we can do with DNA."

"So," Jake interrupted. "Your research can lead to cures or ways to reverse these genetic flaws?"

"Not exactly. More like DNA weapon research."

"DNA weapons? I've never heard of anything like that." Jake took a step back. "Okay, now you're scaring me."

Kyli laughed and stepped closer to Jake and in a soft tone said, "What if I told you I could read your DNA, find out your genetic failing point then make a liquid or aromatic drug that, when introduced into your system, would attack your body at your weak spot and kill you within forty-eight hours without leaving a trace?"

"That doesn't sound moral...or ethical."

"This had nothing to do with morals or ethics nor is it considered medical research. I've only experimented on mice."

"Well, now I feel better." Jake said sarcastically. "Did it work?"

"It did." She pointed to a wall with several cages. "The first experiments had limited success, but three years of trial and error perfected the process and now we have a one hundred percent *kill ratio.*"

"Kill ratio? Who are you people?"

"I told you it was technical. Remember, forewarned is forearmed."

"What does that mean?" Jake was uncomfortable. What kind of lab was Wiley operating? Even more important, what did Bentley get him involved in and did he even know about this?

He was having difficulty grasping the gravity of her work, but the look on Kyli's face let him know she understood his confliction.

"Jake, you of all people know these are dangerous times." Kyli explained. "We're not the only ones who know the implications of DNA string manipulation. We cannot protect against what we don't understand. We must know how it works or else we're vulnerable to attack by those entities out there—and there are plenty—that would not hesitate to use this as a weapon."

"So you aren't DNA assassins, you're what, DNA guardians?"

"Don't be so short-sighted, Jake. That's how people die."

Her words struck a nerve. "Protecting yourself with guns and knives I understand, but this is scary."

"It's very scary. Let me give you a plausible, albeit simplified, example and you can see just how scary it could be." Kyli walked over to a large metal door that resembled a small version of a bank vault door. "Let's say a country hostile to the United States, China for example, developed a contagious formula that would fatally attack anyone who did not have a specific Chinese marker in their DNA. All they'd have to do would be to introduce the contagion at strategic locations. Large international airports would be the most effective spots in which to release the contagion and move it worldwide the fastest. By the time anyone could figure out what was happening, the world's population would decline. Within a matter of months China would be able to obtain world domination. Got your attention yet?"

"I'd never thought about anything like that. Is it really possible...I mean with humans?"

"If I can do it with mice, I can do it with humans." Kyli pointed to a large metal door. "Enough about that. Any idea what this is?"

"Let me guess. The vault."

"Yes it is." Kyli walked to the door. "Only Mr. Wiley's card, password, voice authentication, and retina scan will unlock this door."

"What's in there?"

"You'll have to ask Mr. Wiley. I'm not at liberty to discuss the contents of the vault." Kyli grabbed Jake's hand and pulled him toward the bio lab exit. "We'll talk about it at lunch. I'm hungry."

"But, you know, right?"

Kyli gave an impish grin, her eyes sparkling as she led him away.

†††

The Hotel Carpinus was in the neighboring village of Herent across the canal from MEtech. For the second time that day Jake was a victim of Kyli's heavy foot, this time in her Mini Cooper. They arrived at the hotel in ten minutes.

She pulled the car to the front door of the hotel and shut off the engine. "Grab your bag." She unlocked the hatch.

"I thought we were having lunch?"

"We are." She said. "Let's get you checked in first. I made our lunch reservations here as well. You'll like it and the food in the restaurant is splendid."

When they walked into the lobby, Kyli went to the registration desk and spoke to the man in Dutch. The wallpaper behind the man had gold and white vertical stripes, the colors complimented the rest of the lobby's furnishings.

Kyli signed the hotel registry and the man handed her a key. She signaled for Jake to follow her. "You're in room seven. Lucky number seven."

"Superstitious? Not what I would have expected from a scientist."

"Why would you say I'm superstitious? Seven happens to be my lucky number. It might end up being yours too." She laughed and motioned toward a hallway. "Let's check it out."

There was that glisten in her eyes again. Jake didn't know what to think. Was she flirting? Kyli was friendly and certainly attractive but he'd just met her. He hadn't even thought about another woman since Beth's death and wasn't sure if he was ready for anything other than business.

He followed her to his room. She opened the door with the key and entered, holding the door open for Jake. "Your room, Mr. Pendleton." She imitated a bellboy.

Kyli took the bag from his hand and tossed it on the bed. She turned and moved toward him. She stopped close, in his personal space. Jake felt uneasy. She arched her back pushing herself closer to him. Her amber eyes full of mischief. Her perfume invaded his nostrils, Chanel Chance. Beth's favorite perfume. Why hadn't he noticed it before?

His body stirred, head spun, and he felt flush again. He tried to say something, anything, but nothing came out.

She raised her chin and said in a sultry whisper. "Jake? Do you know what I really want? Right now?"

He couldn't speak. He just shook his head like a schoolboy trying to be cool but failing miserably.

"I really want to get something to eat. I'm starving." She turned and walked out of his room.

He lowered his head and followed her out of the room. *I'm such an idiot.*

CHAPTER 17

THE FIRST NAME on the list was a waste of time. The man knew nothing, so Kaplan and Chase went in search of the next lead. The pair located the second source but he denied any knowledge of the terrorist cell in Hajjah or the abduction of Hunt. Kaplan's instinct told him the man was lying. The more Kaplan questioned him, the more the man contradicted himself until finally the man backed himself into a corner. Beads of sweat collected on the man's forehead and then Kaplan turned up the heat.

Kaplan threatened to kill the man's family and expose him as a traitor. The man seemed reluctant at first until Kaplan threatened to turn him over to al Qaeda. Then the man talked. Not only did the Yemeni know about Hunt's abduction, it also turned out his brother was a member of the terrorist cell. He was only trying to protect his brother by lying to Kaplan.

Kaplan needed more information. He needed names and places. Needed facts. He pressured the man but at the first mention of Hashim Khan, the man shut down. Kaplan was close, but was running out of time. The terrorist cell wouldn't keep Hunt alive for long. He needed to confirm that Khan was involved with the Yemen cell...and with Hunt. The interrogator went to work.

Chase drove back to the safe house while Kaplan held the unconscious man in the back seat. The quick blow to the back of the man's head had dropped him.

The back room in the safe house was empty and dark—no windows—the coldest room in the house. With a temperature around fifty-five, it was ideal for what Kaplan had in mind. He needed the man to talk, to tell him everything. Anything short of that would prove very painful to his captive. He understood the man's reluctance, once he gave Kaplan the information, there would be a warrant for his death, his brother's death, and the deaths of his entire family. A warrant not from Kaplan, but from Khan.

Kaplan found all the materials necessary for the makeshift interrogation room. He stripped the man then secured his feet to a metal hook anchored in the floor. He bound the man's hands with flex cuffs, doused him with cold water, and forced the naked man to stand in the cold room.

Every time the man would start to fall, Kaplan would slap him then douse him again in cold water. The shivering started in less than an hour when the man's body temperature started to fall.

He questioned the man repeatedly but the man's fear of Khan outweighed Kaplan's efforts.

Several of the Delta brick's team assisted Kaplan with his interrogation. But nothing seemed to weaken the man's resolve.

After six hours, Kaplan grew impatient. He knew eventually the man would succumb to this technique but some prisoners had lasted over forty hours before they talked. The luxury of time was not something he could afford. The clock was ticking and he knew the longer it took to find Hunt, the greater the odds she would not be alive.

Kaplan cleared the room except for Chase and ordered Chase to guard the prisoner while he left the room.

Ten minutes later Kaplan returned with an eight-foot board and a backpack. He and Chase tied the man to the board, feet first then hands. Chase wedged something under one end of the board elevating the man's feet slightly above his head. When the prisoner was secure, Kaplan reached into his backpack and pulled out a roll of cellophane.

"Sir. You can't do—" Chase started to object.

"I can and I will Captain." Kaplan interrupted. "There are too many lives at stake here. This man knows something. Without that information people will die. What this man knows can save those lives."

Chase said nothing.

Kaplan wrapped the man's head in cellophane and grabbed the water bucket. "Last chance asshole."

The man laid stoic. He began to chant.

Kaplan started pouring water over the man. Water quickly worked its way under the cellophane and licked at the man's head. The man's gag reflex kicked in. He bucked against the board, bulging eyes revealed his fear of drowning.

After thirty-three seconds the man begged for mercy. Kaplan was impressed; the average was fourteen, even though on rare occasions a few al Qaeda terrorists had been known to last nearly two and a half minutes.

Kaplan cut the cellophane away from the man's head. "Ready to talk now?"

CHAPTER 18

"Mr. WILEY SAID you had a full day in store for me, what will we be doing?" Jake asked.

"All work I see." Kyli said. "We'll get to everything in due time. Mr. Wiley wanted me to show you around the classified electronics lab first."

"I thought we already did a walk-through."

"Nope. That was the assembly area. There's a secure room where high-priority items are housed."

Before they left for lunch, Kyli removed her lab coat and hung it on a hook by the lab door. She wore a black dress, cut slightly above the knee with black pumps, a classy yet professional look. A smile never left her face. Full of non-stop energy, she stirred something in Jake he hadn't felt in a long time—feelings he thought were dead. It gave him a glimmer of hope that he could have a life after Beth. But still, there was the anger. Yet now the anger was mixed with feelings of betrayal of his love for Beth and a newfound excitement he felt when he was with Kyli.

Kyli's cell phone beeped announcing the arrival of an incoming text message. "It seems," she said. "You've got a video conference to sit in on. Mr. Wiley will be here in a few minutes. Follow me."

"Where to now?"

"The conference room, where else?"

Less than five minutes later, Wiley entered the room. "Kyli, Jake and I need a few minutes."

Kyli walked to the door. "I'll be in the bio lab if you need me." She winked at Jake.

Jake tried not to react. *Stay focused.* He followed Wiley's lead and sat down.

Without speaking, Wiley walked over to a podium and started typing on a computer. A fifty-inch monitor mounted on the wall lit up. Speakers on the wall crackled then three figures appeared on the split-screen monitor—Bentley and Fontaine on one side, Gregg Kaplan on the other.

"What's up, Scott?" Wiley sat next to Jake and spoke into the three-winged audio device in the middle of the oval conference table.

Bentley was the first to speak. "Good and bad news to report. The good news is we've located Isabella Hunt. Jake, Mr. Wiley has agreed to assist me on this mission, which includes having you help rescue Isabella. Something you said you wanted to do."

"Yes, sir. Very much." Jake said.

"We've put together an extraction plan but due to terrain, some logistic issues, along with the political unrest in the region, this will have to be a night op with no chance for detection. Gentlemen, this is a hostile country so this mission is silent in, silent out. We can't afford any blowback. The United States will disavow any involvement. This is totally unsanctioned, if anyone gets caught, they're on their own."

"I hope that was the bad news too." Jake said.

"I'm afraid not, Jake." Bentley glanced at Fontaine then back at his camera. "Gregg will brief you on the bad news. Go ahead, Gregg."

"We located and detained one of the locals who knew about Isabella and the al Qaeda cell here in Yemen." Kaplan paused. "After some...enhanced interrogation, we've learned that the cell has already left Yemen and is enroute to Western Europe. We don't know where but apparently Isabella does. That's why it's imperative we rescue her ASAP before al Qaeda attacks and a lot of people die."

"George." Bentley said. "You take it from here."

"According to Gregg's source, Isabella is being held in the Hajjah Palace." Fontaine and Bentley disappeared from the screen and a satellite view of Hajjah appeared. "The palace is here." A circle electronically drew around a building.

"As you can see, the palace is surrounded by a rock wall and the front gate is well guarded twenty-four hours a day."

The screen rotated and a topographic view of the area popped up. "Our problem is that there is literally no level ground in Hajjah. It is built on a mountain."

The view expanded outward. "The highway passes at the base of mountain leaving only one road in and out of town."

"That confirms what our inside source told us." Kaplan said. "She volunteered to assist us with our infiltration."

"As you can see here," Fontaine continued. "With all the roadblocks and checkpoints along the highway, access or exit by vehicle is out of the question. With all the political turmoil in the region, we've determined that our only option is to drop you in from overhead. You'll have to locate, extract Isabella, and escape on foot undetected."

Bentley and Fontaine reappeared on the screen.

"What if she's injured and unable to travel on foot?" Jake asked. "We can't just leave her there."

"We can't take that risk." Kaplan said. "Figure something else out, I'm not leaving her there."

"George?" Wiley spoke for the first time since the conference call started. "There might be another way."

"If you have an idea, I'd like to hear it." Bentley said.

"Is there any place in town that's remotely level, like a large parking area or a field? I only need four or five-hundred feet." Wiley asked.

"There is one area where kids play kick ball or soccer games. It's about fifty feet wide and maybe, repeat, *maybe* four hundred feet long. It isn't totally level, it has a gentle slope toward the edge of the mountain." Fontaine brought up the satellite image again and electronically circled the area. "It's a dark area at night, no lights at all."

"Can you zoom in, George?" Wiley asked.

"Sure." The image zoomed in closer. "How's that?"

"Good. Now tilt the topo so I can get an idea about the side of the hill." Wiley said.

The image rotated. The topographic view revealed the vertical terrain of the mountain.

"It'll do." Wiley said. "A couple of buildings will add to the challenge but an approach and departure can be accomplished."

"E. W.?" Bentley interrupted. "What are you talking about?"

"Scott, I have two prototype gliders that are rigged for this type of night time op. Infrared heads-up displays and a silent electric motor for self-launch capability. You can fly in, locate and rescue your asset, and fly out. No one will ever know you're there…or even been there for that matter."

"Kind of ballsy, don't you think?" Jake asked. "And who exactly is going to fly the gliders?"

"It's been a long time, but I've flown a glider before." Kaplan said. "I'm sure it'll come back to me."

"Okay, for the record, I'm not flying with Gregg." Jake said. "Who's going to fly the other one?"

Wiley ignored Jake. "Scott, I can have Jake and the two gliders in Aden by tomorrow evening. We'll arrive shortly after dark. The gliders will be ready within a couple of hours after we arrive. I'll need you to make arrangements for two tow planes at Aden. George and I can work out the details of mission planning."

"Alright E.W. I'll take care of it." Bentley said. "Gregg, we'll be in touch soon so wait for instructions. Jake, control yourself, do I make myself clear?"

Jake paused. He knew the number one priority was to rescue Isabella. "Yes sir, I promise."

Wiley interrupted. "Jake will be fine, Scott. You have my word."

The monitor blinked then went blank.

Jake looked at Wiley. "How did you think of all that stuff so fast?"

"Fifty years in the business. That's where experience trumps youth." Wiley pushed up his glasses, swiped his hair, and smiled. "You're not afraid of heights, are you?"

CHAPTER 19

WILEY PRESSED THE intercom button, "Have Kyli meet us in the RF lab."

"RF lab?" Jake asked.

"Radio frequency. How soon we forget."

"That was fast thinking." Jake said.

"You haven't seen anything yet, junior." Wiley smiled. He opened the door. "I have plenty of tricks up my sleeve."

The RF lab was a side room with Plexiglas walls adjacent to the main electronics lab floor. One wall was a showcase of gadgets MEtech had created. On the top shelf was a device Wiley called the *spook radio*. A device that monitored as wide a frequency band as possible targeting only signals of interest, which allowed the operator to identify and track the signals while remaining anonymous.

Kyli arrived at the RF lab door the same time as Jake and Wiley. She slid her key card through the reader, opened the door, and entered the lab. Jake followed. Wiley was speaking to someone in the electronics lab when the door closed—another soundproof room.

"I assume you'll be leaving soon." Kyli said.

"I think so. I don't really know yet." Jake smiled. "I guess I'm not part of the fraternity yet so I haven't been given the key to Wiley's cryptic communication."

"Don't worry, you'll catch on soon enough."

Moments later the door clicked and Wiley entered. He walked over to the showcase wall, removed a box, and laid five items on a table in the center of the room. "Kyli, I need you to bring Jake up to speed on the RTI. When he's got it, bundle it in the backpack. We're taking it with us tomorrow. I'll be in my office. After you finish, you can take him back to his hotel. Why don't you show Jake around town tonight but make sure he gets in early, tomorrow's a long day."

Wiley turned and left before Jake could verbalize the questions formulating in his mind.

"This must be big." Kyli said.

"Why is that?"

"We haven't used the advanced RTI in the field. We've done dozens of tests under different scenarios but never a live mission. It's still in the experimental stage so this is very exciting. You get to be the first."

"What is RTI?"

Kyli grabbed Jake's hand and pulled him toward the worktable. "Radio tomographic imaging. It will allow you to see through walls, literally. You will be able to locate and track moving people or objects in a given area."

"I like this toy already. It's like Superman's x-ray vision."

"It's not that simple." Kyli held up four ball-shaped objects. "First, you have to put these in place. One at each corner of the structure you want to look into. Radio transceivers—they transmit and receive radio signals."

Jake picked up one of the balls. He noticed the thick rubber studs protruding from its surface. "Might be easier said than done."

"Not really, but I'll get to that in a minute." She took the ball from Jake's hand and placed it on the table with the others. "You know, the Patent Office is full of some really good ideas that just haven't been perfected to their full potential."

"Wait a minute." Jake said. "You're telling me that Wiley raided the Patent Office and stole someone's idea. That's illegal."

"Steal is such an insensitive word, Jake. Borrow is more appropriate. Borrowed concepts are never used commercially. If Mr. Wiley comes across an idea he and a few others feel are commercially viable products then we kind of *leak* a better way of doing it back to the originator and let them perfect their invention. Wiley likes to make ideas work and understands there is no need to reinvent the wheel."

"So, where did he *borrow* this idea?" Jake asked. "Or should I not ask?"

"No that's fine. You should know." Kyli smiled. "This idea came from the University of Utah. But their computer display and software were lacking. They used transceivers spaced roughly six feet apart lining the entire perimeter. So many, in fact, that it was impractical for real world application. For an average sized building, they might need dozens, perhaps hundreds of transceivers. Grossly underpowered and inadequate to do the job. And their monitor display was almost illegible. Each person showed up as a blob on the screen. It literally served no useful purpose in the covert world, so Wiley improved it.

"The concept is the same but our design far surpasses anything they had considered possible. We use four transceivers, one on each corner. Radio signals are bounced off targets and the returning echoes provide the target's location and speed relative to the transceiver. The data from each transceiver is received by the computer and displayed on the screen. Individual targets are distinguishable by their mass and frequency. Our program has a database that allows you to mark and label each target and the computer will monitor their movements allowing us to track each target individually."

"Do the targets ever get confused?"

"Not a chance. Not with Wiley's design. Everything and everyone has its own distinct frequency signature, so once you tag a target, the computer will always distinguish it from all other targets."

Kyli flipped on the computer. "Because RTI measures shadows in radio waves created when they pass through a person or object, our display will also accurately depict stationary objects."

"What if the building has multiple levels or a basement?" Jake tapped on the monitor. "Can it account for that?"

"That's the beauty of these." She picked up a transceiver ball. "First these are shock-proof, so you can throw them where you need them. That allows you to place them discreetly reducing your odds of being detected. You just need to make sure they are at least ten feet away from the structure. Second, they are self-orienting. They operate with a tiny gyro inside, they automatically level themselves then locate their siblings—the other transceiver balls. But the best feature of all is what happens next. When initiated by the computer, the transceivers will literally draw a 3D model of the building on the display. At ten feet from the building, we can deliver two sub-levels and four above ground levels. At twenty feet spacing, six above ground levels, and so on. You get the picture. We're always limited to two sub-levels though."

"Why doesn't Wiley leak this to the creators?" Jake rolled the ball on the table noticing the rubbers studs stop the ball from rolling. "This could have some very useful real-life benefits for law enforcement and fire departments."

"It certainly could. And the original model has been used for those exact purposes. But you can see the problems if the advanced RTI fell in the wrong hands. That's why the bureaucracy won't let it reach commercial use. Now let me show you how the software works."

Jake spent the next three hours with Kyli learning the intricacies of the RTI including troubleshooting in the event any unforeseen circumstance arose.

"Okay, let's pack this up so it's ready to go." She dropped a padded backpack on the table. "Everything has a pouch. Load it up."

It took Jake less than a minute. "All finished."

"Good job, Jake. Let's go." Kyli motioned toward the door. "I have a big night in store for you."

Jake felt the conflict playing tug-of-war with his emotions.

"Jake, do I make you nervous?"

"No, not at all." He lied.

CHAPTER 20

Mosque De Trappes
Trappes, France

HASHIM KHAN MET with the leaders of the Trappes Islamic Association in a room behind the men's prayer room. The imam, or worship leader of the mosque and the TIA, wanted assurances from Khan that the planned attacks would not implicate the Muslims of Trappes. He gave them that assurance—he lied.

Deception had become an integral part of his life. A part of his life he prayed would not keep him from Paradise. With the growing trend of political correctness among Muslims trying to break the *terrorist* stigma, deception was a necessary evil.

Earlier in the day, Khan had picked up a shipment of laser printer toner cartridges from the shipping company in Versailles. Contained in those crates were five well-hidden, lead foiled covered cartridges with C-4 explosives packed inside plastic coated and sealed rollers. All made possible by the creative ingenuity of the Hilal Shipping Company of Aden, Yemen.

Martyrs from the Yemen cell arrived in Paris on separate flights originating from varying locations, each with specific instructions. Step-by-step directions allowed them to never cross each other's paths, and arrive at the Mosque De Trappes at designated times. All five were safely tucked away in the basement dormitory making final preparations for the suicide attacks. Each man was given his own cot, his own prayer blanket, and his own footlocker to store the last of their possessions. Possessions that would be shipped back to their families with praises of each man's martyrdom. He had given them one week to prepare. Seven days to make peace with Allah. Seven days to cleanse themselves.

Seven days to live. Seven days until Paradise.

TIA followed Khan's orders—acquiring everything on the list. Now it was his time to go to work. He scanned the material on the tables. After he assembled each unit, filling each of the cylinders with explosives and steel balls then wiring them into the fabric, the suicide vests weighed roughly thirty-five pounds. Hidden beneath overcoats, the C-4 blast would kill anyone within a forty-foot radius. The power of the explosives would cause major structural damage as well as amassing multitudes of casualties.

Khan used extra precaution since the Australian cell had been taken out. The world authorities now suspected there might be further attacks and tightened security. He'd planned for that scenario.

His martyrs in France would leave hundreds dead, an effective blow against the infidel.

Khan planned the attacks and only Khan knew when and where the attacks would occur.

Attacks.

Plural.

He'd chosen two of Paris' icons, guaranteeing high tourist attraction and high body count. But that was only half his plan. The major blow, the highest body count, would come later when he attacked an unsuspecting United States location. A location where large numbers of unsuspecting men, women, and children jammed into unsecured areas.

When Khan attacked there, the death toll would reach into the thousands. America and the world would soon realize that no place was safe. And once again, al Qaeda would be responsible for the free world's stripping its citizens of their rights and privileges—all in the name of security.

The free world would evolve into a police state.

CHAPTER 21

JAKE STEPPED OUT of the shower just as his cell phone started ringing. He towel dried his thick dirty blond hair as he walked toward the phone. He looked at the Caller-ID. A number he didn't recognize.

"Jake Pendleton."

"Jake, I just wanted to let you know you can sleep in tomorrow morning. Kyli will pick you up around noon. I'll bring you up to speed when we leave for Yemen. We need to arrive after dark so we'll eat on the plane. Kaplan and someone from the Delta team will meet us in Aden."

"Have you found another pilot?"

"Don't worry, Jake. We'll have two pilots."

There was a knock on Jake's door. He wrapped the towel around his waist.

"Sir, if that's all..."

"One more thing Jake. Kyli's a free spirit, don't let her get you in trouble."

"I can handle Kyli, sir." Another knock on the door. "You have nothing to worry about."

"Good to know." Wiley clicked off the phone.

"Just a second." Jake threw the towel on the floor and pulled on his pants.

Without a shirt on, Jake opened the door. She stood in front of him wearing a layered gray dress with black nylons and knee length fur-lined boots. The purple streak in her hair was gone. She had thrown her black jacket over her shoulder.

"What the...? Why aren't you dressed? You need to get your ass in gear mister or we're going to be late."

"I didn't know I was under a time constraint. I'll be dressed in a minute."

He started to close the door when Kyli pushed it open and walked in. "Hurry. I'll be waiting..." She sat on the couch. "...right here."

Jake grabbed his clothes and took them into the bathroom. "I just got off the phone with Wiley. He says you're trouble and I should stay away from you. Is that true?"

"You spent all day with me, Jake. I'm a scientist, what do you think?"

He walked out of the bathroom buttoning his shirt. "I think there's something neither one of you is telling me. Something between the two of you. He sounded either jealous or protective. I'm not sure which. My guess is he's either your lover or your father."

Kyli doubled over laughing. "You're wrong on both accounts. If he were my lover then there'd be something wrong with both of us. I just turned twenty-eight and he's seventy-one. That'd make him a creep and me very desperate, which I assure you I am not. Of course, if he were my father, then my name would be Kyli Wiley. How cool would that be?"

"Then what is it? It's more than employee, employer." Jake slipped on his shoes and grabbed a jacket.

"Mr. Wiley's oldest daughter, Mira married Michael Wullenweber, my father. My parents met in Germany and lived there until my father died. I was five. Elmore Wiley is my grandfather. He moved my mother and me to the States and has taken care of me ever since."

"Elmore? Seriously?"

"Seriously. And don't you dare tell him I told you either." Kyli got up and walked toward the door. "Are you ready?"

"You still didn't tell me where we're going."

"I'll let you figure it out. Where are we? Geographically I mean."

"Belgium."

"What month is this?"

"Last time I looked it was October."

"There you have it. All the information you need. You're supposed to be so smart, you figure it out. You're in Belgium in October. Where are we going?" Kyli opened the door.

"I don't know. I give." Jake threw up his hands.

Kyli slapped him on the chest. "Oktoberfest. It's party time." She walked out the door.

Maybe Wiley was right. She could be trouble. A scientist with a wild streak, the combination might be entertaining.

✝ ✝ ✝

The nightstand clock displayed a blurry 10:30 the next morning. His head pounded. His stomach felt like a volcano about to erupt. Jake couldn't remember much about last night—his memory erased like a cleaned chalkboard. *How much did I drink?*

The last time he'd been that drunk was on graduation night from the Naval Academy in Annapolis, where he graduated Valedictorian. He suffered a two-day hangover that time. The next closest he could remember was one night he and Beth drank too many Margaritas in the hot tub at his mountain retreat in Ellijay, Georgia.

His last memory of Oktoberfest was the large stein of beer forced on him by Kyli, his third. Nothing after that. *What happened last night?* More importantly, how did he get back to the hotel? He lifted the sheet on the bed. And where were his clothes?

He tried to sit up. The room spun and he fell back onto the pillow. He rolled over and a wave of nausea hit at what he saw next.

Kyli's purse and jacket were stacked on a chair. Her bra was on the floor and her nylons wadded up on the couch.

Shit. Not now. He found Kyli attractive but he'd never slept with a woman he'd only known for one day. Less than a day. How could he face Wiley? Her grandfather, for crying out loud.

A click at the door grabbed his attention as the door swung open. Kyli walked in with an aromatic pot of coffee and pastries on a silver platter. "Look who rose from the dead."

She put the tray on the coffee table by the couch and picked up her nylons and bra. "Oops." She stuffed them into her purse.

She walked to the window and parted the curtains allowing a strong beam of sunlight to brighten the room. "Time to rise and shine, lightweight. I would have thought a Navy man could hold his liquor better than that."

"What the hell do you mean 'lightweight'?" He squinted. He pointed to the chair. "Did you stay here last night? Did we...uh, you know?"

"Did we partake of carnal pleasures with each other?" She laughed. "Is that what you're asking, lover boy? Don't you remember?"

He shook his head. "I don't remember much of anything about last night."

"I guarantee you one thing." Kyli leaned over the coffee table and lifted the coffee pot. "If we'd...uh, you know, you would *not* have forgotten about it."

"What the hell did I drink?" He put his head between his hands. "How did I get out of my clothes?"

"If you can't remember, I'm not telling." She poured two cups of coffee. "Cream and sugar?"

"Black. Thanks." He reached for the cup. "You didn't answer my question. What happened last night? Did we...?"

"Jake, you were so plastered. Even if you wanted to, you couldn't have. But you did have fun." She waved her iPhone. "I have pictures. Did you know you're a horrible dancer?"

"We danced?" He rubbed his eyes. "Oh no."

"*We* didn't dance. You danced." Kyli held up her phone again. "Like I said, I have pictures."

They talked for a while longer. After two cups of coffee, he was able eat a couple of pastries. His vision cleared, as did his head. But any memory of the night before had vanished into the wind. He could only rely on Kyli's version and he didn't like what he heard.

"Wiley wants you at the office around noon. Are you going to make it?" She walked over to the chair and picked up her things.

"Yes. I'll make it." Jake massaged his temples. "What are you going to do while we're gone?"

"My good friend Kates is flying in tonight." She pulled her keys out of her purse. "We're going to Paris for a few days. We'll probably go to the Eiffel Tower. Maybe even the Louvre. But definitely Champs Elyses."

"Her name is Kates?"

"Kates. With an 's' on the end. Not Kate. Not Katie. Kates." Kyli grabbed her stuff from the chair and moved toward the door. "I'll be back in an hour. Be ready."

"Where you going?"

"Home. I live in a flat about three blocks from here. I needed to clear the cobwebs out of my head too, you know."

"Just leave all your things here." She said. "The room's been booked for a month. Be sure to wear comfortable traveling clothes, Wiley will provide everything else."

"Why do you call him Wiley? Why don't you call the old man 'grandfather' or 'gramps'?" Jake feigned a smile. The volcano wanted to erupt.

Kyli put her hands on Jake's chest, stood on her toes, and gave him a kiss on the cheek. "Thanks for going with me last night. We had fun, whether you can remember it or not." She opened the door, looked back at him and said. "By the way, anyone ever tell you you're a good kisser?"

She closed the door and left.

Jake's head spun. The wave of nausea overwhelmed him. The volcano was erupting. He ran to the bathroom and heaved into the toilet.

CHAPTER 22

ISABELLA HUNT HAD lost track of time. She was able to keep up with her days and nights for a while but with the continual darkness of her prison, the drugs, and the beatings, they started to run together. When she was abducted from Hilal Shipping in Aden, the terrorist attacks planned for Paris were only two weeks away. She had to figure out how to escape—how to get away from her captors and warn Bentley.

She'd given up on a rescue; there wasn't enough time left. A rescue now would waste precious time. Time the CIA needed to track down the two terrorists cells and neutralize them. During her last communication with Fontaine, he'd indicated Jake and Kaplan were in Australia planning to neutralize the cell that planned to attack Sydney.

She prayed they were successful.

Hunt's years of conditioning and her strong will were keeping her alive. Her athletic prowess helped minimize the impact of the beating she received from the man she called Rotten Teeth. But she was getting weaker. It had been many hours since she drank the tainted liquid, days since she ate. Her refusal had meant more beatings. Her strong instinct for survival forced her to eat and drink even though she knew it would keep her in a drugged stupor.

She worked on her bindings, trying to free her hands. They wouldn't budge.

The bolt on the wooden door clanked and the door swung open. The smallest man entered with food and drink. He sat in front of her and prepared to feed her.

"Cut loose my hands." Hunt said. "I am too weak to escape. The bindings are too tight."

"I can not. My orders are clear." The man said. "If you do not eat, I am to give you this." He pulled a syringe from his pocket and held it close to her face.

Feeling defeated, she opened her mouth.

Ten minutes later she had eaten everything the small man brought and drank two full glasses of water. She felt much better. *Maybe the meal wasn't drugged.*

The small man got up to leave. "Please, cut me loose. I need to go to the bathroom."

"I will let someone know. My orders are clear. If I free your restraints, they will cut off my hands." He picked up the tray, turned, and walked out.

Ten minutes later two men entered the room. It was too late. The food had been drugged and she could barely hold up her head.

She felt the flex cuffs being cut free. She tried to move, now was her chance. Maybe her only chance. Her body wouldn't respond. Then panic overwhelmed her, she felt the men removing her clothes.

Her greatest fear, on the verge of being realized. The men were going to rape her.

Her mind was aware but her body immobile. Whatever they gave her had just about paralyzed her limbs.

They dressed her in a gown as thin as a sheet, and placed her on a cot. Her head resting on a pillow.

She tried again to move. Her legs and arms felt too heavy to lift.

She heard another man enter the room. She felt him lift her gown, exposing her body and knew the moment was coming. She wanted to die. The man's hand groped at her, pawing at everything that made her a woman. She knew she was in Hell. Then he stopped and pulled the gown over her. When he spoke, she knew who it was—Rotten Teeth.

"Tomorrow we will talk again." Rotten Teeth said. "If you do not tell me what I want to hear, then you will die. But before you die, I will let you feel a real man inside you.

Then I will let each of these men take you as well. And with each one, I will remove a body part, stemming your blood with fire. You will die a very slow and painful death."

She saw a syringe being inserted in her arm.

Rotten Teeth pushed on the plunger.

Her world went black.

CHAPTER 23

THE LAND CRUSIER pulled up to the west end of Yemen's Aden International Airport as the last hint of daylight left the sky. The abandoned hangars were dark. Kaplan could barely make out movement on the ramp.

"I cannot believe I had to make that miserable drive again." Kaplan said. "They really should work on the roads in this country."

"You're kidding, right?" Chase replied. "The road from Sana'a to Aden is one of Yemen's best. Some of the other so-called highways are nothing but livestock trails."

"Let's go check it out." Kaplan motioned to the shadow on the ramp. "Wiley said the C-130 is about an hour ahead of his Lear."

Earlier in the afternoon, Kaplan and Chase received a briefing from Fontaine and Wiley. The plan was set in motion, all the arrangements had been made with only two details left unfinished. One minor, one major.

Bentley was only able to secure one aircraft to use to tow the gliders. Oddly enough, the plane had to fly to Aden from Sana'a. Kaplan and Chase were well under way by the time that happened.

A double aero tow, although not commonplace, was still considered safe. It had been years since Kaplan flew a glider, he hoped it was like riding a bicycle and would come back to him.

The major detail left undone was the inability to secure a boat to rendezvous with them in the Red Sea. A detail that should scrub any mission. But Bentley and Wiley were still pushing forward.

Kaplan had been worried about Isabella Hunt. Her fate bothered him more than he first realized. Ever since he learned of her capture, he had a pain in his stomach like he'd been punched.

The Delta team did their part. The recon of the Hajjah Palace and the landscape surrounding it went undetected, all data relayed to Kaplan and Chase, and then to Fontaine via secure satellite uplink. Wiley and Fontaine devised a plan. The final details of which would not be disclosed until Wiley arrived.

Kaplan and Chase arrived at the back of the C-130 aircraft as the crew unloaded the last section of the composite gliders. The cargo bay was lit only with red light, imperceptible more than fifteen feet to the sides of the aircraft.

Within twenty minutes the crew had assembled both gliders and snapped instrumentation harnesses into the cockpits. Kaplan watched in amazement. He and Chase walked over to the two men who stood next to it. In a quiet voice Kaplan said, "You guys look like a pit crew at the Daytona 500."

"We've had plenty of practice," the shorter of the two said. "Mr. Wiley had us assemble and disassemble these four times this afternoon before loading them. Are either of you Gregg Kaplan?"

"At your service." Kaplan said.

"Sir. If I may, you're flying this one here. How about a quick run-down of the sailplane?"

"That would be great, it's been a while since I flew. I could use a refresher."

"These sailplanes are Wiley's special hybrid models. These are the only two. The aircraft are made of lightweight composite. Very tough though, almost indestructible. One of Wiley's requirements for these aircraft was their structural integrity. They can reach speeds of up to 150 knots—with no ballast. Another feature is they are undetectable on radar. Another one of Wiley's inventions, the special composite absorbs radar waves so there's no reflection. Without a visual confirmation, no one knows you're out there."

"Black gliders. Don't know that I've ever seen that before." Chase said.

"Technically, they're not black. They just look that way in the dark." The man said. "It's a very dark gray mixed with an olive drab."

"Duck blind colors." Chase interrupted. "Those are the colors most widely used for duck hunting."

"Better camouflage at night. Even on a full moon, you just can't see this glider without light. And on a night like this, with a little cloud cover, forget about it." The man said. "You could fly right down someone's throat. They could be looking right at you and they wouldn't see you coming until it was too late."

"What did you just snap in?" Kaplan asked. "Some sort of portable instrument panel?"

"It's Wiley's all-in-one special." The man pointed to the instruments with a red laser pen. "You got your basic three. Altimeter, airspeed indicator, and heading indicator. You also have this special GPS locator, preprogrammed by Wiley himself. Voice-activated headset here, along with these." He held up a pair of oversized eyeglasses.

"And those are?" Kaplan asked.

"These are the bomb for night flying. Lightweight. Easy to use. Just flip this switch here." The man toggled a switch and the eyeglasses lit up pale green. "Night vision made easy. The GPS will line you up, the glasses will make you think it's high noon. Every landscape detail will be visible."

"Looks like he's thought about every phase of the mission." Kaplan said. "Except one. Who's going to meet us at the rendezvous point?"

CHAPTER 24

WILEY'S BLACK LEARJET lined up its final approach for a landing to the west on Runway 26. Somewhere near on the airfield, Jake knew Kaplan was waiting. The last time they saw each other, they exchanged harsh words. He wondered how Kaplan would react when he saw him.

As the lights from the city of Aden rose to greet him, he tensed in anticipation of landing. The Lear's tires barked slightly then the Lear taxied off the runway onto the ramp in front of the abandoned hangar, Jake strained his eyes but saw nothing, wondering if the C-130 and Kaplan had arrived. The aircraft slowed, turned around, and then came to a stop. Through the window Jake saw a large shadow looming next to the Lear. *They're here.*

It had only been a few days, but it seemed longer since Jake had last seen Kaplan. So much had happened since he met Wiley. He felt different. He realized his anger was holding him prisoner. It had become his crutch to deal with guilt. He was prepared for the mission, Wiley made sure of that, quizzing him on details for nearly two hours during the long flight from Belgium. He wondered why his anger felt subdued. Was it because of Wiley?

He thought about the last few days. Could it be because of her? Like the moon's playful reflection dancing on the water, thoughts of Kyli mesmerized him. Every time he looked at Wiley, he thought about her. In one day's time, her spirit had changed him. He was beginning to realize that he had to let Beth go. He couldn't change the past. He'd killed the man that had taken her life. O'Rourke had paid his penance. Like Kaplan said, it was time to move on.

"Jake. We'll talk to Mr. Kaplan, then we'll mobilize."

The air stair door lowered and Kaplan climbed onboard the Lear and took an empty seat. Wiley introduced himself.

Kaplan stared at the old man. "Hey, don't I know—".

"No." Wiley interrupted.

Kaplan turned to Jake. "No screw ups this time, Jake. Isabella's life is at stake."

"No problem, Gregg. Let's just get Isabella out of there."

"You boys shut up and listen. We don't have time to waste on any issues between the two of you." They both nodded. "We have less than thirty minutes. Our timing must be dead on or we're up the proverbial creek. We get one shot at this. Mr. Kaplan, did you get a thorough briefing on the sailplane and its systems?"

"Yes, sir. Your man was very informative and his briefing quite thorough."

"Are you comfortable flying solo?"

"I think so, sir." Kaplan said. "I wish I had an opportunity to practice my landings but it'll come back to me."

"Who is flying the other glider?" Jake asked.

Wiley ignored him. "Mr. Kaplan, you're flying the number two aircraft. When the sailplanes release from the aero tow, you'll release first, then number one will release and drop the towline. All you have to do is follow the leader. Stay right on its flight path or slightly above it. The lead glider will set up the proper approach angle. You just do what it does and go where it goes and you should have no trouble. Understand?"

"Yes sir." Kaplan sounded confident.

"Who's flying the lead glider?" Jake interrupted again.

Wiley looked at him, then turned to Kaplan. "A walk in the park it won't be. There are still a couple of issues getting up to Hajjah, but we'll handle those on a real-time basis."

"We?" Jake said. "Are you flying the lead glider?"

"I am." Wiley said. "I have over a thousand hours flying sailplanes. Do you have a problem with me going along? I did plan this mission by the way."

"No sir. I'm glad you're going." Jake stuttered. "No disrespect, but aren't you a little—?"

"I hope for your sake you weren't going to say *'old'.*"

"Jake's right, sir. This is a dangerous mission. There could be shooting." Kaplan said. "We don't want anything to happen to you."

"You boys don't get it." Wiley said. "That's exactly why I'm going along. There can be absolutely no shooting. This is silent running. Someone has to keep you two in line. We have a strict timetable. In and out, no screw-ups or we're all dead."

† † †

Ian Collins stepped out of his rental car and tossed the keys to the valet. The Renaissance Concourse valet grabbed the keys mid-flight.

"Welcome to the Renaissance." The valet handed Collins a ticket stub.

"Thank You." Collins spent many determined hours eliminating his Irish brogue. Other than his size, no other feature about him could stand out. He needed to be just another tall man.

He grabbed the ticket, stuffed it into his back pocket, and headed to his sixth-floor room. Everything had fallen into place. His plan was ready for execution.

People were creatures of habit. Most people never varied their daily patterns. They became predictable.

Old people were the worst. They had routines. Routines they didn't want to change. Routines that kept them in their comfort zone.

Routines that made them vulnerable, something he was counting on.

Routines that got them killed.

As expected, when he arrived at the mansion earlier in the day, it was empty, the servants sent home for the day. The wealthy owners wouldn't return home for several hours, which allowed him all the time he needed to rig the incendiary devices. A setup he knew would guarantee results.

Effective, failsafe, and totally untraceable.

How much easier could these old fools have made it for him?

Every night before bedtime, a glass of milk and a handful of old people pills. Then off to bed.

While he was in the home rigging the device, he put the sedative in the milk, enough to make them sleep through an earthquake.

Collins collapsed on the hotel bed. A quick nap, supper at Spondivits, a seafood restaurant three blocks from the hotel, and then a quick drive down I-85.

The assassination was planned with detailed precision, but this time he wasn't getting paid. No funds secretly deposited in his Cayman account or his Swiss account. No one to notify once the deed was done.

This job was personal.

CHAPTER 25

JAKE STILL COULDN'T believe Wiley was going on the mission. The man was over seventy and had no business putting himself in harm's way. The success of the mission was critical and he didn't need an old man slowing him down. He and Kaplan needed to get in quick, locate and secure Isabella, and get the hell out of there.

But something else was eating away at Jake and he couldn't put his finger on it. Was it because the old man was Kyli's grandfather? Or was it something else? Wiley's take-charge demeanor was both annoying and comforting. The man was smart enough to plan it, even control it from a distance, but was he capable of executing the plan if things went wrong?

Somehow Jake had a hunch Wiley could handle it. With all his eccentric behavior, the old man did seem capable of the physical challenge, not that it mattered. Kaplan and Wiley were the only ones capable of flying the gliders. They were both required for the mission.

The Delta recon team, the funny platoon Kaplan called them, had done their job. Chase left as soon as Jake and Wiley arrived. He told Jake he was returning to Sana'a and planned to pack up his squad for the return to Oman where another special assignment awaited their special skills.

Wiley signaled for Jake and Kaplan. "We don't have much time so let me fill you in on what's about to happen."

Four crewmen from the C-130 started hand-towing the two black gliders toward the end of the runway. The darkened end of the runway abutted a road that ran along the waterfront. Very few cars traveled the road at this hour.

With the exception of the approach lights to Runway 8, that end of the airport was a black void.

"If you'll look to the north you can see an approaching aircraft." Wiley pointed to the white light in the distant sky. "That's our tow pretending to be on a training flight with a student pilot and a flight instructor. The plane will land facing us, turn around on the runway, and takeoff in the opposite direction. When it does, we'll be in tow."

"What about the tower?" Kaplan asked. "They'll see us. They'll see the gliders go right past the tower. We'll be made."

"Got it covered." Wiley said. "When the aircraft turns around, we have less than three minutes to be in the air and out over the water where it's dark. So when I tell you to move, move fast. Get strapped in and ready to roll. My men will handle the hook-ups. Jake, you're with me. Understood?"

"Understood." Jake said.

"I hope you know what you're doing." Kaplan said.

"Oh ye of little faith." Wiley grinned. "Watch and learn."

†††

Two air traffic controllers in the control tower at Aden International Airport watched the small single engine training flight enter a right downwind leg for a landing on Runway 26. The request made, for training purposes was to roll out at the end of the runway, turn around, and takeoff in the opposite direction. It was not the norm, but neither was a training flight in Yemen. Training flights routinely asked air traffic controllers to accommodate out of the ordinary requests, traffic permitting, for the purpose of flight training.

The absence of other aircraft in the vicinity of the airport prompted the air traffic controller to issue a combined clearance. "Runway 26, cleared to land. Runway 8, cleared for takeoff."

With the clearance in hand, the small high-wing aircraft followed perfect traffic pattern procedures, turning on final approach for Runway 26. The aircraft landed just past the numbers and made the long rollout toward the opposite end.

As expected, the air traffic controllers observed the small airplane spin around on the runway and come to a full stop. As soon as the aircraft stopped, the unexpected happened.

The runway lights and electrical power for half the town of Aden failed. The airport was plunged into total darkness. A few headlights from distant cars traveling along the highways were the only lights visible. The aircraft's lights were no longer visible either.

"Takeoff clearance cancelled." The chief controller yelled into the microphone. "Takeoff clearance cancelled."

The radio was dead.

It took three minutes for the back-up generators to power up the control tower. Equipment began to glow as it came back to life. Runway lights grew brighter. A minute later all power was restored in Aden.

The chief controller scanned the length of the runway and taxiways, expecting to see the small aircraft. The runways and taxiways were empty. He scanned the surrounding skies.

Nothing.

The training airplane had vanished.

He picked up the phone.

†††

"How the hell did you pull that off?" Kaplan asked into his voice-activated headset. The old man had surprised him with his creativity. He never thought of killing the power to the airport *and* the town.

Wiley replied. "I called in a favor."

Kaplan watched the pilot of the tow aircraft cut all the aircraft's lights the moment the runway went dark. The pilot's instructions from Wiley were to keep the aircraft stationary on the middle of the runway and wait for the bang on the fuselage—the signal from the ground crew that the gliders were set.

With the entire area dark, Kaplan watched the ground crew move the two gliders into position behind the tow aircraft, attach each with a detachable rope roughly two hundred feet in length. One behind the other in tandem. After the slack had been removed from the towlines, one of the ground crew ran to the idling aircraft and slapped his hand on the fuselage then ran clear.

By the time the lights came back on to the airport and town, the three aircraft were far enough over the water to avoid visual detection.

As per Wiley's instructions, the pilot of the tow aircraft flew straight for exactly three minutes, turned to a heading of 020 degrees for exactly two minutes before turning inland. Kaplan matched each maneuver. His anxiety about flying soon left him. The controls were light and responsive. Although he knew it was dark, the night vision display unveiled everything as if it were daylight. He saw several boats scattered across the open water pulling all-nighters to bring in as big a catch as possible.

"We're not out of the woods yet." Wiley said. "It's roughly 350 kilometers to Hajjah—we disconnect from tow at three hundred."

"Miles, please." Jake said. "It's been a long time since I've used kilometers. How many miles?"

"Jake, you better get used to kilometers. But miles it will be for tonight." Wiley said. "215 miles to Hajjah. Roughly a 185 miles to disconnect."

"Why aren't we out of the woods?" Jake asked.

"Very soon Yemen's army personnel will detect the tow aircraft." Wiley explained. "They might or might not launch to find out why it left Aden after the power outage. And without running lights. I don't imagine the authorities will be too happy with our pilots."

"I thought the Yemen army was an allied force." Kaplan said.

"Officially, maybe." Wiley explained. "Reality is a whole different matter. Many leaders, or at least several of the top-ranking officials in the Yemen army are in cahoots with al Qaeda terrorists. Never trust Yemeni leaders. Yemen is overrun with al Qaeda. The leaders are paid off."

"What if they do launch?" Jake asked. "We're sitting ducks up here."

"Depending on when they launch depends on which course of action we take. If they launch too soon, we disconnect and scrub." Wiley said. "Otherwise we play it by ear."

Disconnect and scrub? Did Kaplan hear Wiley right? He couldn't let that happen. He wouldn't let Wiley pull the plug. They had to save Isabella.

He had to save Isabella.

CHAPTER 26

JAKE DIDN'T LIKE blind trust and Wiley wasn't being forthright in sharing his plans. Maybe Wiley didn't trust him or was afraid he'd look bad if he had to change plans at the last minute. Or maybe he was just winging it as he went along. Either way, Jake didn't like being left in the dark.

Bentley apparently trusted Wiley and Jake trusted Bentley's judgment, even if Bentley had sent him into exile. An exile induced by himself.

In the Navy, he was a planner and an analyst. And he was damn good at both. He knew he had a gift. A gift he developed at an early age when his father taught him to play chess. Requiring him to predict his opponent's play at least four moves ahead honed his skills as a strategic planner. By the 6th grade, he was winning chess tournaments. He developed insight into things many others didn't grasp—except Wiley. The old man was smart, too smart. As difficult as it might be, Jake had to trust Wiley.

If the Yemen army launched early, would Wiley indeed abandon Hunt? She might not even be alive. He wondered how Kaplan would handle that. Abandoning Hunt? The possibility she was already dead? Jake knew his friend was tough but he also knew if the rescue was abandoned, Kaplan wouldn't handle it well.

His thoughts were interrupted when Kaplan asked a question.

"When do we know we are passed the abandon stage?" Kaplan asked.

"It's an hour and a half to disconnect if all goes according to plan." Wiley spoke like a team leader, an air of authority in his voice. "Our first objective is to get north of Taiz, that's where the first launch would originate. There is nothing in Aden. If they launch while we're south of Taiz, we have no choice but to scrub the mission. There is no backup. We can't stay attached and we can't make it to Hajjah. If we can get to the 150-mile mark, there is a possibility of success. I have a backup plan but the element of danger escalates to the point where I don't know if it's worth the risk."

"It doesn't matter what the risk is." Kaplan said. "If there is a backup, I say we use it."

"Last resort only." Wiley said.

Jake thought he sounded irritated with Kaplan. Then Wiley surprised him.

"Jake, take the controls." Wiley said.

"Sir, I have no idea what to do." Jake protested.

"Take them. Now." Wiley commanded. "I'll explain everything to you."

The next hour went by fast. He didn't have to do much while the gliders were still in aero tow. Except when they talked, it was relatively quiet. Only air noise passing over the glider. Kaplan was silent. No more questions. Jake suspected Kaplan was getting a refresher on the controls while Wiley was instructing him.

The silence was interrupted by a steady tone. Wiley spoke to the pilot of the tow aircraft, "Give me maximum climb rate. We have ten, twelve minutes tops before we disconnect. I need all the altitude you can give me."

"What's happening?" Kaplan took the words out of Jake's mouth.

They've launched four aircraft from Taiz. Their speed implies helicopters." Wiley said. "We're at mile one thirty now, not far enough but we'll go for it anyway. Listen carefully, if we don't do this exactly right, we're all dead."

†††

Five minutes later Jake was startled by another alarm tone in the cockpit.

"That's not good." Wiley said. "They just launched fighters from Sana'a. Time for us to say goodbye to our tow. Gregg? Are you ready?"

"Let's do it." Kaplan said.

"Remember don't light up until you see me light up. Heading 3-3-0 and do not exceed 120 knots. It'll seem like you're going straight up." Wiley said. "Oxygen nose clips on. Got it?" Wiley asked.

"Got it." Kaplan said. "Oxygen on. Ready to go vertical."

"Jake, hold on tight here we go."

"Mr. Wiley? Won't the fighters see our jet exhaust or heat signature?" Jake asked.

"Not with my custom exhaust shroud." Wiley explained. "Unless they're directly behind us, we'll be invisible."

Jake couldn't see Wiley's face, but he was sure the old man was smiling.

Wiley seemed to be enjoying the adventure. The thrill. He didn't disconnect, he waited. The fighters got closer. Jake squirmed in his seat. According to the electronic screen, ten miles and closing.

"Sir, shouldn't we disconnect now?" Jake asked.

"Not yet." Wiley said. "Let them get closer. We need to eke out as much altitude as we can before we break away."

Five miles and closing.

"Sir?" Jake wanted to question Wiley's judgment. Maybe the old man was, in fact, too old.

The fighters were at three miles and closing when two bright flashes appeared.

"Missiles." Wiley shouted. "Disconnect, disconnect."

They had reached an altitude of 10,430 feet when Kaplan disconnected from Wiley's glider. Wiley released Kaplan's towline then disconnected from the tow aircraft.

"Jake, turn to heading 3-3-0, nose up, activate JATO bottle on my mark." Wiley sounded off in perfect cadence. "Now."

Jake was slammed against the back of his seat from the sudden increase in thrust and acceleration. The JATO rocket, an acronym for jet-fuel assisted takeoff, was a system designed to provide overweight aircraft with additional thrust for takeoff. Wiley's adaptation was a sixty-second burn of a single small rocket bottle that would automatically jettison after burn.

"Nose up, nose up." Wiley commanded Jake. "Speed 120, no faster. Control your speed with your angle of climb—it's very steep."

"Roger that." Jake replied.

"Kaplan? How you doing back there?" Wiley asked.

"I'm right on your tail." Kaplan shouted. "Behind and to the left. Whoa, what a ride."

The two gliders climbed higher and higher.

The sky grew bright below them followed by the reverberation of the explosion, louder than the JATO rockets.

"I can't believe they shot down the tow plane." Jake yelled. "We just got those two killed."

"Collateral damage." Wiley said.

"Who were they?" Kaplan asked. "Yemenis?"

"No. I'm afraid not." Wiley lowered his voice as the JATOs burned out and automatically disconnected from the gliders. "The young men were from the Delta unit you worked with in Sana'a. Bentley had trouble finding local pilots so they volunteered. They understood the risk, I explained it to them personally."

"Son of a—" Kaplan started.

"Nose over slightly." Wiley interrupted. "We have a mission to complete. Best glide speed. Stay on heading. We have 55 miles to go. Even with the tailwind, it'll take nearly an hour. We are, oddly enough, right on schedule. Gregg, I need you to stay focused."

"I'm focused. I'm focused." Kaplan said. "Just really pissed off."

"No more pissed off than I am." Wiley said. "Like I said earlier, you can't trust the Yemenis."

Jake looked at the altimeter, 19,670 feet above sea level. With a landing elevation of 5700 feet, they had roughly 14,000 feet to lose in 55 miles.

He did the calculations in his head.

They weren't going to make it.

CHAPTER 27

"I DON'T WANT to be an alarmist." Jake said. "But we have a bigger problem. Based on my calculations, we can't make it to Hajjah."

"Mr. Wiley?" Kaplan asked. "Is Jake right?"

"Jake doesn't have all the facts." Wiley said. "It's going to be tight. No margin for error."

Jake felt a pit in his stomach grow. He looked out the window at the Earth below. Nothing. Nothing but a black void. He knew the terrain was rugged. He confirmed it when he switched on his night vision goggles.

The JATO bottles had rocketed them upward thousands of feet. During all the excitement, he'd forgotten about their main objective—rescue Isabella Hunt. Landing safely on the ground in Hajjah very well might be the easy part. No telling what awaited them upon arrival. If they made it.

The visibility was nearly unlimited beneath the cirrostratus layer of clouds that hovered above them. To the northeast, he could see the city lights of Sana'a. They looked close but he knew they were at least thirty miles away. Using his NVGs, he could see the outline of the coast of the Red Sea to the west. After they extracted Hunt that would be their next stop.

For the next thirty minutes, Jake watched the altimeter as the gliders gradually drifted toward the mountains below. He planned to switch off his night vision goggles so at least he wouldn't see it coming. They'd just plow into the side of a mountain and death would be instantaneous.

Jake gazed at the GPS display and compared it to the darkness. The display showed Hajjah to be fifteen miles ahead. In the distance, Jake could see a sparse smattering of lights. They were too low. Flying a glider in Yemen. At night. In the mountains. A hell of a way to die.

He thought back to all those aircraft accidents he'd investigated. The wreckage. The carnage. He never dreamed he'd be part of one himself. Of course, they were going relatively slow in comparison to the accidents he investigated in his prior life. A life that seemed so distant. And yet, it had only been seven months.

Their speed might make a crash survivable. So instead of instant death, he could expect to be maimed for life. Maybe captured alive in Yemen and tortured. *Great. This just gets better every second.*

The glider jolted hard. A wave of fear passed over Jake. "What was that?"

"What I've been waiting for." Wiley answered. "With this wind, we'll get to take advantage of some ridge lift. Not a lot, mind you, but enough to get us to our landing site. I'll take it from here, Jake."

"It's all yours." Jake watched Wiley gently maneuver the glider along the lift line. The altimeter started rising. The angle from the glider to the lights ahead continually increased to a comfortable margin.

"Kaplan, you doing okay?" Wiley said.

"No sweat." Kaplan said. "I'm probably a good hundred feet above you now."

"Yeah." Jake said. "You think it's due to less body weight?"

"I have a visual on the landing site." Wiley announced. "Kaplan, can you confirm a visual?"

"Yes sir. In sight." Kaplan said. "But I'm too high so I'm going to swing a little wider and line up for a straight-in."

"That's fine. Just don't get too far out." Wiley said.

"No sir." Kaplan said. "I'll keep it a little high and slip it in if I need to."

Jake was nervous. How good was the old man, he wondered? It didn't take him long to find out.

With expert precision, Jake watched the old man bank the glider on a final approach to the landing site. With his NVGs on, the site looked small—too small an area to safely land the glider.

The old man didn't seem concerned. He set the flaps. His speed control, precise. Wiley was flying a perfect glide slope. Jake relaxed a little.

The edge of the mountain came at them fast. The closer they got, the easier it was to read the slope on the landing site.

Slightly uphill. He knew it would be no challenge for Wiley. Kaplan might be a different story.

As the glider flew past the edge of the cliff, Jake tensed his body. Wiley eased back on the joystick and pushed out the air brakes. The glider decelerated rapidly and touched down without a sound on the clay surface. It was over. They made a safe landing. Jake exhaled. He hadn't realized it until that moment he was holding his breath.

On Wiley's command, they climbed out of the glider and pulled it as far from the main landing area as possible. A quick glance around. No one in the small village had been alerted to their presence.

Jake looked back toward the edge of the cliff. He could make out Kaplan's glider—it was coming right at them.

Too fast and too low.

CHAPTER 28

KAPLAN STUDIED THE landscape through his night vision heads-up display. Baraka was right, the entire village of Hajjah was built on a hill—more like a mountain than a hill. The mountainsides were terraced leading up to the top where the town of Hajjah was situated. Most of the terraces appeared to be thirty to forty feet in height. The streets were switchbacks winding from the top of the mountain to the valley below. Both sides of the streets were lined with small-whitewashed houses.

The cliff at the approach end of the landing site had the steepest drop, approximately 500 feet. The field was located immediately past the edge of the cliff. A death wish landing site. If he ran out of altitude before the field, he'd smack into the side of the mountain like a bug colliding with a windshield.

Through his night vision goggles he watched the other glider land. He saw Jake and Wiley move their glider out of the way giving him more room to land. Good. He wanted as large a landing area as possible.

He'd never landed a glider at night. For the record, he'd never flown a glider at night. The NVG display made it easier, though. But even with the NVG display, the landing site didn't look the same. Depth perception was different at night and he was having some difficulty making the adjustment. Unfortunately he didn't have the luxury of time. He had to do this right the first time.

He was too low and his airspeed too fast, a combination that allowed him to fix both—once. There was no such thing as a missed approach in a glider, no going around for a second attempt. He had one chance and that was it. He eased back on the joystick and his airspeed slowed, the proper glide path regained.

He sensed something was wrong. What had he forgotten? He glanced down and noticed his speed across the ground was too fast. Then he realized his mistake. He hadn't deployed the flaps. Short final approach was no time to forget procedures that important. It hadn't occurred to him before, even with his flat angle of descent.

Kaplan deployed full flaps. The affect was a quick increase in lift, which ballooned him well above his desired glide path. The end of the landing site was approaching fast. He was running out of options.

The glider slowed to the proper airspeed but he was still too high. He had to react or the glider would touch down at the end of the landing site, overrun, and crash.

Slip.

That's what he'd do. He'd slip the glider down. An uncoordinated maneuver that resulted in an excessive rate of descent but might allow him to lose the extra altitude he'd gained with the flaps.

"Let it work. Let it work."

It worked. He lost enough altitude, which allowed him to reestablish the proper glide angle. He did a final check on short final. Speed, check. Altitude, check. Flaps, set.

Then it happened. An unexpected gust of wind blew up the side of the mountain—ridge lift. He was a hundred feet from the landing site and the updraft had taken him well above any semblance of making a safe landing.

Kaplan panicked.

He could think of only one thing, drag. He needed extra drag and a lot of it.

Kaplan jammed the air brakes full forward. The spoilers on the top of the wings popped up. It was like the glider hit a wall in mid-air. The nose pitched down and the glider dove for the ground.

Too much. Too much.

Fifty feet to go. He was descending too fast.

He glanced at his airspeed. Too slow. If the glider stalled he would crash into the side of the mountain.

Kaplan retracted the air brakes and felt the glider surge forward. Airspeed increasing. No altitude left, he was at the edge of the landing site. The edge of the cliff. He was going to hit hard.

Kaplan pulled back on the joystick. Further, further. The nose of the glider pitched up as it slammed into the clay surface. The impact caused him to bite his lip. Warm blood trickled down his chin. He felt something give in the back of the aircraft. The tail groaned then kicked up.

The nose of the glider plowed deeper into the landing site. The right wing caught the ground and the aircraft pulled to the right. Loose clay sprayed across the canopy as the glider slid sideways.

Kaplan looked out of the cockpit and saw Jake and Wiley running away from their glider. He was sliding right at them. Not good.

As the glider skidded, the left wing dug into the clay. The friction slowed his forward momentum but he was still on a collision course for the other glider. He braced for impact.

A second later the left wing of Kaplan's glider skidded underneath the other glider lifting the tail five feet in the air.

The glider stopped, damage done.

Not only had Kaplan wrecked his glider, he might have damaged Wiley's other glider as well. He had single-handedly ruined the mission and possibly alerted the entire village to their presence.

CHAPTER 29

JAKE AND WILEY ran toward the sailplane, helped Kaplan get out of the cockpit, and sought cover behind an old shed adjacent to the landing site.

"Do you think you could've made a little more noise, Gregg?" Jake studied the surrounding buildings for signs of movement. "You got blood on your shirt."

Kaplan ran his hand across his mouth. "I bit my lip."

"Mr. Kaplan, what happened?" Wiley asked.

"A gust from the mountain." Kaplan said. "I ballooned at the last minute. I didn't know what else to do but jam on the air brakes."

"Gregg, I've seen dozens of aircraft accidents." Jake said. "But that's the first one I ever witnessed."

"Maybe we should trade places, see how well you do."

"Quiet. Both of you." Wiley demanded. "Mr. Kaplan, you made enough noise to wake the dead. I'm afraid someone might have heard and will come investigate. Don't worry about the aircraft. I'll take a look at them when it's safe to move around. For now, keep alert for anyone approaching."

"Yes, sir." Kaplan said. "Sorry about the glider."

Wiley motioned for them to stay put then he moved away in a crouching trot.

"I thought you said you knew how to fly." Jake turned to Kaplan. "If you can manage to be quiet, maybe we can look around and make sure the coast is clear."

"Wiley said stay here." Kaplan said.

"Stay here then." Jake whispered. "I'm looking around."

Jake spent the next ten minutes slipping from building to building, shack to shack, looking for any signs of movement. Just as he was convinced they were in the clear, he saw the figure of a woman in a burqa walking down the hill directly toward Kaplan.

He backtracked in an attempt to approach the woman from behind as she drew closer to Kaplan. The closer she moved toward Kaplan, the closer Jake moved toward her, quarter angling her from behind. He needed to make sure she didn't cry out for help. They had been lucky so far. No one else showed interest in Kaplan's mishap with the glider.

The woman was almost on top of where he'd left Kaplan when he noticed Wiley approaching from the opposite quarter angle. Jake knew Wiley was cutting off any angle she had for escape. She needed to be silenced. Gauging from Wiley's speed and angle, Jake would reach her only a second or two before Wiley.

Jake moved swiftly and silently. The woman seemed intent on reaching her destination, not looking from side to side. She was close. Close enough to recognize the gliders in the darkness. He had to make his move now.

With less than ten steps before he caught her, he broke into a run. The dirt crushed between his shoes and the rock hardened earth—clearly audible with each step. Jake was close enough to grab her when she spun around.

She pointed a gun at Jake's chest. It was too late for Jake. There was no avoiding a point blank range shot. He didn't know whether to dive straight into her or hit the ground. A decision he never got to make.

As the woman spun around and raised the pistol, a black figure appeared behind her simultaneously clamping a hand over her mouth and removing the pistol from her grip. Kaplan.

Jake's heart raced.

The pistol fell to the ground. Kaplan jerked the headwear from the woman and turned her to face him. Then they spoke.

Jake was confused.

Wiley walked over and picked up the pistol. "Is this the woman from Sana'a?"

"Yes." Kaplan whispered. "This is Baraka."

Wiley handed her the gun.

"I was near Palace, heard noise. I come make sure nothing wrong." She pointed at the tangled gliders. "Can still fly, yes?"

"That remains to be seen." Wiley said. "Come with me Jake, let's clean up Mr. Kaplan's mess."

†††

Jake and Wiley separated the gliders. Jake pulled Kaplan's glider free while Wiley lifted the tail of his glider. They worked in quiet synchrony, moving the gliders then inspecting them.

Wiley's glider was unscathed. Scratches of no consequence on the tail. Kaplan's glider was not so lucky. The right wing had been damaged by the wing low impact. The left wing tip dented from the slide into the other glider. Neither of which seemed to concern Wiley. He reached into the rear of his glider and pulled out a small leather tool wrap.

With several adjustments to the right wing, made from inside the cockpit, Wiley had cinched the wing back to its normal position. Then he pulled out a roll of black duct tape.

Wiley held up the roll. "This, young man, should be in every first aid kit."

Jake controlled his laughter. Wiley seemed prepared for everything.

"I built these aircraft tough." Wiley explained. "Designed them for rough terrain. Built to take abuse. They're strong but not indestructible. Fortunately Mr. Kaplan was probably only going about forty miles per hour when he had his first impact with the ground. And since he didn't hit anything stationary, the damage was minimal."

Wiley pointed toward the cliff. "Now let's line them up and ready them for takeoff." Wiley said. "Then we'll grab our gear and go retrieve Ms Hunt."

Jake and Wiley pulled the aircraft in line for their eventual takeoff, Kaplan's glider first followed by Wiley's. Wiley reached into the cockpit of his glider and flipped a switch, a retractable motor and propeller popped up from the tail of the aircraft.

"If we had motors," Jake said. "Why the hell did we have to use those crazy jet bottles and then have to worry about making it to this town?"

"These retractable engines are electric and totally silent." Wiley explained. "Battery power for these aircraft is the one area I had to scrimp on. Batteries are heavy and I couldn't afford to put on any more weight by using longer lasting batteries."

"But if we weren't going to make this landing spot, we would have used them, right?" Jake asked.

Wiley said nothing.

"Right?"

"No, Jake." Wiley said. "The use of these before takeoff from here was never an option. We either made it on the JATO bottles or we didn't. Their use is mission critical and only to be used strictly for takeoff and enroute to our rendezvous point."

"So you would have let us crash land…at night, in this God forsaken part of the world?"

"If we couldn't make this spot, then yes Jake, I would have force landed away from our destination."

Jake followed Wiley to Kaplan's glider. Again, Wiley reached into the cockpit and flipped a switch. The retractable motor and propeller popped loose but failed to extend.

"Not good." Wiley said.

"What is it?" Jake asked. "Why didn't the motor come up?"

"Apparently Mr. Kaplan's landing has jammed the mechanism." Wiley grabbed his tool bag. "We'll have to pry it loose. If we can't get this to retract, it will critically reduce the aircraft's gliding distance."

"Then what?" Jake asked.

"Then we won't make our rendezvous point." Wiley said. "We'll have to land before our destination and hoof it out. But that isn't our biggest obstacle."

"How could it get any worse?"

"We might lose our cover of darkness."

CHAPTER 30

JAKE CHECKED HIS watch for the fourth time in ten minutes, 3:59 a.m. local time. Wiley had been working on the retractable electric motor mechanism for twenty minutes. They were getting further and further behind schedule. According to Wiley's initial timeframe, they should be entering Hajjah Palace at this very moment, but the old man refused to split the team up and send him ahead to start setting up the RTI.

Kaplan had been helping Wiley with the glider, offering an apology every few minutes. Jake could see Wiley's frustration. The man was used to success. His missions ran smooth because of his keen insight and attention to detail. Wiley worked at a feverish pace wiping the sweat from his forehead. Jake noticed even the plunging temperatures of the cold night air wasn't enough to calm Wiley's exterior. For the first time, he noticed Wiley's cool demeanor starting to deteriorate.

"There." Wiley said. "It's the best I can do."

"The best you can do?" Kaplan asked. "Does that mean it's fixed?"

"It'll have to do. The motor is up and locked into position and functioning. You'll have power for takeoff and climb out. The arm won't fully retract so there will be a drag issue to contend with later. The mechanism will travel about halfway provided you don't drain the battery. So try not to run it dry before we get to altitude." Wiley patted the tail of the glider. "You wrecked it. You fly it out."

"I'll make it work, sir." Kaplan tried to sound confident.

"You two gear up. Grab the equipment bags. Baraka and I will get a head start," Wiley said. "We're running out of time so we need to hustle."

Jake stared at the fading lights of the Palace as a blanket of fog settled onto the mountaintop, they could use the reduced visibility to their advantage, he thought. Three men wearing backpacks followed Baraka through the unlit streets of the mountaintop village of Hajjah. Stealth was important, as was silence. They were lucky that Kaplan's glider mishap didn't disturb any of the village's residents. Looking up, the Palace entrance was only six hundred feet from the landing site. Almost three hundred feet of that was vertical which meant climbing several tiers of switchback roads. A much longer hike.

Jake glanced at his watch as they approached the Palace. *Another twenty minutes gone.* He was winded and breathing heavy. He could hear Kaplan doing the same. Wiley and the woman didn't seem fazed by the uphill trek or the thin atmosphere.

By the time they reached the stone wall surrounding the Palace, the fog had reduced the visibility to less than fifty feet. Glancing down from the hilltop, the landing site and the gliders were no longer visible.

"Jake, grab the RTI bag and let's set it up." Wiley whispered.

"On it." Jake replied.

"RTI?" Kaplan said to Jake. "What the hell's he talking about?"

"Radio tomographic imaging. After I set up the nodes..." Jake held up four small knobby balls. "...Radio transceivers, we'll be able to see, identify and track everything in the Palace."

"That's impossible." Kaplan said.

"You Army boys don't know much." Jake said. "I used the system at Wiley's lab in Belgium. It works. And it's cool."

"Is there anything the old man can't do?" Kaplan asked.

Jake smiled. "I don't think so."

"I can't bring someone back to life after they've been shot for talking too loud." Wiley interrupted. "Your voices carry. Now shut up and get to work. Jake, go place the nodes around the palace. Quietly."

Wiley turned to Kaplan. "Stay here. I'll show you how this works as the nodes come online."

✝✝✝

Kaplan watched as Wiley fired up the mini-computer monitor and activated a program icon he'd never seen before. The dark screen showed a small bar graph and the words "SEARCHING FOR NODES."

"Now pay attention." Wiley said. "As Jake positions each node, the bar graph will give us signal strength."

Kaplan watched as four bars relayed signal strength to Wiley's computer terminal. Then the words "BUILDING CARTOGRAPHY" appeared.

"What's it doing now?" Kaplan asked.

"It sends radio waves throughout the Palace and gathers data. This takes about two minutes then it will build a 3D image of the interior of the Palace." Wiley pointed to another small icon in the upper right hand corner of the monitor. "After it builds the architectural database, I'll tell it to image life forms. Then we'll locate and tag everyone in the Palace. If anything moves that isn't a life form then the computer will adjust and annotate."

"How does something that's not alive move?" Kaplan said.

"Think about it, Gregg." Wiley said. "Anything inanimate that isn't moving when the database is built will show up as fixed...a permanent part of the structure, like a desk or a box. But say some one moves the box. The computer will compensate and tag it by changing the box's color denoting it as movable."

"And you invented all this?" Kaplan asked.

"No." Wiley said. "Just substantially improved it."

Baraka stepped over and pointed to the monitor. "Is Hajjah Palace. I have been there before."

"That's good." Wiley said. "Because when we locate Ms Hunt, you'll have to lead them to her."

Wiley clicked the *"LIFE FORM"* icon. The words *"THERMAL SCAN IN PROGRESS"* popped up in the center of the screen.

Kaplan studied the monitor.

"THERMAL SCAN COMPLETE."

"IMAGING LIFE FORMS."

Kaplan watched as the computer populated the 3D image with depictions of every living body in the Palace. "Now what?"

"Now comes the hard part." Wiley said. "We have to figure out which one of these is Ms Hunt, tag her as friendly and then tag the rest as unfriendly."

Jake returned with the empty RTI bag. "I see you've already imaged."

"Looking at this," Wiley said. "We have six life forms. The two outside we know are sentries. Which leaves three unfriendly and one friendly inside. So who is who?"

"I help." Baraka pointed to the ground floor on the monitor. "No place here for hostage. All open space. Like museum. Two on bottom are guards. They have guns."

"Then I'll tag these as unfriendly as well as the sentries out front." Wiley clicked and each life form turned red and was designated with a number. "Which means one of these two is Ms Hunt."

"Well that's easy then." Jake said. "One image is in a hallway here." Jake pointed to an image on the second floor. "The other is inside a room. That has to be Isabella. They wouldn't leave her in the hallway."

Wiley tagged the other life forms, one red, and the other green. "Now when you enter the compound." He pointed at Kaplan and then to Jake. "You go first and Jake, you go second. I have to tag you as well so I don't turn you the wrong way. Baraka will already be in the compound distracting the sentries and I'll have tagged her by the time you two enter."

Jake checked his weapons. "Anything else?"

"You two keep this in mind," Wiley said. "If you don't do exactly what I tell you, when I tell you, this mission will fail."

CHAPTER 31

THE DRIVE SOUTHBOUND on Interstate 85 from Atlanta to Newnan didn't take Ian Collins as long as he'd anticipated. Atlanta airport traffic was light and he'd made good time on the interstate, reaching Newnan ahead of schedule.

Collins took the Col. Joe M. Jackson Medal of Honor Highway exit and pulled into the drive-thru at Arby's. After paying for his food, he drove east then turned south on Shenandoah Boulevard. A few minutes later Collins turned into the parking lot of the Heatherwood Baptist Church. The parking lot was empty so Collins pulled behind the church and backed his rental car into a corner spot near a tree line.

At this hour there was still a stream of traffic on Shenandoah Blvd. and Lower Fayetteville Road. Too many cars to make the quarter-mile walk to the mansion without running the risk of being noticed. He needed to make sure he wasn't seen by anyone. No one could have any recollection of a pedestrian in the area late at night. *That* might raise suspicion and, for now, this needed to be considered an accident.

So he waited.

He sat in the dark car, ate his Arby's sandwich, and waited.

Waited for the traffic to wane and for the elderly occupants of the mansion to settle in for the night. For them to start their nightly routine and drink the sleeping agent that would render them unconscious.

Then they would sleep.

Until they died.

† † †

Jake crouched behind a boulder and signaled to Kaplan that Baraka was approaching the two sentries. He motioned for Kaplan to move across the walkway for a better vantage point. A clear line of sight was needed to eliminate the two guards.

Before Jake and Kaplan advanced toward the Hajjah Palace, Wiley handed them each a tranquilizer pistol equipped with its own version of a sound suppressor. Wiley's tranquilizer gun was virtually silent, even quieter than a silenced handgun. No one in the village would be alerted to their presence.

Baraka's task was to distract the sentries and lure their attention away from the path leading to the Palace so Jake and Kaplan could take their shots and move to the next stage of the mission.

"All right men, get ready." Wiley's voice crackled in Jake's headset. "Baraka is almost there."

Jake didn't know what distraction Baraka would use only that she said she could handle her assignment. From his vantage point, he could see both guards. One much shorter than the other, both dressed in uniform attire.

Jake watched the woman move toward the palace, stop, and pull something from the shrubs next to the walkway. A small bag. Without hesitation, she held the bag in front of her and continued toward the palace.

As she approached the entrance, one of the guards, the taller of the two, raised his hand signaling her to stop. The woman ignored him and kept walking toward the entrance. The short guard raised his rifle. Jake felt his stomach tighten. Then she spoke and the man lowered his rifle.

Jake signaled Kaplan and they both took careful aim at their designated targets.

As the woman approached the taller man, he slapped her with the back of his hand. She fell to her knees.

Wiley's voice in the headset, "Now."

Jake and Kaplan fired at the same time striking their targets in the neck with the darts. Jake watched both men grab their necks and fall to the rocky ground. The sedative worked fast rendering its victims unconscious.

"Well done." Wiley's voice again.

The darts could be removed after fifteen seconds but had to remain attached for at least that length of time. Wiley told Jake the dose he used guaranteed unconsciousness for at least six hours, depending, of course, on the size of the person. Jake and Kaplan's only instruction was to make sure their shots were on target. *"You hit them and my formula will take care of the rest."* Wiley had said.

As instructed, Jake followed Kaplan into the compound where he moved the unconscious men into sitting positions on either side of the oversized double doors of the palace. Jake pulled the darts from the men's necks, placed a plastic cap over the needle and put them in his coat pocket.

"What do you see?" Jake whispered into his headset.

"When you walk in the front door, there will be a wall on either side for the first five or six feet. Like a foyer area, then the room opens up. There will be four columns positioned equal distance around the center of the room." Wiley said. "To the right is the stairwell to the upper floors and in front of the stairwell is what looks like a table. Both men appear to be sitting at the table."

"Any movement upstairs?" Jake asked.

"No." Wiley said. "My bet is the guard is asleep."

"When we open the door, both men will be alerted. Probably with guns pointed our direction." Kaplan said.

"Again, let Baraka go in first." Wiley said. "At the very least she has to get them to lower their weapons. When they have relaxed their guard, I'll signal and you two can take them out."

Baraka gathered her bag, "I go now."

"You are very brave." Jake said. "Be careful."

†††

Collins finished his sandwich and threw the garbage on the back floorboard of the rental. He pulled out his newly purchased e-reader, flipped on the mini-light, and read to pass the time.

Dressed in full black, he was ready for his revenge. He would blend into the darkness and furtively take the next step in his complex plan to draw his prey to him. He read until it was time, turned off his e-reader, grabbed his pack from the back seat, and started the quarter-mile trek to the mansion.

Avoiding the streetlights near the Heatherwood Baptist Church, he walked behind the church through a parking lot to the tree line on the northern boundary of the property. Tucked behind a tree, he waited. Within a minute, there was a break in the traffic—no cars in sight—he darted across four lanes and a median and into the woods at the corner of Forest Road and Shenandoah Boulevard.

He retraced his path from earlier when he had planted the device. The same path he'd used several times earlier while he observed the patterns of the elderly couple. The old man, a retired public servant with some elevated status, was of declining health and had been unable to drive for almost a year. The woman was still in good health for her age, working in her garden plot and swimming daily in the pool that overlooked their private pond.

The Forest Road property contained a large secluded home with a guesthouse. The thick copse of trees that masked the main house from the guesthouse, also gave the owners a false sense of security. Those same trees provided Collins several prime viewing locations into the rear of the home. Another mistake the owners made—no window treatments. Through his high-powered binoculars, Collins recorded their movements by viewing through the glass enclosure.

He watched the old man and woman pour their nightly drinks, sort through and swallow their pills, and retire for the night.

Collins checked his watch.

Right on schedule.

CHAPTER 32

JAKE FOLLOWED BARAKA through the front door. She moved toward the middle of the room while he and Kaplan hid behind the wall to their immediate right.

The bottom floor of the Hajjah Palace was a spacious, open room with ornate carvings along the woodwork and stone finishing. Its dirty walls revealed the outlines of picture frames and murals that once hung many years ago. The palace was long overdue for restoration like so many of Hajjah's other buildings.

Jake didn't care. These people lived in squalor. They allowed all their historic architecture to decay with time. The desert took its toll on more than just the people trying to carve out a living in the desolate region.

The men yelled at Baraka when she entered the room. Jake heard guns clattering and his pulse quickened. Baraka was talking fast in a language he didn't understand. He knew she was nervous by the pitch in her voice. Kaplan said she was a woman of conviction and he was confident in Kaplan's judgment.

After a few seconds of shouting the voices calmed yet remained tense. Baraka's speech got louder as she repeated the same words.

Jake extended his mini-mirror around the corner to observe what was happening. One man held a knife to her throat while the other man pointed a gun at her. The men were similar in height but one was thin and the other overweight. The thin man was older, he held the gun.

She kept talking. Her speech rapid fire. Jake's finger tightened on the trigger. The woman held out the bag and said something. The man grabbed the bag and dumped the contents on the table. Food.

The older man held up a finger and shouted. The overweight man lowered the knife. Baraka's speech slowed to normal. She gathered up the food and stuffed it back in the bag. The older man pointed toward a back room somewhere behind the stairwell. Both men put their weapons on the table and moved away. As they did, Baraka dropped the bag on the floor, reached under her burqa, and pulled out a gun.

"Shit." Jake dropped the mirror. "Go."

Jake and Kaplan ran toward the men. The older man moved for his gun and Kaplan fired a shot. The dart hit him in the neck and he fell to the floor. The overweight man knocked the gun from Baraka's hand, grabbed his knife from the table, and pushed the blade to her neck.

Jake moved to the left, Kaplan to the right.

"Shoot." Baraka shouted.

As Jake and Kaplan moved farther apart, the man focused on Kaplan.

"Shoot." She said again.

The man yelled something and Kaplan moved to the man's far left. As he turned, Jake took the shot. The dart hit the target. The man fell and so did Baraka. She grabbed her neck but blood was already oozing through her fingers.

"We have a problem." Kaplan said into his voice-activated microphone. "One of the men cut Baraka in the neck and she's bleeding."

"I okay," she said. "I okay."

"Whatever you do, do it fast." Wiley said into their headsets. "The guy upstairs is moving your way."

Jake leaned over and moved Baraka's hand from the wound. "She's right, Gregg. It'll be okay."

"How the hell do you know?" Kaplan said. "You're no doctor."

"No. But I do know what a neck wound looks like that isn't okay." Jake started dragging the old man against the wall. "Just hold pressure, it'll slow in a few minutes."

"I hold pressure." Baraka said. "Go get girl."

"Are you sure? Kaplan asked.

"I sure. I sure." She said. "Go get girl."

Jake moved the other unconscious man against the wall, removed the darts, and motioned to Kaplan and they started up the stairs.

The stairway went up fifteen steps then made a ninety-degree left turn at a landing. Because of the high ceiling downstairs, Jake made the assumption that the next flight would be equally as long.

Jake went up the left side of the stairwell while Kaplan went up the right side, two steps below Jake.

"He's coming down on your side, Jake." Wiley's voice. "Remember, no gunfire. Shots attract attention."

Jake motioned to Kaplan to move to the left side of the stairwell behind him. Jake moved higher in the stairwell, now two steps from the top of the first flight of steps.

"He's just around the corner." Wiley's voice. "Go for casualty, but no shots. I repeat no shots."

Jake eased his tranquilizer pistol into the holster and pulled out the Benchmade knife Wiley gave him on the airplane, a spring-assisted with a 3.25-inch blade. He silently opened the knife and locked the blade. Jake took another step. One step below the landing, back against the wall.

"Jake, stop right there." Wiley. "He's less than two feet away and about two feet higher. Wait for him. When he makes a move, you'll know what to do."

Wiley was right. The man in the stairwell was impatient and Jake was ready.

He saw the barrel of the man's weapon, a pistol, break the plane of the wall. Jake knew he had to move fast. Keeping his head and body behind the wall, Jake calculated where the man's hand was, reached around the corner of the wall with his right hand, and sliced in a downward thrust where the man's arm should be.

Jake felt the blade strike the man's wrist, slicing through sinews and tendons. He felt warm blood spill onto his arm and hand. The man's gun clambered onto the floor. Jake heard the man scream followed by footsteps running up the stairs.

Jake chased him up the stairs. The hallway was long and straight. The man grabbed a chair and held it out as if mimicking a lion tamer. The chair seemed small in front of the large man. Jake estimated the man weighed two-eighty and stood six feet tall. But he was injured. The man's right arm was useless.

Jake pulled out his tranquilizer pistol and fired. The man anticipated the shot and blocked it with the chair, the dart lodged under the seat. He yelled and threw the chair at Jake. Then he turned and ran.

A mistake.

Jake was close enough when the man started running to catch him in a short distance. Jake was a sprinter and the man was slow. Jake tackled him from behind and landed on top of the facedown man. Although he'd never used the move before, he learned it at The Farm when Bentley sent him for skill craft training.

Jake grabbed the man's head from behind, right hand under his chin, left hand on the back of his skull. He pulled back on the man's head. The man thrashed about grabbing at thin air and attempting to buck Jake loose.

Jake pulled back harder, craned the man's neck backward, placed his knee at the base of the man's neck, and then he yanked hard to the right. He felt a small crack but the man kept moving.

Jake turned harder.

A louder pop and the man's legs stopped moving.

Jake gave another twist.

The man's neck cracked loud and his body fell limp. A last gurgling exhale left the man's body.

When Jake turned around, Kaplan was gone.

† † †

Gregg Kaplan followed Jake up the steps in the Hajjah Palace. Blood spattered on the walls and steps from where Jake slashed the last remaining terrorist's wrist, causing the man to drop his weapon and flee. The large man screamed, turned, and fled up the stairs and down the long hallway.

Kaplan wasn't accustomed to someone else taking the lead in an operation, especially someone with as little experience as Jake. But Wiley didn't give him a choice. He'd never understood why Director of Central Intelligence Scott Bentley had handed Jake off so fast to Wiley. Kaplan had Special Forces training and had served in combat. Jake was a rookie and his impulsiveness made him a loose cannon. Danger and killing were new to him. He was still dealing with the loss of his fiancée. It didn't make sense to hand Jake off to a stranger just to get him away from Washington and the pressure Bentley was receiving from Senator Richard Boden. But politics was Bentley's problem and whether he agreed with it or not, it was the DCI's decision.

Kaplan noticed Jake seemed to know exactly what to do when he was faced with the terrorist at the corner of the stairwell. He was quiet and effective. Jake slashed the knife exactly where it was needed. When Wiley said "*casualty*" and "*no shots*," Jake, without hesitation, holstered his weapon and wielded his knife. Maybe Bentley did know what he was doing, and there was more to Wiley than just making spy toys.

Kaplan saw Jake sprint down the darkened hallway. Low wattage lights hung from the ceiling—bare bulbs in wire cages. Kaplan watched Jake jump the man from behind and twist the man's neck while the man tried to buck Jake off. He followed Jake until a voice in his ear told him to stop.

"Gregg, stop." Wiley's voice. "Turn around. Go back down the main hall past the stairs and take the first left."

"Got it." Kaplan replied. "What about Jake?"

"He can handle himself." Wiley said. "He knows what to do."

"Apparently."

Kaplan retraced his steps, ran past the stairwell and turned down the first corridor to the left.

"End of the hall." Wiley's voice. "Second door on the right."

Kaplan ran the thirty feet to the door and tried the knob.

Locked.

The light was dim so Kaplan fished out his MagLite mini and shone the beam at the locking mechanism.

A warded lock, which meant he needed a skeleton key.

Kaplan heard a groan on the other side of the door. Isabella.

More groaning.

"Isabella."

Kaplan stepped back and kicked hard into the massive door. It didn't budge. Although the exterior of the palace was in disrepair, the interior structure was built to withstand time. The huge planks of wood that framed the doorway were more than a match for any man. He needed the key.

Kaplan turned to go search for the key, Jake was standing next to him.

Jake held out his hand. "Looking for this?"

Kaplan saw the skeleton key dangling from a leather strap.

† † †

Something aroused Isabella Hunt from her drug-induced stupor but she was too groggy to tell what it was. Or, if in fact it was just another dream. She thought she heard screaming. A man screaming. Not a yell, but a scream. The sound of fear—or injury. And then a loud banging from somewhere in the building.

Maybe it was just a dream. She'd had plenty of them while she'd been held captive in this God forsaken place, wherever it was. She thought she'd heard Gregg Kaplan yelling for her, coming to save her. But that, too, had been in her dreams. Gregg would kill all the guards, burst through the door, take her in his arms, and sweep her off to freedom. Just like in a Harlequin romance novel where the hero rescues the damsel in distress. But this time the voice was different than in her dreams. It was louder and more distinct.

Hunt jumped at the sound of the key in the lock. A sound she'd become accustomed to hearing, but not at this hour of the morning. The familiar clank as the solid shafted bit key released the locking mechanism. The squeak of the hinges as the massive wooden door opened wider.

In the darkness she could discern only two beams of light entering the doorway. Frozen with fear and groggy from the drugs, she tried to move. She didn't have strength to resist.

She heard his voice again. "Isabella."

She felt herself being lifted off the cot. "Isabella. I've got you now. You're safe."

This was no dream, this was real.

It *was* Gregg Kaplan.

CHAPTER 33

KAPLAN SEARCHED THE dungeon-like room with his Maglite until the beam of light found the cot. Isabella Hunt was curled in the fetal position. A pit grew in his stomach as he rushed to her.

"Isabella. I'm here." He said. "You're safe."

He brushed her matted, blood-dried hair away from her face. "Isabella? Can you hear me? It's Gregg."

"Gregg, she's been drugged." Jake said. "We need to get her back to the gliders. It'll be light in less than an hour and we need to be as far away from here as we can."

Kaplan scooped her up in his arms, resting her head against his shoulder. "It'll be okay now."

"Gregg?" she whispered. "Is it really you? You came for me?"

"It's really me, here to take you home."

"I'll arrange the scene," Jake said. "Make it look like she overpowered the guard and escaped through a window."

Isabella groaned as Kaplan lifted her into his arms. "How are you going to do that?" he asked.

"I have an idea. Just go. Get Isabella to the glider. I'll be a couple of minutes behind you." Jake ran down the corridor and out of sight.

Kaplan carried Hunt down the same bloody steps. Baraka was waiting for him at the landing, still holding pressure to her wound.

"Is woman okay?" Baraka asked.

"She's been beaten and sedated." Kaplan said. "But she'll live. How's your neck?"

"Bleeding almost stop." She said. "Must take woman to small airplane. Baraka is fine. Have friends in Hajjah, can hide there."

Kaplan carried Hunt out of the Palace and down the winding walkway. At the bottom of the second switchback, Kaplan turned left toward the gliders.

Baraka stopped. "I go now. Good luck, Mr. Kaplan."

Kaplan stopped. "Thank you, Baraka, for everything. We couldn't have done it without your help. You have avenged your family."

The woman hurried out of sight.

With Isabella in his arms, Kaplan ran all the way to the gliders. He found Wiley waiting, the equipment already stowed in the aircraft for their trip to the Red Sea.

"Because of weight distribution she must ride with you." Wiley said. "Where's Jake?"

"Jake said he was fixing the scene to look like an escape. How? I don't know."

"He'd better hurry or his ass gets left behind." Wiley said. "Besides, he's wasting time."

"Gregg." A tear rolled down Hunt's cheek.

Wiley looked at Kaplan. "Be careful."

"I'll be fine." Kaplan slipped Hunt into her seat and strapped on her harness. "We'll be fine."

† † †

Jake found a metal tray full of untouched food near the entrance to Hunt's prison cell. He grabbed the tray and flung food on the floor of her room. He ran back to where the dead man lay and smashed the tray against the side of the man's head—hard enough to break open the dead man's flesh. Then he ran back to the prison room and tossed the tray on the floor. He needed to make it look like Hunt escaped rather than being rescued.

Metal utensils were on a nearly table so Jake grabbed a knife, smeared it in the man's blood, and dropped it by the puddle of blood. Next he picked up the dead guard and tossed his body down the stairwell. Now he needed to fake an escape by Isabella.

He moved through each corridor, opening and closing doors until he found what he was looking for. Curled on the floor in a utility closet was a rope. He couldn't have planned it any better.

He forced open a window, tied off one end of the rope to a column inside the room, and tossed the rope out the window. He turned to leave then realized he should ensure authenticity.

He grabbed the rope and climbed out the window and lowered himself toward the ground. He met the end of the rope ten feet above the ground. No way down but drop. He let go of the rope and fell.

The hard ground sent shockwaves through his legs. His knees buckled as he hit the ground. *Get up.* The pain radiated along his spine until his head throbbed. *Get up. Shake it off.*

His headset crackled, then Wiley's voice. "Jake, get down here or get left behind."

He pushed himself up using the wall for balance. He bent over, hands on knees, took three deep breaths, and ran. "On my way."

When Jake reached the gliders, Kaplan had just finished strapping Hunt into her seat. "How is she?"

"She'll be fine." Kaplan said. "Now can we get out of here?"

Wiley got in the glider and activated his customized avionics and instrumentation. "Jake, get in and let's go."

"Gregg, after you clear the edge." Wiley said. "Climb out at sixty knots on a heading of 2-6-0. We'll be right behind you."

"Roger that." Kaplan's voice in Jake's headset.

Jake activated his night vision goggles just in time to see Kaplan's glider cross over the edge of the cliff and out of sight below. Two seconds later the glider reappeared in a climbing right hand turn.

Jake felt Wiley accelerate their glider toward the edge of the cliff, his specialized electric motors totally silent. The glider crossed the edge of the cliff, a split second of weightlessness, and then the downward G-force pull of the climb. Wiley banked the glider to the right until rolling out on the same heading he gave Kaplan.

Jake took a deep breath. "We might just make it after all."

"We're not out of the woods, yet." Wiley said. "That was the easy part. The hard part is still to come."

CHAPTER 34

Mosque de Trappes
Trappes, France
3:00 a.m.

HASHIM KHAN WOKE up early from a restless night. Something he'd heard the day before troubled him. Something the imam had casually mentioned when he was reading a Paris newspaper.

He left the solace of his private room and returned to the room where the imam had been reading. He looked at the table where the imam read the paper. But now the table was bare. He checked around the room and finally found what he was looking for in the trash receptacle.

Khan spread the tabloid across the table, leafing through it page-by-page, searching for something, the details of which he couldn't remember. Then he discovered what had troubled him, a small sidebar article. The planned closure of one of his targets, the closure planned on the day of the attack. It was too late to change targets—he needed another option. Only one came to mind.

The five men he'd picked for this mission were young, naïve, and scared. He'd given them seven days to prepare. Seven days to make their peace. Seven days to live. They'd accepted their mission with pride. They accepted their fate.

But in seven days the target would be inaccessible. He needed to move up the date of the attacks. The young men were ready. They would do their job. He would tell them later that the time frame had changed.

Today they could cleanse.

Today they could shave.

Tomorrow they would die.

†††

The gliders flew in tandem, Kaplan and Hunt in the lead, Wiley and Jake in the rear. The useful life of Wiley's custom-made batteries was forty-five minutes. In order to gain maximum altitude with the time available, Wiley said best rate of climb was required until the low battery warning light came on. The eastern sky was waking up behind them, slowly illuminating the flight ahead. Soon the sun would show the way. The NVGs had already been turned off and stowed away. Twilight was giving way to daylight.

Something had bothered Jake about Wiley's reluctance to use deadly force on all of the men at Hajjah Palace. It made no sense to leave witnesses—witnesses that had seen them—had seen Baraka.

"Mr. Wiley, what about the men at the palace? They know we were there. Rescued Isabella. They'll go after Baraka. They'll kill her."

"Relax, Jake. I've got it covered."

"If you don't mind me asking, how?"

"Ever heard of a smart bomb?"

"Sure, but—no way." Jake said.

"In exactly ten minutes, a smart bomb will strike the Hajjah Palace. Any evidence of our presence will evaporate and no one will be the wiser."

"Dammit. Don't you think you should've shared that information?"

"You didn't need to know."

"So, all that work I just did, arranging the rooms, jumping out the window—"

"All for naught, Jake."

"Great." Jake could sense the old man was grinning at his expense.

Jake looked down at the barren terrain. The mountains were almost behind them. In the far distance he could barely trace the outline of the Red Sea shoreline. They'd traveled twenty-five miles in total silence and climbed to an altitude of 12,000 feet when the *LOW BATTERY* light turned on. Time to retract the propeller and glide. He hoped their altitude was high enough.

"My battery light just came on." Kaplan broke the silence. "Time to retract."

"Ours too." Jake watched Wiley shut down the electric motor and retract the propeller. The engine slowly lowered itself back down into the tail of the glider.

Jake watched as Kaplan lowered his damaged motor. It moved down and stopped. Up a little, then back down and stopped. Jake knew Kaplan was working the mechanism as far down into the fuselage as possible to reduce drag. Jake checked his GPS unit, Kaplan would need his glider as drag-free as possible because they still had fifty miles to travel.

"What did you mean when you said the hard part was yet to come?" Jake asked. "Aren't we going to make it to the rendezvous point?"

"Unless we get spotted and shot down," Wiley said. "We'll make it to the drop. It's just I've never ditched a glider before and we very well might have to put down in the Red Sea."

† † †

Kaplan worked the electric motor as deep into the well as he could before the battery was fully drained. The noise stirred Hunt from her drugged state with a jerk.

"Isabella? Are you awake?"

"Gregg? It wasn't a dream? You did come after me."

"Yes I did." Kaplan said. "But I had help. Jake is with me—and the old man he's working for now."

Kaplan explained about the mission in Australia and the trouble Jake caused by shooting Mustaff Bin Yasir. Senator Richard Boden was breathing down Bentley's neck so the director sent Kaplan to Yemen and physically delivered Jake to El Paso, leaving him with the old man.

"What does the old man do?" She asked.

"I'm not real sure, something with radio frequencies and microwave signals. He's got a gadget for everything it seems." Kaplan turned his head around and smiled at Hunt. "If it weren't for him, we'd never have been able to rescue you. He planned this whole mission."

"I was afraid I'd never see you again." Hunt said. "I don't know how long I was in that place. I started losing track of time. I stopped eating and drinking. I figured they were drugging me. Then a man would ask me questions and hit me."

Kaplan heard Hunt sobbing. "You're safe now, Isabella."

"I never saw him." She sniffled. "All I know is his breath was like...like...road kill. The stench was nauseating."

"There were five men in that building, Jake killed the one guarding your room." Kaplan noticed the outline of the Red Sea becoming more distinct as the first beams of sunlight illuminated the glider's cockpit. "Jake made it look like you overpowered him and escaped while the others were asleep. They're as good as dead when their handler finds out you're gone."

"Are we talking about the same Jake I know?" Hunt asked. "That doesn't sound like him at all."

"No kidding." Kaplan smiled to himself. "I didn't think I could ever work with Jake again, but in just two days, Wiley has changed him. Wiley has some sort of control on him. Helped him move past his anger. And the funny thing is, I don't think Jake has realized it yet."

"What do you mean?"

"He's more in control. He takes the lead without being told and instinctively knows what to do. And it hasn't even been a week since he blew Yasir's head off."

Kaplan deliberately omitted the details of Jake's loss of control when he accused Jake of being just like Laurence O'Rourke. Details that Isabella Hunt didn't need to know. Details no one needed to know. That incident was between Kaplan and Jake. One day Kaplan would make Jake apologize or he would make Jake pay—no one points a gun at him without consequences.

"Gregg." Wiley's voice. "I need you to pull up and to the right. Let me take the lead then you can fall in behind me."

"Roger that." Kaplan eased back on the stick and turned slightly to the right. The glider's speed slowed as it gained altitude. To his left he watched Wiley ease the glider underneath his wing and out in the lead. *The old man was good.*

Kaplan lowered the nose and maneuvered his glider behind Wiley and Jake, keeping no more than about a fifty-foot distance.

A sudden flash from behind caught his attention. "What the hell was that?"

Wiley's voice came over the headset. "Smart bomb just leveled the palace. The main reason I was in a hurry to get us out of there."

"What about Baraka? The rest of the village?"

"Relax, Mr. Kaplan. Best thing about a smart bomb is that it only takes out the intended target. The worst thing that happened to the rest of the village was being abruptly awakened from their slumber. Any trace of our extraction has evaporated. And in al Qaeda's eyes, so has Ms Hunt."

Kaplan had to admit it, the old man had thought of everything.

"By the way, how's she doing?" Wiley asked.

Kaplan turned around and noticed Hunt's eyes blinking. "She's fading in and out, but she'll be fine when the effects wear off. She needs medical attention, though."

"Gregg?" Hunt's voice weak and slurred. "I was afraid I'd never see you again."

"It's okay. We're together now, that's all that matters."

"No, Gregg. Listen. Khan's…planning an attack…in France."

Her speech was slurring again. She'd gone through waves of coherence and incoherence ever since they left Hajjah. "Isabella, you can tell me later. Save your strength." Kaplan said.

"You…don't…understand. You have…to stop…"

"Shh. It's going to be okay. You can tell me later. There's nothing we can do about it right now anyway."

"There's something else I want to tell you, need to tell you. She paused several seconds. "I…I—."

"I know, Isabella." Kaplan whispered. "Me too."

CHAPTER 35

JAKE WAS TROUBLED by the last thing Wiley said. "What do you mean, 'ditch?' I thought you had this all worked out."

"I do." Wiley paused. "More or less."

"More or less? Care to explain?"

"Like any mission, there's always a level of uncertainty." Wiley gave the glider a gentle course correction to the left. "You've heard the old adage 'if all goes according to plan.' In case you didn't notice, very little has gone according to plan. We spent way too much time repairing Mr. Kaplan's glider."

Wiley held up his wrist and pointed to his watch. "It's already 6:30 local time. The sun's been up for thirty minutes. This rendezvous was supposed to happen under the cover of darkness. By now, our connection has had to move back offshore for fear of being spotted. The last thing we can afford is an international incident. This is a country we're not supposed to be in and this mission is not sanctioned. It doesn't exist. We might end up ditching in the Red Sea."

"What about Isabella?" Jake asked. "She's still weak and not up to something like that."

"Not a lot of options, Jake." Wiley said. "We knew the risks when we agreed to this mission. We're all expendable."

"If you don't mind me asking, what is the plan?"

Wiley continued. "Our original rendezvous was on a little sandy island just off the coast called Al Bodhi. We had seventy-six miles to travel from Hajjah. No problem, plenty of altitude."

"And now?" Jake asked.

"Al Bodhi offers no protection. It's a flat sandy island with a lagoon in the middle." Wiley explained. "Under the cover of darkness, we could have landed, unloaded into a skiff and met up with another larger boat farther out in the Red Sea."

Wiley banked to the left. Jake noticed the coastline of the Red Sea stretch in both directions beneath them.

"Al Bodhi's off to the right." Wiley said. "Now we have to go about thirty miles farther to the Al Zubayr Islands. The archipelago is full of scuba diving sites. Our rendezvous will be on the backside of a volcano across from Saddle Island. Our transport is disguised as a live-aboard dive boat equipped with a medical bay and two medics."

"I see it on the GPS." Jake said. "Can we make it?"

"I'm confident we can." Wiley said. "But if you haven't noticed, Mr. Kaplan has been losing altitude at a greater rate than us. He will have trouble making it to the landing site. And even if he does make it…"

"What?" Jake said. "Even if he makes it, what?"

"The Zubayr archipelago is not soft and sandy like Al Bodhi. It's hard and rocky and unforgiving. If he makes a landing like he did in Hajjah, they'll both be injured. Or worse."

"What about that thing we did going into Hajjah?" Jake said. "You know, uh…ridge soaring. That's it. Where we climbed a few hundred feet."

"Problem is, Jake, we're over water. No updrafts over water, especially this early in the morning. We took advantage of the winds in the mountains to gain extra altitude. Now we have no mountains and no land." Wiley paused. "As far as ridge soaring, Mr. Kaplan will have to make it to the northernmost island in order to get the first and possibly only chance at ridge lift and even then—"

"Even then." Jake interrupted. "It might not be enough."

"Exactly."

Jake didn't say anything for the next thirty minutes. Wiley explained the situation to Kaplan and he said he understood what had to be done, including the consequences of failure. Jake knew Kaplan would be extra cautious with Isabella on board. Even though Jake didn't like it, he knew Kaplan had strong feelings for her. But there was something else eating away at him. He couldn't quite put his finger on what it was, though.

There was tension between Kaplan and himself. They had been close friends, even confidantes when they first met in Savannah, Georgia earlier in the year. Kaplan had been involved, from an air traffic controller's standpoint, in an aircraft accident investigation. Early in the investigation Jake suspected it wasn't an accident but the result of sabotage. As Jake unraveled the truth, he exposed his own boss as a conspirator. But worse than that, Jake uncovered Kaplan's long-time girlfriend as an accomplice. Maybe Kaplan held that against him.

The same event that took the life of Jake's fiancée also took the life of Kaplan's girlfriend. But her death was fast. She died on the spot, in front of Kaplan. Jake's fiancée, on the other hand, lingered in a coma for days, began to recover and then without warning died. It's possible, even probable, that Kaplan blamed Jake for her death too.

At some point, Jake knew, he'd have to make amends. He wanted to have that opportunity.

At some point, but not right now.

CHAPTER 36

KAPLAN SAW THE Zubayr archipelago island chain stretch out in front of him from north to south spanning fifteen miles from end to end. He counted fourteen islands. The northernmost island a tiny dot even from his low altitude of three hundred fifty feet. The glider in front of him a half a mile and at least another hundred fifty feet higher had just passed the first island.

The second island in the chain was much larger, maybe three quarters of a mile by half a mile, with a large peak in the middle. The ripples in the waters of the Red Sea indicated a strong wind from the south. He knew this was his best chance, maybe his only chance, to gain back some precious altitude—at least enough to carry him further down the archipelago. The question in his mind, how much altitude could he gain before he lost the lift from the peak? A question soon answered when he saw Wiley make a climbing left turn gaining several hundred feet before turning south toward the rendezvous point.

The jolt from the updraft caught Kaplan off guard. He rolled into a gentle turn and spiraled upward, making sure he kept the glider inside the updraft. Kaplan's altimeter climbed ever higher. Now he was faced with a choice, follow the chain of islands, hopping from one to another adding extra miles to his route but remaining close enough in case he needed to find another ridge to steal altitude from. Or, make the straight line shot to the rendezvous point like Wiley did but it left him vulnerable over the open water.

Wiley told him his prototype gliders were rated at slightly better than a 60:1 ratio. He ran the rough calculations in his head. *Piece of cake.*

Kaplan lost the updraft at exactly a thousand feet, turned to the south and followed Wiley's glider on a direct line toward the rendezvous point. Halfway across the span of open water he realized he'd made a mistake in his calculations as his altimeter passed through six hundred feet. Coupled with a headwind slowing his progress across the water and the extra drag from the jammed retractable engine, he wasn't getting the 60:1 glide ratio Wiley bragged about.

Not even close.

† † †

Jake studied the island in front of him as Wiley finessed the glider closer to the landing spot. The island had a large volcano crater on the eastern side, blown out to the southeast from a previous eruption. A column of steam rose from within its center. Wiley's landing spot was west of a smaller crater on a plateau next to the western shoreline. Jake noticed all the islands in the Zubayr archipelago were littered with craters, all of them black and barren, but this large crater was the only one that appeared active.

As they approached the landing site Jake could see the blackened earth covered with thick vegetation.

And rocks.

Lots of rocks.

A large boat was anchored just west of where Wiley was preparing to land. A large red and white dive flag was mounted on top. Two skiffs were beached on the western shore and two figures stood by each.

"Is that our welcoming party?" Jake asked.

"Yep. Two crew, two medics." Wiley said. "Turn around and see how Kaplan's doing, will you?"

"He's back there a good ways, maybe a mile." Jake said. "He looks a little low."

† † †

Kaplan watched the glider in front of him kick up a cloud of black dust as it touched down. Four figures scurried toward the glider as Wiley and Jake popped the canopy and crawled out. Two men pulled the glider toward the skiffs, a distance Kaplan estimated at fifty, maybe sixty feet.

"Isabella, are you buckled in?" Kaplan asked.

"Aren't we a little low, Gregg?" Hunt asked. "I don't know much about flying but we look like we're too close to the water."

"We are low. It's going to be close." Kaplan said. "Hold on tight."

Once again Kaplan was staring ahead at a glide path that was too shallow—too low. He noticed the shoreline as they approached the landing site. The black sand ended abruptly several feet from the water's edge then leveled out. Covered with vegetation and small rocks, the landing site was far from ideal. That is, if he could even make the landing site.

He kept the glider lined up on the same line Wiley used. The black sandy beach rapidly approaching. The water even faster. Wiley had incorporated a three setting flap system, each signified by a catch when the flap handle was pulled. Kaplan pulled on the first notch of flaps.

Better.

The glider slowed and the glide path angle improved. Kaplan pulled on the second notch of flaps.

Much better. *We might just make it.*

Kaplan relaxed a little. He hadn't realized until that moment just how tight his grip was on the controls. He wiped his sweaty palms on his pants.

He pulled out the last notch of flaps. His glide angle improved again. Momentarily. Drag caught up and his airspeed slowed. Kaplan lowered the nose to compensate and kept his airspeed just above a stall, that moment when airflow over the wings was insufficient to maintain lift, and the aircraft stops flying.

That moment came as Kaplan's glider was twenty feet from the black sandy beach. The glider skipped on the shallow water and onto the beach where it dug in nose first. Water and black sand sprayed across the canopy. The four-foot lip from the beach to the plateau that Kaplan was aiming to clear was approaching faster.

"Hold on." Kaplan yelled.

The glider dug into the black sand deeper as the glider slowed. The nose of the glider caught the lip with too much forward speed.

Kaplan heard Isabella Hunt grunt as the glider came to an abrupt stop. He felt the pain of the harness straps digging into his chest, shoulders, and waist. Then came a feeling he didn't recognize. The glider was still moving, rotating forward. And upward.

"Whoa." Hunt screamed. "We're going over."

The glider stood on its nose. Kaplan stared at the ground, harness pulling against the weight of his body. What seemed like an eternity to Kaplan, was only two seconds. Then the glider fell backward onto the beach.

"Remind me never to fly with you again." Hunt said.

"Any landing you walk away from is a good landing."

✝✝✝

Jake was the first person to reach Kaplan's glider. By the time he opened the canopy, both crew and medics had arrived.

"Another nice landing, I see." Jake said. "Will you give me lessons?"

"Very funny, smartass." Kaplan reached his arm out to Jake. "Give me a hand, will ya?"

Jake pulled Kaplan out of the glider while both medics attended to Isabella Hunt.

"We need to get her to the boat." One of the medics said.

The two crewmembers gently removed Hunt from the glider and carried her to the nearest skiff. One of the medics walked up to Kaplan. "Are you injured?"

"Only my pride." Kaplan said. "Go. Take care of Isabella, please."

Jake helped Kaplan unload Wiley's equipment from the glider. One of the two crewmembers returned to the glider after the skiff left with the medics to take Hunt to the larger boat anchored three hundred feet from shore.

After everything was removed from the gliders, Jake, Wiley, and Kaplan loaded the remaining skiff and were taken to the larger boat. *The Toymaker* was a one hundred twenty-five foot yacht that resembled a live aboard dive boat in every way. The dive deck was equipped with a full complement of tanks, wetsuits, masks, and fins.

"The Toymaker?" Jake laughed when he read the name painted on the transom. "Seriously?"

"What?" Wiley grinned. "I've been a certified scuba diver since I was thirteen. This is a very versatile vessel with many uses above and beyond just a dive boat. Inside you'll find all the comforts of home along with some 'specialized' equipment. I designed the hull myself. In the right conditions, she'll do forty-five knots."

"Why am I not surprised?" Jake noticed the men onshore tying the two gliders together with ropes, one behind the other. "What's to become of your sailplanes?" He pointed toward shore.

"I can't allow them to be retrieved." Wiley explained. "They are unique and the technology is classified. We'll be boarded in Djibouti and I can't run the risk of them being discovered and us being tied back to the explosion in Yemen. There is a trench in the sea floor about five hundred yards south of here. We'll tow them to the trench and scuttle them to the bottom."

"A trench?" Jake asked. "How deep?"

"I'll drop them at about 600 meters." Wiley said. "About two thousand feet."

"Two thousand feet." Jake said. "The Red Sea is that deep?"

"You *did* see the volcanoes?" Wiley said. "There are spots that are over ten thousand feet deep. Now, let's go check on Ms Hunt and find out what she knows."

Jake and Kaplan followed Wiley down below deck to the medical bay. The medics had Isabella Hunt already hooked to an IV. Her face was pale and Jake could see she'd lost a lot of weight.

"How is she?" Kaplan asked

"She lost consciousness as soon as the IV started working." One of the medics said. "She's dehydrated and they'd been drugging her for days. I drew a blood sample to see what's in her system. She'll need to sleep for now."

"As soon as she's conscious, I want to speak to her." A familiar voice said from behind them.

Jake turned around.

CIA Director Scott Bentley.

CHAPTER 37

COLLINS LEARNED PATIENCE from the beginning of his life as an assassin. As a hit man for the Irish Republican Army, his first assignment required him to remain stationary for over twelve hours before his prey and the right opportunity to kill came his way.

It was cold in Ireland the night of that assignment. Wet snow bit at him for hours, chilling him to the point of shivers. Yet he waited. Waited and watched until his target drove up after a long night of 'pub hopping.' The explosives Collins had planted in the man's detached garage were enough to bring down an office building, overkill for the small garage. But he accomplished the kill. Along with the garage, the man's entire home was demolished by the explosive device.

Technology had come a long way since those days. And so had his expertise. He'd learned the tricks of the trade, far superior to others in his line of work. He learned tragic accidents *do* happen and he used that to his advantage. The more a target appeared to be a victim of random misfortune, the less attention it garnered from the authorities.

Collins calculated the response times from the local fire and police departments. He knew exactly how long he had to incinerate the home, return to his vehicle, and flee the scene before local authorities arrived.

Now was the time.

Collins removed the wireless device from his backpack and toggled the switch. If all went according to design, there would be no initial explosion, just a massive flame fueled by the owners' gas line. The explosion would come later, after the fire was fully involved, the home ablaze, and he was far from the scene. He knew the heat from the pyre would destroy any evidence of arson.

He picked up his binoculars and studied the rear of the home, the kitchen below the master bedroom fully visible from his vantage point. A flicker of light grew larger. Flames shot upward from behind the stove engulfing the cabinets above. He smiled. The device had worked as planned.

He listened for any sounds emanating from the residence other than the sounds of the fire itself. None. He'd disabled every smoke alarm he could find. If he'd missed one, he would have known by now.

The downstairs filled with heavy black smoke, flames barely visible as they spread across the ceiling. The rustic beams made perfect kindling, ignited quickly and burned hot for long periods of time. The all glass prow-shaped rear wall blew outward, glass crashed onto the back patio. Flames curled around the roofline, crawling laterally from room to room, feeding itself on the old home.

Time to go.

He stuffed his binoculars and the wireless device into his backpack, slung it across his shoulder and ran toward his car.

When he reached the edge of the woods he could hear the blazing roar of the fire behind him. The streets were empty. He ran to his car. In the distance he heard the faint sound of sirens.

He tossed his backpack on the seat, started his car, and drove to the edge of the parking lot. To his left he saw flashing lights rounding the curve a half a mile north of him on Shenandoah. He turned right just as a ball of fire ballooned over the tree line in front of him. The sound wave that followed rocked his vehicle. He turned right, west, on Lower Fayetteville Road and saw flashing lights ahead so he made another quick right on Stonebridge Boulevard and entered a residential subdivision.

An approaching fire truck had unexpectedly cut off his planned escape route on Shenandoah. His alternate route cut off by a police car. Meticulous planning is the key to success. Plotting several different escape routes had always been a requirement for Collins. *Plan for the unexpected* had been his axiom. It had kept him alive all of these years. And out of the hands of authorities.

Collins weaved through the Stonebridge subdivision until he reached Newnan Crossing Boulevard. He turned north. By the time he reached the traffic signal at Col. Joe M. Jackson Medal of Honor Highway, the night air was filled with sirens from all types of emergency vehicles responding to the blaze.

In his rear view mirror Collins could see the orange glow from the fire. He turned left when the light changed to green then made an immediate right onto Interstate 85 and drove toward Atlanta.

Collins hummed a John Prine song he heard on the radio, "Sweet revenge, sweet revenge, without fail."

CHAPTER 38

8:00 a.m.
Herent, Belgium

KYLI PLACED HER hand on her friend's shoulder. "Kates. Kates, wake up. We need to get moving."

"Come on, Kyli." Kates whined. "It's early and I have jet lag."

"If you want to see Paris today, you need to get your ass in gear." Kyli said.

"This is Europe, for crying out loud, how far can it be?"

"The drive is three hundred fifty kilometers." Kyli ripped the sheets off Kates.

Kates was one of Kyli's best friends from high school. She slept in gym shorts and a t-shirt. Her long brown hair tangled and matted. All Kyli could see were Kates' long legs that seemed to stretch for eternity, a physical trait Kyli envied.

Kates opened her blue eyes as she grabbed for the covers. "Kyli. I don't know what a kilometer is. Well, I know what it *is*, but I don't know how far it is."

"Fine." Kyli ripped the covers off the bed again. "It's like a hundred and eighty miles."

"Three hours then." Kates grabbed for the covers again. "And the way you drive, probably less."

"Nope." Kyli struggled with Kates over the covers. "Like you said, this is Europe. The drive is more like five hours. So let's get moving. You can sleep in the car."

Kates sat up in the bed. "Your grandfather's Mercedes is a car." She said. "A Mini Cooper is *not* a car, it's a shoebox with wheels."

"Maybe so. But it's fun to drive." Kyli opened the curtains. The sun highlighted the purple walls. " So, what do you want to see first?"

"You know what's on my list." Kates grabbed a towel from the closet. "I want to see the Eiffel Tower, Champs Elysees, and the Louvre. Those are a must."

"We'll walk Champs Elysees tonight." Kyli said. "It's pretty at night with all the lights. The Louvre takes a lot longer than the Eiffel Tower so we can do the tower in the morning, it's on the other side of the river, then we'll head over to the Louvre and stay as long as you'd like."

"Tell me about that guy your grandfather brought over with him." Kates' flipped the towel onto her shoulder. "Is he cute?"

"Jake?"

Kates nodded. "Is there somebody else?"

"No. Just the one. He's cute and single." Kyli said. "He has thick, wavy, dirty blond hair, and a good body. Sparkling blue eyes. He's so serious. I had fun messing with him when he was here. He got blitzed when I took him to Oktoberfest so the next morning I told him he was a good kisser."

"You kissed him?"

"No." Kyli said. "Just told him that to mess with his head a little. I set him up. When he passed out on the bed, I stripped his clothes off, put my bra on the floor, left my nylons wadded on the couch, and looked unkempt like we'd slept together. When he woke up, he nearly freaked out. He couldn't remember a thing. I almost felt sorry for him…but not enough to tell him it was a joke."

"How old is this guy?" Kates asked.

"He's older, maybe the age gap is too much."

"How much older?" Kates asked.

"I don't remember exactly." Kyli said. "I think Grandpa said he was thirty-three or thirty-four. Something like that."

"Kyli. You're twenty-eight. That's only six years." Kates threw her dirty clothes at Kyli. "I'd say he's a prime target. Hell, you've dated guys older than that."

"Yeah, I know, but I didn't really *like* them. Besides, I don't think he's *mentally* available."

"What? Is he psycho?" Kates asked.

"No, not at all." Kyli said. "Actually he's very intelligent. I should have said I don't think he's *emotionally* available. His fiancée was killed in March and I don't know that he's ready to move on yet."

"Kyli, you're smart and like to have a good time. Maybe he needs some of that right now." Kates said. "Where is he now?"

"He's off with Grandpa on another one of those 'top-secret' missions." Kyli made quotes with her fingers. "Somewhere in the Middle East. Grandpa's probably already gotten him killed. That'd be my luck. But if he comes back—."

"Watch out, Jake." Kates laughed. "Here comes Kyli."

†††

Hashim Khan planned a busy day for the five men in the basement. He awakened them an hour before dawn. "Today will be a glorious day." He said to them in their native tongue.

"Please accompany me to the men's prayer room for morning prayer." Khan said.

Khan and the five men spread their prayer mats in the Mihrab, a semi-circular niche in the mosque facing the direction of the Ka'ba in Mecca. Prayer was required five times a day. Their lives were centered on prayer. So important, prayer was designated the second Pillar. Islam has five obligatory acts or Pillars. The Qur'an presents these pillars as a framework for worship and a sign of commitment to the faith. *Shahada,* the reciting of the Islamic creed in Arabic. *Salat,* Islamic prayer. *Sawm,* fasting during Ramadan. *Zakat,* almsgiving. And *Hajj,* the pilgrimage to Mecca.

The first prayer must take place before dawn.

After prayer was complete and the mats placed in the designated area of the mosque, Khan called them together to explain the turn of events, the change in plans that moved their attacks to the next day.

Khan noticed four of the men eagerly awaited the mission. Their destiny in Paradise. The youngest, however didn't react with the same enthusiasm as the others. He was somber and withdrawn. This one, Khan decided, he would watch.

After the meeting, the five men were sent to cleanse and purify their souls. Hair would be cut. Faces would be shaven. A necessary step before the glory of tomorrow. The remainder of the day they would spend in prayer in preparation for Paradise.

Khan left the men in the imam's care while he drove into Paris. One last look at his targets. One last glimpse at the historic landmarks before their destruction. The evil West would get what it deserved—death and destruction—and it would be swift and without warning. Many would die, perhaps thousands. Many more would be injured. When the dust settled, the Infidel would again know the power of Allah.

They would know fear.

CHAPTER 39

Tadjoura Trough, Gulf of Aden
100 Miles East of Djibouti
4:30 P.M.

JAKE WAS THE first to notice when Isabella Hunt regained consciousness. Her eyes distant, pupils dilated, and brow creased with a troubled look on her face. He nudged Bentley with his elbow, "Sir. Isabella's coming to."

Kaplan moved to her bedside and grabbed her hand. "How do you feel?"

One of the doctors examined her then turned to Bentley, "She's all yours, sir. She'll be a little groggy for a while but she should be able to answer questions. Just don't push too hard, she's been through a lot."

Five minutes later Jake heard Hunt give Bentley news causing his pulse to quicken. Hashim Khan had planned two terrorist attacks in Paris. His mind was clouded with only one thought. *Kyli and her friend are going to Paris.*

Jake grabbed Wiley's arm. "Sir, Kyli and her friend…uh Kate—"

"Kates?"

"Yeah that's it, Kates. They are on their way to Paris now." Jake said. "They're planning on staying for a few days. We need to contact her and tell her to get out of there."

"I'll go to the bridge and use the satellite phone." Wiley said. "You find out what you can from Ms Hunt."

Wiley turned and left the small room.

Hunt revealed the information she'd gathered while working for the Hilal Shipping Company in Aden. Two simultaneous attacks were planned for high-profile Paris landmarks specifically chosen by Khan to guarantee a high body count. She didn't know the landmarks nor did the man who owned the shipping company. Khan never shared his targets with anyone.

After twenty minutes, Hunt stopped talking. Jake, along with Bentley and Kaplan had absorbed and processed the information Isabella Hunt had shared with them. If the timetable Hunt laid out was accurate, Jake had ample time to avert the strike on the French targets. He needed to get to Paris as soon as possible. If Bentley couldn't get him there, he knew Wiley could.

Wiley came back with a distressed look on his face. "I can't get in touch with Kyli."

"What do you mean?" Jake asked.

"I called her apartment, no answer." Wiley said. "I called the office and they said she wouldn't be back for a few days. So, naturally I called her cell phone next…"

"And?"

"And my office manager in Leuven answered."

"She must have forgot to unforward her calls." Jake said.

"That's what I thought too." Wiley said. "But she answered Kyli's actual phone. Kyli left it at the office. I have no way of getting in touch with her. Sometimes Kyli does personify the absent minded professor."

"What about her friend? Can we get her number?"

"Already thought of that, Jake. I had my office manager call Kates' mother in Florida." Wiley shook his head. "Kates doesn't have international service."

"Scott," Wiley said. "Jake and I need to go to Paris. If you can get us to Sigonella, I'll make arrangements to have us picked up there. I'll also alert the French Gendarmerie."

"Sorry, E.W." Bentley said. "You can't go. I'll send Gregg with Jake. You and I have business that can't wait. Not even for your granddaughter."

† † †

Jake and Kaplan were picked up by a helicopter and transported to an aircraft carrier patrolling the Gulf of Aden. They touched down on the deck of the USS Abraham Lincoln, a Nimitz class nuclear-powered super-carrier. Jake and Kaplan were allowed thirty minutes to rest, eat, and change into flight gear. They were then loaded into separate F/A 18F Super Hornets.

Five minutes later Jake and his pilot were catapulted into the air over the blue water. The rapid acceleration and resulting g-forces sent a wave of nausea through him but he forced back the bile as the jet fighter rocketed into the afternoon sky. He'd flown in a fighter jet once before and he didn't like it then either. The hotshot pilots always wanted to impress their riders—or more accurately themselves—by over-controlling the aircraft at the sake of their riders' stomachs. Another sick rider, another tale for happy hour. On his first flight he'd vomited in the *sic-sac*. He vowed it wouldn't happen again.

The first thirty minutes were spent in silence, the only noise being the communications between the pilot and the air traffic controllers. Jake couldn't help but remember something Wiley had said to him while they were on Wiley's Citation jet enroute to Belgium, *"In all likelihood, the next few days will be life altering for you."* It seemed like such a long time ago and so much had happened since Wiley spoke those words. He'd been running on pure adrenaline. It felt like days since he'd slept and he was exhausted. He needed to rest, it would be a long night and he and Kaplan would probably spend it awake.

"Sir?" The pilot broke the silence. "This flight is quite irregular. You and the other man must know someone pretty important to pull this off. I've only seen this once before...it was terrorist related."

"Captain?"

"Yes, sir."

"This mission is classified and never took place," Jake spoke into the fighter's intercom. "A lot of lives are at stake. The order came from the top."

"I hope you stop the bastards, sir."

"Me too, Captain." Against his closed eyelids, Jake saw Kyli and her pleading face. "Me too."

CHAPTER 40

Northern Red Sea
35,000 Feet
7:00 P.M.

JAKE WATCHED THE last of the day's light lose its battle to darkness while the underside of KC-10 tanker aircraft loomed above the F/A 18F's canopy. With a supersonic range of just under 1900 miles, the Super Hornets were incapable of making the nearly three thousand mile hop from the USS Abraham Lincoln in the Gulf of Aden to the Naval Air Station Sigonella in Sicily without refueling along the way. And the only option available was the tanker that was already in the eastern Mediterranean preparing for a refueling exercise with a combat squadron based on a carrier currently patrolling the Mediterranean. With one phone call before the helicopter picked up Jake and Kaplan, Bentley had overridden the Mediterranean carrier's objective with a mission priority status issued by the President.

According to Hunt's briefing, the explosives were shipped to a small French Islamic community west of Paris called Trappes. Khan was to setup in the Mosque de Trappes and ready five suicide bombers for the two unknown targets in Paris. The only additional information she could provide was that Khan had assured his superior that the targets were guaranteed to be highly visible and packed with tourists. In Paris, that list was long. But with five more days, Jake assumed he and Kaplan would be able to cull the list of probable targets down to a manageable number.

Although a former Naval Officer himself, Jake had never experienced an aerial refueling. His job was strictly an intelligence officer deployed on the USS Mount Whitney. Jake watched the drogue, or basket as the pilot called it, inch its way down from the tanker. The F/A 18F pilot extended the probe on the nose of their aircraft and, with perfect precision, maneuvered the probe into the funnel-shaped basket.

Within a few minutes, the pilot disengaged from the basket, retracted the probe and banked to the left allowing the aircraft Kaplan was in to move forward and connect to the basket.

"My orders are to leave and proceed to NAS Sigonella as soon as we refueled." The pilot accelerated toward supersonic. "Your friend will catch up to you in Sicily."

Jake activated his microphone. "Gregg, try not to hold up the show too long. We've got work to do."

"You know, Jake." Kaplan replied. "If I wasn't surrounded by all these squids—"

"Yeah, yeah, I know." Jake interrupted. "You'd kick my ass. Adios, my friend."

Jake felt the power of the F/A 18F as the pilot pushed the aircraft through transonic to supersonic.

"We'll be there in about an hour." The pilot said. "So enjoy the ride."

Jake watched the airspeed and altimeter climb. After a few minutes the aircraft leveled off at 40,000 feet and Mach 1.56.

Wiley told him the black Learjet would meet them in Sicily at NAS Sigonella. The fighters were instructed to taxi next to the Learjet, then he and Kaplan would transfer directly to Wiley's jet and be airborne for the Paris-Charles de Gaulle Airport within minutes.

Jake played it through in his mind, over and over. He and Kaplan would make an unannounced visit to the Mosque de Trappes. If Hunt's information was accurate then they would catch Khan off guard. The last thing Khan would expect would be for them to walk through the front door. The only thing troubling him, the one thing he couldn't shake from his mind, was how he would find Kyli and her friend and get them out of Paris. It wasn't safe and Kyli's carefree nature could put her and Kates in danger.

France had become a boiling pot for trouble. With their liberal laws coupled with the high Islamic population, it was a haven for terrorists. Bentley had insisted the French government render assistance in tracking down and stopping the terrorist attacks, but even they had a reputation for non-cooperation when it came to issues inside their own borders. They held disdain for Americans and were reticent about sharing vital information.

One hundred miles out, Jake's pilot slowed to subsonic speed and started a descent. At 20,000 feet, they leveled off and slowed to 400 knots on the airspeed indicator.

Jake heard a crackle in his headset then Kaplan's voice.

"Hey, does this thing have a horn?" Kaplan said.

"Where are you?"

"Turn around and see for yourself."

The F/A 18F Kaplan was in had rejoined formation and Jake had never noticed.

"Prepare for landing." The pilot interrupted. "Welcome to the hub of the Med."

Established in 1959, Naval Air Station Sigonella is the U.S. Navy's second largest security command, second only to the one located at Naval Support Activity Bahrain.

Jake hadn't anticipated Kaplan's aircraft catching up to his flight, but obviously Wiley had. As the Super Hornets taxied to a remote location on the airfield, Jake noticed the black Learjet idling on the ramp.

As if on cue, when the Super Hornets canopies opened so did the Learjet's cabin door. Jake and Kaplan were relieved of their flight suits and helmets and escorted by Naval personnel to the awaiting Learjet. Three taps on the fuselage by the Naval personnel outside and the Learjet started taxiing. In and out in less than five minutes, just like Wiley said. Jake had learned to expect nothing less from the old man.

Now came the hard part—convince Kaplan to go along with his plan. First thing in the morning, right through the front door of the Mosque de Trappes. Armed. And ready for action. But Jake knew it would be a hard sell. Kaplan was Mr. Conservative, concentrating on thorough planning before execution. Gregg always touted the hallmark of Special Forces planning—PACE—primary, alternative, contingency, and emergency. There was a time and place for all that planning, but not this time. The element of surprise meant attacking now. They had to neutralize the cell. Jake needed Kaplan's help, but if he had to, he'd go it alone.

CHAPTER 41

National Gendarmerie Invention Group Garrison
Satory, France
Midnight

OVER AN HOUR after arriving at the Charles de Gaulle airport, their escorted vehicle pulled inside the gates of a square building with a large open courtyard in the center. Jake studied the building; it was old, in need of repair, and bland. The exterior of the red brick building was covered with black mold.

The National Gendarmerie Intervention Group, or GIGN as their driver Philippe called it, was officially operational in March of 1974 as a result of the Munich massacre during the Olympic Games of 1972. In 1973, the GIGN became a permanent force of the French National Gendarmerie and is considered their elite Special Operations counter-terrorism and hostage rescue unit.

Jake and Kaplan were escorted inside the building. A cloud of cigarette smoke hung in the air, its stale pungent stench filled Jake's nostrils. They were escorted to the GIGN's commanding officer, Lieutenant Travers Heuse. Not what Jake expected, younger—mid forties—and short. In his mind, Jake had pictured an older, conservative man.

Heuse wore faded jeans and a wrinkled white button-down shirt with the sleeves rolled up revealing a tattoo on his right forearm. His necktie was pulled loose and a tweed jacket was draped over the back of his chair. He sat behind an oversized mahogany desk smothered with stacks of papers, an old computer, and an untouched cigarette burning in an ashtray.

"Messieurs Pendleton and Kaplan." Heuse pointed to two chairs. "Please, make yourselves comfortable. I understand you've had a long day. Or should I say a long two days?"

"Please, Lieutenant, call me Jake."

"But of course, Monsieur Jake." Heuse smiled. "And you, Monsieur Gregg?"

Kaplan smiled at Heuse's sarcasm. "Oui."

"We have been fortunate, messieurs." Heuse said. "The Mosque de Trappes is but ten kilometers from this office. Right under our noses, so to speak, eh?"

"That is fortunate." Jake said. "Have you sent someone to stake out the place?"

"Stake out?" Heuse had a puzzled look on his face.

"Observe." Kaplan said. "Do you have someone observing the Mosque?"

"Ah. Oui." Heuse looked at his watch. "I have sent men to drive by Mosque at irregular time intervals. They will stop surveillance in one hour for the night."

"Why are they stopping?" Jake asked.

"Your own intelligence reports indicate we have five more days." Heuse said. "We have the luxury of time. The GIGN has arranged hotel rooms for you in Versailles, just a few blocks from here. I will send a car for you in the morning and we will resume around ten."

"Ten?" Jake couldn't believe the lieutenant was so flippant about a potential terrorist attack. An attack that could kill or injure dozens, maybe hundreds of French men and women as well as many tourists. Including Kyli and her friend. "Shouldn't we get started earlier?"

"No, monsieur. The GIGN needs its rest too." Heuse stood and spread his arms. "Now come, Philippe will take you to your hotel. Get some rest, tomorrow might be another long day."

✝✝✝

Hotel de Ville
Versailles, France
6:30 A.M.

Jake got up early thinking about Lieutenant Heuse's perspective. If Isabella Hunt was right, they did have time on their side. The only problem with waiting was that sometimes plans change. Waiting could cause him to miss the opportunity. His instincts told him they needed to strike fast and strike early. If Heuse and the GIGN weren't willing to move, then he would convince Kaplan to help him storm the Mosque.

Jake rapped on Kaplan's door until he heard Kaplan cussing. "Gregg. Open up."

"What the hell, Jake?" Kaplan snatched the door open. His thick black hair was tousled. Eyes bloodshot. "Go back to bed."

"I called Philippe." Jake said. "He'll be here in twenty minutes. Get dressed. We've got work to do—with or without Huese."

"Jake, this is France. The last thing we need to do is piss off the head of the Gendarmerie." Kaplan rubbed his eyes. "We should wait."

"For once, Gregg, trust me." Jake said. "If you'll start getting ready, I'll explain what I have in mind."

While Kaplan dressed, Jake explained the plan he'd been hatching during the night. Kaplan interrupted several times but Jake insisted he be allowed to finish. Jake had covered every angle and was convinced his plan would work. He just needed Kaplan to concur with it.

"Okay, Jake. Give one good reason why I should go along with your plan."

"It's Wiley's granddaughter out there. We owe it to him."

"Is this just about Wiley? Or is this about you?"

"Gregg." He looked Kaplan in the eyes. "If it were Isabella in Paris, we wouldn't be having this conversation, would we?"

CHAPTER 42

PHILIPPE PICKED UP Jake and Kaplan in a GIGN vehicle, a black Mercedes, standard issue. Fortunately, Jake figured, it was early enough in the morning not to draw unwanted attention. As they made their first circle of the block, the mosque appeared tranquil, as did the surrounding neighborhood.

Jake and Kaplan were outfitted with the equipment left in Wiley's jet. Duffle bags for each man filled with articles of clothing and accessories to give them the appearance of tourists wandering the streets of France. Wiley was a resourceful man and had already arranged clearance for Jake and Kaplan to carry weapons without French authority intervention, something Wiley said required him to call in some favors from high-ranking French officials. Heuse had given them both warning about the use of their weapons. *"Strictly self-defense"* were the words he used.

As the Mercedes started its second pass by the front of the Mosque, Jake saw a white van pull out of the mosque onto the roadway. When the Mercedes and the van passed each other, Jake noticed the driver and several passengers in the rear of the van. Something about the driver troubled Jake.

"Did you see that?" Jake asked.

"Is nothing." Philippe said. "Probably on their way to jobs."

"No. Something was wrong." Jake looked at Kaplan. They'd both been trained to be observant. Drilled over and over to unconsciously note minute details that clue them of impending danger. Details so minuscule the average person would never perceive them as a source of trouble or out of place.

"Gregg, did you notice it?"

"It didn't feel right." Kaplan said. "But I can't put my finger on it. What is it Jake? What'd you see?"

"First thing was the driver. He was dressed the part of the faithful Muslim." Jake said. "But his features…behind the beard he was—"

"Caucasian." Kaplan added.

"That's right." Jake signaled for Philippe to pull the car over. "And Hashim Khan is an American traitor. What else, though? Either of you notice the men in the back?"

"No." Philippe said. "They were nothing but shadows."

"Yeah." Kaplan blurted out. "Their faces."

"That's right." Jake pulled out his Glock and screwed on the sound suppressor. "They were clearly Middle Eastern and, more importantly, had shaved their faces. The attacks are going down today." Jake pulled back the slide chambering a round. "Philippe, turn around and catch up to that van."

✝ ✝ ✝

Khan noticed the Mercedes as it passed by his van. The same type that drove by the mosque several times during the night. GIGN. And if the Gendarmerie were onto him then something had gone wrong in Yemen. Hilal had talked. Maybe the woman really was a spy for the West. Either way, they both would die. Khan would ensure it.

In the rearview mirror he saw the GIGN vehicle pull over then make a u-turn. Khan floored the accelerator.

The arrival of the GIGN was unexpected but Khan had planned for the possibility of evading the Gendarmerie. He knew the mosque was under surveillance. Even in France, all of the Islamic communities were scrutinized.

Since the possibility of detection existed, Khan had devised a deception for the authorities.

He grabbed his cell phone and placed a call while weaving the van through traffic, making turn after turn, trying to outrun and outsmart the GIGN men in the Mercedes. After five minutes of evasive driving, a pre-planned route Khan had already driven several times before, his radio blared indicating his shell game was ready to begin.

Khan maneuvered the van to the prearranged switch over, keeping the Mercedes at least a block behind him. When he reached the switch over spot, he glanced in his mirror; the GIGN car was far enough behind to make the switch.

He drove past an identical van that had accelerated into traffic as he turned into a maintenance garage. The bay in front of him had its door open. As Khan screeched the van to a stop inside the garage bay, the door slammed shut behind them.

Khan readied an AK-47 as he waited to see if the GIGN took the bait. The decoy van disappeared down the street and the Mercedes whizzed by the garage with lights flashing and siren wailing.

Khan smiled, the ruse worked. The decoy van had a prearranged pattern to drive, luring the GIGN car farther away from the garage. By the time the GIGN caught up to the decoy and realized what had happened, Khan and his men would be close to their first target.

The garage door in front of Khan's van opened and he pulled out.

† † †

The GIGN Mercedes handled the tight turns with ease but Jake thought that Philippe was holding back on the accelerator. "Can you drive any faster? He's getting away."

"Lieutenant Heuse will not like it if I mess up his car." Philippe said. "I will not lose the van. I know these streets, there is no where to hide."

"You better catch up to him fast or you won't need to worry about Heuse. The lieutenant isn't here but I am." Jake held up his gun. "Do I make myself clear?"

Jake watched the van turn left around a corner nearly a block ahead of them. "You're going to lose them, hurry."

Philippe slammed the accelerator to the floorboard as they rounded the left hand turn causing the Mercedes to lean hard to the right.

"There." Jake pointed. The van was much closer than Jake had guessed but it didn't matter, they were gaining. "Hit your lights and siren. Let's announce our intention. Tell him we want him to stop."

Philippe toggled the switch and the GIGN Mercedes lit up with flashing lights in the windows and the front grill of the car. The van accelerated down the straight road.

"Go. Go." Kaplan shouted. "We can outrun him."

"Let's get this over with." Jake yelled.

The whooping Euro siren disrupted the calm morning as the two vehicles weaved through the small number of cars on the road, the Mercedes gaining precious distance on each straightaway. The chase lasted exactly four minutes, then the unexpected happened.

The van slowed and pulled over. By the time the Mercedes came to a full stop in front of the van, Jake and Kaplan were scrambling from the back seat, weapons drawn and running back toward the van. "Call Heuse, get reinforcements." Jake yelled back to Philippe.

Jake darted forward in the middle of the street. "Hands on the wheel."

Kaplan yelled something in French. "Mettez vos mains sur le volant."

The man put his hands on the steering wheel.

Jake looked at Kaplan, "You speak French, too?"

"Enough to get by. You don't?"

"No. Tell them to get out of the car with their hands in the air."

"Sortez de la fourgonnette. Mains sur la tete. Chacun d'entre vous." Kaplan said.

The doors to the van opened. Five bearded men got out, one from the front, and four from the back.

"Sur le terrain. Face vers le bas." Kaplan waved his gun at them.

"What'd you say?" Jake asked.

The five men lay face down on the grass next to the road.

"Enough to get by, huh?" Jake said.

Kaplan smiled.

"These aren't the men we saw earlier." Jake couldn't believe it. The terrorists had outsmarted them. "Grab the driver. They did a switch somewhere."

Kaplan grabbed the driver from the ground, picked him to his feet and pinned him against the side of the van. "What happened to the other van?" Kaplan asked in French.

Jake kept his gun aimed at the four men on the ground. *How did they pull off the switch?* Khan was smarter than he gave him credit. Khan had already planned for this, was on his way to Paris, and Jake still didn't know the locations of the attacks.

Jake watched Kaplan give the driver a jab to the kidney. The man's knees buckled but Kaplan pulled him upright and slammed the man's head into the side of the van. He didn't understand anything Kaplan was saying but he could tell the man was pleading. After two minutes, Kaplan grabbed the man by the collar and threw him on the ground. Jake heard sirens in the distance. Growing louder.

"They don't know anything." Kaplan said. "They were paid to drive for three to four minutes then pull over. They're a decoy and we fell for it. Khan is gone."

"How do you know they don't know anything?" Jake asked.

"Trust me. If he'd known anything." Kaplan said. "He'd have spilled his guts."

Philippe walked up to Jake. "Lieutenant Heuse wants to talk to you when he gets here."

"Forget Heuse." Jake said. "Take us to the mosque. Now."

"But, monsieur."

Jake moved toward Philippe, putting his face just inches away from the Frenchman. "Take us to the mosque now or a lot innocent people will die. Do you want their blood on your hands?"

Philippe motioned to the men lying on the ground. "But these men, monsieur—"

Kaplan yelled something at the men lying on the ground.

"Monsieur!" Philippe looked at Jake. "You would not dare."

The eyes of the men on the ground grew larger.

Kaplan looked at Philippe. "Yes. He would. And he'd take great pleasure in it I'm sure." Kaplan turned to Jake. "They won't move."

CHAPTER 43

KYLI WOKE UP and looked for Kates. She should have been in the other bed but it was empty. Her head was a little groggy from the drinking she and Kates did at the bar last night, their final stop after an afternoon and evening on Champs Elysees.

"Kates?"

"I'm in here." Kates replied from the bathroom.

Kyli noticed the bathroom light was still off. "What are you doing?"

"I'm going to take a shower, my head hurts."

"I know what you mean." Kyli said. "I don't usually drink so much. We need coffee. Lots of coffee."

Kyli's friend had wanted a 'Parisian experience,' exploring off the beaten path places around town. After they arrived in Paris, they checked into the Marriot Champs Elysees then walked to an outside café where they spent the better part of an hour eating, drinking, and people watching. Kyli had been to Paris several times, but it was the first time for Kates. They started at the Arc de Triomphe, climbed to the top to get a view of Paris. Afterwards, they window shopped, making their way down Avenue Montaigne to look at all the top fashion designer shops.

They ended the day at Place de la Concorde where they found a hole-in-the-wall restaurant and grabbed a bite to eat. Then Kyli took Kates to a nearby bar that played live music. They stayed too long and drank too much. But the night was fun and Kyli was certain Kates would never forget her trip to Paris.

"I was thinking." Kates said from the bathroom. "I'd rather spend more time at the Louvre and maybe we could go to the Eiffel Tower tonight after dark."

"That's a good idea." Kyli heard the shower turn off. "If we get moving, we can eat and catch the bus or Metro. We can be at the Louvre by nine or a little after. Hell, we can probably walk and make it by nine-thirty. It's only about a mile and a half—down at the end of Champs Elysees."

"Bus." Kates stuck her head out of the bathroom. "Or Metro. Maybe we can walk back this afternoon."

"Perhaps. Or we could go straight from the Louvre to the Eiffel Tower." Kyli crawled out of bed. "My turn in the shower."

It wasn't until high school when Kyli met Kates. It was during those years they became good friends. And had been close ever since.

Kyli's thoughts turned to Jake. She wished she could talk to him again but she'd been forgetful and left her cell phone at the office in Leuven. Wiley had whisked Jake off on another one of his secret adventures before she had a chance to really get to know him.

For reasons she couldn't explain, she felt an attraction to him. It transcended a physical attraction, although that was certainly there too. No other way to say it; he was *hot*. Five-ten, slim. And cut. She'd always loved men with blond hair too, and in Jake's case, it accented his sapphire-blue eyes. But no, it was more than his looks. He was also intelligent, but naïve about women. Maybe his fiancée's death had made him vulnerable, unsure how to act.

Maybe it was that side of Jake that drew her to him.

"Earth to Kyli." Kates threw a towel at her. "Hey. It's your turn in the shower."

Kyli looked up. "Okay. Yeah, thanks."

"I've seen that look before." Kates teased. "You were thinking of *him*, weren't you?"

"Who? No. I don't know what you're talking about."

"Don't you lie to me, Kyli Wullenweber." Kates said. "You might be fooling yourself, but you can't fool me. You've been preoccupied with Jake ever since I arrived. He must be something special to grab you like this. You, of all people."

"What is that supposed to mean?" Kyli said.

Kates laughed. "You know damn well what I mean."

CHAPTER 44

JAKE INSTRUCTED PHILIPPE to park the GIGN Mercedes next to the front entrance of the mosque. "Let's go." Jake instructed Kaplan and Philippe.

Weapons drawn, the three men rushed through the front door. The first man Jake saw was the imam. At the sight of the guns, the man turned to flee but Jake grabbed him and placed his barrel an inch from the man's face. "Where are they going to attack?"

The imam's eyes grew large—fear—exactly what Jake intended. Jake had dealt with radical Muslims before, they were all the same, and to get anything out of them they needed to be afraid. Not afraid of dying, dying was the easy way out. They needed to be afraid of living after Jake finished with them. And Jake would make sure every man in that mosque was afraid of living if they didn't cooperate.

The imam raised his hands. "Attacks? I know nothing of any attacks."

Jake slammed his fist against the side of the man's nose. The man fell to his knees, blood poured from his nose. The man wiped his nose with his garment. Blood smeared across the side of his face.

"Monsieur."

"Shut up, Philippe."

"Take him to the men's prayer room. There will be others there also." Kaplan said. "Someone will talk."

Jake pointed his gun at the imam. "Get up. Let's go."

Kaplan grabbed the man by the arm, pulled him to his feet, and led him toward the rear of the mosque.

A door opened into a semi-circular room, the men's prayer room. Prayer mats lay on the floor, all facing the same direction. A man stepped from behind a curtain in the rear with a rifle. As the man raised the rifle, Jake fired three shots in rapid succession. The man fell to the mosque floor.

Jake motioned for Philippe to move left. Jake moved to the right side of the room. Kaplan held the imam in front of him. Jake and Philippe held their pistols ready as they moved slowly toward the back of the room.

Kaplan jammed his barrel into the man's neck. "How many more?"

The imam said nothing.

Kaplan grabbed the man's throat and squeezed. The man's face turned red and he gasped for air. "How many more?"

"Three."

Kaplan relaxed his grip. "Where are they?"

Nothing.

Kaplan pushed against the man with his barrel. "Your choice. Answer or I'll put a bullet in your brain."

"Two in the back." He pointed with a head movement. "And one in the cellar guarding the prisoner."

"Tell them to come out now or they're dead men." Kaplan ordered.

"Raman. Sharif. Do as he says. Lower your weapons and come out." The imam shouted.

Two men appeared from behind a curtain. One hand raised, the other lowered, each holding his rifle by the barrel.

"Drop the guns." Philippe shouted. "Lay face down, hands behind your back."

The men did as requested. Philippe reached into his pocket and retrieved flex cuffs. He cuffed the two men while Jake held his gun on them.

Jake walked over to the imam, grabbed his arm, walked him to a chair, and pushed him onto it. "I'll ask you again. Where are they going to attack?"

"I do not know." The imam pleaded. "Khan told no one but his men. We were never to know until afterwards—Khan's orders."

Jake raised his fist to hit the imam.

"Please, no." The imam cowered. "The man downstairs, the prisoner, he is one of Khan's men. He knows the locations. Khan said he is a failure, a disgrace to Allah. My orders are to hold him here until Khan returns. I fear the fate of the young man under the hand of Khan."

"What about the man watching him?" Jake asked. "Will he surrender or will I have to kill him too?"

The imam shook his head. "He answers to me, not Khan. He will offer no trouble."

Kaplan led the way with the imam to the cellar. The imam was right, his man surrendered his weapon as instructed. Philippe flex cuffed him as he did the others. The prisoner, Khan's failure, was duct taped to a chair. Wearing nothing but a thin robe, he sat there. Legs bound, arms bound, chest bound. A strip of duct tape placed over his mouth.

The imam told the three men Khan had left specific instructions that the young man wasn't to be touched, moved, or fed. The man was a disgrace to Islam, to Al Qaeda, to Allah and would be dealt with harshly. He would never see Paradise. And anyone who touched him would be dealt with even harsher.

"Do you understand English?" Jake asked.

The man nodded.

Jake reached into his pocket and pulled out his Leatherman. He cut away the front of the man's robe from the waist down leaving the young man exposed. "Let me tell you how this works. First I ask you a question. Then you give me an answer. If I think you're lying, I'll cut something off. Each time you lie, I'll cut something else off until there is nothing left. Am I getting through to you? Do you understand?"

The young man nodded.

Jake ripped the tape from the young man's mouth. "Good. Now tell me everything you know about Khan and the attacks he's planned for Paris."

✝✝✝

Khan drove with determination toward downtown Paris. He'd memorized the planned route along with several avenues for escape—something, until now, he didn't think he'd need. But considering the GIGN might be alerted to his plans, the escape routes became viable options.

He'd planned to return to the Mosque de Trappes after the suicide bombings to deal with the young man—an example must be made. By then, Paris would be in mayhem. The national and international medias would swarm into the city. All rescue and law enforcement personnel from surrounding communities would be called into action to help the wounded. The hospitals and morgues would be overrun. Time was on his side. The Islamic nation will have struck again at the heart of the infidel. Al Qaeda would be blamed. Khan would be victorious.

With the gendarmerie alerted to the mosque and his attacks, Khan now knew he couldn't return to the Mosque de Trappes. A possibility he'd planned for, just in case something like this did occur. Now his alternative course of action was sealed, he'd drop off the bombers, his merchants of death, then flee the city of Paris and the country of France. He would flee undetected.

He dropped off the first two bombers across the river from the first target location. Theirs was a simple task. Walk across the bridge, fall in line with the many tourists, and wait for the designated time. Then they could shout their final prayer and detonate the vests. Paradise waited for them.

Khan dropped the second two bombers, his most reliable men, at the entrance to the great museum. Their task was to enter the glass pyramid and descend into its depths. There, they would meet Allah and be transcended to Paradise.

CHAPTER 45

THE YOUNG TERRORIST offered no resistance to Jake's inquiries. Jake recognized the man knew his chances with Jake and Kaplan were much better than the horror of being left to deal with Khan. Philippe radioed ahead to Heuse who would send gendarmerie forces to the two target areas. The descriptions the young man gave Jake of Khan's men were vague. The only useful information vetted was the description of the men's clothing and which entrance would be used at the great museum.

Jake glanced at his watch. Khan had set the time of detonation to coincide with one of America's most infamous dates—9:11 a.m. Sixteen minutes from now. Jake and Kaplan were still five kilometers from reaching the destination Heuse sent them to—the Louvre museum. The target guaranteed to have the highest tourist count. Guaranteed to cause mass hysteria and panic.

As they sped through the cramped and crowded streets, Euro siren wailing, Jake wondered where Kyli was. The city was a tourist Mecca. Thousands flocked daily to visit the Parisian sights. The odds Kyli and her friend were near either of the two targets was remote, but not impossible. How could she have left Leuven without her cell phone? It seemed irresponsible due to the gravity of the situation.

The black GIGN Mercedes sped across Pont du Carrousel toward the entrance to the Louvre Museum. Philippe swerved to avoid a bus full of tourists at the entrance. Jake and Kaplan checked their weapons, loaded fresh magazines, and then tucked their Glocks in their jackets. The sound suppressors removed made for an easy, comfortable fit.

According to Heuse, the Louvre had scheduled an indoctrination ceremony in the auditorium under the Louvre Pyramid for 9:30 a.m. to honor the museum's latest appointment to the Board of Directors, Maximilian DeBrule. Maximum capacity turnout was expected so the ceremony was scheduled early to avoid the peak tourist hours. Louvre security had been notified and asked to calmly evacuate the *Under the Pyramid* level of the Louvre. In reply they had informed the GIGN there was not enough time to completely evacuate the building before the bomb detonated.

Jake checked his watch, 9:06. Five minutes. The Mercedes slowed as the Louvre Pyramid came into view. "What the hell are you doing? Get us to the pyramid."

"We must park and run." Philippe said.

"No." Jake shouted. "Drive across the plaza. We can't waste any more time. Just do it."

"But, monsieur—"

"Just do it. Now."

Philippe floored the accelerator and the Mercedes lunged forward, bouncing over the curb and nearly plowing over a light pole. The Mercedes careened across the Louvre courtyard toward the glass pyramid. Pedestrians screamed and scattered like pigeons being chased by a dog. With its lights flashing and siren wailing, the Mercedes skidded to a stop sixty feet from the pyramid and two feet from a woman who stood frozen by the sight of the oncoming car.

The glass and metal pyramid serves as a main entrance to the Louvre museum. The pyramid was surrounded by three smaller pyramids and sat in the main courtyard of the Louvre Palace.

Jake and Kaplan jumped from the black sedan in a full sprint toward the pyramid when the sound of a distant explosion made them turn and look.

Jake saw a fireball billowing from the Eiffel Tower. Then a second fireball ballooned from the tower. He turned back toward the pyramid when he heard a gunshot from inside the building. Tourists screamed and ran in every direction. Before Jake could react, it happened.

A flash of light from inside the pyramid.

Jake felt a tremor beneath his feet.

†††

Kyli and Kates had just reached the bottom of the stairs beneath the Louvre pyramid when a security guard began announcing the evacuation of the building due to a potential gas leak. The wait in line hadn't taken them as long as Kyli estimated. A ten-minute casual stroll from the Metro station, another ten-minute wait in line and she and Kates were descending below the glass pyramid.

"You have got to be kidding me." Kates said. "I come all the way to Europe and I can't get into the Louvre."

"I'm sure it won't be for long." Kyli reassured her. "Sounds more like a precaution. We'll be back down here in no time. You'll see."

Kyli and Kates turned around and began climbing the stairs when Kyli heard the commotion above them at the entrance. People shouting, pushing, and shoving then a man ran down the stairs past her and continued toward the auditorium.

A guard leaned over the rail, "Halt."

Kyli saw the guard raise his gun. "Kates, run," she yelled. She grabbed Kates arm and started running up the stairs.

The guard fired his gun in the air.

Kyli looked down at the fleeing man and then back up at the guard. She realized the implications. The man who ran down the stairs was Arab—clean-shaven, clutching his jacket. Time with her grandfather had taught her that evil people surrounded them and radical Muslim sects were some of the most dangerous. They had no respect for life or for the lives of women and children. They didn't fight like soldiers, but like cowards. Suicide bombers were worst of all, their objective was to take as many lives as possible.

"Faster, Kates. Faster." Kyli yelled. "We need to get the hell out of here fast."

Arm in arm, the two women ran up the stairs, taking two steps at a time, until they reached the top of the stairs. They dashed for the exit. Hundreds of people were running across the Louvre courtyard, fleeing for their lives. Kyli had a firm grip on Kates hand when they reached the doorway. The two women were in synchronous stride, running as fast as they could, when there was a deafening explosion behind and below them.

The last thing Kyli saw were Kates' eyes as the blast lifted them in the air, ripping their hands free from each other and catapulting them across the courtyard.

†††

By the time Jake recognized what had just happened, the glass pyramid exploded. Glass, metal, and bodies flew outward, tumbling across the courtyard. Windows in the Louvre Palace shattered from flying debris and the shock wave of the explosion. Jake was hit by the concussion wave knocking him to the concrete. Bits of glass ripped and buried into his skin. He felt like he'd just been attacked by a swarm of bees, stinging his entire body.

Jake looked at Kaplan who was struggling to stand, his face covered in blood. A large piece of glass buried in his forehead. He looked back at the GIGN Mercedes; a four-foot piece of twisted metal had sliced through the windshield impaling Philippe to the front seat.

Jake picked up his gun and ran toward Kaplan. "Gregg, you okay?"

Kaplan wavered. "My gun. Where's my gun?"

"Gregg, sit down." Jake looked around. Kaplan's gun was knocked twenty feet away. "I'll get your gun. You stay still."

Jake retrieved Kaplan's gun and looked across the courtyard. Only about a dozen people were still standing. Dozens of bodies littered the courtyard, some intact, others not. It looked like a war zone. Painful moans echoed through the plaza. Smoke billowed from the crater that just seconds earlier was where the pyramid stood.

"Jake." Kaplan pointed toward the crater. "There, it's not over."

Jake followed the direction Kaplan's hand was pointing and saw a man staggering toward the crater, clutching his jacket, and chanting in Arabic. A chant he'd heard before and knew too well.

"Allahu akbar." The man chanted over and over. "Allahu akbar."

Jake yelled. "Stop."

The man reached the edge of the crater and turned toward Jake. His jacket was torn from the blast. Jake recognized the vest, a suicide vest packed with explosives.

The man looked at Jake. "Allahu akbar."

"Allahu akbar, my ass." Jake squeezed the trigger. The man's head recoiled then he fell into the pit.

CHAPTER 46

KYLI THOUGHT SHE was dreaming. Her entire body screamed with pain after tumbling across the Louvre courtyard. In a deafened fog she saw a man walking across the courtyard aiming a gun in the direction of the blast. His torn shirt and pants spotted with blood. The man looked like Jake, but that was impossible. Jake was two thousand miles away. She saw the muzzle flash, his gun recoil, but deafened by the blast, she heard no sound.

The last things she remembered were the blast from under the pyramid, Kates being torn from her grip, and the pain as shards of glass ripped at her skin, stinging and burning. The back of her head felt damp and sticky.

She tried lifting her head, but it wouldn't move. The man who fired the gun turned around and was walking toward her. Her eyes tracked his movements. She struggled to lift her blood-covered arm. All it did was drag across the concrete. She tried raising it again, but only her fingers twitched. "Jake."

A wave of pain flooded her brain and the man disappeared into the darkness.

†††

Jake scanned the courtyard and did an assessment of the situation. There were dozens of bodies scattered across the ground. Some alive, some dead. All bleeding. Jake counted thirteen people standing, moving around checking on the wounded, searching for lost loved ones, and trying to cope with the reality of what just happened.

Jake noticed a young woman nearby, tall and thin, calling a name. The back of her clothes covered in blood, her arms and legs covered in abrasions. At first he couldn't understand whom she was calling. He could see she was scared and wandered aimlessly. Then, as she got closer, he heard the name she called. His heart sank—*Kyli*.

He hurried toward the tall woman. She was at least fifty feet away. If she was Kyli's friend, then he needed to get to her.

He noticed Kaplan sitting against the Mercedes holding a small child, probably unaware of Philippe's dead body behind him. There was a woman rocking back and forth on her knees, the child in front of her looked dead. Dozens survived the blast only to bleed out from fatal penetration of glass shards.

Jake stepped over rubble as he moved toward the tall woman calling Kyli's name when he noticed a woman laying face down, dozens of shards of glass protruding from her back and the backs of her legs. She had the same color hair and size as Kyli. Her face was covered in blood, her bloody arm stretched along the concrete toward him, fingers twitching.

"Kyli." Jake reached down and moved her slightly. The woman was already dead—not Kyli. He let her fall to the concrete.

Adrenaline coursed through his veins, he had to find Kyli. He sidestepped a twisted piece of metal and spotted the tall thin woman again. He took two steps toward her and froze. He heard his name. He looked in the direction of the voice. Blood, glass, and debris covered the concrete between him and the voice.

He heard the voice again and recognized Kyli. She was laying face down, drifting in and out of consciousness. Glass sliced her skin on her arms and legs. A large piece was wedged just below the base of her skull. Her clothes covered in blood. Jake needed to get help.

Within seconds the courtyard filled with police cars and emergency vehicles. It became an amphitheater of noise and a kaleidoscope of flashing lights. Victims wept for those lost and called for those still missing. Sirens reverberated in Jake's ears. He sat next to Kyli, holding her head still until the medics arrived. He looked at his hands. They were covered with blood—Kyli's blood. It was happening again. His mind flashed back to Savannah, when he was holding Beth, his hands covered in her blood. He could think of only one thing.

Khan.

He would hunt Khan down.

Hunt him down and kill him.

CHAPTER 47

KHAN FLED PARIS sooner than he'd originally intended. He hadn't anticipated the gendarmerie closing in on the mosque as soon as they had, almost thwarting the planned bombings. He'd noticed two Americans in the GIGN Mercedes, one fair-skinned with lighter hair. The other his polar opposite; dark skin, dark hair, and dark eyes. The two could be trouble. He wondered if they were somehow connected to the failure in Australia or the explosion in Yemen. If so, they were tracking him so he needed to proceed with extreme caution.

He decided to stick with his original plan, a week in San Sebastian playing the rich Spanish playboy. His French was good, his Spanish better. He'd change his appearance the first full day in Spain, haircut, shave his beard, and a new wardrobe. When he made his connection in Madrid, he knew he'd be scrutinized. His olive skin and dark features would lend him the air of authenticity he needed as a citizen of Spain traveling west for a visit to America for a business conference.

Khan wasted an hour in downtown Paris abandoning the van in a seedier section of the city, leaving the keys in the ignition. He walked to the nearest Metro station, changing trains multiple times until he ended up at the Porte d'Ivry station. He walked the half-kilometer to a nearby garage where a stolen black Audi had been stored.

At each Metro station television monitors broadcast the devastation at the Louvre and the Eiffel Tower. Khan had drastically overestimated the damage the bombs would cause at the Tower. Although closed for inspection, the damage to the Eiffel Tower was minimal and the number of casualties low. Conversely, damage to the Louvre was extensive, the pyramid entrance completely destroyed.

Khan drove the Audi on a predetermined route westward toward the Bay of Biscay via Le Mans, Poitiers, arriving in Bordeaux in early afternoon where he ate lunch at a small sidewalk café and toured a winery east of town. With France on high alert from the bombings, he played the part of the upset Spaniard lamenting the destruction of two of France's icons.

From Bordeaux, Khan drove to Bayonne, France where he left the stolen Audi and retrieved a brand new red flame Volvo C70 convertible with a Spanish registration. His playboy image almost intact, Khan drove the coastline to San Sebastian with the top down enjoying the cooler October weather.

Khan checked into the Hotel Niza as planned, his suite overlooking Isla de Santa Clara. Dozens of boats were moored into the shallow green waters just beyond the beach in Concha Bay. Beyond Isla de Santa Clara stretched the endless blue waters of the southern end of the Bay of Biscay, or Cantabrian Sea as the locals called it. It was almost dark and from his balcony he gazed at the sky. To the west he could see remnants of the wispy, orange clouds that autumn brought.

News reports indicated the death toll at the base of Eiffel Tower was thirty-two with another forty-six injured. He'd expected a higher number. His disappointment was offset by his success at the Louvre. One hundred twenty two dead, one hundred forty eight injured. Another powerful blow dealt against the free world.

Khan was still troubled nonetheless; only one bomb had detonated at the Louvre. The news reports indicated that a second suicide bomber was shot and killed, preventing his vest from exploding. Khan regretted not listening to his better judgment and using a remote detonator.

Yet, he was still pleased with the result. He knew his next attack would stab at the heart of America. A week from today he would travel from Spain to the United States, where he'd launch an attack so brazen, so heinous and despicable, that the country would forget the attacks of 9/11, they would pale in comparison to Khan's devastation.

The infidel would realize there was no safe place to hide.

CHAPTER 48

Brugmann University Hospital
Brussels, Belgium
10:00 P.M.

JAKE RAPPED LIGHTLY on the hospital room
door as he pushed it open. Wiley was sitting in a chair next
to Kyli's bed, Kates in the bed next to Kyli's, both lying
prone, Kyli's head immobilized.

"Well?" Jake said. "How are they doing?"

Jake, Kaplan, Kyli, and Kates had been triaged at a
Paris hospital. Jake and Kaplan were treated for minor
wounds to remove glass fragments and then released. Kyli
and Kates' injuries were more serious. Kates was treated
and remained overnight for observation. Kyli had to
undergo surgery to remove the large glass shard lodged in
the back of her neck. As soon as Kyli recovered from
surgery, Wiley was permitted to provide medical transport
for the two women to a hospital in Brussels. After arriving
in Brussels, Wiley had a team of physicians standing by to
receive and treat the two women.

Wiley stared at Jake. "You looked like someone
peppered you with rock salt."

"I've never been shot with rock salt, but if it stings all
over, then you're right." Jake said.

"Consider yourself lucky." Kates leaned over from her
bed. "They removed a chunk from my ass and it hurts like
hell." She extended her hand to Jake. "We haven't been
formally introduced but I'm Kates."

"I know. I loaded you into the ambulance."

"That was you?" Kates asked. "That whole thing is a
blur. It doesn't seem real except for the pain."

"How's Kyli?" Jake asked. "Has she come around?"

"She'll be fine, Jake." Wiley patted the chair next to him. Jake sat down. "The doctors said she should wake up soon. She's drifted in and out for the last hour. How's Mr. Kaplan?"

"He's doing fine." Jake got up and inspected the bandage on Kyli's neck. "Bentley's down there with him now. I think they're going back to Langley tonight. He got peppered with glass like I did, nothing major except the gash on his forehead. It'll end his modeling career."

Wiley chuckled. "The ladies might find that scar interesting."

"Grandpa, what happened?" Kyli shifted on the bed. "I can't turn my head. Why am I looking at the floor?"

"I'm right here, Kyli." Wiley said. "They have your head and neck immobilized. A piece of glass penetrated your neck and the doctors don't want you moving your head and pulling the wound open. You'll have to lay face down all night."

"What about Kates? Is she okay?"

"I'm fine." Kates said. "But Paris turned out to be a pain in the ass, literally. I had a piece of glass lodged in my ass."

"You got a piece of glass stuck in your ass? That's too funny." Kyli laughed. "Strangest thing. Right after the explosion I saw a man with a gun. He aimed it toward the blast and fired. I know it sounds crazy but I thought it was Jake."

"Your mind does crazy things to you when you're under stress." Wiley said. "There's a good reason for what you thought you saw."

"I know, I know. But it seemed so real."

"It was real." Wiley said.

"I don't understand."

Jake interrupted. "I shot the second terrorist before he could detonate his vest."

"Jake. Is that you?"

"In the flesh."

"Come down here so I can see you." Kyli said.

"You want me to get on the floor? Are you kidding me?" Jake asked.

"No, I'm not." Kyli said. "Please."

Jake sat down on the floor near the head of Kyli's bed and slid sideways until he could see Kyli's face. "Hi there."

"Jake, you look like Al Pacino from *Scarface.*" Kyli said. "What happened?"

"The same thing that happened to your neck and your friend's ass. Jake said. "You two were lucky today. Maybe next time you can remember to take your phone with you."

There was a knock on the door. "Can we come in?" Bentley pushed the door open. Kaplan followed him into the room.

Bentley looked around the room. "I thought Jake was coming up here. I need to talk to him."

"Right here, sir" Jake said.

"What are you doing on the floor?" Bentley asked.

"Talking to Kyli."

"I need to talk to you, Jake." Bentley paused. "Privately."

Jake got off the floor. "I'll be right back." He said to Kyli. He walked toward Bentley. Bentley held the door open while Jake walked into the corridor.

"What is it, sir?"

Bentley motioned for them to walk. "You did a great job in Paris today and I'm proud of you and I know you'll continue to impress Mr. Wiley." Jake started to speak but Bentley continued. "I have some news for you, Jake and there's no easy way to say it."

Jake gave him a curious look.

"Jake. There's been an accident. It's your parents."

CHAPTER 49

Four Days Later
Oak Hill Cemetery
Newnan, Georgia

FOR THE SECOND time in six months, he was here again. This time he was adding two more graves, those of his parents. Six months ago, it was his fiancée, Beth. Much like then, it was a cool, dreary morning. The wet, recently mowed grass left a pungent smell in the air.

Beth was gone and now his parents. He began to understand the words Wiley said to him the day they met in El Paso. *"You're not special, Jake. We're all touched by sadness in life."*

And, for the first time, he felt alone. He was an only child. His parents were only children. There were no aunts, no uncles, no cousins. And all the grandparents had been dead for years. With his parents gone, he was the last Pendleton.

When he'd talked to the fire marshal, no cause had been determined. The marshal suspected a gas leak in the kitchen but the damage had been so devastating that the cause of the fire might never be determined. According to the marshal, the heat produced from the inferno caused the exterior gas tank to explode, further compounding the fire departments efforts to contain the fire.

Jake scanned those in attendance noting his father had made some powerful friends during his days in the military and as a political appointee. Attending was CIA Director Scott Bentley, Former President Jimmy Carter, three United States Representatives, the Governor of Georgia, and two

United States Senators. One of whom was the man who wanted Bentley to deliver his head on a platter, the Honorable Richard Boden, accompanied by his contingent of Secret Service protectors, and as usual, noticeably chewing gum.

Boden was a tall, thin man with thick gray hair. He used a cane and walked with a limp from a gunshot injury he'd sustained in the Vietnam War, a war that had earned him two Purple Hearts and the Congressional Medal of Honor. He'd taken three bullets in his right leg, two of them shattering his knee and destroying the joint. Even with the miracles of modern technology and an artificial knee, Boden still required the use of the cane.

Kyli sat next to Jake while the priest delivered the eulogy. Wiley sat on the other side of Kyli. Seated on Jake's other side was a gaunt looking Isabella Hunt and Gregg Kaplan. Behind them were several rows filled with his parents' friends and neighbors, all there to pay their last respects to a couple whom they'd known for many years.

In front of him were two caskets suspended in mid-air above the excavated burial pits where they would be lowered and covered with Georgia clay and dirt. An American flag was draped over his father's casket, the man given a military funeral for his service to his country and as a public servant.

Beyond the caskets, as if segregated by some unseen force, sat the men of power and politics: Bentley, Carter, the Governor, and the five members of Congress. Behind them and arching around in a semi-circle back toward the caskets were the *guns*. Most were Secret Service. Some CIA. The rest were Georgia State Patrol. All conspicuously armed as if a turf war could break out any second in the historic old cemetery.

At the head of the gravesite stood seven Marines in full dress uniforms serving as Honor Guards.

The priest started the prayer. Jake lowered his head and closed his eyes. As the priest spoke, Jake felt Kyli's warm hand move on top of his. Her touch was soothing, her compassion welcome. Kyli wore a conservative black dress, unlike her usual flamboyant style. According to Wiley, the doctors in Belgium had been overly precautious with Kyli and soon determined her wound not to be as serious as first suspected. She had a healthy glow on her face. The only indication of her injury was the bandage on the back of her neck.

With her other hand, Kyli grabbed his upper arm and leaned close to him. It had been a long time since he'd been close to a woman. He felt a need to be comforted, desperate to have someone care about his loss. His pain. It felt good, and he needed to feel something.

The prayer ended and so did the moment. Kyli sat up straight and removed her hands. He opened his eyes feeling guilty. The moment evaporated, but he wanted it back.

The priest motioned to Jake as previously discussed. He stepped forward and placed a rose on his mother's casket. Two soldiers removed the flag from his father's casket, folded it with military precision, and with gloved hands presented it to Jake. He glanced at Kyli, she was wiping tears from her face. Wiley had his arm around his granddaughter's shoulder. Isabella Hunt had moved next to Kyli and held out another tissue. Gregg Kaplan kept his head bowed.

These were Jake's best friends; he realized that now. They did care for him and even more, what happened to him. They stood by his side now in testament of their true friendship and in return, he'd stand by them.

After the Marine soldiers were dismissed, mourners stood and filed past the open graves to pay their respects. A few women tossed purple orchids, his mother's favorite flower. Many bowed their heads and then made the sign of the cross on their chest. Others just paused and said goodbye.

Bentley walked over to Jake and asked Kyli if he could have a moment alone with him. He signaled Kaplan, Hunt and Wiley to join them. "Jake, we have new information on Khan and his whereabouts. The rest of us are meeting later to discuss with Fontaine what he's discovered. You should to be read in on this."

Wiley grabbed Jake by the arm. "Kyli and I are returning to Belgium, I have business that I must attend to. I want you in that meeting with Bentley."

Jake looked at Wiley and knew Wiley understood how he felt. "I wouldn't miss it for the world. Khan has to go down...and I want to be the one to bring down that worthless piece of—"

"Excuse me." Senator Richard Boden, chewing his gum, placed his hand on Jake's shoulder. "Scott, E.W., if you'll pardon the interruption."

Jake looked at the senator. "This is a private conversation."

"I beg your pardon." Boden removed his hand. "Because I know you're under stress, I'll overlook your insolence. I wanted to pay my respects."

"Thank you, Senator. Now, if you don't mind. I'm a little busy at the moment." Jake caught sight of Bentley standing behind Boden giving him the *"cut it out"* signal by stroking his fingers across his neck.

"Listen here, Mr. Pendleton." Boden's face flushed, jaw noticeably clenched. "I've got half a mind to have your ass hauled in right now for your lack of discipline in the field. I knew and admired your father for a great many years and out of respect for his memory, I'm going to overlook those transgressions. But let me tell you something right here and now." Boden looked at Kaplan. "And the same goes for you too. If either one of you so much as crosses an eye, I'll march your trigger-happy asses to the steps of Capitol Hill and let you face a Senate inquiry about your actions. Do I make myself clear?"

Jake clenched his fists and glared into Senator Richard Boden's eyes.

Boden took two steps back.

Jake took two steps forward, stopped, and then turned away, ignoring the Senator.

CHAPTER 50

HASHIM KHAN'S TRANSFORMATION into a Spaniard was almost complete. After parking his car across town, he spent the first night at the Hotel Niza in a beachfront room on the Bahia de la Concha, and then checked out, all part of his plan. He strolled through the streets of San Sebastian, with each stop his metamorphosis advanced.

Two streets over he found a men's hair stylist where he had his face shaved and hair fashioned in the latest style. Next, he located a stylish clothes boutique recommended by a local. A salesman selected designer clothes, shoes, and accessories for his new wardrobe. His makeover into a wealthy Spaniard was just about complete as he continued down the narrow streets of San Sebastian looking for his final items. The cool sea breeze felt refreshing on his shaven face. Finally, he found the shop he was searching for and purchased posh luggage completing his ensemble.

Returning to his Volvo C70, Khan unpacked his old bags and repacked his new clothes in his new luggage. Everything about him screamed arrogance. The guise was necessary to stave off unwanted suspicion. Of course he'd be noticed, that's what he wanted. Not for what he was, a killer and terrorist, but as an over-indulged man spending his money on booze and women and living a life of debauchery.

Hide in plain sight.

The last items he required proved the most difficult to obtain. When he checked in at the Hotel Maria Cristina under the name Arlo Delgado he had two voluptuous women hanging on his arms. He'd found the hookers on the streets, promised them cash and fine things in exchange for their services and silence. They eagerly agreed to Khan's terms.

Khan plopped down the six hundred Euros per night required for a Royal Suite, paying for a full week in advance, and left strict instructions not to be disturbed. That was three days ago.

The Hotel Maria Cristina, named after the first guest through the doors on July 9, 1912—the Spanish Regent Maria Cristina—rose magnificently above the historic city of San Sebastian.

The first two women didn't work out as well as he'd hoped. They were greedy, too demanding, and too interested in Khan's personal affairs, so one evening they became shark food on the bottom of the Cantabrian Sea.

The same night he'd disposed of the first two women, he met two younger women in a bar on the Boulevard. They were on vacation from the United States and were infatuated with the idea of hooking up with a rich Spaniard and threw themselves at him. Khan bought them expensive clothes, jewelry, and liquor. In return, they kept him sexually satisfied. Mutual benefit. He kept his appearance as a playboy intact. In fact, it was no longer an appearance but a reality. He had become a playboy. The women would go home bragging of their adventures in Spain with a rich lover named Arlo taking with them new wardrobes and accessories, or at least, that's what they thought.

The time had come to make arrangements for his travel to the States. His passports and documents all in order, the drive to Madrid would be uneventful. He knew he would pass through all the security checkpoints without a problem; he had nothing to hide but his true identity. No one would figure it out until it was too late. Not until *after* he'd struck his unprecedented blow. An attack considered unorthodox even by Al Qaeda standards. A despicable act of violence against thousands of innocent and harmless victims.

After supper with the women, he slipped a sedative in their cocktails. A knockout pill to keep them unconscious until morning. He had business to attend to and plans to arrange and confirm. The last thing he wanted was two horny women distracting him and prying into his personal affairs, so it was less trouble to drug them for the night. In the morning when the women woke up, groggier than normal, they would all be naked in the bed, reeking of an overindulgence of alcohol. They'd have sex again. All three of them. Just as they had the last two mornings.

When the women passed out, he grabbed his laptop computer, powered it up, and logged on to a secure server which relocated his IP address around the globe several times allowing him untraceable access to any website. He glanced at the naked women on his bed, they were both very attractive and desire stirred within him. A blonde and a brunette, former college roommates who met their freshman year when they were enrolled in a Spanish class together. Every year since graduation they'd taken a two-week vacation to a different destination in Spain, this year they were indulging his need for sexual pleasure.

But, he had a mission to accomplish. Unfinished business in America. By America's own admission, the infidel could not defend against the "lone wolf" terrorist. And that was how he intended to attack.

He would enjoy the women for another day, partaking in their carnal pleasures, slaking his lustful desires with the women's vigorous sexual appetites. Afterwards, he'd take the women on the same boat ride as the first two whores, a one-way trip to the bottom of the Cantabrian Sea.

CHAPTER 51

FROM HIS WINDOW, Ian Collins watched the third airline jet launch into the late afternoon skies over Atlanta in less than a minute. Thank God for soundproofing. Only the faintest of rumbles permeated the thick walls of the hotel.

He saved the last images on a flash drive. Soon he would take the flash drive down to the hotel's business center and print out the documents, three in all, and return to his room to prepare them for mailing. When the envelope was received at its destination, Collins knew, the effect would be devastating, his ultimate goal.

His obsession with Jake Pendleton had culminated into the brazen surveillance of the man earlier in the day. Collins followed the news stories of the tragic loss of two of Newnan's most prestigious and influential residents from a fire caused by a gas leak. It was payback for the elderly politician's interference that resulted in two bullets being shot into Collins.

He followed the procession of vehicles from the funeral home to the Oak Hill Cemetery and, at one point, actually joined the line of cars then pulled away as they entered the cemetery grounds. As the procession moved toward the gravesite, Collins stopped his car at the section known as the Confederate Cemetery and removed his high-dollar digital SLR camera with its zoom lens.

Collins viewed the funeral through the lens, snapping pictures of those in attendance, focusing on Jake. He made note of Jake's stoic demeanor throughout the funeral. The man and woman sitting to Jake's left seemed familiar, too familiar, then it occurred to him. He'd seen them before. They were with Jake Pendleton in the Friar's Chamber in

Ireland. They were part of the reason for Collins' failure. He would deal with them later.

It was the young woman sitting next to Jake that piqued his interest. She leaned against Jake and held him with both hands. She appeared to be showing him more affection than compassion. This, he found interesting.

Another opportunity to seek revenge on the meddling Pendleton.

Collins used his hotel keycard to access the business center, logged onto a computer, and opened the files on the flash drive. He printed each document on the hotel's laser printer, logged off, removed the flash drive, grabbed his copies from the printer, and returned to his room.

With the photos spread on the table in front of him, Collins carefully affixed a marker, his marker, to each. Their meaning would be clear and the recipient would triple their efforts to locate him. Perfect.

His web was being spun and his prey lured into it.

Jake Pendleton's next funeral would be his own.

✝✝✝

Four miles east of downtown Atlanta in an old brick building on Ponce De Leon Avenue in Decatur was where Bentley told Jake to meet them. He parked on the street two blocks away and walked in the darkness of night to the field office. The building was non-descript other than the red brick. It could have been an office for anything, accountants, lawyers, realtors, or a field office of the Clandestine Services of the Central Intelligence Agency.

Earlier Jake had arranged for a limo to take Kyli and Mr. Wiley to the airport. They were returning to Belgium— Wiley for a few days, Kyli for good. It was a bittersweet moment for Jake. He hated to see her go, the moment at the cemetery still lingered fresh in his mind. But he needed to clear his mind and focus on Khan.

Jake entered through the front entrance, a small foyer enclosed in glass, only to be greeted by a CIA guard who introduced himself as Bruno. The human tank towered over Jake like an NFL linebacker. His arms were the size of Jake's thighs. His intimidation didn't stop with his size. His dark black skin was covered in black attire. Adorned in full bling, Bruno wore a chain-link gold necklace, a gold earring, gold bracelet on his right wrist, and three gold rings.

"You don't look like a Bruno." Jake quipped. "You look more like a bodyguard for a rapper or a bouncer at a nightclub."

"I'm half Italian—satisfied?" He smiled, a gold tooth glistened under the lights.

"Depends on what the other half is."

"You don't want to find out."

"No, I don't think I do." Jake smiled.

Bruno whispered into his sleeve and the door behind him buzzed. Bruno pushed the door open letting Jake walk through. "Director Bentley is waiting, second door on the left."

"Thanks."

The Atlanta operations center was a large room with a dozen men and women sitting behind computer terminals wearing headsets. Five flat-screen monitors lined the rear walls. Huddled in front of one monitor were Bentley, Hunt, and Kaplan. Jake recognized the image on the monitor; it was CIA analyst George Fontaine. Fontaine worked in the Clandestine Imaging Division of the Technical Service of the CIA. The CID's responsibility was technical support to clandestine operations in the form of photography, secret writing, and video surveillance.

"What's up with Bruno?" Jake pointed back at the door.

Bentley turned, "Malcolm? Good guy, but I wouldn't get on his bad side."

"I could've used that intel earlier." Jake said.

"George and I briefed Mr. Wiley on this earlier." Bentley motioned to Jake to take a seat. "You're just in time to hear what we found out."

Jake walked over and stood next to Bentley. "Hey, George."

"Hello Jake." Fontaine was known to be thorough and all business so he wasted no time beginning his presentation. "It took some doing but I think we caught a lucky break." The monitor adjacent to the image of Fontaine showed the streets of Paris after the bombing of the Louvre. "If you'll notice the white van." The picture zoomed in on the driver.

"Khan." Jake said.

"That's right, Jake. I tracked his movements through the use of traffic cams, and found where he abandoned the van. Using the same cams, I verified his identity and followed him to the Metro."

Jake watched the monitor change pictures following the sequence of events as Fontaine explained Khan's movements.

"The French government, at least in Paris anyway, made it easy to track Khan's movements along the Metro lines. They even have cameras in the Metro cars. I followed Khan until he exited the Metro at the Porte d'Ivry station. I used traffic cams again until Khan disappeared into a nearby garage. Five minutes later, this black Audi drove out. It took a few minutes but I finally snagged a traffic cam photo of the driver and guess who?"

The picture on the monitor revealed Hashim Khan.

"The rest was a piece of cake...at least for a while anyway. By now, with the explosions at the Eiffel Tower and the Louvre, every satellite with an angle was aimed at France. He never changed plates so I tracked him to Bordeaux where, it appears, he took a tour of a winery."

"You're kidding, right?" Kaplan asked.

"Trying to look like a tourist, was he?" Jake imitated a European accent. "Bet he even bought a couple of bottles of wine."

"How could you know that?" Fontaine asked.

"Lucky guess." Hunt said.

"He actually bought three bottles and placed them in the back seat which eventually gave away his identity." Fontaine continued his presentation. "I tracked him to Bayonne, France, near the coast where I lost him. The car disappeared into a structure and never resurfaced. It's still there as far as I know. The trail went cold. No movement. No pedestrians. No traffic cams to monitor. I thought we were at a dead end unless his plans were to stay in Bayonne, which didn't make any sense. He knew he was being pursued. He must have seen you two in Trappes when he evaded you.

"At ten minutes intervals, I pulled photos, checking every road out of Bayonne and then I noticed it. A red convertible driving toward the Spanish border. The car had Spanish plates and the driver had black hair, but so does half the population."

"How could you be sure it was Khan?" Kaplan asked.

"The wine bottles are on the seat and you matched the labels to the winery." Jake said. "You already told us that."

"No, I didn't. But I was about to."

"Come on, George. You're making a short story long." Jake said.

"I'll get right to the point. I tracked him to San Sebastian, Spain where he spent one night at the Hotel Niza. Then he changed his appearance and we're working on a hunch now. The car has disappeared. A man resembling Khan in height and build but clean cut and shaven is staying at the Hotel Maria Cristina under the assumed name of Arlo Delgado. We have an asset from Madrid there now, monitoring Delgado's movements. He's taken some photos but, to be honest, I'm not getting anything I can use with our facial recognition software."

"George?" Jake interrupted. "What's your gut instinct on this?"

"I think Hashim Khan and Arlo Delgado are one and the same."

"That's good enough for me." Jake said.

Bentley turned to Jake. "What are you thinking?"

"I speak Spanish." Jake said. "I'm going to Spain. But Wiley took the jet so I'll need a lift."

"I hope you're not chasing a ghost. Otherwise we're wasting valuable time." Bentley handed Jake an envelope. "Wiley gave me this to give to you. He said you'd know what to do with it."

Jake took the envelope from Bentley. On the front was his name, 'Jake' written in Wiley's handwriting. The back was sealed with wax. A deep crimson, blood colored wax stamped with Wiley's ring. He'd seen Wiley wearing the ring and thought nothing of it. Two large interlocking letters, 'GF,' dominated the impression.

He walked away, turned his back to them, slid his finger under the wax seal, and popped it free from its hold on the paper. He slipped out the note and read it in silence.

Jake,

This is 'Eyes Only' information. Scott handed you off to me, which means you still work for me. His interests in this matter and mine differ. He has a separate agenda, one dictated to him by politicians. One he doesn't agree with but can do nothing about.

This is an assignment you must handle alone. Watch your back when you arrive in San Sebastian, lose your friends and come to a place called Peine del viento, Comb of the Wind. There you will meet your blind date. Follow the instructions below and don't deviate from them. You'll be provided with everything you need.

Scott will insist Khan be captured alive. My instructions are simple—kill Khan. I'll deal with Bentley...

Jake read the rest of Wiley's instructions, slipped the letter back in the envelope, dug around in his pocket for matches—something Wiley always insisted he carry—and set the envelope on fire. Holding it with his fingertips, he watched the red and yellow flames devour the envelope until nothing was left. He dropped it to the floor and ground the ashes beneath his shoe.

When he turned around. Bentley, Kaplan, and Hunt were staring at him.

"What are we waiting for? Let's go to Spain."

CHAPTER 52

GREGG KAPLAN WALKED beside Isabella Hunt, Scott Bentley, and Jake Pendleton toward the CIA Challenger jet parked on the tarmac at the Dekalb-Peachtree Airport in Atlanta. It was dark and the night air was cool. Exhaust from the jet's engines flooded the ramp with the smell of kerosene.

"You'll find everything you need in your duffels." Bentley looked at Jake. "Wiley has arranged for weapons and other gear upon your arrival. It'll be waiting for you when you arrive in San Sebastian."

"Seems like old times." Kaplan said. "The three of us flying off to save the world."

Bentley looked at Hunt. "You haven't told him?"

"I haven't had the chance, sir." Hunt said.

"Told me what?" Kaplan was worried.

"Jake, come with me please." Bentley motioned for Jake to follow him to the jet.

"Told me what?" Kaplan looked at Isabella.

She stood in front of him, blocking his view of Bentley. "The doctor said I'm not fit for duty assignment."

"He's probably right. You should take it easy." Kaplan said. "Does he have any work for you?"

"I'm going back to Langley with Bentley. I'll be working as an analyst again for a couple of months." She placed her hands on Kaplan's chest. "But he promised I get to handle this op with you and Jake. You'll be sick of having me in your ear all the time." She smiled.

"You just got out of the hospital. We haven't talked about...things."

They hadn't had time to talk since the rescue in Yemen. Kaplan desperately wanted to have time alone with Isabella but the same day she was released from the hospital they flew to Atlanta to attend the funeral. There was so much said—or not said—in the glider. Hunt had been drugged and she'd said so much. Kaplan could only wonder if she meant everything she said or if it was the drugs making her expressive with her feelings.

The last two missions they worked on together, they were undercover as a couple. Once as vacationers and once as honeymooners. That was when they first kissed, for appearance sake, to strengthen their cover story. He felt something and he was sure she did too. But she'd played it cool, like she does everything. And even as much as he wanted to bring it up, he resisted. He didn't want to jeopardize the mission…or find out he was wrong.

The next op was different. They knew they were under surveillance so they played the loving couple, always touching, always playful.

They'd spent two hours in a bar waiting for a rendezvous. After they made contact and arranged for a meeting the following day, she had insisted they stay in the bar for a couple of drinks.

When they got back to their room, Isabella Hunt continued her affectionate behavior, to keep up the guise he presumed. But her kiss was passionate, long, and wet. He presumed it was the alcohol, so he gently pushed her away. She pulled him closer, pressing herself against him. He returned the kiss with the same intensity. Before he realized what was happening, they were on the bed ripping each other's clothes off. He expected it would stop, the ruse to fool the observers a success.

It didn't stop. She was ravenous. They made love, and then they slept. The next morning, Kaplan was greeted with the familiar cool exterior of Isabella Hunt.

"Don't worry, Gregg. I'll be right here when this is over. When you and Jake finish this op, you'll be back at Langley and so will I. We'll have plenty of time to talk."

A look came across Hunt's face that concerned Kaplan. "What is it?" He asked.

"Don't tell Jake, but I overheard Bentley talking to someone about him. Bentley seemed upset but finally relented and agreed to something."

"You don't know what it is? Did it sound like he was in trouble?" Kaplan rubbed the bridge of his nose. "You know Senator Boden is after Jake, maybe Bentley's going to turn him over to Boden."

"I don't know. I doubt it." Hunt stepped closer to Kaplan. "All I know is Jake won't be returning to the States anytime soon. He'll be staying longer with that Wiley fellow."

"That's what I thought too." Kaplan said.

Bentley stepped out of the aircraft. Hunt stepped back and stood next to Kaplan as Bentley approached. "Gregg, time to go."

Kaplan looked at Hunt and winked. "Yes sir."

Bentley grabbed Kaplan's arm as he started to move. "One more thing."

What's that, sir?"

"After you arrive in Spain, don't let Jake out of your sight."

† † †

Isabella Hunt stood by Director Bentley's side as the cabin door closed and the jet taxied away. She wanted to tell Gregg everything. How she felt. What had happened. The real reason she wasn't going to Spain with him. *I didn't lie to him. Not technically. The doctor did say I wasn't fit for fieldwork. But maybe I should have told him—*

"Did you tell him?" Bentley asked.

"No, sir."

"Are you going to tell him?"

"I'm not sure."

"Don't you think he has a right to know?"

She had already thought about that question and her answer as well. The dilemma had been on the forefront of her consciousness every minute since her rescue.

"I'm sure Gregg would think he has a right to know, but as far as I'm concerned, it's my problem. I'll handle it alone."

"Isabella, at some point you have to tell him."

"No, Director, I don't. And maybe I never will."

CHAPTER 53

KHAN WAS THE first of the naked trio to stir as the morning sun streaked through the suite's windows. He wasn't a large man, average height and build and rather non-descript in his guise as a Spaniard, but he was cunning and ruthless. Whatever he wanted, whatever he desired, whatever he planned, he would take extraordinary measures to accomplish. He slipped from between the two naked women and padded in bare feet across the suite to the wet bar where he started the coffee brewing to help clear the cobwebs from his head. He would miss their sexual energy realizing he might never again find two more submissive women eager to please him the way these American women had.

All of the arrangements had been finalized the night before while the women slept. The attacks on the American soil would send shock waves across the globe. The West would soon realize their vulnerabilities. Nations would lock down their borders. Personal liberties would be stripped from the people and Al Qaeda would get the credit—an Islamic World Order would rise from the sand and dominate the world. 9/11 would pale in comparison.

He'd also activated his contingency plan after he noticed the man following him the previous day. Seeing someone once or twice in this coastal resort town might qualify as a coincidence but sighting the same man a half dozen times set off alarm bells in his head. He needed a backup plan and that was his expertise. He always had a backup plan—and a backup to the backup. The success of any plan was being prepared for the unexpected. Khan was ready.

† † †

Jake stretched, working out the kinks from sitting too long as the CIA Challenger jet descended over the Cantabrian Sea toward a spit of land along the Spanish-French border. Located along the Bidasoa River in the port town of Hondarribia, the San Sebastian airport was sixteen kilometers east of town. He'd been to Spain once before—when he was seventeen—not the northern coast but southern and central Spain. He struggled to remember what it was like but he could only conjure vague recollections of Madrid, the bull-fighting arena in Valencia where he'd met the toreadors, and the Mediterranean coastline. Even though he was only in his thirties, it was too long ago to vividly recall.

He'd spent the hours on the jet thinking about the note Wiley left him and his impending rendezvous at Peine del Viento—Comb of the Wind. He detected a tone of anger in Wiley's words, his granddaughter harmed in the Paris attacks, and the man, who seemed to always be in control, wanted revenge.

So did Jake.

The jet landed then turned around and taxied back down the runway until it reached an exit to the ramp. Before the pilots could shut down the engines, two Spanish customs and immigration officers were walking toward the aircraft. After a cursory search of the cabin, the men left.

"That was quick." Jake said. "I imagine Bentley ran interference since they didn't look for squat."

"Just checking a box." Kaplan pointed out the open cabin door. "Here comes our ride."

Jake and Kaplan grabbed the duffle bags and went to meet the agent Bentley sent from Madrid. As they reached the light gray sedan, a small man got out and opened the trunk. "Christopher Perez." He stuck out his hand. "Call me Chris."

Kaplan grabbed his hand and gave it a shake. "Gregg Kaplan. This is Jake Pendleton."

When Kaplan released his grip, Perez rubbed his palm, opening and closing his fingers. "Quite a grip you got there, Kaplan."

Perez slammed the trunk closed. "Let's go. I secured three rooms in town about three blocks from the Hotel Maria Cristina, where Mr. Arlo Delgado is staying. I have a man watching the hotel right now. So far today, Delgado hasn't left the hotel."

"Have you seen him yet? Can you ID him as Khan?" Jake asked.

"Inside that folder you'll find all the photos we have." Perez accelerated the sedan away from the airport. "You can compare them yourselves. The descriptions match in every way. But, as you can see, even our best photo isn't a full frontal."

Jake held up two photos. "That's our man, I'd bet my life on it. Only without the beard and the hair. Look at the eyes, that's how you can tell. Dark and evil."

"I don't know, Jake." Kaplan said. "We'll need better confirmation before we make a move on him. Let's get there and take a look for ourselves."

"I'm telling you, that's Khan." Jake said.

Twenty minutes later the three men entered the Pension Santa Clara. Jake and Kaplan carried their duffle bags while they followed Perez to his room where he gave the two men weapons.

"There you go gentlemen." Perez pointed toward the bed. "Glock 19, nine millimeter handguns with screw-on suppressors, three nineteen-round magazines each with hollow-point bullets. All ready to go. Bentley said if either of you need fifty-seven shots, you deserve to be dead."

Jake checked his watch, a quarter after one. According to Wiley's note he needed to be at Comb of the Wind by 2:30 to meet Wiley's contact. He'd thought about it on the long flight to Spain and couldn't imagine what Wiley could offer that Bentley and Fontaine hadn't already briefed them on. If he'd learned anything from Wiley, it was not to underestimate the man. He was a man with unlimited resources and unlimited connections. Jake supposed being in the spy business for over fifty years brought a lot to the table.

He also suspected Bentley had told Kaplan to keep an eye on him, and make sure he didn't do something rash— like kill Khan before the CIA could get to him.

But that's exactly what Jake intended to do.

CHAPTER 54

JAKE'S FIRST ORDER of business was to lose Kaplan and Perez. He had a plan he hoped would work. According to Perez's man, room service just delivered a large meal to Arlo Delgado's suite. Figuring it would be at least an hour before Khan showed himself, Jake made his first move.

"Let's eat, I'm hungry." Jake said. "I'm sure there's a café close by."

"More like a dozen or so within three or four blocks. This is the Old Town part of San Sebastian. It is considered a pedestrian area," Perez explained. "Everything is within walking distance."

"We can eat later." Kaplan argued. "We have work do to."

"Look Gregg." Jake stuffed his Glock in the back of his pants and the magazines in his jacket pocket. "I'm going to get something to eat while we have a few minutes. We might not get a chance later—once Khan is on the move. You two can come with me or you can sit here and starve. Your call."

"Fine." Kaplan seemed reluctant to start an argument in front of Perez. "Let's just make it fast. I want to be there when Khan comes out of the hotel."

Perez opened the door. "I know a place where the service is fast, the food good, and the prices reasonable."

The three men exited Pension Santa Clara to a walking street labeled San Lorenzo. Within a few minutes they stepped inside a modern and welcoming café called Sidreria Donostiarra.

"I thought you said reasonable prices." Jake said. "Have you ever looked at the menu?"

"The food is excellent." Perez laughed.

"Why did you bring us here?" Kaplan grumbled.

"Because the desserts are to die for." Perez said.

"Odd choice of words." Kaplan said. "Because if we miss Khan, that might be what happens."

They were seated at a table next to the window where Jake watched the hordes of pedestrians stroll by as if they had nowhere to go. No one seemed in a hurry. The trio ordered sandwiches and waited too long before the order was brought to the table. Jake glanced at his watch, 1:45. It was getting close to time for him to elude Kaplan's constant monitoring of him and make his way to Piene del Vientos where he was to meet his blind date.

Jake finished his sandwich well ahead of the other two. "That was good." Jake stood up. "Time to make a head run."

"Don't take too long." Kaplan complained. "We're short on time."

Jake could tell Kaplan wasn't expecting him to disappear this soon. "Keep your sense of humor, Gregg. We might need it later."

Jake scoped out the location of the restrooms as soon as they arrived at the café, noting who went in and when they came out. The men's room was the first room down the hall and he could tell by the floor plan that it backed up to the kitchen. He saw men waiting outside the door several times so he knew it was a one-man facility. The women's room was at the end of the hall and he'd noticed numerous occasions when more than one woman entered at a time. And each time the door opened, Jake could see the reflection of outside light—meaning it had a window. He just hoped the window was large enough to squeeze through.

Jake walked down the hall, glancing back to see Kaplan's watchful glare. He grabbed the knob. Locked. As he knew it would be. Jake bounced up and down enough to let Kaplan see his urgency, and then he walked to the women's room. He gave Kaplan a *'what the hell'* look and stepped inside. Jake had watched this room carefully, he was sure it was empty.

Jake opened the door and slipped inside, locking the door behind him. He heard a shuffle behind him.

"I beg your pardon. This is *not* the men's room."

Jake turned. A brunette was standing at the mirror touching up her makeup. She was older, he guessed mid-forties and wore a tight black dress, spiked heels with ankle straps, and was quite attractive.

"I'm sorry. I thought it was empty." Jake pleaded his case. "And I really have to get out of here."

Not part of Jake's plan, not Plan A, anyway. "Look, I can't hide in here much longer. I was having a drink at the bar and asked a woman for a date. Her boyfriend wasn't very happy about it."

"Not a smart move." Her eyes scanned him up and down. She smiled. "You should have waited for me. You're luck might have been better."

Think fast, Jake. "Now I wish I had. You're a beautiful woman. Get me out of here and I'll buy you dinner. Can I can meet you somewhere?" He couldn't believe what he was saying.

She laughed. "You're cute. Not very smooth, but cute."

Jake walked to the window and opened it as far as it would go. The opening was large enough to crawl through. Now to see how gullible the woman was.

"Are we on?"

She grinned. "We're on. When and where?"

"How about at the end of the Boulevard by the water. Say, six o'clock? Then we'll go wherever you'd like. I owe you that much." He pulled himself to the window ledge.

"I'll be there." Her voice turned sultry. "Let me give you a little push."

"Thanks." He moved through the window opening and felt the woman's hand run up his leg to his groin, then squeeze his buttocks.

"Nice and tight." She said. "That's why I love younger men."

He felt himself flush. He crawled out the window and dropped to the ground.

At first, he thought he'd made a mistake. The area behind the café was blocked off with no apparent way out but up—and no way to get *up*. He followed a wall that led him through a maze of nooks and crannies until he caught a glimpse of a street. He exited through a barred six-foot gate, fortunately not locked, which landed him on a narrow pedestrian street. He glanced at his watch, 2:00. He had to hurry; he had over three kilometers to run and only thirty minutes to get there. He had a problem, though. He'd lost his bearings in the maze and had to regain them fast without exposing himself to the café he'd just exited.

He used the shadows stretching from the structures around him to help him get his bearings. Soon he was standing on the Boulevard, the main walking street in Old Town San Sebastian.

The opportunity made him smile, a vendor was renting bicycles to tourists. Jake paid the man double, explaining he'd left his ID in his room, and then started pedaling down the route he'd already planned prior to their arrival in Spain.

By now, he concluded, Kaplan would have discovered he'd slipped out of the café and would be contacting Bentley. When he returned, he knew Kaplan would be mad but he'd get over it. Then together they would track down Arlo Delgado—Khan.

CHAPTER 55

GREGG KAPLAN STARED at the bathroom door, waiting, wondering what was taking Jake so long. He almost went after him when he saw Jake go in the women's room instead of the men's room but Perez talked him out of it. "When you got to go, you got to go." Perez said. Now Kaplan was getting suspicious.

He panicked when the door opened and the person Kaplan saw leaving the restroom was not Jake but a woman. He rushed down the hall pushing two women from the restroom entry and burst inside. He pushed open the stall doors. Nothing.

Perez followed behind Kaplan, tapped him on the shoulder, and pointed to the open window. "Looks like he ditched us."

"Son of a bitch." Kaplan stormed out of the room looking for the woman in the black dress. "Bentley is going to be pissed. We need to find the woman who just came out."

"You mean the hot one? She's over at that table." Perez pointed to a couple seated at a rear table.

It was definitely the woman who had been in the bathroom with Jake and she was whispering in the ear of an older man with a shaved head and goatee. She had her purse tucked under her arm and started to stand when Kaplan walked over to the table. "Excuse me, ma'am. But did a man come in the restroom while you were in there?"

"Yeah. He told me what happened with your girlfriend." She said. "Seems he made a mistake and was afraid you were so upset with him that you might try to do something about it."

"I'm not here with a girlfriend. I'm here on business." Kaplan grabbed her arm and squeezed. "Now where did he go?"

"Oww. That hurts." The woman frowned. "I don't know where he went. Out the window." She yanked her arm free.

Kaplan motioned to Perez. "Come on, let's move."

"Where to?"

"The Hotel Maria Christina." Kaplan motioned at Perez's cell phone. "Call your man and tell him to be on the lookout for Jake."

"What do you think Mr. Pendleton is going to do?"

"I don't think, I know. Jake missed Khan in Paris. Wiley's granddaughter was injured and hundreds of innocent people were killed and even more injured. Jake is going to kill Khan." Kaplan started running. "We have to make sure he doesn't get to him first."

"That doesn't make any sense. He knows we're staking the place out. He knows we're watching."

"One thing I've learned about Jake is he's unpredictable." Kaplan pulled out his cell phone and pressed the speed dial for CIA Director Scott Bentley. "That's also what makes him dangerous."

"But he still has to get through us to get to Khan."

"You don't understand. If Jake went after Khan, then he's already gotten past your man and Khan is as good as dead."

†††

Jake pedaled across the courtyard in front of the San Sebastian Town Hall, past the carousel, and down Paseo de la Concha, the two-and-a-half kilometer walkway next to Playa de la Concha—shell beach. The late October sky was laced with streaks of cirrus clouds, sun sparkling off the ice crystals high above. The winds were light and the temperature unseasonably warm for the time of year. Jake noticed dozens of sun worshippers along the beach in a last ditch effort to grab a suntan prior to November's impending chill.

Even at low tide the beach narrowed into non-existence as he approached Pico del Loro, a rocky finger that jutted out into the crystalline waters of Bahia de la Concha pointing toward Isla Santa Clara, the small island that guarded the entrance to the bay. Across the road from the rocky abutment, atop a hill sat Palacio de Miramar.

Five minutes later he reached the stone walkway of his destination, Piene del Vientos, the Comb of the Winds. The uneven stones were too rough to navigate on the bike, so he dismounted and walked the bicycle to the end of the walk.

Metal structures mounted into rocks stuck outward from several places in varying angles each with curved prongs resembling a metallurgical project gone wrong. It reminded him of oversized forks with damaged tines whose handles had become infused into the stone. What an odd place for a clandestine meeting, he thought.

Jake scanned the site and counted eighteen people, mostly couples and a few individuals seeking a moment of solitude. Conversations were dampened by the roar of crashing waves against the rocks and stone sea walls. The sound of the waves gave him a peaceful feeling. There was something about the water, he thought, the sound of waves crashing against the rocks and then receding back to the ocean that relaxed his mind.

He'd memorized Wiley's message.

Every word.

Jake's eyes landed on the only person that fit Wiley's description. He expected a man but it was a woman wearing the green fleece, standing alone, gazing out over the water. She had olive skin and long red hair that draped down the back of her fleece. Directly in front of her, roughly twenty feet out was one of the metal sculptures jutting horizontally from a large rock out in the water.

Immediately to her right sat a couple on top of the three-foot rock wall that separated the walkway from the sea. The blonde woman crossed her legs in the lotus position while she scanned through pictures on her digital camera.

Further to his right, another twenty feet or more was a young blonde girl lying on her side gazing into the sea. Tendrils of her stringy blonde hair flapped with the breeze. She wore a pink short sleeve shirt and low-rise jeans with tattered bottoms.

He dug in his pocket and pulled out a city map of San Sebastian. Why all the cloak and dagger baffled Jake. He had seen these tactics used in movies. Wiley told him that in the world of espionage, old tactics and cryptic communication still worked. But this wasn't espionage, it was about acquiring information to help him find a killer. He'd learned to trust Wiley' wisdom. So if this was the way Wiley wanted it, then he would follow orders.

He smiled. *In a way, it is kind of cool.*

He approached the woman in the green fleece from behind. He spoke fluent Spanish. "Pardon me? Can you help me with directions?" He held out the map. "I seem to be lost."

The woman turned around and for the first time he saw her facial features. She was late twenties, dark green eyes and dark eyebrows that didn't match the rest of her features. He realized her hair was dyed red but it complimented her olive complexion. She'd pulled a wide strand of hair over her left cheek. When the wind blew, he could see a three-inch scar.

She took the map from his hands. "Where do you want to go?"

"Monte Igueldo. Do you know the way?"

The woman pointed to the top of the hill to her left. "There is Monte Igueldo. You went right when you should have gone left."

"You look familiar. Have we met before?" Jake asked.

"No, I don't believe so."

"Do you have a brother named Marco? I think I see a family resemblance."

"Marco died last year. I have no family left." She said.

That was it, to the last word. Perfect. The message exact, identity confirmation complete.

"Do you have something for me?" Jake asked.

She dug underneath her fleece and pulled out a sealed manila envelope. "You are to treat this with the same scrutiny as his first message—eyes only."

"Got it." Jake understood. Burn after reading. "Do you work for him? Are we allowed to talk?"

She smiled. "Once we confirm identities we may talk freely. My name is Francesca, I'm an Emissary."

Emissary. There's that word again. "You work for Wiley too?" Jake asked.

"He told me you called him 'the toymaker' the first day you met."

"I did."

"So did I." Francesca said. "Wiley says we think alike but I doubt it, you're still a rookie."

"Rookie? How old are you?" Jake studied her face. Her green eyes were penetrating. She seemed tough. He motioned to her check. "Get that in the line of duty?"

She rubbed her fingers over her scar. "Not that it is any of your business, but it is a reminder of a run in I had with an irritable Irishman."

"Maybe Wiley's right, we are more alike than you think. I had a run in with one of those as well."

He had so many questions he wanted to ask. About her. About Wiley. But he didn't have time. "Are you working with me on this?"

"No." She smiled as she started to leave. "Wiley said you're on your own. Sink or swim. I think you'll be surprised at what you read. If you don't get yourself killed, I'll see you again…if not, it was nice meeting you."

Jake stared as she walked away. She never looked back, never turned around, and disappeared out of sight.

He opened the envelope and read the information twice, committing every detail to memory. He was indeed surprised at what the documents contained. Vital information he needed if he wanted to kill Khan. Information that neither Bentley nor Kaplan had access to. Information that would get him to Khan, but might get him killed doing it.

The element of danger just increased tenfold.

CHAPTER 56

K YLI WULLENWEBER AND her grandfather, Elmore Wiley landed in Brussels earlier in the day. She'd slept almost six hours on the flight back from Atlanta so she decided to go by the office to take care of her backlog of work. She'd been out of the office for several days, recovering from injuries caused by the explosion at the Louvre and attending the funeral of Jake's parents.

She stared at her computer monitor in a daze, not focusing on her work. The last few days were surreal. Jake had saved her life in Paris, killing the second terrorist before he detonated his suicide vest, a blast that would have killed her. Jake stayed with her at the hospital during her recovery until CIA Director Scott Bentley delivered the news of the tragic fire that took the lives of his parents.

She wanted to comfort Jake at the funeral, but the reality was she hadn't known him long enough. As a matter of fact, she barely knew him. So why did she feel such a strong connection to him? It wasn't just Paris, she felt the first pang when he left for Yemen with her grandfather. This was all new to her, these feelings. She'd had previous relationships, some she'd thought at the time were serious, but she'd never felt like this.

Come on Kyli, get a grip.

Jake still had issues with the tragic loss of his fiancée seven months ago. Wiley had explained the entire incident to her before Jake arrived in Belgium. At times, he'd seemed withdrawn, but it was always short lived. She knew Jake was interested in her. She could tell. When she stood close to him, he seemed nervous. She felt him shudder when she touched him. He needed time to cope with his past and she was willing to grant him as much time as he needed.

She shut down her computer, locked her desk, grabbed her coat, and walked to the elevator. Her backlog would have to wait until morning. Wiley had dropped her off at MEtech so she was without a car and needed a ride home.

When the elevator reached the lobby, Kyli walked over to the reception area. The office manager was shutting everything down for the day.

"Getting ready to lock up?" Kyli asked.

"Yes Dr. Kyli. You are the last to leave, as usual."

"I know it's a little out of your way, but would you mind taking me home? Mr. Wiley left me without a car."

"I don't mind at all." The woman made a few keyboard strokes. "Let me set all the alarms, and we'll be on our way." She paused. "Mind if I ask a personal question?"

"I don't mind, go ahead."

"Why do you refer to your grandfather as Mr. Wiley?" The woman typed in the last alarm sequence. The monitor started counting down. Sixty seconds to arming. "I mean we all know he's your grandfather. It's not a secret."

The two women walked through the door.

"He prefers to keep it formal unless we're alone. Most of the time it's out of habit."

Ten minutes later Kyli climbed out of the car, thanked the woman for the ride, and climbed the steps to her apartment. She inserted her key and unlocked the door. Inside she found her luggage exactly where her grandfather said it would be, on her bed, along with a note explaining that he would be out of town for the next few days on business. She smiled. *Yeah, spy business, I'm sure.*

She unzipped her bag and began to unpack. She noticed the curtains were drawn, not how she'd left them. She assumed her grandfather was being protective and closed them for her. She tossed her dirty clothes in the hamper and walked over to the window.

She grabbed the curtains with both hands and spread them apart. A reflection in the glass stared back at her. She spun around and saw a large, silver-haired man dressed in black standing in the middle of her bedroom pointing a gun at her.

She stared at his eyes.

One blue.

One brown.

She screamed.

CHAPTER 57

KAPLAN SHIFTED IN the passenger seat when Arlo Delgado walked through the main door of the hotel, on each arm a beautiful woman. A blonde and a brunette. The late afternoon sky was streaked with contrails from a day's worth of airline traffic overhead. Delgado was dressed in white linen pants, a blue floral print shirt, and a backpack. Both women wore white ribbon and lace tunics, bathing suits visible underneath. An oversized beach bag thrown over the shoulder of the brunette. The women wore flip-flops. It appeared the three were headed to the beach for the day. He studied the man through his binoculars, was he Khan…or not?

A taxi pulled in the circular entrance to the hotel and stopped, allowing Delgado and the women to climb inside. "Don't let them out of our sight." Kaplan said to Perez.

Kaplan jumped when something banged against the right rear door of Perez's car. The door opened, a man jumped inside. Kaplan had already drawn his gun and was twisting around when the man grabbed the barrel and shoved the gun into the car's seat.

"What the…?" Kaplan's anger ignited when he recognized the man. "Dammit, Jake. I ought to shoot you anyway. Where the hell have you been?"

"I told you. I had to go to the bathroom."

"Cut the bullshit, Jake. Where did you go?" Kaplan reiterated.

"I was in my room. The bathrooms at the café were in use."

"So you went out the window in the ladies room?"

"Seemed the quickest way." Jake said.

"And you were in your room?"

"I just said that. Hard of hearing, are you?"

"Gentlemen, please." Perez interrupted. "Delgado and the women, they're getting away."

"Follow them." Kaplan ordered. "You drive, I'll handle Jake. Like you said, looks like they're going to the beach."

"They're not getting away and they aren't going to the beach." Jake said.

"How do you know?" Kaplan asked.

"Drive to the middle finger pier at Puerto de San Sebastian." Jake said. "Khan's rented a boat for the evening. Apparently he likes taking women on sunset cruises. Not that I blame him, they are pretty hot."

"How do you know this?" Kaplan asked. "Wiley?"

"I have my ways, Gregg." Jake said. "Now stop wasting time with the interrogation and drive to the marina."

Kaplan stared at Jake in disbelief. Should he trust Jake? He knew Jake was up to something, but he couldn't figure out exactly what it was. If Jake was going to kill Khan then Khan would already be dead. Jake had the opportunity. Was Jake really in his room this whole time? He and Perez didn't check the rooms when they found Jake had escaped the café through the window so technically it was possible. Unlikely, but possible. Where else would Jake go? None of it made any sense to Kaplan.

"Well?" Perez said.

"Do like he said. Drive to the docks." He continued staring at Jake. "You better be right and you better not try anything outside of our orders. Bentley gave me instructions to keep you from killing Khan at all cost…including the use of deadly force."

"What purpose would that serve? If Khan is dead then how will we know what the U.S. target is?" Jake said. "And one more thing. When we get to the port and you've seen that I've been truthful, I'm taking charge of this operation."

✝✝✝

Delgado and the two women climbed out of the taxi and walked to the end of the finger pier where a water taxi was waiting to take them to the 40-foot cruiser Delgado had rented for the evening. The same cruiser he rented before with the same provisions. The boat wasn't due back until 10:00 a.m. the next morning. More than enough time to take the women for a long leisurely sunset cruise, feed them their last meal, perhaps indulge in carnal pleasures one last time, then send them both to the depths of the Capbreton Canyon in the Bay of Biscay where they will spend eternity inside the sediment over four thousand feet below the surface.

A small water taxi carried them to the vessel moored a few hundred yards out on the clear waters of the Bahia de la Concha. Delgado let the two women climb onboard first, tipped the water taxi driver, and climbed onboard pushing the bow of the small boat away from the cruiser with his foot. The water taxi motored back to the docks.

Delgado flipped the switch activating the blower, letting it run a few minutes while it exhaled any fumes that might have built up in the engine compartment prior to starting the engines. The women wasted no time removing their tunics and climbing onto the bow of the boat to catch the last of the sun's rays.

He stared at the women through the windshield of the cruiser; they were both beautiful. The brunette wore a pastel twist bandeau top; her bare shoulders glistened in the sun as she smoothed tanning oil across them. A silver Nautilus pendant hung from a chain and dipped precariously into her cleavage. Her pastel low-rise bottom matched her top. Her thick long hair was pulled back in a ponytail and draped down her back.

The blonde wore a ruby red thong bottom. Her tanned buttocks shimmered as the suns rays reflected off the water.

Draped around her waist was a gold triple belly-chain. She wore a matching ruby red goddess enhancer top although she needed no enhancing. Perfect in every way. He preferred blondes and would miss her the most.

He started the engines, released the mooring ball, slipped the engines into forward, and idled out of the bay.

†††

Jake argued with Kaplan all the way to the docks. As Perez parked the car, Jake pointed out Khan getting into a small water taxi with the two women. "Look, it's very simple. You two do as I say and we capture Khan. If you don't like my proposal, then we go our separate ways right now."

"What's your plan, swim after them?" Kaplan's face was flushed. "Who the hell do you think you are, coming in here with this take-control attitude?"

"Stay here then." Jake got out of the car. The two men followed him. "You see, when I found out about Khan renting the cruiser for the evening, I rented a twenty-two foot fishing boat equipped with fishing gear and tackle. I thought we'd just do a little fishing with Khan in sight at all times. And if we get the chance to take him at sea, even better."

"Really?" Kaplan's face softened and he looked calmer. "You did that already?"

"I did. And unlike Khan." He looked at Perez. "Or Delgado if you prefer, our boat is docked right here. All we have to do is jump in, fire it up, and go."

"Jake, I'm impressed. Since you're obviously more prepared than we are, it's your show…for now, anyway." Kaplan conceded. "But, if you try anything."

"Thanks for the vote of confidence." Jake pointed toward a gray fishing boat near the end of the outside finger pier. "Now let's roll."

"You going to tell me where you went and how you know all this?" Kaplan asked as they reached the boat.

Jake stepped close to Kaplan and put his arm on Kaplan's shoulder. "All in due time, my brother. All in due time."

CHAPTER 58

KHAN FELT THE last of the sun's warmth against his face. The blazing sun had almost reached the horizon when he cut the engines. He crawled up the steps and through the windshield door onto the bow where the women were laying on their towels. In his hands he held a bottle of red wine and three glasses.

As soon as the cruiser cleared the Bahia de la Concha, both women stripped off their bathing suit tops. Three miles from shore, they removed their bottoms and oiled their skin again. The *all-body* tan seemed important to the women. They were proud of their young, taunt bodies and showed no hesitation in shedding their clothes around Khan.

He liked it.

"Girls, a little toast." He poured three glasses and handed each woman a glass. "To our last night together in Spain, may it be a night we will remember forever."

"Here, here." The women said in unison as they clinked their glasses together.

It will certainly be a night I'll remember forever. He took a drink from his glass.

The women downed their glasses and Khan refilled them. He left the bottle with the women and retreated to the cabin where he retrieved a second bottle. He opened it, poured another glass for himself, then handed it to the women through the bow hatch. Yes, it would be another good night.

Earlier he'd noticed a small fishing boat on the horizon but it never got closer than a half a mile from his boat. He watched the men through his binoculars while they trolled along the walls of the Capbreton Canyon where the sea bottom drops thousands of feet. The men were drinking and laughing and never appeared to pay his boat any attention. Now the boat was a tiny speck in the distance. He was being paranoid. Maybe the man he'd spotted in town wasn't watching him. He wasn't one of the men on the fishing boat, Khan was sure.

Khan heated up the dinner he'd had catered for the trip by a five-star restaurant in Old Town. He set the table on the stern deck and called the women when it was ready. The sun had set and only a few of the brightest stars were beginning to light up the sky. Tiki lights were strung along the roof on the aft deck, soft music played in the background. A naked blonde and a naked brunette, both giggling, came down the stairs through the windshield door.

"Oooh, something smells good." The blonde said. She walked to Khan and kissed him hard. "I'm hungry."

The brunette slipped her tunic over her oil soaked naked body. "We need food so we'll have energy for later." She placed the second bottle of wine, half empty, on the table and tossed the empty bottle overboard.

Khan grabbed the already loaded plates from the galley and placed one in front of each woman. The blonde slipped on her tunic. Khan returned to the table with his plate and sat down. The three of them raised their glasses to the center of the table and made another toast. "Ladies, you're the most fun I've ever had." Khan said.

Both women giggled then the blonde spoke. "We decided to give you a special treat tonight, so save room for dessert."

† † †

Jake kept enough distance from the cruiser without losing sight of it. He'd made a couple of close passes for appearance sake so Khan could verify that the occupants of the boat were indeed fishermen out having a good time. As good fortune would have it, Perez caught a good-sized fish while they were near Khan's vessel. The three men shouted and yelled validating themselves as fishermen, high-fiving, and toasting with beer. He only hoped Khan was watching and his ruse had dispelled any suspicion the terrorist might have.

It seemed to work. Now, with only the stars aglow in the sky, Jake motored away from the cruiser with the fishing boat's lights on, then turned them off and maneuvered back to within a half-mile distance. He zoomed in with his night spotting scope. Khan was laughing and drinking and seemed more interested in the two naked women than in whether or not someone was tracking him. No better distraction than beautiful women.

A mistake Jake planned to capitalize on.

Jake noticed the cruiser had a large swim platform. That would make it easier to board the cruiser without alerting Khan.

"Now what?" Kaplan asked.

"We wait." Jake handed Kaplan the spotting scope. "We wait and watch."

"You're kidding, right?" Kaplan said. "Since when did patience become one of your virtues?"

"Even a blind squirrel finds an acorn every now and then."

"And now you're a bad philosopher too?"

"We could be out here a while." Perez said.

"Yes, we could. But this is our best chance to take Khan alive." Jake unzipped a duffle bag that had been tucked under the seats and pulled out night vision goggles.

"What else you got in there?" Kaplan asked.

"Three semi-automatic sniper rifles, ammo and some Snickers bars."

"You're kidding, right?" Kaplan asked.

Jake stared at Kaplan then looked at Perez and smiled. "Yeah, I'm kidding."

CHAPTER 59

TWO BOATS FLOATED aimlessly half a mile apart, bobbing up and down like a cork on a fishing line. As time passed the Cantabrian Sea grew choppy, waves slapping against the hull grew louder so Jake eased the smaller vessel further from the cruiser.

Khan and the two women had been in the cabin for over an hour. Tiki lamps still lit up the aft deck, their vivid colors played across the water like Christmas tree lights. Before the women went below deck with Khan, Jake watched them take turns dancing with the terrorist. Each one removed their tunics and taunted and teased the man.

After an hour and a half, Jake grew impatient. He was about to suggest they move closer to the cruiser when Khan appeared on deck alone, stumbling toward the stern as the boat pitched in the waves.

"Looks like we've got movement." Jake said.

Kaplan grabbed the spotting scope, Perez his binoculars.

"Who is it?" Kaplan asked.

"Khan. And he's alone." Jake watched through his night vision spotting scope.

Khan walked midway across the deck, turned around and returned to the helm. The tiki lamps went out and the aft deck plunged into darkness.

"I can't see anything." Kaplan said.

"Me either." Perez.

"I'll give you the play by play." Jake zoomed his scope in as close as it would get him. "He's digging around in the back for something. Wait, he pulled something out and dropped it on the swim platform."

"He's not going diving, is he?" Perez asked.

"What'd he pull out?" Kaplan.

"I can't tell, just two lumpy shadows on the swim platform. We're a long way away and the lack of clarity with this scope is making identification difficult. Whatever they are, they're small and compact. Too big for fins, definitely two, though."

The fishing boat slowly rotated parallel to the swells and the boat rocked side-to-side. "I can't see shit with the boat moving like this. Perez, fire up one engine and put the bow into the waves." Jake ordered.

Perez did as instructed and the boat stopped rocking.

Jake located the boat again with his goggles. "Khan just put something large on the platform, maybe a tank or something."

"You think he's going diving at night?" Kaplan asked. "Doesn't make sense."

"Unless." Jake drew out the word. "Unless he's leaving the women onboard and making for shore."

Perez laughed. "It's over forty kilometers to shore...twenty-five of your miles, he'd never make it."

"Maybe someone's picking him up. Maybe he's about to blow the boat up and kill the girls." Kaplan said.

"Nope. That's not it either." Jake stared intently through the spotting scope. "He just brought one of the women on deck and laid her across the transom. Now he's going back inside."

"What is he doing?" Kaplan.

"He's bringing out the other woman. He laid her down next to the first one. Neither one is moving." Jake lowered his scope. "He's disposing of the women. Fire up the other engine and get us over there ASAP. Full throttle. We take him now."

Jake reached into the duffle bag and pulled out a sniper rifle. Then another. Then another.

"You weren't kidding about the rifles." Kaplan grabbed one from Jake. "Where did you get these?"

"Don't ask." Jake studied Khan's movements on the back of the boat. "He's wrapping something around their legs. Son of a bitch, we're not going to make it. We're not going to make it."

Jake jumped when the rifle blasted a shot toward the cruiser. He saw Khan look in their direction after Kaplan fired. Khan moved at a frenzied pace. A splash and only one woman remained on the transom.

"Dammit." Jake shouted. "He dumped one. Explain it to him again, Gregg. Or better yet just kill him."

Kaplan fired another round. "I'll never hit anything with the boat moving like this."

Another splash. "Oh my God. They're both gone. The bastard killed them both." He looked at Perez. "How deep is it here?"

Perez fiddled with the depth gauge. "In feet, a little over four thousand. If he weighted them, they're gone. There's nothing we can do."

"Yes there is." Jake grabbed a rifle and took aim at the cruiser. "We can kill that bastard."

"No, Jake." Kaplan yelled over the roar of the two outboard motors. "Alive. We need Khan alive."

"Fine." Jake resolved. "We take him alive. Then we torture his ass to death."

CHAPTER 60

KHAN HEARD THE shot off the starboard side of the cruiser in the distance but saw nothing, just a black void across the dark sea. He'd tied the brunette's feet to the weight when he heard engines roar to life from the direction of the shot. He hoisted her over his shoulder and tossed her in the water. Next he pushed the weight overboard and the brunette disappeared into the black water, plunging her to the bottom of the deep-sea trench known as the Capbreton Canyon.

With renewed urgency, he shackled the blonde to the weight, tossed her into the water, and pushed the weight overboard. She sank out of sight as the weight dragged her down.

Another shot rang out from the right side of the cruiser; the roar of the unknown boat's engines grew louder in the darkness. He scrambled to the cabin, trying to keep his sea legs while the cruiser pitched and rocked, grabbed his automatic rifle, and returned to the deck. Stopping at the helm, he turned the ignition to each engine and they roared to life. He pushed the transmission levers into forward and jammed the throttles down. The cruiser lurched forward as the bow pitched upward with each new wave. He knew his initial bearing to San Sebastian so he made a sweeping left turn back toward shore. Now the oncoming craft was to port, a better angle for firing from the helm.

More gunshots, bright flashes in the distance, wood splintered down the side of the cruiser. He raised his rifle and unloaded fifty rapid-fire rounds at the mystery boat. He needed to get away; his craft could reach smooth water speeds in excess of sixty kilometers per hour but under these sea conditions, much less—maybe forty-five—if he was lucky. Probably not enough to outrun the smaller craft.

He turned on the GPS-coupled autopilot with his preloaded coordinates and activated it. Now he was hands-free to seek cover and engage the oncoming boat.

Another blast caused a side window on his boat to explode, glass shards rained down across the deck, two of them nicking his face. Close. But the muzzle flash also highlighted the enemy vessel, enough for him to know where to aim, and now he could identify the faint outline of the boat itself. It *was* the gray fishing boat from earlier in the day. He'd been duped. When he saw the men catch the big fish and start celebrating, he'd erroneously made the assumption they were just men fishing the lip of the canyon. As they trolled their craft away from him toward the horizon, he'd forgotten they existed.

How could he have been so stupid? Now he was in a firefight in the middle of the sea. It was three armed men in a smaller, more maneuverable boat against him.

He knelt down behind the seat, resting his rifle on the railing for as much stability as he could get in rough seas. The gray outline of the fishing boat skipping across the tops of the waves seemed ominous as it closed in on his craft but it also offered him a good target. He took careful aim and squeezed off more rounds. He heard the rounds make contact with the smaller boat, and then it swerved taking a parallel track across the water.

More muzzle flashes and he ducked. Holes ripped through the port side, splintered wood fragments flew across the deck. He could make out the silhouettes of the three men, two holding rifles, one piloting the boat. He fired another burst and all three men ducked out of sight. Right where he wanted them, he thought.

The first shadow to reappear was the man at the helm. Khan had a clear shot and he took it. The man fell out of sight and the boat veered away and slowed.

One down. Two to go.

Three more shots hit the back of the cruiser. With each flash, Khan saw the outline of the boat. It was coming directly from behind. Not an ideal angle. He ducked and crawled to the back transom. As he reached the stern, he raised the rifle and leveled it at the boat. For the first time, he noticed fishing rods in rod holders whipping on the back of the boat. The boat was twenty meters behind and gaining. He readied the rifle and fired, unloading round after round into the hull of the boat until the rifle clicked.

Empty.

He made his way to the helm, keeping his body low, grabbed his ammo, reloaded the rifle and readied it for firing. He still had plenty of ammo and a handgun stored below deck. He returned to the rear transom and looked out. The boat was gone.

Three shots rang out from the right side of the cruiser. One grazed his left shoulder. He'd been in gun battles before, but not on a boat in the middle of the sea. He suppressed the pain and aimed the rifle toward the fishing boat. He fired and both men ducked. One of the outboard engines on the fishing boat burst into flames. He kept firing. And screaming. Screaming at the infidels.

Two men in the boat rose up and fired, one right behind the other. Semi-automatics. Inferior weapons to his automatic yet effective with the cadence the two men used to return fire. He heard one of the fishing boat's engines groan and the boat lost speed. Both men turned toward the failing engine so he unleashed another hailstorm of bullets. The cruiser pulled away from the boat and within seconds was out of sight.

He got lucky and he knew it.

The cruiser made a correction to starboard—to the right—as programmed into the autopilot.

His backup plan. He'd eluded his pursuers. Eliminated the women.

Now for his escape.

CHAPTER 61

JAKE COULDN'T BELIEVE he'd just watched Khan send the two women into the depths of the sea. They were gone, with no chance of rescue. By now, they were already several hundred feet below the surface and, if they weren't dead before, they were now. Khan just killed two more innocent victims. He would pay for that act of cruelty.

As Perez steered the fishing boat, Kaplan took a shot at the cruiser in an attempt to disable the vessel, then Khan unleashed a barrage of bullets into the side of their boat. All three men ducked for cover. Perez steered a course parallel to Khan. With the cruiser to their right, Jake and Kaplan fired. A window shattered and Khan disappeared.

A moment later Khan reappeared and peppered their boat with a spray of bullets. Perez went down. He'd taken a round in his right temple and his lifeless body crumpled in the middle of the boat. As Perez's body fell, the boat turned hard left almost knocking Jake overboard. Jake grabbed the railing as he was being thrown over then pulled himself toward the helm as the boat swerved out of control.

Regaining control of the helm, Jake piloted the craft directly behind the cruiser. He used the hull for protection by keeping the bow high in the water. By the time Jake realized his mistake it was too late. Khan opened fire and bullets pierced through the bottom of the wooden hull allowing water to stream into the boat.

Jake steered right and accelerated alongside the cruiser while Kaplan fired into the cruiser's hull. He thought he saw Khan take a bullet, but he definitely heard him yelling despite the roar of the engines. Then Khan reappeared and fired. The fishing boat's left engine exploded from the barrage of bullets but Jake kept pushing the engine, grinding out every last bit of power. Khan couldn't get away. Khan had to be stopped.

He and Kaplan looked at each other and nodded. They lifted their guns over the railing and fired. They alternated shots with such a pace that it was almost as effective as an automatic weapon—right up until the left engine sputtered, coughed, and died.

Khan and the cruiser disappeared into the night.

Jake threw his rifle onto the deck of the fishing boat. "Shit, the son of a bitch got away."

Kaplan kept firing. Firing into the darkness.

For the first time since he had taken control of the helm, he looked down at Perez. It was a clean exit wound, in the right temple and out the left. Perez was dead. His blood drained toward the back of the boat, swirling into the ever-increasing amount of seawater seeping through the bullet holes that had penetrated the hull.

Kaplan yelled and threw his rifle onto the deck. "Now what?"

Jake had already turned the boat toward shore. "Back to San Sebastian. Let's hope the starboard engine holds, it doesn't sound good."

"How far to shore?"

"Twenty two miles. At this speed." Jake made the mental calculations. "If the engine holds up, probably an hour. More if we start losing power. But we have bigger problems than that." Jake pointed to the deck. Three inches of water was standing, loose items floated toward the stern. " The marine radio took a bullet and my cell phone is dead."

Kaplan pulled out his phone. "Mine too. What about Perez's phone?"

Jake searched through the dead man's pockets. He held up the phone and water dripped out. "Drowned. And if we don't plug a few leaks, we won't make shore before we sink."

† † †

Khan dropped to a sitting position on the deck while the autopilot guided him toward his backup escape route. Everything went awry because he had gotten sloppy. A mistake he won't make again. As the adrenaline from the shoot out wore off, the reality of the last few minutes sank in. His chest tightened, he couldn't breathe. *Relax. Relax.* He tried to use reason and calm himself down but nothing worked. He felt his pulse race. He forced himself to take long, slow breaths. He curled into the fetal position on the open deck. Khan considered himself brave, but he'd never been so close to death.

Khan didn't know how long he'd lain there. Did he pass out? When he mustered enough energy to climb back to the helm, he could see lights dotting the shoreline. He checked his GPS—twenty kilometers to go—he'd been out for over half the trip, twenty-eight kilometers had passed behind him already. At his current speed, he'd make Orio in thirty minutes.

† † †

Jake fought the growing swells as the crippled fishing boat made its way toward shore. It didn't take Jake long to figure out that every time the boat planed out, it took on water faster. He had to slow his speed so the boat would ride in bow-high thus extending how long it would take to reach shore. Kaplan was bailing water non-stop with the only bucket on board, a one-gallon bait bucket. The big problem was the boat took on almost a gallon by the time he could bail a gallon.

Over the course of the last thirty minutes, he and Kaplan had exchanged duties several times. Kaplan was bailing again.

The boat was sitting lower in the water. A rogue wave washed through the vessel adding another five inches of standing water.

"This is hopeless." Kaplan shouted. "I can't keep up with it any longer."

"Take the helm, I'll bail some more." Jake ordered. "We're still ten miles out."

"Forget it." Kaplan pointed at the engine. "We're not going to make it."

Jake followed Kaplan's finger. The starboard engine was smoking and leaving a trail of oil in the water. As the rpm's slowed, Jake added more throttle until it was all the way forward. Five minutes later, the motor spit its last breath and the boat was now at the mercy of the sea.

"We're still nine miles out, give or take." Jake said. "How far can you swim?"

"Tonight? Nine miles. Give or take."

Jake had more in-the-water experience than Kaplan and was mentally prepared for what was in store. A long, exhausting, and laborious swim in cold water. With water temperatures in the sixties, exhaustion time was two to seven hours. Cold water robs the body's heat 32 times faster than cold air. As the body's core temperature dropped, Jake knew what to expect. At 96.5 degrees, shivering begins. Amnesia at 94 degrees. Unconsciousness at 86 degrees and death at 79. Once they hit the water, they had to keep moving or drown.

Under normal circumstances, they would be motionless in the water, conserving energy while they waited to be rescued. But these weren't normal circumstances. They were nine miles out to sea, no one knew where they were, but most of all, they had to stop Khan.

Jake grabbed his duffle letting the water drain from the bag. He dug around and pulled out six Snickers bars. "Here. Start eating."

Kaplan grabbed the packs. "You really did have Snickers in there."

"Boy Scout motto. Be prepared. Eat it all, you're going to need all the energy you can muster."

The next five minutes were spent in total silence. The only sound was the waves slapping the sides of the sinking fishing boat. The two sat, ate, and rocked with the boat. Jake could see the apprehension in Kaplan's face as the boat sank lower and lower into the water.

"How good a swimmer are you?" Jake asked.

"At this point, what does it matter?" Kaplan stuffed his garbage in a side pocket of the console on the boat. "You're in charge, I'll just follow you."

"It's all about pacing." Jake wasn't good at giving words of encouragement, but he felt Kaplan needed to hear something positive. Jake was a strong swimmer, very strong, and as a child competed in swim tournaments with the school swim teams. "We'll take it slow and steady."

"Slow and steady. Roger that." Kaplan sat on the rail and unlaced his boots.

"What are you doing? Leave your boots on."

"But I can kick better without them."

"Trust me on this."

Kaplan laced up his boots. Jake grabbed two life jackets and tossed Kaplan one. Next he grabbed two flotation-approved seat cushions. He rummaged through the boat's compartments, found a flare gun and stuffed it, the weapons, and ammo into a wet bag then sealed it tight.

"Put the life vest on, get a good grip on the cushion, and let's go. Remember, keep the cushion underneath you for extra buoyancy. We'll need all the help we can get." Jake sat on the edge of the railing. "The water will be cold."

Kaplan sat next to Jake on the railing. "Tell me something I don't know."

Jake smiled. "You see, you did keep your sense of humor."

CHAPTER 62

DARKNESS STILL DOMINATED the night sky except for the twinkling of stars and galaxies millions of light years away. He studied the sky, doing his best to recognize some of the constellations he'd learned as he prepared for the final phase of his mission.

The engines droned on, rpms out of sync. Still no sign of dawn. The closer Khan got to shore, the rougher the seas, but the cruiser handled them without yielding. He'd feared the damage from the hailstorm of bullets might have compromised the vessel.

The cruiser's GPS guided him right to the mouth of the Ria del Orio where he had to negotiate a ninety degree left turn into the river's channel behind the rock mounds of the jetties. Walls of water crashed into the jetties as the relentless incoming tide pounded against the rocks. Once in the channel, however, the waters became tranquil. Smooth as glass. A welcome relief from the nonstop tossing of the waves over the last few hours.

He eased the damaged cruiser through the channel and behind the breakwater walls of the marina. Using only one engine to reduce the noise, he nosed the cruiser straight into the reserved slip, a prior arrangement he was glad he'd made. Thank Allah.

The marina's slips were on multi-fingered floating docks. By request, his slip was located at the end closest to the mouth of the breakwater, which unfortunately meant he had to walk past dozens of boats to exit the marina. Sound carried in marinas, he knew, and at 4:00 a.m. it would be easy to attract unwanted attention unless he was very quiet. The last thing he needed was a nosy boater to come up on deck to see who had just motored in so early in the morning. He must avoid detection.

Tying off the bow and stern with lines required him to jump off the boat on the floating finger piers. He gingerly stepped out, tied off the port stern then the port bowlines followed by the starboard side in reverse order, securing the lines taut to keep the cruiser secured in the middle of the slip. He didn't have the luxury of time. He needed to make a pass through the cabin and deck, removing all items that might tie him to the missing women, grab his personal articles, and leave. He anticipated he had two, maybe three hours at best, before his bullet-riddled hull attracted attention at the marina and law enforcement officials would be summoned to the scene. They would scour the cruiser from bow to stern looking for clues to indicate what had happened...and to whom.

Barefoot, Khan tiptoed down the floating dock carrying every identifying article he could find. He'd kept his room at the Hotel Maria Christina clean. Whenever he left, he carried everything he needed with him in a backpack just in case he had to make an unanticipated getaway. He could never be too careful. Khan followed the winding sidewalk and up the pedestrian ramp leading to the marina parking lot where his leased car and new identity waited underneath the autopista del Cantabrico bridge.

The carefully selected parking space was seldom used since it was located at the far end of the lot next to a metal garbage drum. He rifled through the articles disposing of everything that connected him to the past week. He opened the trunk and pulled out another backpack with all new credentials. He cleaned and bandaged his shoulder. It was a flesh wound and hadn't bled much. He threw everything old in the garbage drum, doused it with lighter fluid he'd stored in the trunk, and set the contents of the drum ablaze.

Arlo Delgado ceased to exist. He was now Esteban Menendez, astronomer at Planetario de Pamplona—the

Pamplona Planetarium—on his way to Madrid to catch a flight to the United States to attend an astronomy conference in Manhattan.

A backup plan...always have a backup plan.

† † †

Fuerte de Socoa
Saint-Jean-de-Luz, France

Exhausting was underestimating the intensity of the nine-mile swim to shore. It was grueling, backbreaking punishment. Fortunately, the incoming tide, large swells, and strong winds pushed them toward shore at a much faster pace than Jake expected. Kaplan had fallen behind a few times but Jake knew Kaplan's Special Forces mindset wouldn't allow him to quit. The water was cold and each time Kaplan lagged behind, he complained of the shivers. Jake mimicked a drill sergeant and Kaplan would snap out of it and start swimming at a faster pace.

Twice he thought he saw fishing boats heading out for a day of fishing, neither close enough to get a visual on the two men in the water. He'd tried using the remaining flares to grab their attention but they were duds. He'd been able to launch one flare before he and Kaplan jumped in the water but that was hours ago. Because of the roughness of the water, Jake imagined only the crustiest old salts would brave the brutal Cantabrian Sea.

It was daylight now and the sky was bright although a high overcast layer obscured the sun. The wind and tide were taking them well east of San Sebastian. At first he'd resisted but he knew the two of them couldn't overcome the current and wind so he allowed it to take them where it wanted. And where it wanted, he found out, was nearly thirty kilometers east of San Sebastian on the French shores of Saint-Jean-de-Luz.

Jake guessed they were about one kilometer from shore when he noticed the breakwaters protecting the small town. Waves slammed against the stone walls sending plumes of water skyward, at times nearly ten meters high, jetting up and over the walls. Fortunately, he thought, the current would place them west of the breakwaters at the foot of a stone building that resembled an ancient fort.

They were close, maybe forty meters from shore when Kaplan let go of his flotation cushion and swam ahead. "Jake. We made it."

At the same time, Jake felt his feet hit a rocky bottom. "Gregg, wait." He yelled.

A ten-foot wave swelled behind Jake, allowing him to ride the wave on his cushion like a body board shooting him past Kaplan by ten meters.

The same wave picked up Kaplan, spun him sideways and crashed him into the rocky bottom.

Jake stood in knee-high water. He looked back as Kaplan surfaced. Blood streamed down his face, a gash across the top of his forehead.

"I'm okay." Kaplan stammered.

Another wave, a more powerful wave, picked Kaplan up and hurled him into the tiered rock bottom.

"Gregg." Jake shouted. He took two steps forward when he caught a glimpse of Kaplan's life vest then it disappeared. Until the sea released its grip, Kaplan would remain under water.

Jake waded through the sea foam, reaching his hand into the water, grasping for any part of Kaplan. In his peripheral vision he saw another wave coming. His hand latched onto something, Kaplan's life vest. He grabbed it and ducked underwater allowing the wave to hammer over the top of him. He held on tight as the water dragged him and an unconscious Kaplan along the bottom.

As the water receded, he grabbed Kaplan's vest and pulled him toward shore—dry land only a few meters away—when another, smaller wave broke and pushed them closer. Jake fell on his haunches and felt the sharp rock dig into his leg. Adrenaline numbed the pain. He rose to his feet and leaned into his efforts to drag Kaplan to shore. Two feet of water, five meters to go.

He heard it before he saw it. Another mammoth wave bearing down across the rocky bottom with its sight set on them. Water rapidly receded underneath his feet as the wave sucked in as much as it could before spewing it out. With a thunderous crash the wave broke two meters in front of him. He pulled hard dragging Kaplan toward dry land. He stepped in a hole and fell. The wave cascaded over him driving Kaplan over him like a bulldozer through a pile of dirt.

His whole body ached. He was bruised and scraped. He stood, grabbed Kaplan's vest and pulled him up the rocky slope. For the first time, he noticed the unnatural position of Kaplan's leg.

He rolled Kaplan to his side and checked for breathing.

Kaplan coughed up water. "My leg. My leg."

"Your leg's broken. It looks bad." Jake said. "You got a good-sized knot on your head too."

"But we made it, right?"

"Yeah, buddy. We made it." Jake looked around. "I don't know where we are, but we made it. You stay here while I go get help."

"I'm sure as hell not going anyplace."

Jake looked at Kaplan's leg. "Right."

CHAPTER 63

JAKE SAT ACROSS the hospital café table from Lieutenant Travers Heuse of France's GIGN. The same man he'd met days before in Paris, wearing the same blue jeans, the same tweed jacket and with another smelly cigarette dangling from his lips while he spoke.

"So Khan got away?" Heuse asked.

"He did."

"Any idea where he's going this time?"

"No."

"This is getting to be like a bad habit. Me sitting with you after you let Khan get away...yet again."

"I don't like it either." Jake stared at the inch-long ash dangling from the end of Heuse's cigarette, waiting for gravity to pull it loose. "I'd like to go check on Gregg."

"He's still in surgery. They must put a temporary pin in his knee." Heuse pulled the cigarette from his mouth, tapped the long ash loose, letting it fall to the floor. "The break was not good. The doctor said Monsieur Kaplan will limp when he walks. The rocks are treacherous in the heavy surf, no?"

"It was just the highlight of a nine mile swim."

After he'd left Kaplan on the rocks, he'd climbed the sloping cliffs then scaled the rock wall surrounding the fort. Within minutes of locating a staff member, there were a dozen or more people lining up to rescue the crippled Kaplan from the rocky beach. Then they were transported to the hospital in Biarritz where he was treated for minor abrasions and a sprained ankle.

Kaplan wasn't so lucky. He'd suffered a concussion, three broken fingers on his left hand, and his left leg was broken at the knee. When Jake pulled him from the water, Kaplan's left leg made a twenty-degree bend at the knee in the wrong direction, out to the side. Jake knew months of physical therapy and rehabilitation lay ahead for Kaplan.

"Monsieur, you have been most troubling for the French government. Might I suggest you leave France and not return for a long while."

"And he'll be happy to oblige you, Lieutenant." Jake recognized the voice. DCI Scott Bentley. "As soon as Gregg is released, we'll be out of your hair."

"Admiral, Sir." Jake stood to his feet, and then he remembered Bentley's orders about protocol—or rather the lack of it—and discretion. Jake motioned with his hand. "Director Bentley, Lieutenant Travers Heuse." Why is Bentley always showing up unannounced?

Heuse looked nervous. He obviously knew who Bentley was from their dealings over the Paris debacle, but face-to-face with one of the most powerful men in the world, Heuse looked intimidated. Jake fought back a smile.

"Director?" Heuse said. "To what do I owe the privilege?"

Bentley ignored him. "Jake, go to Kaplan's room and wait for me. I'd like to have a moment alone with Lieutenant Heuse."

"Yes sir."

✝✝✝

The medics helped a sedated Kaplan into the CIA Challenger and prepped him for the flight to Washington, DC. One of Wiley's two Citation 750s sat next to it on the ramp just west of the main passenger terminal at the small French airport.

"Where's Mr. Wiley?" Jake asked.

"I don't know for sure, but I suspect El Paso." Bentley opened his leather portfolio briefcase and pulled out a large brown envelope. "He and I have a meeting tomorrow at The Greenbrier in West Virginia."

Jake stared at the envelope barely listening what Bentley was saying. "The Greenbrier. The hotel with the bunker?"

"One and the same. Elmore said he's sending you to New York?"

"So I've been told." Jake wondered if Bentley had information on Khan. The material he'd gotten from the redheaded woman named Francesca at Peine del Viento in San Sebastian was speculation but so far, Wiley had produced good intel. "New information on Khan?"

"No, Jake. I'm afraid not." Bentley sidestepped. Jake could tell he was uncomfortable. "You can read this on the plane." He held it out then pulled it back as Jake reached for it.

"What?"

"Listen, Jake. There are many things that have happened over the last few months that you thought was misfortune. But what's in this envelope removes many doubts." Bentley extended the envelope to Jake but held on to the end.

Jake's stomach tightened.

"You're going to be enraged. Now, more than ever, you'll need to focus. You must control your emotions. I think Wiley has done a great job with you. He says he's done nothing, but I see a difference." Bentley pointed toward the Challenger. "And so does Gregg. I don't know why you dumped Gregg in San Sebastian. I don't want to know. I suspected you struck out after Khan on your own. But obviously you had some other motive. What's in this envelope isn't about Khan, it's about you."

Bentley went silent.

He surmised the director was letting the words sink in...and they had. "What about me?"

"This is your past, your present, and might very well shape your future. It depends on what you do with it. How you handle it."

"Sir, you make it sound terrible."

"Jake, the contents of this envelope will enrage every cell in your body." Bentley let go of the envelope.

CHAPTER 64

IAN COLLINS CHECKED on the woman. She'd been drugged since they arrived at his villa on Ios. Same drug he'd used on the cheerleader in Dallas eight months ago. Same drug he'd used many times. It's greatest benefit; it kept her quiet and compliant.

He was setting a trap. A trap for a man he despised. The man who had remained just out of his reach. The man who'd ruined his life and his livelihood. His hatred consumed him. He could not rest until the man met the same demise as his parents.

He kept the woman in the basement of a two level building located at the highest point in the small harbor town. Down there she would never be heard. Eventually he would move her to another location, someplace a little more obscure. He could never be too careful.

By now, the man would know. The anger must be welling up inside him. He would be blinded by it. He would be able to think of only one thing. The same thing that had driven Collins for so long.

Revenge.

Collins had baited the hook. It wouldn't be long now, a few days at the most and the man would come looking for him. Looking to kill him. Blinded by hatred. And that would be his downfall. And in some sick way, Collins would be sad, for the man had proven to be a most formidable opponent. And even though they'd only squared off once, the man had gotten the upper hand and won the round. The match wasn't over yet, though.

No. The next round, the final round would be his victory.

The trap was set and waiting, and soon the man would walk into it.

Soon, Jake Pendleton would be dead.

† † †

Esteban Menendez checked into Manhattan's plush Excelsior Hotel, the site of the astronomer's conference to be held over the next two days. The highlight was the Hayden Planetarium inside the American Museum of Natural History, which was directly across the street. His tenth floor hotel room offered him a bird's eye view of the museum. He had no intention of attending the conference. He planned to strike fast—then disappear.

He checked his watch, 8:00 p.m., one hour until his contact would pick him up at the hotel entrance. He unpacked, putting his things away in the drawers, closet, and the bathroom. He wanted to give the appearance he had settled in for several nights.

It was his first time back in the United States in fifteen years, ever since he switched his allegiance to Islam and worked his way through the ranks of Al Qaeda. It shouldn't have been so easy to get into the inner circle of the terrorist organization, but it was. He'd successfully planned many attacks throughout the world and, though not his fault, had paid dearly for the unsuccessful ones.

This would be his final mission. All preparations were made and this attack was a lone wolf attack, the hardest for the infidel to defend against. His only problem, he didn't want to die. He knew from his brush with death at sea. Now, more than ever, he wanted to live.

This attack would happen. Al Qaeda would get its rightful credit and all appearances would be Hashim Khan died in the most atrocious act of suicide bombing the country had ever witnessed. Khan would fake his death and disappear. Disappear without a trace. Not the CIA. Not Al Qaeda. No one would find him.

Ever.

He'd been planning this attack for more than a year. No better place to get lost in a crowd than New York City. One more name change. One more identity alteration. One last temporary disguise. He'd arranged everything in advance, without stepping one foot in the country. His new credentials, all U.S. were sitting in a safety deposit box at a bank in Midtown Manhattan. He had the key to the box. For the right price, anything could be moved without fear of exposure. It's all about whom you know and how well you pay. Mostly, how well you pay.

Tonight he must work to get his plan ready. He would rig the explosive charges and ready them for activation. Tomorrow was a big day. Tomorrow the world would witness the most egregious terrorist attack in history. Hashim Khan would die in a blaze of glory.

Tomorrow he would become, once again, a citizen of the United States of America.

††††

Over the Atlantic Ocean
45,000 Feet

Jake sat in the leather chair with the unopened envelope Bentley had given him in his lap. It'd been there for over three hours. Part of him wanted to open it, but Bentley's last words were ominous.

Two days ago, or was it three? He was at his parents' funeral in Newnan. Kyli was by his side. It hadn't been that long since he'd seen her but he missed her. He missed her smile, her innocent, flirtatious teasing. The more he thought about her, the more he felt it. Maybe it wasn't so innocent. When this was over, after he'd killed Khan, he knew he would be returning to Belgium. Then he would see if there was anything there.

Wiley's emissary in San Sebastian had left him with intel on Khan and his next target. Intel he now knew was gathered by the Korean woman he found in Mustafa Bin Yasir's tent in Australia and by the gendarmerie in Trappes after they did a thorough search of the mosque. Now Jake knew the target city, New York, and the presumed occupation and alias. Astronomer, Esteban Menendez.

He placed the unopened envelope on the empty seat next to him and grabbed the laptop. Wiley spared no expense, wifi capability with close to high-speed internet on all his jets. He turned on the computer and launched the web browser. He started with a Google search "esteban+menendez." He clicked 'Search.' The search found nothing. Next he typed in "astronomy+new york." Bingo. A conference of astronomers from all over the globe started tomorrow in New York. A two-day gathering at The Excelsior Hotel in Manhattan of the GAF—Global Astronomy Federation.

Jake had a hunch there was a connection but what was Khan's target? Khan wanting to blow up a hundred aging astronomers was not what he'd expect from someone as evil and devious as Khan. There had to be more. Something else he wasn't seeing. Something he was missing. But what?

Jake grabbed the flight phone and placed a call to Langley. On the second ring, a familiar voice.

"George. Jake Pendleton. I need you to look something up for me."

"Jake, you know I can't do that without the director's authorization and the director won't arrive for another three or four hours."

"George, listen carefully." Jake's tone changed. "I'm playing a long shot here, but I might know how to track down Hashim Khan. To see if I'm right, all I need you to do is check the names on a hotel registry. I'll be in New York in a couple of hours, I don't have time to wait for Bentley…and neither do you."

Fontaine said nothing. Then, "Jake, I could lose my job if—"

"You won't lose your job, I promise. But you might save a lot of lives. Now hack into The Excelsior Hotel."

"Give me a minute or two."

Jake looked at the envelope again. Plain. Brown. 9 x 12. Thin, not much inside to contain such horrendous news.

"Okay, Jake. I'm in."

"Great, can you read me all the names of guests that start with 'M'?"

"Sure, you ready?"

"Ready."

"McCall, McCullough, Medici, Meliksetian…I think that's right, Mendelsen, Menendez, Mills, Mlyar, Montgomery, and Mudali. Any of those who you're looking for?"

"No, George. I'll keep trying though. Thanks."

"Wait. Jake, maybe who you're looking for is using a different name or a different hotel."

"Possibly. I was just playing a hunch. I was wrong. I'll have to keep searching…but just in case, will you be there for a while?"

"Bentley's got me here all night."

Jake hung up. Number six on the list. He hated lying to Fontaine but he didn't want him alerting Bentley who, in turn, would send his own assets after Khan. "I gotcha now, Khan."

He typed in the location of The Excelsior Hotel on Google Maps. Right next to Central Park. He did a search for events in Central Park but nothing out of the ordinary that would draw much interest came up. He studied the map. American Museum of Natural History was right across the street from The Excelsior. He did another search, typed in the museum name and astronomy and waited. Almost instantly the number one search grabbed his attention, a link to the New York Times. He clicked it.

The page loaded slower than he wanted. Before the page loaded he knew what Khan was planning, the headline said it all. And it could be the most heinous of all attacks. He stared in disbelief.

HAYDEN PLANETARIUM TO HOST OVER 4000 FROM CITY PUBLIC SCHOOLS.

Khan was planning to kill thousands of school kids. He read the article. The American Museum of Natural History was hosting *School Space Day* for public schools from all over New York City. And the biggest surprise of all, Senator Richard Boden, the Democrat from New York, would be keynote speaker for the event. He read on, and then he looked at his watch and the date. If he was right, he only had six hours before busloads of children from all over New York City filed into a potential disaster. And if Jake was successful, by the time the first busload arrived, Khan would be dead.

Jake leaned back in his seat, content in his plan to kill Khan. He grabbed the envelope and ripped open the seal, and let the contents slip into his hands. At first, he didn't understand what he was looking at, two newspaper articles and a photograph. He stared at the one on top, a newspaper clipping of Beth's obituary with a shamrock taped to it. The second, a newspaper article about the tragic fire that took the lives of his parents with two shamrocks taped to it.

"What the…?"

He flipped to the last sheet, a photo of him at his parents' funeral, just days ago, with a target symbol drawn on his face.

When the impact hit him, it hammered him. Every sinew in his body tightened. Waves of rage coursed through his veins. The airplane's cabin closed in on him. He began to sweat. His hands trembled.

Collins.

Ian Collins had killed Beth. The son of a bitch murdered Beth and his parents.

The bastard.

Bentley had forewarned him, and he was right. This was the worst thing he'd ever read. He felt his anger swell but this time it wasn't Laurence O'Rourke's face he saw, it was that blue-eyed, brown-eyed, streaked-haired Irishman, Ian Collins.

And Collins would have to pay. Jake would track Collins to the depths of Hell and back if he had to, but Collins would pay.

Collins would pay with his life.

Then another revelation hit him. He picked up the photo of him at his parents' funeral. The bastard was there at the cemetery. Watching. Watching him grieve. The sick bastard was there.

He grabbed the laptop with both hands and hurled it across the cabin where it smashed onto the galley floor. "You'll suffer, you son of a bitch."

That was the moment he felt it, cold and empty inside. Now, only one thing in life mattered.

Jake had to kill Collins—or die trying.

CHAPTER 65

ISABELLA HUNT PICKED Kaplan and Bentley up from the CIA hangar at the Dulles International Airport. She drove a white, non-descript Company van. Bentley's bodyguards assisted Kaplan to the back of the van. With the pin in Kaplan's leg and the cast preventing his knee from bending, a car would make transportation difficult. Bentley had urged Kaplan to check into a hospital, but Kaplan refused. He said he wanted to sleep in his own bed. He'd volunteered to come to Langley the next day for a full medical evaluation.

She'd spent the past two days regretting she didn't tell Kaplan everything. It had been bothering her for a long time. Despite what she'd said to Bentley, maybe Kaplan did have a right to know. But still, it was her problem and she'd always handled her own problems her own way. And always alone. She wasn't used to sharing or having others take the reins in her personal life.

Maybe she'd try to bring up the subject later with Kaplan.

Maybe.

Hunt pulled the van into the entry lane at CIA Headquarters allowing the guards to check all credentials. Even though the director was with them, certain security precautions and protocols were still required. After the van was scanned and identifications authenticated, the van was allowed entry onto the grounds of the spy agency. Hunt pulled to the underground entry and dropped off Bentley. His bodyguards exited the van first, checked the area then opened the door to the bulletproofed armored van. The two linebackers escorted the director into the HQ building as Isabella Hunt drove away.

"I'll be your chauffer for the next few days, Mr. Kaplan." She quipped. "May I take you somewhere? Perhaps the pool, I understand you enjoy swimming."

Kaplan played along. "No, Miss Hunt, I think I'd like to go home. And I'll probably require some assistance after we arrive. I hope that won't be a problem for you."

"No sir, Mr. Kaplan." She turned around and smiled. "I aim to please."

"How's your leg?" She asked.

"Hurts like a son of a bitch."

"Your fingers?"

"Not so bad. I've broken fingers before, just tape 'em up and go. Of course, now I have these fancy little splints. Not sure I like them."

"How's Jake?"

"He did all right. I can't figure him out though."

She turned the van onto Kaplan's street. "What do you mean?"

"He ditched us in Spain, then he reappeared like nothing had happened with a boat he'd rented and everything arranged. Like he knew ahead of time what Khan was doing. The CIA had no knowledge of any of it. And not only that, he had acquired weapons and ammo and provisions...if you can call candy bars provisions."

"Did you ask him about it?"

"Oh yeah. And I got some smart-ass reply. He avoided saying anything definitive. The thing is...if he hadn't done that, Khan would be long gone and we would probably be dead."

Hunt pulled into Kaplan's driveway. "But Khan is long gone. He got away and you two almost died."

"If it weren't for Jake, I would be dead right now. He's very resourceful. And something tells me he knows Khan's location and is already on his trail.

"You think?"

"I'm sure of it."

She got out and opened the door for Kaplan. He leaned on her as she walked with him to his front door. His keychain got caught in his finger splints and he dropped his keys on the front porch.

Hunt leaned down and grabbed them. "Allow me, sir."

She got the correct key on the second try. "Now, may I assist you to your room?"

"Maybe the couch for now." Kaplan hobbled toward a seven-foot leather couch in the middle of his den. "I think we have a few things to talk about, don't you."

"I don't know, Gregg. I don't want it to get complicated." In reality, she knew it was already complicated. What she really meant was she didn't want it to get more complicated. Her condition was her problem, why should she make it his as well? She should spare him the inevitable—it would be the right thing to do—but her heart wouldn't let her. She was selfish and she wanted this time with him, however brief it might be. What she knew was the right thing to do and what she wanted to do were raging a battle inside her consciousness. It wasn't fair. Just when she'd found someone, this happened. And her next decisions, she knew, would be the hardest she'd ever made.

CHAPTER 66

AT PRECISELY 7:00 A.M., Khan's contact picked him up in front of The Excelsior Hotel in a black sedan; there were hundreds of black sedans with tinted windows in the city so it went unnoticed.

"Is everything in place?" Khan slid to the middle of the back seat.

"Exactly as instructed." The driver merged into traffic then drove five blocks and pulled into an alley behind an abandoned West Side Manhattan building.

The sedan stopped at the rear entrance, a service door opened, the sedan drove in, and the door closed behind them.

The open expanse on the ground floor was lit only with suspension lights dangling from the ceiling and what little sunlight found its way inside. Parked to one side was a box truck disguised as catering truck. As instructed, Khan's contact had the three men load the truck prior to his arrival then leave. Time was running out, he still had several tasks to complete before he brought death to the infidels. At the top of his list, go to the bank to pick up his documents. He needed to be ready to disappear as Esteban Menendez and Hashim Khan at the same moment the museum came crashing down on top of four thousand infidel children.

In four hours those names would become history. One an alias for the other, which would become the most infamous of all. Forever the name Khan would hold a new connotation; it would rank with the likes of bin Laden, Hussein, and Hitler. The modern world would cringe at the sound of the name.

Hashim Khan.

He would get to watch history unfold from the quiet little Midwest town of Cottleville, Missouri just outside St. Louis. He would live a sedentary life of leisure as a retired computer programmer made wealthy from a buyout of his software company. The life he would live as a man known as Paul Scot Rayburn, which was a play on his true identity from years ago. Raymond Paul Scott from Bozeman, Montana.

He'd already purchased the 4300 square foot home nestled on a thirty-five acre spread. Using photos sent by a real estate agent, he'd had the entire estate furnished, ready for his arrival. Everything purchased under his new identity. Title to the property, paid for in cash by his legal representative, along with two new vehicles, a Ford F-250 pickup and a black BMW 750 Li sedan.

Khan planned to remain in New York City for two days, blending into obscurity, before flying to St. Louis where a limo would deliver him to his new life in Cottleville. He'd taken great measures to ensure he would be untraceable to his former life. He'd spent a lot of time and money to find the right broker for the job, a broker who made his living by discretion, and was rich from it. He was Khan's only loose end, he'd eventually eliminate.

He didn't know which would be worse, if Americans discovered he was still alive and captured him or Al Qaeda. The Americans would detain him, probably take him to Guantanamo Bay, subject him to grueling interrogation but in the end he was still an American. He'd be given his civil rights, injected into the judicial system where he'd be locked away in solitary confinement for decades while his lawyers battled his fate in the courts with appeal after appeal. In the end, he'd get the needle.

If Al Qaeda found him first, he would have to endure agonizing torture, as his skin was slowly peeled, layer-by-layer. They'd keep him alive as long as possible to maximize the pain. Days. Perhaps as long as a week. Then he would die the worst death imaginable. Anything the Americans did would pale in comparison to the sadistic manner he'd die at the hands of Al Qaeda.

Khan spent over an hour inspecting and verifying the supplies in the catering truck. Along with the catering order placed by the museum, Khan's special equipment was packaged as he requested.

He summoned his driver, "Take me to the bank."

Fifteen minutes later Khan slid out of the sedan and walked into the elaborate bank lobby. Marbled floors and mahogany furnishings adorned the exclusive global bank. Khan stood in line at a desk waiting for his turn while he scanned the lobby. Most people weren't paying attention to their surroundings; they were focused on concluding their banking business and getting on with their lives. Two women and one man sat in a waiting area; one woman fiddling with her iPhone, the other woman reading a magazine, and the man reading the *New York Times*. Nothing looked out of place to Khan.

Khan stepped up to the woman behind the desk and presented the key. She smiled and pressed a button on her phone, spoke softly to someone, and within twenty seconds Khan found himself being escorted to the safety deposit box vault. The man inserted a bank master key after Khan inserted his key. The man turned both keys simultaneously and the door to the box popped open. The man pulled out a long metal box, locked at one end. The man removed Khan's key, handed it to him, and pointed to a small room with a heavy red velvet curtain used for privacy.

"Please let me know if you need anything," the clerk said.

"Thank you." Khan took the key and the box into the small room, placed the box on the table and pulled the curtain closed. He opened the box. Inside the metal box was another box, locked with a five-digit combination, Khan's box. He dialed in the combination and opened the box. Everything was as he'd expected. Inside the smaller box, a sealed package. Khan broke the seal and removed the contents, exchanging it with the documentation and credentials of Esteban Menendez. When he walked out of the bank, he walked out as Paul Scot Rayburn. What was left of Esteban Menendez would remain in the vault for another twenty years until the lease ran out. By then, the world would have changed and the long-dead astronomer's credentials would be meaningless.

When Khan reentered the lobby, he noticed the two women were gone but the man was still there—still reading the *Times*. Khan exited the bank to his waiting black sedan.

† † †

Jake noticed the man when he walked in the bank's lobby and how different he looked from the man from Paris and the man that had shot at him on the Cantabrian Sea. Yet still, there was something familiar about him. His mannerism, his hunched shoulders. But when he saw the man's eyes he knew.

Khan.

Thanks to Isabella Hunt's knowledge of Hilal Shipping Company's banking practices, Wiley's information was correct, as usual, and now Jake had him. Khan was getting ready for a one-way trip to hell. Jake knew the most dangerous part was to ensure the threat against the museum and the children had been neutralized before he took Khan down. Had Khan already planted the device...or devices? And how did Khan plan to detonate? So many hanging questions made Jake realize the volatility of the situation.

He debated calling Bentley for reinforcements, but finally ruled it out. Time was not his ally. It was too late. Bentley would have assets close by but he could not risk them tipping off Khan. What if he failed? He couldn't live with that either. He formulated a plan to stop Khan. The terrorist had eluded him twice before, but not this time. Not again. Jake knew he had to stop the bombing then kill Khan...in that order.

If Khan recognized him, Jake knew it would be over before he could do anything about it. He had to remain undetected until he'd ascertained how Khan planned to blow up the museum. He'd been staking out the bank since the doors opened for business, studying every man that entered. He couldn't afford to let Khan get away. Khan wasn't the only master of disguise; Jake created his own illusion for the terrorist. The Yankees ball cap, glasses, oversized bowling shirt and cane didn't warrant a second glance.

He hadn't had to wait long before the man entered. After he tagged his target and was certain it was Khan, he waited. His plan was already in place. Jake had a taxi waiting outside, meter running.

Khan walked back through the lobby, glanced his way but failed to recognize him. The terrorist continued out of the bank where the black sedan was waiting.

While he waited in the lobby, Jake pretended to read the *New York Times*. After Khan left, he folded the paper, tucked it under his arm, and followed Khan onto the street.

Two vehicles back, Jake's taxi was waiting, meter running. He crawled into the back seat, and gave the cabbie instructions. The driver nodded and followed the black sedan for the next twenty blocks until it pulled into an alley and stopped. Jake jumped out and sent the taxi on its way. He had studied a map in the back seat of the taxi, following along as they drove. Khan stopped five blocks from the museum. His heart raced with anticipation. This had to be it.

CHAPTER 67

ISABELLA WATCHED HIS eyelids grow heavy. Gregg's pain medicine made him drowsy. He was resisting, she could tell.

"Gregg, go to sleep. We can talk later."

"But—"

"Shh." She placed her finger on his lips. "We'll talk later."

That was three hours ago and she still hadn't decided what to do. She was a woman and wanted to share this with him. In her mind she could see how the next few months would play out. His leg would heal; he would take time off work, and spend it all with her. They would travel and do all the things couples do, just in a compressed time frame. They would make love every day, taking in as much of each other as they could...

Then it would be over.

The morning after they had made love in Tripoli, it started. Early morning headaches and nausea. Two weeks later the headaches were followed by vomiting, which oddly seemed to make the headaches go away. From her symptoms she reasoned she was pregnant. How could she have been so stupid? There were so many other signs, but she just ignored them. Once, on her mission in Yemen, the headache was accompanied by blurry vision, which exacerbated the magnitude of the headache, followed by a brief loss of consciousness. She blew it off as fatigue and stress from the mission.

The symptoms were all there, and lurking somewhere in the back of her psyche she knew it was serious, yet she refused to acknowledge it. To be struck down by something she couldn't see and couldn't control was too frightening. So she ignored the symptoms, again and again, as if that would make it go away.

After the CT scan upon her return from Yemen, the doctors told her she had a cerebral aneurysm, fixable only by surgery. The silent killer could strike at a moments notice. Once ruptured, she'd be only minutes from death. But the recommended surgery was too risky—nearly a 75 % mortality rate.

It was at the suggestion of Elmore Wiley that she consult a physician in Belgium who had developed a new, less-risky surgical procedure to repair the aneurysm. Using a camera and robotic tools, the physician would go in through the veins and insert a surgical mesh or screen to permanently correct the aneurysm. His mortality rate was under 30 %. Still risky but much better odds. And with it, the possibility of getting her active lifestyle back.

No, she couldn't tell Kaplan. He would insist on putting his life on hold and staying by her side. It wouldn't be fair to him.

Their feelings for each other would have to languish and fade away. Isabella's eyes filled with tears. She gently kissed the sleeping Kaplan. Her heart ached for what it may never have.

†††

Khan signaled the driver to stop outside the rear entrance of the abandoned building. He got out of the sedan and waved the driver on. He pulled the keys from his jacket pocket, looked over his shoulder as he walked toward the small door next to the vehicle entrance he'd used earlier.

The building was empty except for the box truck. Across from the truck was a small office with a gym bag sitting on top of an old wooden desk. He walked into the office, unzipped the bag, and pulled out coveralls and a cap that matched the logo of the catering service along with a company identification badge, a fake driver's license, and cargo manifest.

He removed his jacket and pulled on the coveralls, zipping them within two inches of the top, just enough to show the white button down shirt underneath. He slipped the ID badge onto the left breast pocket, his driver's license into his pocket, grabbed the manifest, and walked out to the truck leaving his personal belongings in the bag on the desk.

Startled by a noise above him, he jumped. He looked up and saw birds flying around overhead. He opened the cargo door to the truck and climbed inside. He moved three boxes to the side to get to the five packages he was after, four small ones and one large one.

He opened each package and activated the device inside, closed and resealed them. It was time and he was ready. An hour from now he would take his place in history. An hour from now New York City's first responders would again be rushing to a major calamity with visions of September 11th filling their infidel minds as another New York City building collapsed to the ground killing its occupants.

But this time it would be worse.

Mothers and fathers would be unable to protect their children as the world watched them die.

Four thousand children.

Khan climbed into the truck, started the engine, used the remote to open the back door, and drove out. His next stop, the loading dock at the American Museum of Natural History.

†††

Jake exited the taxi and, as soon as the sedan dropped off Khan and drove away. He ran down the alley toward where the man disappeared. When Jake reached the door to the building he realized there were no windows on the ground level. He tried the door handle. Locked. He stepped back and looked up, a fire escape, but the ladder was fifty feet farther down the alley.

Khan was inside and Jake needed to find out what the terrorist was up to. He ran to the ladder and climbed to the second floor level. Next he walked down the rickety metal structure to the windows where Khan had disappeared. An anchor in the brick mortar gave way under Jake's weight and the platform moved banging against the side of the building. Startled birds flew from their nests inside the building, most escaping through broken windows.

Jake crouched then eased up to eye level with the windows. He saw Khan dressed in some sort of uniform walking toward a box truck with a catering service logo painted on the sides. Khan went inside the back of the truck, out of sight, then after a few minutes came back into view. Khan closed the cargo bay door, climbed into the driver's seat and started the engine.

Jake scanned the room from his lofty viewpoint for exits—only one—directly below him. He needed to get off the fire escape and into a position to follow the truck, even though he already knew where the truck was going. When Jake moved, the platform slipped again as a cement anchor broke free from the concrete wall. If the fire escape fell, he'd fall with it.

Desperately trying to stabilize his weight distribution on the platform, he slowed his steps. The metal door beneath him rolled up and he heard the catering truck accelerate toward the door. He was in plain view for Khan to see him.

He reached the end of the platform by the metal steps at the same time the truck exited the building. Jake lay prone on the platform until the truck turned the corner and drove out of sight. Sliding down the ladder by cupping his feet and hands around the outside of the rails allowed gravity to pull him to street level.

He recalled the envelope Bentley had given him. The clippings with the shamrocks. He let his anger build like a swelling wave gathering strength. He focused on his two targets. Connected only by his lust for revenge, he saw the faces of the two men he would kill.

Khan and Collins.

He sprinted out of the alley and onto the sidewalk as fast as he could toward the museum. Without breaking stride he darted across West 79th Street raising his hand at oncoming traffic to avoid being hit. Tires screeched and horns blared as Jake continued to run toward the museum.

When Jake rounded the corner, the catering truck was stuck in traffic two blocks ahead of him. He steadied his pace to keep equal distance from the truck. He couldn't risk being seen by Khan. He slowed his breathing and blended with the crowd of people on the sidewalk. After he killed Khan, he still had unfinished business with Ian Collins. He hated Khan but it was a personal vendetta against the Irishman. Collins had systematically destroyed everything around Jake.

An eye for an eye.

CHAPTER 68

KAPLAN WOKE UP in pain but with a clear head. With every heartbeat, every pulse of blood through his body, his leg throbbed.

"Isabella?" Kaplan called out.

No answer.

He'd slept several hours, he didn't know how long but it was much needed rest. It had been the early hours of the morning when they'd dropped Bentley and his bodyguards off at Langley and Isabella had driven him home.

While he slept, he dreamt of the night he and Isabella made love. The romantic atmosphere of the Mediterranean was overwhelming and perhaps underestimated. Doors to the balcony opened to their adobe style villa in Tripoli, the warm breezes from the blue sea washed over their naked bodies. The private balcony in the bedroom offered spectacular views as the full moon bounced beams across the water illuminating every curve on her dark skin. The balmy night turned steamy as they made love, exploring each other as new lovers do, passionately and longingly.

He'd battled his feelings for her the entire time she was in Yemen, a trip he didn't want her to take. He knew she'd been ill after that night in Tripoli. Food poisoning she'd tried to tell him. Stood to reason since he'd been plagued with stomach issues after that trip as well. Then she was gone, just like that, off to Yemen. He knew it was one of the many drawbacks of working for the Clandestine Service, no normal life. No time to foster personal relationships.

Somehow they could make it work. They could both resign and live comfortably on contract jobs. In effect, they would still be working for Bentley, just not on the United States Government payroll.

"Isabella?" Kaplan called out again.

Nothing.

He rolled off the couch using his crutches to hoist him onto his foot. He positioned them under his armpits and hobbled around the room.

"Isabella."

He turned toward the front door and saw the note folded tent style on the dining table. He figured she went back to Langley anticipating he would sleep longer and would return soon. But that wasn't what the letter read. Not even close. After he read her words, he felt light-headed. He grabbed a chair, letting his clutches fall to the ground, and plopped into the seat.

He let the note slip from his fingers. It floated to the floor.

He lowered his head.

Isabella Hunt was gone.

†††

Khan ground the gears to the truck every time he started to move forward. He'd always had trouble operating a stick shift and now he wished he'd learned the intricacies of using a clutch.

The light turned green, Khan pressed heavy on the accelerator, and then let go of the clutch. The truck bucked again and moved forward slowly gaining speed.

The next light was green, one block to go. He saw the service delivery entrance sign for the American Museum of Natural History located at the rear of the museum. He cleared the guard post with his identification then pulled past the delivery ramp. Now he had the challenge of backing it down the ramp, between two other trucks, and not smash into the concrete abutment at the bottom of the ramp.

A young man walked out on the loading dock and waved him directions, guiding him between the two trucks. Slow and steady. He didn't know how truck drivers negotiated hills of any kind. Three pedals and only two feet. He kept a foot on the brake and a foot on the gas, which worked fine until he stopped and the engine ground to a halt. The young man looked perturbed, hands propped on his hips and a frustrated look on his face.

Khan restarted the truck, feet on the clutch and the brake when he realized he could let gravity roll the truck down to the loading dock. Fortunately, he thought, he didn't have to worry about driving the truck out.

Khan had researched the architectural layout of the museum, specifically for structural integrity and located the four most critical load-bearing points under the museum. The destruction of those, coupled with the blast from the truck would ensure the collapse of the museum onto its own footprint.

After Khan opened the cargo door the young man approached with a hand truck, Khan pointed to the boxes. "Only the ones marked *AMNH* are yours. The rest are my next delivery."

"You're late."

The young man's sarcastic tone caused Khan to smile knowing soon the young man would be buried beneath tons of rubble.

"Where's the bathroom?" Khan asked.

The young man pointed. "Down that hallway on the left."

"Thanks."

Khan waited until the young man left with his first load and then reached into the smaller boxes, pulled out the devices and placed them in a large backpack. He headed for the sub-basement to install the explosives.

†††

Jake rounded the corner to the loading dock and saw Khan disappear into the building with a pack strapped on his back. He was winded but he knew what he had to do. He found his way from the ramp to the loading dock, then walked over and looked inside the back of Khan's truck.

"Hey, what the hell are you doing?" A voice said from behind him.

"Where did the driver of this truck go?"

"You can't be here. This is a secure area." The young man said.

"Look, kid. I don't have time for games. One more time, where is the driver of this truck?"

"I don't know. He asked about the bathroom. Now you have to leave or I'm calling security." The young man grabbed the radio from his belt. "Now leave." He used the antenna to point the way for Jake to get off the loading dock.

With as much force as he could muster, Jake's right fist punched forward, slamming into the young man's solar plexus rendering him unconscious. The radio flew from his hand as he flew backwards. Jake watched the young man slide across the smooth concrete. He grabbed the young man by the ankles and dragged him into the cargo bed of the truck and wedged him behind the large box.

He opened the small boxes. Empty. Next he opened the large box, the one concealing the young man from view and found what he needed. From his tradecraft training Jake knew the box contained enough explosives to nearly level the entire museum, but he noticed something else. Something he'd already found indicative of Khan's traits. Khan's overconfidence made him neglect a small detail. The explosives were not tamper resistant. It was a careless mistake.

Jake removed the cell phone and disabled the explosive by removing the blasting caps. Four small boxes. Four smaller explosives. Khan was probably installing the devices somewhere in the substructure of the building. Jake needed to find out where and fast.

He ran in the direction of the restrooms. When the young man was talking to him on the loading dock, he had noticed a fire evacuation plan mounted on the wall. It was a large diagram of the level he was on and smaller diagrams of all floors, including a subbasement below him. That would be where Khan would plant the explosives. He knew it as soon as he saw the diagram.

He had one last thing to do. He dug into his pocket and pulled out his own cell phone, punched in the secret number, the one only a select few people knew, and hit send.

He located the door to the basement and descended into the lowest level. It was musty and dank. The hum of machinery used to keep the museum operating drowned out most noise. Although not an architect, he had earned a degree in aerospace engineering at Annapolis and had worked on the structures team several times while employed by the National Transportation Safety Board. He scanned the large diagram next to the exit and located the four most probable structural points for Khan to use. Jake knew if Khan blew out the main supports, the superstructure of the museum could collapse. He ripped the diagram from the wall and set out to locate the bombs, or Khan, but preferably, both.

CHAPTER 69

THE AMERICAN MUSEUM of Natural History was a large complex consuming an entire city block. Its subbasement was a concrete maze of tunnels, pipes and wiring. Conduits ran along the ceilings linking miles of electrical wiring to a hub located in the central part of the basement. The hub was housed inside a thick wire mesh cage with "HIGH VOLTAGE" placards mounted around the outside. The lighting was dim, air stale, and it reeked of mold and mildew mixed with rodent feces and urine. To his good fortune, a utility ladder was propped against a wall next to the exit door.

He grabbed the ladder and, using stolen blueprints of the building, located the first two major support columns. He attached the explosive devices to the concrete masses using black duct tape. The blueprints indicated the basement was roughly 600 feet by 600 feet. The support columns he'd identified were spaced 400 feet apart. He strapped the devices as high as possible near the junction of the pillars and the concrete ceiling. With the load bearing supports gone, the center section of the museum would collapse, pulling the exterior walls with it. His plan was to blow a crater in the building's lowest level and allow gravity and failing structures weakened by the blast, to cave into the void, sucking down over four thousand men, women, and children into the bowels of New York City.

Artifact storage rooms lined the catacombs of concrete tunnels. Artifacts being recycled or damaged found their way into these rooms. Khan didn't care, soon enough it would all be one big pile of rubble.

He strapped the third bomb into its strategic spot when he heard a noise and realized for the first time he wasn't alone in the subbasement. Subconsciously he placed his hand on his weapon. Time was critical. Whoever had joined him down here was a potential threat. He was confident he hadn't been followed and was certain whoever was in this foul-smelling environment with him was probably museum maintenance. But he'd been sloppy in Spain, let his guard down, left details unchecked, and was almost killed. As soon as he attached the last explosive, he planned to track down the intruder and remove him.

He moved to the fourth and final support pillar and readied the device. He detected movement along a far wall; he placed the device on the floor and leveled his gun—a rat. As he turned back to retrieve the device from the floor he detected movement in his peripheral vision, something moving toward his head.

† † †

From where Jake stood he had three choices, straight ahead into the middle of the basement, the corridor to the left, or the corridor to the right. According to the diagram, the corridor in the middle led to an electrical service unit containing breakers and the emergency shutdown panels, not a likely choice for Khan. The corridors to the left and right circled the perimeter of the basement and led to each of the main load-bearing support pillars. Which direction did Khan go?

Jake needed to deactivate as many of the devices as possible before he confronted Khan. Any slipup and Khan could send out the signal and all the remaining devices would detonate. He had to get this right the first time.

Over the course of the past few days, Jake had noticed two important characteristics about Khan's habits; he always had a backup plan but, more important, he was predictable. Jake knew he could use that to his advantage to bring down the terrorist. Khan's thinking was undeveloped, how he'd made it this far amazed Jake.

He knew his dilemma, did Khan go left or right? He needed to retrace Khan's path disabling the devices along the way. Jake's training taught him that inherent human behavior was typically predictable. When the masses came to a crossroad, 75% had a tendency to turn to the right. Odds Jake bet his life on.

He ran two hundred feet down the corridor to the right, making a counter-clockwise sweep through the subbasement to locate and neutralize the explosive devices. He located the first support column. Nothing. He didn't know what to expect but he did expect to find something. He studied the column, tracing its lines from the floor to the black ceiling, noticing only that the top of the column appeared to be painted black. He started to move on when he realized it wasn't paint, it was tape—black tape.

He retrieved a Maglite from a pocket of his cargo pants. He used it to locate the device and realized his next obstacle—the bomb was out of reach. How did Khan get up there? Jake looked around for something to stand on but found nothing. Just below the tape were metal electrical conduits and below that cast iron plumbing pipes. He jumped, stretching his fingertips as high as they would go but the pipes remained out of reach.

Only one thing left to do; use the column as a one-step ladder to gain the extra height he needed to grab the pipe. He stepped back five paces and ran at the column, placing the soles of his boot three feet from the floor and launching himself upward. His right hand grasped the pipe. The pipe shifted, water trickled from the joints, but he held on tight. He swung his left hand up, grasped the pipe, and pulled himself upward until he could reach the tape.

Hanging from the pipe with his left hand, Jake used his right hand to dig into his pocket and grab his knife. He opened it with the flick of his thumb, and sliced the tape. He pulled the tape loose, removed the device, disarmed it, and dropped to the floor, leaving the inert explosive device dangling from the tape at the top of the support column.

The next column in his counter-clockwise pattern was nearly four hundred feet down the dank corridor. When he reached the column he spooked a rat from its bunker and it scurried out of sight down the next corridor. He repeated the same procedure as before. In quick succession, he had defused the second apparatus and was running another four hundred feet to the next column. He realized he might be getting close enough for Khan to hear him so he altered his gait in an attempt to make less noise when he ran.

When he reached the third column, he stopped and gazed down the adjoining corridor leading to the fourth support. Khan. He noticed Khan was just over half way down the corridor with a utility ladder in one hand, a roll of tape in the other, and a backpack slung over his shoulder. He had to move fast. He'd rendered three of Khan's bombs inoperative, one in the truck and two in the basement. Two left and then he'd worry about Khan.

Jake bolted up the third column and disarmed the device. He couldn't run straight at Khan down the last corridor, the terrorist would see him and have time to detonate the remaining device.

He recalled the diagram of the floor plan, corridors around the perimeter and halfway down each corridor was another tunnel that led toward the center electrical room. Backtracking two hundred feet to the center corridor, Jake spotted a crowbar on the floor near the turn. *Perfect.* Jake didn't want to shoot the terrorist until all the explosives were disabled. He picked it up and ran toward the center of the structure. Circling around the electrical service room, Jake found the adjacent corridor and ran to cut off Khan's route.

When he reached the last corridor, he stopped and peeked around the corner. Khan was kneeling over his backpack obviously rigging the final device. Jake moved further down the corridor toward Khan, ducking in every nook and cranny along the way to conceal his approach. He was thirty feet from Khan when he felt something on his leg. A rat. There were several more around him. He instinctively swatted the rat scaring them away—in Khan's direction.

Jake saw Khan jump at the sound of the rats scurrying, raised his pistol in the direction of the rats, and then lowered it when he realized it wasn't a threat. Jake was close enough and had his chance. Khan was distracted. Approaching from behind Khan and slightly to his right, Jake raised the crowbar and took a baseball bat swing at him—head high.

Khan must have seen him because he ducked, rolled ten feet away, leveled his pistol, and took a shot in Jake's direction. Jake felt the bullet whiz past his head. He hurled the crowbar at the terrorist. The metal shaft struck Khan in his right arm forcing the gun from his hand and knocking him to the ground. Khan screamed and grabbed his arm. Jake saw blood ooze through the man's fingers.

Jake dove for the device and in seconds had deactivated the detonator.

Five down.

Now for Khan.

But Khan was gone and so was his gun.

CHAPTER 70

KHAN DUCKED WHEN he detected movement too large to be rats out of the corner of his eye. Someone was threatening his mission. His first thought was to kill the intruder but the man with the wavy blond hair moved with lightning speed. He looked familiar. Was he the man in the car in Trappes—the one he saw as he shuttled his martyrs to their deaths? And then he made another connection as well. He was looking at one of the men from the fishing boat in Spain, the man giving the orders.

Khan rolled with his pistol leveled and fired but the shot missed, ricocheting off the concrete wall. As he went to fire again a black metal rod struck his arm knocking the gun from his hand.

Pain shot through his arm as he felt the metal tip rip through his skin at his elbow. He heard bone crack. His arm became warm as blood soaked through his sleeve and ran down his arm. He clutched his elbow with his left hand, blood ran through his fingers.

The blond man dove for the bomb. Khan grabbed his gun and ran toward the exit. He knew there were three smaller devices and one large one still in the truck. All four were armed and once he'd cleared the block he'd detonate them. It would still have the same cataclysmic effect. The museum would crash to the ground killing thousands.

He ran fast, ignoring the pain in his arm. This madman had been tracking him from France to Spain to New York. He had underestimated him. Khan needed to escape, go underground, and not resurface for a long time…years perhaps. It would be more difficult now; he was injured and needed medical treatment. They would ask too many questions at a hospital or clinic. Too many eyebrows would be raised. He couldn't afford the risk. He'd have to alter his plans yet again.

He heard footsteps, running footsteps, from behind and moving toward him fast. He turned and saw the madman gaining on him. He increased his pace as much as he could. One hundred feet to the exit. He kept running. Fifty feet to go when the madman shouted. He ignored him and kept running.

Khan heard the pop and felt the stabbing pain in his leg at the same time. It felt like a fiery hot poker had been thrust into his leg, deep into his thigh. He fell to the concrete with a busted right arm and a bullet in his left leg. His hope for escape was gone.

† † †

Jake's anger drove him. As soon as he'd disabled the fifth and final bomb, his anger kicked the door open and demanded revenge. *It's my turn now.* He drew his Glock and pursued his quarry. He was faster than Khan, much faster, and gained on him with every stride he took. The man was fifty feet in front of him.

He stopped, leveled his gun, and fired. Khan dropped to the ground clutching his leg. Jake started walking toward the terrorist when Khan raised his pistol at Jake.

Jake dove to the ground and saw the muzzle flash. The bullet pinged against a water boiler behind him. He couldn't let Khan leave the basement. Jake raised the muzzle of his gun toward the ceiling and shot out the lights around him plunging his corner into darkness. Now he could see Khan, but Khan couldn't see him. He hoped.

Khan pulled himself away from the exit side of the corridor, dragging his injured leg behind, and took refuge in back of a large air handler unit. Jake made his move toward the exit, shooting out lights each time he moved. Every time

Khan appeared, Jake drove him back into hiding with bullets.

"Give it up, Khan." Jake shouted. "There's no way out except through me."

"Who are you?" Khan shouted.

"Doesn't matter. Your only chance to live is to give yourself up."

"Were you the one in France? And in Trappes?"

"Yes."

"Spain? On the boat?"

"All of the above."

"How did you track me? I have to know."

"You're sloppy Khan. You leave a trail everywhere you go and before long, all the breadcrumbs lead to you."

"If I come out, are you going to kill me?"

As much as he wanted Khan dead—for Wiley, for himself—he felt he owed it to Bentley to give the terrorist at least one chance to surrender. If Khan refused, then Jake would kill him. "That depends on you." Jake said.

"What do you mean?"

"If you throw out your weapons and do as I say, I'll take you in alive. My guess is you'll end up at Gitmo for a long time."

Jake heard shuffling and suspected the injured man decided to give himself up. Not like an al Qaeda terrorist. But Khan was an American after all, a mastermind of evil but with an apparent desire to live.

Movement.

Khan had somehow managed to pull himself to his feet and hobbled into the corridor. Jake aimed his Glock dead center on Khan's forehead as the man gradually emerged. Soon, Khan was in full view. He'd ripped his sleeve and made a makeshift tourniquet on his leg. His arm bloody, he walked and looked like a zombie. If he so much as flinched, Jake would send him to the land of the dead.

Jake noticed the cell phone in Khan's hand. "It won't work, Khan. I've disabled your bombs."

"Perhaps there is one you don't know about."

"You're a failure, Khan."

"It is you who has failed. Say goodbye."

Khan pressed the button.

CHAPTER 71

NOTHING HAPPENED. HE checked the signal strength; even in the subbasement he had three bars *and* 3G. Then he heard ringing. The cell phones. And no explosion.

"But how could you know?" Khan asked.

"I didn't. But I found the box in the truck and disabled it. Your overconfidence made you overlook one important detail; the bomb wasn't tamper resistant. Easy to defuse. You'll be remembered as a failure, an embarrassment to al Qaeda. You're no terrorist; you're just a pathetic excuse of a human being who believed killing children would give him martyrdom."

Khan flushed, body temperature rose, face turned beet red. Was the infidel right? Was he a failure? Or was this man that good? He had failed this mission, he saw that now. He had one last chance to make a name for himself—to save face—one final chance for al Qaeda to be heard.

"Give it up, Khan?" The man pointed to the exit. "Any second now, a dozen men will come through that door. When they do, you're a dead man."

Khan stepped back until he was even with the exit. "You're bluffing."

"Am I?" The man said. "I called for reinforcements before I followed you down here. The museum has been evacuated, Khan. Your plan failed."

Pounding sounds of footsteps filled the stairwell behind the exit door and Khan knew the madman spoke the truth.

The perpendicular corridor leading to the electrical service room was directly across from the exit and Khan was standing in the middle of the corridor. He feared death, but now he felt trapped. To give up was to admit failure. He ripped open his coveralls and revealed an explosive vest and grabbed a dead man's switch from his pocket.

With a click, it was armed.

Khan held up his arm. "Then you will die with me."

✝✝✝

Jake was squeezing the trigger, ready to blow the man to Hell, when he saw the suicide vest. He couldn't shoot now. The only thing stopping the detonator from activating was the pressure from Khan's finger. If Jake took the shot, Khan's finger would relax, the spring-activated switch would push forward triggering the detonator, and the vest would explode. At a distance of thirty feet, Jake might survive the blast, but the men coming down the stairwell would die.

A suicide vest could do a great deal of damage to people, especially when it's been loaded with shrapnel…nails, pellets, glass. But what it couldn't do was bring down the museum and, based on the small size of the vest, wouldn't do much structural damage to the basement. Jake had already ensured the safety of those above, what few remained. He played it through in his mind, after his phone call, the entire area would have been cordoned off and everyone—men, women, and the thousands of children—herded far enough into Central Park to remain clear of danger in the event Jake failed to stop Khan.

But now he had to figure out how to get out of the subbasement alive. The pendulum had swung and Khan held the upper hand.

For the moment.

Jake didn't know what type of squad was on the other side of the exit door. It could be New York City beat cops, or a SWAT team. He hoped it was a team trained to contain this type of situation. But, whoever it was, he was glad they were here. It gave him the distraction he needed. Khan was preoccupied with whoever was in the stairwell and retreated toward the center of the basement.

Jake took advantage of the situation and backtracked through the dark corridors, working his way through a maze of boilers, water tanks, air handlers, generators, and diesel fuel tanks until he spotted Khan sitting against the wire cage of the electrical service area. Khan chanted something Jake couldn't understand, but he knew its meaning. Not a good sign. Jake realized Khan had resigned to die.

Khan held the dead-man's switch in his injured right hand and his pistol in his left hand resting it on his injured leg. Jake aimed his weapon at Khan. This time the terrorist could not get away. A penance had to be paid for all the lives he took. The people in Paris. The two young women he dumped into the sea. Khan wasn't just ruthless, he was evil.

The squad stormed through the exit door.

All hell broke loose.

CHAPTER 72

IT TOOK THREE hours for the rescue workers to find Jake. He was pinned beneath a water storage tank that was blown off its supports from the shock wave of the blast. He was alive. Considering how close he was to Khan when the New York City SWAT team unleashed a hailstorm of bullets, he was lucky.

After the first barrage of bullets, he dove to the basement floor behind a double-wall of solid concrete blocks used to support the water tank. The blast was almost immediate, toppling the tank and wedging him between it and the wall...unconscious from the concussion wave.

Two SWAT members were killed from head trauma, the rest suffered the same injury as Jake, temporary deafness and disorientation. The same effect as a flash-bang in confined quarters.

While he lay there waiting for the first responders to dig through the rubble, locate him, move the tank, and pull him free, he could think of only one thing.

Ian Collins.

Unfinished business.

Jake had gone rogue and left Bentley out of the loop until the last minute. *Off the reservation* as he heard it described many times. His phone call wasn't well received by Bentley. The director said nothing except he'd handle the evacuation. The tone in his voice relayed his dismay with the situation. But as Wiley reminded him the last time they spoke, Jake didn't take orders from Bentley.

He'd successfully completed the mission, but by whose measure? Bentley's mission was to capture Khan and put him through rigorous interrogation in an attempt to get at the terrorists further up the al Qaeda food chain. Wiley wanted Khan dead, his note to Jake was clear. Wiley told Jake on the first day that the number one priority in his business was to meet the objective. The how didn't matter.

Jake had followed Wiley's instructions. Even though he didn't technically *kill* him, Khan was dead—a failed martyr on a failed mission. But he still felt an allegiance to the CIA director. Bentley had been the one who had taken him under his wing. Not once, but twice. The first time while Jake was a naval intelligence officer on the USS Mount Whitney. Bentley had recruited Jake to work directly under him at the Pentagon. The second time just seven months ago when Jake's world turned upside down in Savannah, Bentley recruited him to go after the man he thought, they all thought, had killed Beth. Now the truth had been revealed, Ian Collins was the killer. And Ian Collins would pay with his life because now it was personal.

The New York City Fire Department used a pneumatic jack to push the tank away from the concrete wall and pulled Jake to freedom. The dust from the explosion had caked his clothes and face with a powder white dust. He'd cupped his undershirt over his nose to help filter the air until the sediment settled to the basement floor. FDNY tried to put him on a gurney but Jake refused.

One of the firemen told Jake they didn't know he was in the basement until Senator Richard Boden sent them back down with instructions not to come back up until they'd found him. Seems Boden might have had a change of heart since the funeral.

Smacking his gum, Boden greeted Jake on the loading dock while armies of reporters from the media waited outside for them to appear.

"I'm not going to do it." Jake wiped the dirt from around his face. "I work in the Clandestine Service. The last thing Director Bentley needs is for you to make a public spectacle and expose the identity of one of his operatives."

Boden frowned. "Mr. Pendleton, you're not even supposed to be in this country. As a matter of fact, this wasn't even CIA jurisdiction. So you have a choice to make. One, you can walk outside with me and become a real American hero—"

"Or what, you'll have your goons haul me off?"

"Or two, you can kiss your CIA job goodbye. As a matter of fact, I'll make it my personal business to make sure you never work in this country again."

Jake saw through the senator's ulterior motive. He didn't have a change of heart, it was election year and the voters were only days away from going to the polls. A feather in his cap at this eleventh hour would cinch his reelection.

"Senator? You know, the way I see it is like this. I'm going to walk out of here and you're not going to do a damn thing about it. Because if you so much as think about it, I will go to the press and explain how if you had had your way, I would be in jail and the museum would be in total ruin, thousands of innocent children and one dumbass senator would be dead. Now get the hell out of my way or you can kiss your reelection goodbye."

CHAPTER 73

The Greenbrier Hotel
White Sulphur Springs, West Virginia

JAKE STUDIED THE historic landmark as the limousine approached the north entrance. Bentley had casually mentioned he and Wiley would be here for a meeting, which was good, Jake wanted to talk to both men.

This was his first visit to The Greenbrier, but he was familiar with the resort's history, as were all Annapolis graduates. Beneath the resort was a massive underground bunker that, during the Cold War, was meant to serve as an emergency shelter for the United States Congress. Although never used for that purpose, the bunker was readied, maintained, and staffed for more than thirty years for the government in the event of a national or international crisis. If that had occurred, the property would have been conveyed to government use and would've become the emergency location for the legislative branch thus allowing the United States government to continue uninterrupted operation.

After the explosion at the American Museum of Natural History in New York and his subsequent fallout with Senator Boden, Jake refused to be treated. He had taken a taxi back to the airport where, once onboard Wiley's Citation, he cleaned up and changed clothes while the flight crew flew him on the one-hour hop from New York to the Greenbrier Valley Airport in Lewisburg, West Virginia.

When the Citation decelerated on the seven thousand foot runway, Jake noticed a ramp overcrowded with business jets of all types. Falcons. Challengers. Sabreliners.

Citations. Bentley's Challenger jet and Wiley's personal Citation 750 were among the more than two dozen stylish business jets. The flight crew parked the Citation next to Wiley's other jet. Jake planned to arrange transportation to The Greenbrier, but the chief pilot for Wiley's personal aircraft yelled out to Jake. "Mr. Wiley sent a limo to pick you up and take you to The Greenbrier. You're to go to the north entrance and he'll meet you there in thirty minutes."

"He thinks of everything." *How the hell did the old man know I was coming?*

Twenty-five minutes later the black limousine pulled up to the north entrance of The Greenbrier. Nestled in a valley in the Allegheny Mountains, the Greenbrier was a lavish resort. Jake couldn't help but notice a similarity in architectural style between the White House in Washington, DC and The Greenbrier Hotel except the Greenbrier was several times larger. As the limo pulled under the portico, Jake scanned the manicured lawn, the groomed hedges, and blooming flowers. Even in early November they were meticulously nurtured.

Jake crawled out of the limo and was greeted by the hotel staff. "Are you Mr. Pendleton?" The man asked.

"I am."

"Right this way, please. Misters Wiley and Bentley are waiting for you in the lobby."

For the last two hours, Jake had thought about what he wanted to say to both men but was still unsure how to broach the topics certain to be considered classified. But he had to know the truth and the only way to find out was to ask. Point blank.

"I'll follow you." Jake said to the man.

He followed the man through an open room and into a large lobby.

The man pointed to the far wall. "There they are, sir."

"Thank you."

Bentley and Wiley stood side-by-side underneath an oversized archway embellished in green and white striped wallpaper. The furnishings were bathed in vivid colors; coral, green, pink, turquoise, and lavender with textures ranging from velvet to leather. Jake walked across the black and white marble checkerboard floor until he reached the men.

Wiley smiled while Bentley showed no emotion. Each man wore a jacket and tie; Bentley had his signature leather portfolio briefcase tucked under his arm and Wiley a black nylon briefcase draped over his shoulder. Jake could tell neither welcomed his arrival at The Greenbrier.

Uninvited.

Wiley stuck out his hand. "Congratulations, Jake. A job well done. You stopped the attack and killed Khan. You saved a lot of lives today."

"I didn't kill Khan, he blew himself up." Jake expected a response from Bentley, but got nothing.

Wiley continued. "I'm a little surprised to see you here. How did you know where to find me?"

Jake focused his gaze on Bentley. "Yesterday the Director mentioned he had a meeting with you here. I have a question that needs answering and it is important both of you are together to hear it."

Wiley looked at Bentley. "Okay, Jake. What is it?"

Jake fished around in his back pocket and pulled out the newspaper clippings Bentley had given him. "I have some questions about these." He handed them to Wiley.

"This is not the place." Bentley said.

"The three of us need to take a walk." Wiley signaled for the two men to follow him. "Now."

Jake saw the look on Bentley's face turn to apprehension. He followed Wiley and Bentley who were walking shoulder-to-shoulder whispering. Whispering and arguing. They walked through the lobby and out a rear door into the gardens and onto a red-bricked path. Wiley asked

Jake to fall back. Wiley passed the news clipping to Bentley, who held them for a few seconds then passed them back to Wiley. Bentley shook his head. They whispered some more. Jake strained to hear but the men kept their voices too low.

He followed them to a small pavilion called The Spring House, nestled on the rear lawn. The twelve-column white structure held a copper dome covered in patina. Red, white, and blue swag banners drooped between each post. Under the dome, a spiral brick floor with a black rail fence surrounding a sulphur spring.

As he watched the two older men with the manicured lawn in the background, he noticed something familiar. Déjà vu. Bentley and the old man, face-to-face, in hushed conversation. He'd seen this before and now he knew when. And where.

Wiley motioned for Jake to join them.

The three men stood silent around the rail. Jake could tell they were pondering what to say to him. He'd asked a question they didn't expect and weren't in agreement on how to proceed.

Wiley spoke first. "Jake, you remember the day we met in Texas? When Bentley brought you to me?"

"Yes."

"Do you recall asking me about my emissaries, I told you that soon you would see it was a lot more?"

Jake nodded.

"Maybe that time has come? But Scott has a couple of things he wants to ask you first."

Jake looked at Bentley.

Bentley's piercing look didn't faze Jake. He stood resolute. This time he wouldn't back down.

"Jake, I only want to know two things. Why didn't you call me sooner? And did you really call Senator Boden a dumbass?"

Jake looked at Bentley then glanced at Wiley. Wiley gave a slight nod.

"Do you remember the last thing you said to me before you left me in El Paso?" Jake looked at Bentley.

"Refresh my memory." Bentley said.

"You said until you tell me otherwise, I take orders from Mr. Wiley. You never said otherwise, so I tailed Khan and followed him into the museum. If I'd called for reinforcements sooner, Khan might have been tipped off before I had a chance to defuse the bombs. So, while Khan was underground and had no clue what was going on above him, I felt it was in our collective best interests to handle the situation on my own. If your storm troopers would have invaded the place too soon—"

Bentley cut him off. "And Boden?"

"The idiot wanted a three-ring media circus and I refused. How many times have you told me that clandestine means executed in secrecy? Then he threatened to have me fired, picked up by the FBI, so I explained it to him the only way he could understand. Then I left."

Jake took a deep breath and continued.

"I want to know about Beth. I want to know about my parents." Jake took the article from Wiley's hands. He turned to Bentley. "And I want to know about Ian Collins."

Bentley raised his hand. "Easy Jake. You're a very smart man with uncanny intuition. There is much more involved than what you see on the surface. And that's one reason I put you with E. W. Your potential would be better served outside the constraints of the federal government. The Clandestine Service is not the place for your talents, which is why Mr. Wiley has been training you. Testing you on many levels, cognitive skills beyond any tradecraft skill you could learn with us. He's been grooming you to work for him, seeing if you have what it takes to become one of his emissaries."

"What the hell is this with this emissary thing?" Jake could feel the tone of the conversation changing. "Why me? What about Gregg? Or Isabella?"

Bentley glanced away. "Ms Hunt is no longer with the Agency."

"What?"

"She resigned yesterday, but I tore up her resignation letter. Told her she could take a leave of absence for now in case she changes her mind. She's a good agent and I don't want to lose her."

"Why did she leave?"

"Jake, you know I'm not at liberty to discuss her personal details."

"Does Gregg know?" Jake asked.

Bentley said nothing.

"Does Gregg know?" Jake repeated.

"I don't know. I haven't said anything to him. Nor will I."

"As far as Mr. Kaplan is concerned." Wiley spoke up. "He's very good at what he does, but he's a military man to the core. He's by the book and in my world his cover would be blown in an instant. Then he'd be dead. I'm looking for people who don't look like what they are, who are quick on their feet, and can think outside the box. They have to bend the rules, possibly break them, in order to succeed in their missions. You proved that in Paris, in Spain, and then again in New York...even if you did piss off a senator...and the director."

Jake's head was in a whirlwind. Had he heard Bentley right? Did the director just say he wasn't right for the Clandestine Service? And Isabella? "Director, what are you telling me?"

"I'm telling you I think you should consider working for Mr. Wiley and the Fellowship." Bentley said.

"Fellowship?"

"Jake." Bentley again. "The CIA has become just like every other federal agency, too politically correct. We are rapidly being neutered by those in Washington like Senator Boden and our current administration. But the last decade has seen the demise of our power. My budget keeps getting sliced off in chunks and my funding for covert ops nearly eliminated. So a long time ago, those of us who could see the path this country was taking established ways of getting around the bureaucracy. The Fellowship was born."

Wiley did his familiar hair swipe and stepped closer to Jake. "Myself and a few others started the Greenbrier Fellowship back when President Jimmy Carter outlawed political assassinations. The new path this country was taking would eventually lead us to where we are now, and several of us foresaw the future. Our country began to believe we can have freedom without a price and that's where the Fellowship comes in."

Jake looked at Bentley.

Bentley nodded. "You should consider Mr. Wiley's offer."

"I'm sure it's a great offer but I've known you for a long time…and you've known me for a long time."

"You should reconsider."

"What if I still want to work for you?" Jake asked.

"You can't."

"What are you saying, Admiral?"

Bentley said nothing.

He looked at Wiley and saw no expression. He looked back at Bentley. "Admiral?"

"I'm letting you go, Jake." Bentley said. "Effective immediately, you're fired."

Words he'd never expected to hear, especially from Bentley, but for some strange reason they didn't bother him. All the years he'd worked for Bentley as a Naval Intelligence officer—both on the USS Mount Whitney and in the Pentagon when Bentley was Chairman of the Joint Chiefs—then again as a covert agent with the Clandestine Service after his former career as an aircraft accident investigator came to a rapid end on St. Patrick's Day in Savannah, Georgia. Just over seven months ago he felt like his world was falling down around him. And now, it didn't seem to matter.

Something still bothered him. The two old men never answered his questions. Jake stared at Wiley. "Why were you at Beth's funeral?

The older men looked at each other. Wiley spoke first. "What makes you think that?"

"It took me a while to figure out where I'd seen you before and now I know. You were there." Jake stuck his hands in his pockets and looked at Bentley. "When you walked away from me, you walked across the lawn to Mr. Wiley. So my question is," Jake looked back to Wiley. "Why were you there?"

"Scott wanted me to look into a suspicion he had." Wiley glanced at Bentley. "His suspicion was correct."

Jake studied the two men. Deep in the recesses of his mind, he'd always suspected. Too much left unexplained. He glared at Bentley. "You knew all along Collins killed Beth, didn't you?"

Nothing.

"Why didn't you tell me? Didn't think I could handle it?"

"Maybe I should have. All I had were hunches, nothing conclusive." Bentley explained. "I had our men sweep the room and they found a shamrock...but it was Savannah and St. Patrick's Day after all. The nurse said she found it on the floor. I pulled a toxicology screen and found she'd been poisoned."

"Why the hell did you keep this from me? A shamrock? That's the bastard's calling card." Jake's face flushed.

"This is why I didn't tell you. I knew you'd go off half-cocked in search of Collins." Bentley said.

"That decision was mine to make." Jake's voice grew louder. "Dammit, you should have told me. Maybe I could have done something about it. My parents might still be alive."

"You're right, Jake. I should have told you, I'm sorry." Bentley exchanged glances with Wiley. "There's something else I haven't told you. About your parents."

"What about my parents?" Jake's voice cracked.

"They're not dead." Bentley shifted his weight from one to another. "I have them in protective custody. They're living in one of my safe houses in D.C."

"But, the funeral?" Jake's brow furrowed. "The caskets?"

"All a ruse to keep them safe until we find Collins. I'm sorry I kept this from you but I needed it to look real. For their sake, your reaction needed to be genuine."

"You son of a bitch." Jake clenched his fists. "First you don't tell me Collins killed Beth and now you tell me my parents have been alive all along. You *let* Collins burn down my parents' house."

"I've had a guard living with your parents since Beth's funeral. We located Collins after he killed Beth and sent a team to take him out." Bentley glanced at Wiley, then to Jake. "Somehow Collins got the drop on my men, got them to reveal your father was involved and had pressured me into sanctioning the hit on him. Then he killed them. During the operation, one of Mr. Wiley's emissaries was injured, the other survived unscathed. But ultimately, Collins got away."

Jake turned to Wiley.

"Remember your blind date?" Wiley asked.

Jake nodded.

"Collins put that scar on her face. It will serve as a permanent reminder of her failure on that mission." Wiley touched his cheek.

"That's why I had your parents under protection detail. I knew, sooner or later, Collins would try to kill your father." Bentley moved closer to Jake. "If it weren't for my guard, they'd be dead."

"That doesn't excuse you from not telling me." Jake's voice grew louder.

Wiley grabbed Jake's arm. "Come work for me, Jake, and you'll have an understanding of a world beyond anything you've ever imagined." Wiley reached into his briefcase and pulled out a folder. "This will be your first assignment."

"What is it?"

"Come to work for the Fellowship and you can have it. Trust me, you want this assignment. Right now, more than anything else in this world. Accept, and I'll explain everything."

He thought about it for a few seconds. Bentley had just dropped two bombs on him, both betrayals in Jake's eyes. Even if the director hadn't fired him, he knew he could never work for the man or the agency again...not after covering up his parents' deaths.

He wasn't sure why but he extended his hand to Wiley. "I accept."

Wiley shook his hand then passed him the folder. While Wiley and Bentley watched, Jake read the file. A sinister smile crept across his face.

Once again, the old man was one step ahead of him.

CHAPTER 74

JAKE JUMPED FROM the speedboat and pulled the photo from his coat pocket. While Wiley retrieved his backpack, Jake compared the photo to the hillside as it sloped upward in front of him. He spotted the villa, his destination. The final chapter of the ordeal in Savannah that had plagued him for months was closing forever. When he finished his business here, Ian Collins would be dead.

Twelve hours earlier when Jake accepted Wiley's offer, the two older men—Wiley and Bentley—returned to their meeting while Jake waited in the luxurious lobby of The Greenbrier Hotel. He talked to his parents on Bentley's secure phone. He felt like he was getting part of his life back. Afterwards, he took time to memorize every detail in the file Wiley left with him. Two hours later, he and Wiley were in the same black limo on their way to the Greenbrier Valley Airport.

The closest airport to Ios with a runway long enough to accommodate Wiley's jet was on the Greek island of Thira, thirty-five kilometers south of his destination. Wiley had arranged for a speedboat to pick them up on Thira and take them to Ios.

"How did you find out where Collins was hiding?" Jake started the query as soon as they were wheels up to Thira.

"My intel network was able to trace him from the letter he sent to Bentley. It wasn't very difficult...which bothers me. This is probably a trap."

"A trap? Why would he bother?"

"Think about it Jake. He's taunting you. It's you he's been after all along and he's baiting you to come to him. Otherwise we would never know where he was. He left

subtle clues he knew we would find. Clues that led us to Ios.
He'll be waiting for you, rest assured."

"Then I guess I'll have to be smarter than him." Jake
fell silent. "What's with this Fellowship thing?"

"The Greenbrier Fellowship..." Wiley leaned back in
his leather chair, interlocked his fingers and rested them on
his stomach. "...has seventy members from all over the
world. Originally it was much smaller and all the members
were Americans but as our arena of operations grew, the
need to bring in more members from other parts of the
world increased. Our members are people of influence and
power, like Scott Bentley, in the fields of business, military,
media, politics, banking...the list goes on. We only meet
once a year at The Greenbrier Hotel but we have smaller,
committee style meetings every quarter at different locales.
We discuss a lot of the world's issues and sometimes,
however rare, we decide intervention is necessary."

"What do you mean by intervention?" Jake asked.
"You mean assassination?"

"If necessary, yes." Wiley pulled a newspaper from his
briefcase, drew a circle around a small news clip, and
handed the paper to Jake. "A lot of times our intervention is
more subtle."

Wiley told Jake how his 'emissaries' technically worked
for him but were involved in special projects for the
Fellowship. The old man pointed to the newspaper article
and explained about the recent uprisings in some Middle
Eastern countries such as Yemen, Bahrain, Libya, and
Egypt. The Fellowship had emissaries in place in each of
those countries working with the locals to bring about
instability. The Fellowship anticipated the domino effect
would occur once the first nation had its uprising. Citizens
would rally against their leaders and regimes would fall,
usually in bloodshed, and hopefully a democratic society
would rise in its place.

Jake and Wiley followed the narrow streets of Ios as they wound their way up the hillside toward the villa where the Irishman lived. The arid landscape was cluttered with whitewashed stone houses, churches and local businesses. Tenders were shuttling hundreds of passengers from a cruise ship moored in the harbor to shore. The waterfront had become a beehive of tourists, swarming in and out of every shop. He was glad to escape that madness.

"No toys on this one?" He had learned Wiley was much more than just the toymaker; he was a resourceful man and a wise counselor.

"No toys, Jake. This one's old school." Jake saw Wiley staring at him. "In a few minutes you're going to have to make some life and death decisions." Wiley said.

" I know." Jake said. "And I'm going to kill that Irish bastard once and for all."

"That's not what I mean. This time it will be harder." Wiley continued. "You're going to be tested, conflicted, and possibly disappointed. Use your skills. Listen to what you know and make your decision. Follow your instincts."

"What the hell are you talking about?" Jake asked. "Why does everything have to be so cryptic?"

"Jake, I'm putting my faith in you to make the right decision. Like I said earlier, old school." Wiley paused. "Now let's get to work."

Jake listened, not really sure what Wiley was talking about. He'd noticed the man had a flair for dramatics. He just chalked it up to another of the old man's eccentricities.

Even in early November the weather on Ios Island was warm and sunny. Both men were dressed like tourists in white pants and floral shirts.

Jake was no longer the man he once was. Death had hardened him. Now, he knew Collins had murdered Beth and then tried to execute his parents. His anger fueled his hatred. He realized, as Wiley had forewarned, he was walking into a trap. He'd played it through in his mind dozens of times in the past few hours, thought of every scenario, but he couldn't help from feeling there was something he was still missing.

The Irishman had lured him to a final showdown, but for what purpose?

Jake and Wiley were halfway to the villa when Wiley stopped. "Jake, give me your gun."

"What?"

"Give me your gun." Wiley reiterated. "You have to go in unarmed."

CHAPTER 75

"UNARMED. ARE YOU crazy?"

Wiley hesitated, then pulled out a photograph and handed it to Jake.

He studied the photograph for a few seconds and the missing piece fell into the puzzle. "Guess I'm the collateral damage this time?"

"She's my granddaughter." Wiley said. "She's all I have left, I'm sorry. He said you have to go in unarmed or he'll kill her. I had no choice."

He handed the photograph back to Wiley, reached behind him, pulled out his Glock, and handed the pistol to the old man. "Collins doesn't leave witnesses, you know. After he kills me, he'll come after you. Then, when he grows tired of Kyli, he'll kill her as well." Jake turned and walked up the hill.

When he reached the villa he peeked in a window, Collins appeared to be asleep in the chair. His face was the same but his hair was full silver, the white blaze against the darker hair gone. His eyes were closed, an e-reader in his lap under his left hand, his right hand to his side.

Jake stepped back and slowly turned the doorknob, unlocked. He assessed the doorway for traps then pushed it open.

The Irishman's villa was lavishly furnished, pictures of his homeland Ireland dotted the walls. The front door opened into a large living area where Collins had a solid cherry computer desk, big-screen television, matching leather sofa, and recliner—which he was sitting in. Behind Collins he could see a breakfast nook and a large kitchen.

Jake kept his eyes trained on Collins as he entered the room, not knowing what to expect next. Then it happened.

"Jake Pendleton." Collins spoke behind closed eyes. "I've been expecting you."

Collins opened his eyes and Jake's world flashed back. One blue eye, one brown eye. He recalled the man from Savannah and the chamber in Ireland. Collins was the scariest man he'd ever met.

Collins raised his hand, exposing his silenced Beretta. He pointed it at Jake.

"As you requested, I'm unarmed." Jake raised his arms and turned a full circle. "Now, release Kyli."

"All in due time." Collins smiled. "Don't you want to hear why I killed your fiancée and your parents?"

"Not particularly, no."

"But you must." Collins said. "I insist."

"You killed Beth." Jake interrupted. "But not my parents. They're still alive."

"You're bluffing." Collins' expression changed, brow furrowed, and his cold, mismatched eyes seemed to darken. "I saw the newspapers. I read the reports."

"All fabricated for your benefit and you fell for it." Jake said. "Bentley had been waiting for you to make your move for months. That's why he had guards watching my parents."

Collins fell silent. A man who abhors failure, especially his own. "Now, I'm going to kill you." Jake said.

"Unlikely, Mr. Pendleton, as I am the one holding the gun. I allowed you to find me. And you should ask yourself, why?"

"Let Kyli go first, then you can explain it to me."

"That is not going to happen." Collins walked over and tapped the spacebar on his computer keyboard. "You see, Jake. I don't trust you."

When the side-by-side monitors came to life, Jake saw the two live video feeds, one of Kyli and one of a timer.

The monitor on the left showed Kyli, bound and gagged in a small room. The reflection of sunlight danced back and forth along the wall behind her. The monitor on the right displayed a timer attached to explosives attached to a boiler. The room was dim and shadowy and the timer was set at forty-five seconds.

"Insurance." Collins said.

"Let her go. I'll do whatever you ask."

"No, Jake, it's not going to be that easy. You see she has feelings for you. I could tell at the funeral when she—"

"You're a sick bastard, you know that?"

"Like I was saying, the young woman obviously has feelings for you but that's a life from which you will deprived...by me."

"Where is she?"

"In the basement, behind that door." Collins pointed to a door in the hall. "When I leave here, you'll have to get to her and deactivate the explosives. It will be a race against the clock. Quite frankly, I think you're too coward to try to save her."

Years of playing chess had taught him to analyze every move, strategize attacks, anticipate counterattacks, and think at least four moves ahead. But most of all, learn your opponent's weaknesses. Jake stared at the monitors assessing the rooms in the video feeds for options.

"You left your fiancée alone in the hospital and because of that she's dead. Are you man enough to try to save this one...or will you run to save yourself?" Collins pointed to the basement door with his pistol. "What will it be, Mr. Pendleton?"

Jake said nothing.

"Decision time." Collins pointed his Beretta at Jake's head.

"Drop the gun." Wiley shouted. The old man was pointing Jake's gun at Collins.

"Mr. Wiley, get out of here. He has Kyli. He'll kill her. Look at the monitor." While Collins was focusing on Wiley, Jake slipped his hand into his front pocket.

"Let her go." Wiley moved closer to Jake while keeping his gun trained on the assassin. "I agreed to your terms, I met my end of the bargain. I delivered Jake to you, as you demanded, unarmed. Now release my granddaughter."

"Dammit. Get out of here." Jake said.

"She's all I have left, Jake." Jake noticed sweat running down the old man's forehead. His voice cracked. "Let her go Mr. Collins."

Collins laughed.

"We had a deal."

"Sorry, old man. I just cancelled it." Collins pressed the *Enter* key, the counter started. He turned and fired at Wiley.

Wiley fell to floor grasping his shoulder, his gun tumbled in front of Jake's feet. Before Collins could move, Jake dropped to a knee, flipped open his knife, and hurled it at the assassin.

Collins fired and missed.

Like a spear, the razor-sharp blade impaled Collins' left leg. He dropped his gun and clutched his wound with both hands.

Jake grabbed Wiley's gun and glanced at the timer. 30 seconds left. Jake reached down and pulled Wiley to his feet.

"Must...save...Kyli." Wiley said.

Collins moved for his gun.

Jake focused on the Irishman as he reached his long arm toward the Beretta. Jake fired and the bullet pierced Collins' hand. "Decision time, Shamrock."

"Jake." Wiley interrupted. "Kyli. Save Kyli."

20 seconds.

Jake saw Collins' face twitch. The Irishman's plan had backfired and the big man looked worried. "Only a few more seconds and none of this will ever matter again."

"Jake." Wiley shouted.

"Mr. Wiley, get out of here…now." Jake noticed Collins was sweating. "Ian, you killed the woman I loved, now I'm going to kill you."

15 seconds.

"I can stop it." Collins said. "All I have to do is hit the escape key."

Jake aimed his Glock at Collins. "Stop it then."

Collins pressed the escape key. The counter kept counting down.

10 seconds.

Collins pounded the keyboard. "I don't know what's wrong. It's not stopping. We must get out of here now."

Collins started to move and Jake fired.

Ian Collins' head exploded, his lifeless body fell to the floor.

Jake glanced at the monitor.

5 seconds.

Wiley fell to his knees. "Oh my god. What have you done? What have I done?"

Jake grabbed the old man, threw him over his shoulder, and ran for the door. As he crossed through the threshold, the villa exploded.

EPILOGUE

3 Days later
Athens Medical Center
Athens, Greece

JAKE WAS TALKING to Kyli when The Toymaker regained consciousness.

The blast had hurled Jake and the old man thirty feet in the air before they crashed into the stone villa across the narrow street. The thick exterior stone walls of Collins' villa remained intact after the explosion. Windows blew outward, glass and debris covered the streets. When Jake came to, smoke was billowing from the windows. He heard the firefighters say that the floor had collapsed and crumbled into the basement where everything soon engulfed in flames.

The old man suffered first and second-degree burns, a concussion, broken left wrist, left clavicle fracture, and multiple contusions. Jake escaped with only minor burns, bruises and a knot on the back of his head when he was thrown into a bicycle parked in front of the adjacent villa.

Kyli leaned down and kissed Wiley on the cheek. "I'm glad you're okay, Grandpa."

"Kyli? Is it really you?" Wiley tried to rise up but Kyli pushed him back down. His voice weak and strained, almost faltering. "I thought you were dead. What happened? Where's Jake?"

"He's right here." She said. "He's fine. He saved your life...and mine."

"Jake...come here." Wiley said.

Jake stood and walked to Wiley's bedside. "How are you feeling?" Across the bed from him, Jake saw tears well up in Kyli's eyes.

"Blown up." Wiley grabbed Jake's arm. "How did you know Collins was lying?"

"Simple, it was exactly as you said, a trap. Collins was trying to trick me into the basement."

"Obviously...Kyli wasn't in the basement."

"He had her locked up." Jake paused. "Just not in the basement."

"How did you know that?" Wiley asked.

"From the data you gave me and what I gleaned from Collins' villa." Jake said. "The information was all there, all I had to do was put the pieces together."

"I don't understand." Wiley said.

Jake glanced across at Kyli, then back to her grandfather. "At first, I was shocked when I saw Kyli on the monitor and was ready to comply with Collins' dare. Then I remembered what you said as we arrived on Ios. I knew the only way Collins could be found was if he wanted to be found. It all made sense to me then."

"Jake, who's talking cryptic now?" Wiley lifted his head from his pillow. "How did you know Kyli wasn't in his basement?"

Jake smiled. "My first dealing with Collins goes back eight months. I studied everything I could about that man. One thing he always does, is keep women for his own pleasure. After you and I were out of the way, he was planning to have Kyli to himself." Jake glanced at Kyli. "You're lucky. When Collins doesn't kill a woman, he makes them wish they were dead."

"He was a scary bastard." She said.

Jake turned back at Wiley. "The video feed was the biggest give away. He used the video to try to lure me into the basement, where I would have been blown up. Then he would have killed you and left you in the rubble."

"But you couldn't be sure." Wiley said.

"I was one hundred percent certain she wasn't in that basement. I spent a lot of time on boats and ships when I was at Annapolis, and then again in the Navy. First time, for several weeks on one of the Academy's forty-four foot sloops. Then for several months on the USS Mount Whitney. When I saw the video feed of Kyli, I knew she was on a boat. The sun's reflection off the water is unmistakable, the way it shimmers and dances across a room. I realized then Collins' plan was to kill both of us, get to his boat, and sail away with Kyli onboard." Jake looked at Kyli. "Eventually, he would have killed you too. Probably dumped your body at sea."

"Where did you find her?" Wiley asked.

"It took a couple of hours to get back on my feet." Jake walked around Wiley's bed and stood next to Kyli. "While you were on the helicopter ride here, I went down to the waterfront looking for Kyli. It took me a while, but I finally found her on a sailboat moored in the harbor. First, I checked the docked boats, and then I rented a skiff and searched the boats in the harbor. I knew I found the right boat as soon as I read the name on the transom."

"What was it?" Wiley asked.

"*Shamrock's Revenge.*"

"I'll be damned. What about the authorities?" Wiley asked. "Any trouble with them?"

"None. I told them we were walking up to see the church at the top of the hill when the villa blew. Wrong place, wrong time."

"Kyli, I need to speak to Jake alone." Wiley stared Jake in the eyes while he spoke to Kyli.

"But, Grandpa, you just woke up," Kyli protested.

"Fifteen minutes."

Kyli smiled and walked to the door. "Fifteen minutes." She walked out.

Wiley grabbed Jake's arm. "Jake, I owe you an apology for—"

"You don't owe me anything." Jake placed his hand on Wiley's hand. "I understand why you did what you did…and I'm not upset. If I were in your shoes, I would have done the same thing. And I'm holding you to your job offer."

Jake heard the door open behind him.

"Nice work, rookie."

Jake turned around and was surprised at who he saw. "What are you doing here?"

"I told you if you didn't get yourself killed, I would see you again." She walked to the hospital bed and handed Wiley a large manila envelope.

Wiley took it and placed it on his lap. "Jake, I believe you already know Francesca. I had to fight with her over which one of you got to kill Collins. You both had grudges to bear."

Jake placed his hand on his cheek. "Collins do that to you?"

"Yes." Francesca said. "One day, maybe, I'll tell you about it."

Jake looked at Wiley. "What's she doing here?"

"She was on Ios, in case we failed." Wiley explained. "Her instructions were to kill Collins if he came out of his villa and we didn't."

"After the explosion," she said. "When I knew Mr. Wiley was being taken care of, I stayed around to make sure Collins was dead." Francesca smiled. "After the authorities found his burned body, I left and came to get you."

"To get me?" Jake looked at Wiley for an explanation, but none came.

Jake looked back at Francesca. "Get me for what?"

Francesca pointed to the envelope on Wiley's bed. "That is our next assignment."

"Our?"

Wiley handed Jake the envelope.

"We're working together on this one." Francesca turned and walked toward the door. "Come on, rookie, we have a plane to catch."

Jake looked at the old man. "What about Kyli?"

"She'll be fine." Wiley smiled. "There's plenty of time for you and Kyli. Right now, I need you."

He glanced at Francesca then back to Wiley. "We're leaving now?"

The Toymaker nodded. "Welcome to The Greenbrier Fellowship."

ACKNOWLEDGMENTS

While playing around in literary wonderland, I've discovered how important it is to have friends in your corner, whether it be to offer advice, criticism, or support. Before I mention them, I want to thank the most important people—the readers. If you've followed me from *The Savannah Project*, or whether *The Toymaker* was your first of my novels, I thank you for your support.

The idea for *The Toymaker* came from a man I met a few years ago whose identity, for obvious reasons, I can't reveal. It was actually the suggestion of my wife to include his character (and title) in this book.

There are several others I wish to thank for their contribution. G. J. (Cos) Cosgrove, Jeannine DeBrule, Tim and Kathy Eyerman, Debbie Mastro, Cheryl Duttweiler, Arlene and Terry Robinson, and fellow author Richard C. Hale. Also to the character contest winner, Kyli Wullenweber, for making such a great leading lady.

Once again, for another awesome book cover, I want to thank my good friend, Mary Fisher.

Saving the best for last, the force that keeps me driving forward, my wonderful wife, Debi. As I've mentioned before, you are my biggest fan, toughest critic, and best friend. Thanks for your undying support. I love you.

CHUCK BARRETT

AUTHOR NOTES

As you know by now, no one setting defines this book. *The Toymaker* moves fast and from locale to locale. That happens when you're chasing a terrorist. Throughout this story, Jake Pendleton gets to utilize some really cool gadgets along his journey. All of the technology mentioned in this book is real and exists today in some form or another. With that twisted disclaimer, I did take literary license to *enhance* the features of a couple of the technologies to advance the story.

The copper mesh tent, and everything associated with it, is accurate.

Miniature drones with varying capabilities are in existence today and utilized by the acronym agencies, Special Forces, and even intelligence organizations from other countries. The wasp is my creation. The idea for the wasp came from an actual miniature hummingbird drone. It's real—Google it.

The radio tomographic imaging (RTI) technology is real and was invented at the University of Utah. Elmore Wiley's version offers enhancements above and beyond the original design…but well within our technological capabilities.

The world of DNA, and what can be done with it, makes technological leaps and bounds daily. Do not be too quick to rule out the possibility of DNA assassinations. It has likely already occurred.

Which, lastly, brings me to Elmore Wiley's special gliders. Motorized gliders exist. Composite gliders exist. The jet-assisted-take-off (JATO) add-on was my enhancement. JATO technology exists and has been in use for many years—just not on a glider to my knowledge. Every other technology about those gliders exists today, including the ability to mask them from radar detection. So I figure if some nut can strap a rocket to a backpack and fly through the mountains with nothing else on but a flying squirrel outfit, then I can strap a JATO bottle to a glider.

It's all within the realm of possibility.